Claudia Carroll was born in Dublin, where she still lives, along with several imaginary boyfriends. She has worked extensively as an actress on the Irish stage, but is probably best known for her role as TV's Nicola Prendergast in the long-running RTE soap opera, *Fair City*, a character she describes as 'the horrible old cow everyone loves to hate'.

Her most recent novel, *Remind Me Again Why I Need A Man* has been optioned by Twentieth Century Fox as a TV series. Claudia isn't married and the book's title comes from a phrase she finds herself using quite a bit. Similarly, 'I Never Fancied Him Anyway', is something she often finds herself saying, particularly after a really lousy date.

D0544450

Also by Claudia Carroll

HE LOVES ME NOT . . . HE LOVES ME
THE LAST OF THE GREAT ROMANTICS
REMIND ME AGAIN WHY I NEED A MAN

I Never Fancied Him Anyway

Claudia Carroll

TRANSWORLD IRELAND

TRANSWORLD IRELAND
an imprint of The Random House Group Limited
20 Vauxhall Bridge Road, London SW1V 2SA
www.rbooks.co.uk
www.transworldireland.ie

I NEVER FANCIED HIM ANYWAY
A TRANSWORLD IRELAND BOOK: 9781848270077

First published in Great Britain
in 2007 by Bantam Press
Published in 2008 by Transworld Ireland

Addresses for Random House Group Ltd companies outside the UK
can be found at: www.randomhouse.co.uk
The Random House Group Ltd Reg. No. 954009

The Random House Group Limited supports The Forest Stewardship Council (FSC),
the leading international forest certification organisation. All our titles that are
printed on Greenpeace approved FSC certified paper carry the FSC logo.
Our paper procurement policy can be found at
www.rbooks.co.uk/environment

Typeset in 12½/15½pt Bembo by
Kestrel Data, Exeter, Devon.
Printed in the UK by
CPI Cox & Wyman, Reading, RG1 8EX.

2 4 6 8 10 9 7 5 3 1

For Clelia Murphy.
The funniest person I've ever met, ever.

Acknowledgements

Huge thanks, as always, to my miracle-worker agent, Marianne Gunn O'Connor. As if she didn't pull enough rabbits out of hats for me, she's also sold my last book, *Remind Me Again Why I Need A Man*, to Fox TV, which has optioned it as a series. The girl is just incredible. Best thing about being her client though, is that you also get to become her friend.

Very special thanks to Pat Lynch, always so patient, always so supportive, always ready for a Thursday night out on the town!

Francesca Liversidge is my wonderful editor and I owe her so much. She is beyond fabulous and just makes my job so easy. Thanks also to everyone at Transworld, especially Lucie Jordan, Laura Sherlock, Vivien Garrett, Richenda Todd and Rebecca Jones. I couldn't be luckier to be working with all of you.

Special thanks also to everyone at HarperCollins in New York; especially Claire Wachtel, Jonathan Burnham and Loretta Charlton. And a big 'Hi' to the amazing Karen Glass; I can't wait to work with you!

Thanks to Gill and Simon Hess, Helen Gleed-O'Connor and, of course, Declan Heeney for all their patience and support. Although I will continue to nag you all until I get an invite to the Christmas party.

I'm so grateful to Vicki Satlow, who I've never actually met but who does so much work selling my books around Europe, it's unbelievable. I'm still proudly wearing the Italian T-Shirt!

Thanks to all my family for everything, especially Mum and Dad who put up with my bullying them into buying yet more books all the time.

Thanks to Susan McHugh for being the most patient reader alive. And Sean and Luke!

And thank you to my magic circle of old and dear friends: Karen Nolan and Larry Finnegan, Pat Kinevane, Marion O'Dwyer, Alison McKenna, Fiona Lalor, Frank Mackey, Sharon Hogan, Karen Hastings, Kevin Reynolds, Ailsa Prenter and all the Gunn family. How all our respective livers have survived these years, I do not know.

Special thanks to Anita Notaro, a great neighbour and a great friend. And huge thanks also to Patricia Scanlan, Sarah Webb, Morag Prunty, Geraldine Nolan and Derick Mulvey for all of your help and support.

And of course to Clelia Murphy, who really, honestly *is* the funniest woman alive.

In ancient Greek mythology, Apollo fancied Cassandra so much that he bestowed on her the gift of prophecy.

Unfortunately, Cassandra wasn't all that pushed about him, so, as a punishment, Apollo twisted her brand-new gift into a curse. She could still foretell the future, but as long as she lived, no one would ever believe her.

In other words, she rejected him, so he made sure the rest of the poor girl's life was a living, breathing misery.

But then, that's fellas for you . . .

OK. To begin at the beginning . . .

Dublin, 1985
Our Dining Room

'He claims that he loves me, he's just not *in* love with me, which makes me think he's put me into the sister category and that I'm just completely and utterly wasting my time with this guy. We've been going out with each other for nearly three years and do you know what he gave me for my birthday? A foot spa. I ask you. A *foot spa*. That's the kind of gift you give to an elderly infirm relative that you don't even like.'

'Aunt Lizzie?' I tried my best to interrupt her but she was still in full rant-mode.

'All I want to know is this. When am I ever going to have what your mother has? A beautiful daughter, this beautiful home and a husband who actually wants to spend the time of day with her. So is there something fundamentally unmarriable about me? Why are the men I go out with such complete and utter wasters? Or am I the problem? Could it just be possible that *I'M* the problem?'

'Is it my go yet?' asked Aunt Lizzie's friend, Mary, keeping her voice deliberately low so that my mother wouldn't overhear in the kitchen. Mom didn't approve of her pals pestering me for free psychic advice. At least not during homework time.

'No, don't even answer her,' snapped Aunt Lizzie. 'If I talk fast enough then you can't interrupt me. OK, here's the question. Is George the man I'm going to spend the rest of my life with? Because if he isn't, then I might as well cut my losses and get out now. So come on, Cassie, break it to me gently.'

'It's your perfume,' I said simply.

'My *what*?'

'He hates the smell of your perfume.'

'Are you kidding me? I'll have you know I wear Elizabeth Taylor's Passion, only one of the priciest ones around. Cost me a packet.'

'Stop wearing it and within six months you'll be married.'

Aunt Lizzie looked at me, stunned. 'Are you serious?' she asked, eventually.

'Yup.'

'Can you see it?'

I closed my eyes and screwed up my face. Yes, there it was. Clear as crystal. Easy.

I'm in Donnybrook church, standing beside the altar, trying not to trip over Aunt Lizzie's big meringue of a dress. I look up and there's George, sweating nervously and fixing his buttonhole. I can hear an organist playing the Ave Maria and I'm smelling – what is it? – something strong, pungent, a bit yucky … lilies. Yes, definitely lilies.

Then I look down and see what I'm wearing.

Oh rats. Serves me right for thinking all of this was too good to be true …

'I'm certain,' I said firmly. Aunt Lizzie beamed. She pushed aside my homework where it was carelessly spread out all over our dining-room table and hugged me tightly.

'You're a very special girl, Cassie, I hope you know that.'

'Mmm,' I said, pulling away from her. The stench of perfume was getting to me too.

'And if there's anything you want,' she said, dropping her voice so that my mother wouldn't overhear through the half-open kitchen door, 'you know, a treat, or money – well, anything, really, just let me know.'

'There is,' I said.

'Name it.'

'Please, please, *please* don't make me bridesmaid. You'll only put me in lemon-yellow chiffon.'

'Done,' she said, all aglow, suddenly delighted with life again.

'Right, you've had your turn, over to me,' said her friend Mary, plonking herself down on the dining chair beside me and sounding like an even bossier version of Penelope Keith from *The Good Life*. If that was possible.

'Aren't you going to say congratulations?' Aunt Lizzie tossed at her, a bit smugly. 'You know, bride-to-be and all that?'

'Yes, congratulations, whatever,' snapped Mary, sounding about as far from delighted as you could possibly get.

'Sorry, didn't quite catch that?'

'Don't make me say it again, it hurt my teeth the first time.'

Now, at the time, I thought Mary was an ancient, wizened-up old crone, who always wore heavy, paperweight glasses with her hair scraped back into a bun, almost a caricature of the prematurely ageing schoolteacher, who'd remained a lifelong spinster, completely devoted to her students. In actual fact, though, she was probably only in her late thirties, tall, imperious and, as my mother used to say, 'a bit highly strung'.

Put it this way, you sure as hell wouldn't have wanted to go into her class without your maths homework done.

'So, he's called James,' she said to me, cutting directly to the chase. 'But that's pretty much all I have to go on, for now at least. He's the new art teacher in the school and we shared a moment in the staffroom yesterday.'

'What kind of moment?' asked Aunt Lizzie.

'Eye contact,' replied Mary defensively.

'Eye contact? That's it? You only ever looked at him? You mean you haven't even spoken to him yet?'

'No, and I'd appreciate it if you'd stop pressurizing me, Lizzie, thank you very much. I'm slowly building my way up to a conversation. My way.'

'So, you *didn't* talk to him, you *didn't* exchange numbers and he *didn't* ask you out?'

'Yes,' said Mary. 'A classic case of girl doesn't meet boy.'

'Shh,' I interrupted the pair of them. I was getting another flash and they were distracting me.

'What do you see?' asked Mary.

Claudia Carroll

I couldn't bring myself to tell her, but oh boy, this was when I really hated my gift.

I can see Mary in the staff toilets, bawling crying in front of the sinks. Her mascara is dribbling down her cheeks and then ... yes, there's another woman there, holding Mary's hand and telling her not to worry, that it's his wife they should all be feeling sorry for ...

'What is it?' Mary demanded, clocking my fallen face.

'I ... I don't think he's the man for you,' I said slowly, 'but—'

'Oh, that is so UNFAIR!' snarled Mary.

'Yeah, well, so's my cellulite,' said Aunt Lizzie breezily.

'Shh, gimme a sec,' I whispered, waving at them to keep it down.

'What? What are you seeing?' the pair of them hissed at me.

Another flash ...

It's Mary, but this time she's looking an awful lot happier. She's wearing a pretty summer dress and is ... definitely abroad, somewhere hot and sunny, sitting at a pavement café drinking funny-looking pink stuff, with a very tanned, swarthy-looking guy holding her hand and saying words I don't understand ...

'*Eres la mujer de mis sueños.*'

'What did you say?' asked Aunt Lizzie.

'Sounded like Spanish,' said Mary in her bossy school-marm voice. 'Repeat clearly, please?'

'*Eres la mujer de mis sueños,*' I said slowly, not having the first clue of what I was actually saying. It could have been something rude for all I knew. 'There's a man in a flowery shirt holding your hand and saying it to you, and I don't think you're in Ireland somehow. It's hot and sticky and your nose is all red and peeling. All I'm sure of is that you're very, very happy.'

Mary looked at both of us, like someone having an epiphany. 'You are the woman of my dreams,' she said, stunned. 'That's what it means. You are the woman of my dreams.'

'Oh please, there isn't a man alive who would come out with that drivel,' snapped Aunt Lizzie, a bit put out at all her new-found bridal thunder being stolen from under her. 'Have you been confiscating *Jackie* magazines from first-years again?'

'I think . . .' I said, not quite sure how to articulate this overwhelming feeling I was getting.

'What?' both Mary and Aunt Lizzie demanded in unison.

'Well, the man I'm seeing is definitely single now, but he . . . well, he might have been married before.'

'Ha! A divorcee,' sneered Aunt Lizzie triumphantly.

17

'Isn't that a bit like drinking out of someone else's wine glass? Or shopping in the "reduced to clear" rack?'

'He must be Spanish,' said Mary, totally ignoring her. 'He has to be. And there was me only thinking about spending the long summer holiday in Catalonia—'

'Will you pair stop pestering Cassie and let her get on with her homework!' my mother screeched from the kitchen, as Mary and Aunt Lizzie scarpered quicker than teenagers caught smoking, leaving me quietly to get back to learning my spelling.

I should point out that, when all of the above happened, I was seven years old.

Chapter One

Twenty-one Years On

'ASK CASSANDRA'
ALL YOUR PROBLEMS, SPIRITUAL AND
PSYCHIC, ANSWERED
You can write to Cassandra care of:
Tattle **Magazine,**
Tattle House,
Fleet St,
Dublin 2

Dear Cassandra,

I am your number-one fan. No, really. Well, me and all the girls in my class, that is. Well, except for my friend Amy who says psychics are just lucky guessers half the time, but don't pay any attention to her. Ever since she passed maths, she's turned into, like, such a know-all.

Anyway, I'm not messing, me and all the girls get *Tattle* magazine every Thursday and yours is the first column we all, like, read. So, to cut to the chase, here's my question. I was at Old Wesley to celebrate getting the Junior Cert results last Saturday night and I met the man of my dreams. For def-in-ite. He's in fourth year at Clongowes and he's, like, sooooo yummy. So far we've been to the movies (once) and his house (also once) for a DVD, so I've seen him twice, had three phone calls and forty-two texts (well, forty were from me, but two were replies from him, like, so that's still cool). And it's not even a week till our anniversary next Sat, so it's really only our half-week-versary, so I reckon he must be pretty knickers about me too. Woo-hoo!

I'm in lurrrrvvvvve and my friends are all mad jealous. So, here's my question, and please don't laugh 'cos I'd be totally, like, MORTO. Is it possible to meet your future husband at fifteen? When will we get married? How many kids do you think we'll have?

Thanks a million,

Lovestruck in Loreto College

PS: my friend Sinead wants to know if you have any psychic feelings on whether or not she'll get back with her ex. I can't write his name because he could easily read this and then Sinead would be, like, totally devo. She's hardly eaten since he dumped her and now the jammy bitch is down to eight stone.

OK. First of all, there's something I need to explain. I never set out to be a psychic. I mean, it's not as if it's a career choice you might make or anything. But, whether I like it or not (and most of the time, I *don't*; it can get a bit embarrassing at times and, in spite of what people think, it doesn't work for either lottery numbers or Grand National winners), the thing is that ever since I was a small child, I've been able to see things. Not all the time, I hasten to add; it's not something that's on tap twenty-four hours a day. But when it does happen, it's so vivid and clear, it can be, well, a bit frightening.

In fact, scrap that, it's terrifying.

You see, the thing I need to explain is . . . I've never yet been wrong. Not once, ever. Which, you'll agree, as responsibilities go, is kind of a scary one.

Anyway, I'm sitting at my desk in *Tattle* magazine's busy Dublin office, letter in hand, madly trying to channel something, when in bursts my friend Charlene.

'Why, oh why, are people so mean to the hot?' she says, theatrically dumping her Prada bag on to my desk (the real thing, no fake leather for this chick) and throwing one immaculately fake-tanned bare leg over the other.

'Charlene, it's only four-thirty in the afternoon. Shouldn't you be rolling over for your second sleep?'

'Ordinarily yes, except that I've just been fired.'

'Not again?'

'Apparently our esteemed editor didn't like my last book review.'

'The one where you said, and I quote, "No home should be without this book, even if it's just to prop up a wonky table leg"? Charlene, is it any wonder she fired you? You told me you never even read the book.'

'What can I say? It had a really boring title and, anyway, I had something better to do.'

I know I sound a bit unsympathetic, but the thing about Charlene is, she's always losing jobs. All the time, always. In fact, it's fair to say that she loses jobs the way the rest of us lose car keys. So far, on *Tattle* magazine, she's been the restaurant critic (fired because she doesn't eat fish, wheat, gluten, meat or pretty much anything that's ever been fermented, except alcohol) and the theatre critic (fired because she walked out of a performance of *Hamlet* at the interval and made up the ending. She might have got away with that one, except that, in her infinite wisdom, she mistakenly wrote that all ended happily at the Danish court, as if it were a kiddies' panto.)

Anyway, a couple of things you should know about Charlene:

1. She's stunning, and I really mean stunning, to look at, kind of like Nicole Kidman except with spray tan, all Titian corkscrew curls and big saucer-blue eyes, with a figure so tiny and perfect, you'd think Disney drew her. However, low maintenance this lady certainly ain't. The hair alone takes her two full hours every day, so she can achieve that I-just-fell-out-of-bed look, not to mention home visits from her colourist every thirteen days exactly to maintain her I'm-a-natural-redhead-cross-my-heart image. Charlene has also been know to fly her personal make-up artist to all corners of the globe at the drop of a hat so she can look baby-doll perfect at all times. Which brings me neatly to point number two.

2. She's fabulously wealthy and doesn't actually need to work at all, except that her father (probably one of the most successful people you'll ever meet, who just happened to become a billionaire making, of all things, shower-curtain rings) thinks it does her the world of good to have a focus in life. That, and the fact that he owns the corporation that owns the company that owns *Tattle* magazine. And as Charlene herself puts it, having a 'career' is a really good way to appreciate her shopping time all the more. It also gives her something to chat to her other trust-fund-babe friends about, over three-hour-long, boozy, girlie lunches.

I, on the other hand, do not have a billionaire dad who bankrolls me; I need this job to pay my rent.

'Charlene, I'm sensitive to your . . . ehh . . . torment, but unfortunately, I have to work. My deadline's tomorrow and as usual I've left everything till the last available minute. Now go away, I'm trying to concentrate.'

I'm in a bit of a panic by now, mainly because our editor, or the Dragon Lady, as we all call her behind her back, is forever giving me grief about being unprofessional and missing deadlines and what's even worse, the old she-witch is obviously in a firing humour today.

'Oh come on, Cassie, don't you have any psychic feelings on what I should do next?' she asks me, flicking through a copy of next week's *Tattle* magazine that's lying on my desk. 'My life coach says sooner or later I'm going to have to commit to a career.'

'Commit to a career? You can't even commit to a nail-varnish colour.'

'I know,' she giggles. 'And bear in mind that I don't even think I'll get a decent reference from here. The Dragon Lady says that I have the concentration span of a— Oh wow, look! Twenty per cent off all cashmere at House of Fraser until next Tuesday! Come on, what are we waiting for?'

'Shh, gimme a sec, I just need to think,' I said, turning the letter over and over in my hand, trying to pick something up. Charlene is still warbling on when, suddenly, I get a crystal-clear picture.

'She's going to be an academic,' I say, out of nowhere.

'Who?'

'The schoolgirl in my letter. Straight As all the way. She's going to be offered a scholarship to study in the States. A boyfriend is going to be the last thing on her mind for a very long time to come.'

'Ugh, adolescent hormonal problems,' says Charlene, 'what a snooze-fest. Just tell her there's nothing like a blow dry and a pedicure to solve any problem in the world.'

I frantically scribble down some notes before I forget and Charlene starts slagging off my photo from the top of last week's magazine column.

'We really have got to do something about your hair, sweetie. Don't get me wrong, I love your look, jeans and shirts and, you know, city-chic. It looks great on all you jammy tall bitches—'

'Charlene! Working here! Or at least, *trying* to.'

She blithely ignores me. 'But I'd love to make you, oh how do I put this, a bit less Charlize Theron and a bit more early Madonna. You should tone the blonde down and grow your hair out a bit too, longer hair would really suit you. Just look at me, sweetie, and learn by osmosis.'

'May I remind you, you were the one who persuaded me to go this colour in the first place when I was a perfectly happy brunette. You assured me that blondes have more fun and consequently a higher hit rate with men, and guess what? Turns out they don't.'

'Don't blame me, you're the psychic. You should have known better.'

'Not only that, but you took me to the most expensive salon in town where they subsequently charged me nearly *two hundred* euro—'

'Oh yeah, and I ended up dating that guy who owns the place. I was so in love with him too, I really thought that was going to turn into something deep and committed . . . oh shit, what was his name again?'

'So, basically, you met a man and I met my credit card limit.'

I sigh deeply and go back to my notes as Charlene throws her magazine down, already bored, randomly picks another letter from my pile and reads it out loud.

'Dear Cassandra,

Hi. Long-time reader, first-time writer. I'd never in a million years dream of contacting anyone care of a magazine, only that I truly believe you have a rare and genuine gift, so if you could give me any help/useful psychic predictions about the emotional mini-drama series I find myself cast in, I would be for ever indebted to you.

Like a lot of the problems I read on your page, it

concerns, surprise, surprise, a guy. My boyfriend. My boyfriend who's idea of long-term commitment is to ask me what DVD I'd like him to rent out for later on tonight.

Now, don't get me wrong, I do care about this guy and I do want things to progress, but the trouble is I happen to know a few of his ex-girlfriends and they've all nicknamed him Pattern Man. (And not in the sewing sense, I hasten to add.) His behavioural pattern is as follows: for the first few months after he starts to date a new girlfriend, he's the most ideal guy you could ever hope to be with. Champagne and roses, chocolates, eating out all the time in only the poshest, swishest restaurants: it almost feels like he's showing you off to his mates. Then, after a few months, he starts slipping, getting bored, not returning calls or texts, all the classic signs that relationship fatigue has set in. Then all of his exes have found themselves in the unenviable position of having to give him the old "What's the story, don't you like me any more?" speech and he inevitably says, "Yeah, sorry, babe, relationship fizzle, sure you know yourself," and then, within weeks and sometimes even days, he's moved straight on to his next girlfriend. I honestly don't think this guy has been single for longer than a fortnight in his entire life.

Now, Cassandra, my friends all say this is a classic sign of a guy who loves the thrill of the chase but then gets tired and turned off after a few short months, when the dating honeymoon is over and reality sets in. After that, he starts seeing his girlfriend in her non-date comfy knickers (you know, when you figure, what the hell, I already have my fella, so no need to torture myself with the misery of G strings any more), unwaxed legs and highlights in need of retouching (although this has only happened to me once, cross my heart.)'

Charlene reads on, but I'm actually only half listening to her. There's another letter in the mound on my desk that's, for some reason, drawing me to it. Blue note-paper. Scrawled handwriting. A strong feeling of urgency about it. Immediately, I get an overwhelming sense that whoever wrote this is a little older than those who normally write to me. A woman, I'm seeing, mid-sixties and white-haired, genuinely distressed, badly needing help and not knowing who else to turn to . . .

Charlene is still reading aloud:

'Anyway, to make a long story short, lately I'm begin-ning to feel that it's my turn to get elbowed out of the way and here's the killer sign. It was my thirtieth birth-day last week and he gave me, wait for it, an exercise bike. And there was me dropping hints about how much I loved Boodles jewellery and how fab it would be to have a birthday gift I could love and cherish for ever. I think Pattern Man is living up to his name and that no sooner will he brush me aside than he'll be seen around the town with some twenty-something hot babe.

A newer and probably a younger model, the bastard.

Any psychic advice you might have on the subject would be greatly appreciated.'

'Cassie? Cassie, are you even listening to this? This is a good one. Although God alone knows why this one is even bothering to write to a psychic in the first place. Match dot com was practically *invented* for people like her.'

But she's lost me. I pick up the blue envelope and tear it open. A strong smell of lily-of-the-valley perfume hits me and immediately I get a sense that the lady who wrote this doesn't live alone. There's a man around her, older still, authoritarian, a bit of a bully. For some reason, I'm picking up a strong negative energy and I'm not quite sure why.

Dear Cassandra,

Even as I put pen to paper, I'm aware of how hopeless and pathetic this must sound. Not only am I begging for your help, I'm also shameless enough to ask that you won't actually print this letter. You have no idea how annoyed my husband would be if he thought I'd turned to a national publication in my sheer desperation. I can scarcely believe I'm doing it myself, but if you can't help me, Cassandra, I honestly don't know where else to turn. You're busy, so I'll be brief.

The problem started three months ago, back in July, when we first moved into our new house. Our beautiful retirement home, which cost all of our savings and where I hoped we could see out the rest of our days in peace and serenity. Not to be.

I don't believe in ghosts or hauntings in the real world, Cassandra, but please believe me when I tell you that there's just something about this house. I can't put my finger on it and yet here I am, writing to you, praying that you'll understand and be able to help me.

'Ooh, haunted house?' says Charlene, already bored with her own letter and now reading this over my shoulder. 'Loving it, very *Afterlife*. So what are the symptoms? Or is that the word you use? Hard to know.'

I read on, completely absorbed.

Even though the heating is on most of the time, the house is permanently freezing, there are strong smells coming from one room in particular and, worst of all, things keep getting hurled around, heavy things too. On the rare occasions when we do have people to visit, they never seem to want to stay, nor can I say I blame them. No matter what I do, I can't get rid of this awful, chilling atmosphere. It's suffocating; almost as if the house is trying to drive us away and I don't know why.

I'm frightened, Cassandra, and I'm pleading with you to help me. I would gladly put this house on the market tomorrow, but my husband won't hear of it. He gets very angry with me for even suggesting that there might be something wrong with the place so, for the sake of a quiet life, I put up with it and say nothing.

But I can't take much more. I'm giving you my home number and hope that I'll hear from you. Call any time and if my husband answers the phone, don't worry, I'll think of some excuse to tell him.

Thank you so much. Please understand I'm at my wits' end and have no one else to turn to.

Sincerely,

Worried in Rathgar

'Wow! How cool is that!' says Charlene, kind of missing the point. She leans over and takes the letter from me. 'Your very own personal ghost. Must be like permanently living at Hogwarts.'

I take the letter back and hold it in both hands, turning it over and over, madly trying to tune her out so I can pick something up.

It was late at night when this poor woman wrote to me and the sheer sense of terror I'm feeling around her is making my heart race …

'You could always advise her to move.' Charlene twitters on. 'You know, like the time I sold the penthouse in Marbella after I saw a cockroach run across my parking space.'

'Shh!'

'Oops, sorry. Was I personalizing?'

'I need to go there. I feel I need to visit this house,' I say eventually.

'Why?'

'Because . . . I dunno. I can't make up my mind about this one.'

'You think that's bad? I still can't make up my mind about where I stand on the Paul McCartney/Heather Mills split.'

I'm not even sure I can put into words what's worrying me. All I know is that I have the strongest instinct to go to this house and I'm a great believer in always, always following your gut instincts.

'Oh, it's nothing scary or creepy, it's just that . . .' I look at her, weighing up whether or not I should tell her what's forming at the back of my mind. I decide to go for it, on the basis that no matter how bizarre my job gets (and at times, you just wouldn't *believe* some of the letters I'm sent) Charlene never *ever* makes disparaging comments or dismisses what I do for a living. That's the absolute beauty of her. Yes, she'll put down my hair/clothes/long-term single status without batting an eyelid, but I'm well able for that and will tease her right back, and we'll end up having a laugh, like really good friends can, without anyone taking offence. It's only when people slag off the supernatural and make me feel like a chancer/charlatan/con artist that I get a bit upset. You know, the type of people who, when I tell them what I do for a living, look at me as if I'm barely on nodding terms with reality. It happens, believe me.

'I think I might need to do a clearing,' I say simply. 'There's something in this house, someone trapped. Maybe a spirit that hasn't passed, or rather, that's passed on, but maybe just . . . doesn't know it yet.'

Now I have Charlene's full attention. 'Wow. Dead and doesn't know it. Kinda spooky.'

'Nothing spooky about it in the least. Happens all the time. Spirits are our next-door neighbours, honey, that's all. We've nothing to fear from them; in fact, most of the time, they only want to help us.'

'So you want to go there and do a sort of spiritual spring-cleaning?'

'Ehh . . . yeah, kind of. If you want to put it like that.'

'Right, well, I think I'll come with you for moral support,' says Charlene. 'Over my drop-dead gorgeous body am I letting you face into that alone. Cassie, if I've said it once I've said it a thousand times. You are so amazing at this stuff, why aren't you doing this on television?'

I'm silently blessing her for being such a trooper when she picks up another letter from the groaning pile on my desk and reads it out.

'Dear Cassandra,

I've been seeing a guy for almost two months now and I'm starting to think there's something up. In all that time, he's never as much as laid a finger on me. Not once. He keeps saying it's because he respects me too much and that he's much happier just chatting to me, but I'm a normal woman with normal needs and desires, if you know what I mean, and this is starting to become an issue. Oh, and just to anticipate what any of your readers may think, yes of course I am aware that there are "shag-dodgers" out there, I just didn't think I'd end up going out with one, that's all.

Take my birthday last week, for instance. He came over, watched *Brokeback Mountain* on DVD, then gave me tickets for the two of us to go and see Cher in concert at the Point Depot. I wouldn't mind, but I don't even like Cher. I'd have far preferred to see U2. Then when I tried to kiss him as he was leaving, he gave me a Mediterranean peck on each cheek, told me my make-up was just a shade too dark for my skin tone, and was gone.

It's really starting to drive me mental, Cassandra. This guy can bring me down faster than a bad hair day. If you have any psychic feelings on the subject, I'd be most grateful.

Concerned in Castlebar'

'Well, there's one you don't have to be psychic for,' says Charlene. 'Gay and doesn't know it yet. Gay as Christmas in Bloomingdale's, if you ask me.'

'Hold on, there's a PS,' I say, grabbing the letter from her. '"PS: I don't know if this is any help to you or not, but for some reason, he always smells better than most women." Yup, I'm afraid you're one hundred per cent on the money with this one,' I add, pitying the poor writer but somehow feeling that there is great happiness ahead for her with someone else. Someone foreign – French, I think. I'm seeing dark eyes and olive skin. And I think he could be Scorpio.

'So, do you want me to predict your future?' says Charlene, with the devil in her big saucery eyes.

'What?'

'You and I are going to leave the office right now and go for a lovely soothing glass of champagne in the Odessa bar.'

I groan, staring at the towering pile of letters I haven't

even touched yet. (For some reason, every week I seem to get sent more and more. The Dragon Lady used only to publish about five each week but now it's more like twenty-five and counting.) So much to do . . . but then a nice glass of champagne just sounds sooooo tempting . . .

'Oh come *ooooon*,' pleads Charlene, seeing me wavering. 'When do I ever ask you for anything?'

'Well, I suppose there's no harm in "just the one", is there? Sure I can always come back to work later, can't I? Right then, here's the deal,' I say, assertively. 'One quickie and I'll be back at my desk in half an hour.'

'That's the girl. I've just lost my job and the way I feel right now, Bollinger is my only ally.'

'I'm not actually drunk, I'm more . . . sedated from my misery. But I don't want you to worry about me, ladies. Once I drink myself to sleep, I'll be just fine.'

Six hours later and I'm still plonked on the same big, comfy sofa I've been sprawled out on all evening, a bit pissed and surrounded by the gang, or as Charlene likes to call us, her little circle of love and dysfunction. We're all listening to her best friend and personal trainer who's making us all roar laughing, without intending to, telling us about his latest break-up.

He's chunky, dark, bulked-up, perma-tanned and although his name is Marc, everyone calls him 'Marc with a C'. As well as being hysterically funny, he's also incredibly good-looking, a straight-gay type, which leads to huge confusion in the gym he works at, where his clients include a long list of recent divorcees and newly separated women, all wanting a killer body and a good old self-esteem-boosting flirt at the same time. Marc with a C is always more than happy to oblige because, underneath that wall of muscle and the butch physique, he's actually a sweet, sensitive soul, which kind of explains why his closest pals are all women. I'd nearly go for him if he were straight, and constantly have to remind myself that he's unavailable to me and how much simpler life would be if only he were just a little less attractive and a lot more camp. In fact, not just *camp*, but shortbread-biscuit-tin-covered-in-white-paper-doilies camp.

We've all known him for years, ever since Charlene first converted a room in her house into a personal gym and then hired him to train her there, four times a week. He slags her off something rotten though, saying that the only reason she won't use a public gym is so that no one will see her (a) sweaty and (b) without full make-up.

'Are we *still* on this?' says Charlene from the armchair across from us, sounding, if possible, even more pissed than I feel. 'You broke up with a guy you went on three dates with, one of which involved him sitting through your spinning class, so that doesn't even count. How long since you saw him?'

'Four full days,' says Marc with a C.

'And how long since final contact?'

'One text from me yesterday, to casually remind him about a fitness assessment we had scheduled, which he chose to ignore.'

'Tell the truth.'

A pause.

'OK, seven texts. And before you judge me, just remember you had a fringe in the 1990s.'

'I'm sorry, sweetie, but it's hardly a tragedy.'

'Cassie, I want you to ignore the Tipsy Queen over there,' he says, 'and just tell me if you see a knight in shining Armani in my future. I don't ask for much out of this life, all I want is to be in a deep, committed, loving relationship, for . . . ooh, I dunno, about a week or so.'

'I wish I could,' I say, slurping away on a half-empty glass of champagne, all thoughts of my deadline gone right out of the window, 'but I'm never able to see things when I'm a bit over my limit. You know, like the way you can't drive or operate heavy machinery when you're pissed, you can't make psychic predictions either. Sorry, hon.'

'Yeah, now drink your dinner and leave her alone,' laughs Jo, my best friend and flatmate. 'Cassie's not a performing seal that turns tricks on demand. Besides, the week's only just started; you know perfectly well you'll be back in the saddle by the weekend, you big manaholic. Try walking in my shoes for a bit and you'll appreciate how good you have it. Humpback whales do it more than me.'

'Congratulations, Jo,' says Charlene from where she's now slumped into her armchair. 'I think you just found the title for your autobiography.'

Everyone cracks up laughing and we order another round. Tonight's turned into one of those completely spontaneous evenings that are always far more fun than anything planned and I'm so glad Jo's popped in for a few drinks on her way home from work.

Let me tell you a bit about Jo. She's probably as different from Charlene as you can get, both physically and personality-wise. Sharper than a chilli finger poked in your eye and smart as a whip, she's dry-as-a-bone funny, the sort of woman who should be awarded a black belt in tongue-fu. Honestly, she can have you doubled over with some of her one-liners, although God help you if you find yourself on the receiving end of her merciless teasing, as Charlene frequently does. Looks-wise, she's small and naturally pretty with croppy light brown hair which I cut for her (badly) as she point blank refuses to set foot inside a hairdresser's until Tibet is free. To give you a quick mental picture, if ever they were casting for a Jodie-Foster's-little-sister type, then

Jo's your woman. A fundraiser for Amnesty Ireland, she's also hard-working, intense, disciplined, deeply passionate about human rights and with a social conscience that Nelson Mandela would be proud of.

Put it this way: whereas Jo's personal belief system is that the lack of political will to regulate the arms trade is a major contributory factor to the abuse of human rights in the world, Charlene's is that if Paris Hilton and Nicole Ritchie can't make peace, then what possible hope is there for the Middle East? Jo spends her Saturdays doing voluntary work in our local Oxfam; whereas Charlene believes that wearing second-hand clothes can give you hepatitis. Generous to a fault, Jo would give you her last red cent whereas Charlene practically makes you leave your driver's licence if you dare to borrow anything belonging to her. Two full rooms in her house are devoted to her clothes, which are categorized according to season/day and season/night (not to even get started on her shoe collection, which is stored in a separate walk-in closet approximately the size of our living room), whereas poor old Jo still has the same battered pair of jeans she's been wearing for about five years now.

Don't get me wrong, I love them both dearly, but you couldn't find two women more diametrically opposed to each other, although Jo still has a sort of crusading zeal to reform Charlene. (Without much success; so far she hasn't even managed to get her to switch to coffee with the Fairtrade logo.)

Anyway, back to the Odessa bar.

'Do you realize,' says Marc with a C, sighing, 'that for the first time since I can remember, all four of us are single at exactly the same moment in time?'

'Oh great, thanks so much for that inspirational thought,' snaps Charlene. 'Now I have inner peace. I think you are all aware of my personal goal.'

'To find a husband before you turn thirty,' says Jo dryly. 'Yes, we know.'

'Correction, a rich, *suitable* husband,' Charlene fires back, a bit narkily. One of her trust-fund-babe friends just got engaged last week and it's really annoying her. 'I mean, what is wrong with me? *Look* at me, for God's sake. If I was a man, I'd marry me.'

'Oh, will you stop being such a drama queen?' says Jo. 'You'll only make me pretend to cry. Now can we please get off this subject? This conversation demeans women.'

(Oh yeah, this is a phrase Jo uses a lot. She's very politically correct, something you have to remember when you're in her company; although most of the time we tease her about it and nickname her Millie, short for Millie-Tant. Gettit? She's a good sport though, and is well able to laugh at herself.)

'Besides, that still gives you nearly two full years, same as the rest of us,' says Marc with a C helpfully.

'Here's what I don't get,' I say, taking another gulp of champagne, which immediately goes straight up my nose, making me cough and the others giggle. 'What is the big deal about getting married anyway? Have you any idea how many letters I get from desperately unhappy women stuck in miserable marriages, all wanting to know if there's some light at the end of the tunnel? I'm telling you, girlies, you'd need a heart the size of a marble not to feel sorry for them. I'd far rather be on my own than in a rubbish relationship, wouldn't you?'

'In a word, no,' says Charlene primly. 'If the noughties have taught us anything it's that our mothers' generation got it all wrong. They tried feminism and discovered they couldn't have it all, so if it comes down to a choice, then the minute I get the ring on my finger, I choose to be a happily married, stay-at-home domestic goddess. What's the problem with that?'

'Sweetheart, may I remind you that you use your fridge to keep eye creams in and your oven for storage,' says Marc with a C and we all laugh.

'By your upward inflection, I'm guessing that you meant that remark to be funny, but . . . no,' she throws right back at him.

'Charlene, whatever you do, don't move out of that chair,' says Jo, teasing her. 'I think you may just have stumbled on a portal right back to the nineteen fifties.'

'Explain.'

'In your eyes, the whole feminist movement was just something that happened to other people, wasn't it?' Jo is almost needling her now, sensing her weak spot and going in for the kill.

'Excuse me, Josephine, what is so *wrong* with me wanting to do the wifey thing?'

We're all a bit high on the champagne now and it's making Charlene defensive and Jo argumentative. Happens a lot with this pair, but it's fine, I'm well used to refereeing between them. And invariably they're back to being best buddies five minutes later. Honestly.

'She doesn't mean anything, Charlene,' I say soothingly. 'It's just that up until now your domesticity has been limited to the sowing of wild oats.'

'So, we're all single,' says Jo, matter-of-factly. 'Big fat deal. I'm certainly not going to lose weight worrying about it. I've been on enough crap dates to last me for a lifetime.'

'Besides, we're only twenty-eight,' I say. 'Sure we've *years* of crap dating ahead of us to look forward to.'

'Sorry to break up the party, everyone,' Charlene says, abruptly standing up, still in a bit of a snot, 'but I need the bathroom.'

That's another thing about Charlene; she can't use a public loo and always has to take taxis home whenever she needs to go.

'Her Majesty has spoken,' says Jo. 'If she decrees the night is over, then guess what? So be it.'

'Josephine, are you aware of the health hazard that public toilets can be?'

'No need to get your training bra in a twist, Charlene, I'm merely pointing out that—'

'OK, OK, OK, my darlings, in that case, I have a cunning plan which cannot fail,' says Marc with a C, tactfully skating over the ding-dong that could erupt at any minute between the other two and putting on a ham–actor baddie voice. 'I wouldn't hear of letting you go home on your own, Charlene sweetie, so why don't we all come with you, have a drinkie while you tinkle, then come back here and go to the nightclub downstairs? Odessa is just *such* a hotzone at the moment. It's a one-hundred-per-cent target-rich environment, if you get my drift. So whaddya say, ladies?'

There's a pause as we all look at each other, weighing up who's up for more devilment and who isn't. All eyes eventually settle on me, as normally I'm the first to cave in to any messing that's afoot.

'Sorry, guys, I'm afraid you're gonna have to count me out,' Jo says eventually, stretching and yawning. 'I can't drink another bite. Besides, I've a fundraising meeting at eight a.m. tomorrow so no can do, I'm afraid.'

'I'm going to call it a night too,' I say to catcalls of 'Fader! And who are you going to meet sitting in your kitchen at home? Come out husband–hunting with me!' and Charlene's favourite catchphrase, 'Come on, Cassie, surrender to the random.' 'Oh, guys, I'd love to go on with you but I really have to behave . . .'

'Are you absolutely sure we can't twist your rubber arm?' says Marc with a C with a mad glint in his eye. 'Remember, honey, you're only hot once.'

'Ooh, it's so tempting but . . . no. At this stage, I'm not just late for my deadline, I'm flirting with disaster and I still have *sooooo* much work to do . . .'

'Fine, suit yourself,' he says, fumbling with his jacket. 'Go home to a nice cup of Darjeeling and a HobNob. Stay single. See if we care.'

Now, I'm way too tired and tipsy to do any actual work tonight, but . . . oh, what the hell, I figure as we all drunkenly stumble around looking for bags and coats. I'll just get up early tomorrow and I can still make it. Really early, like six a.m.

Yes. Great plan. If I go straight home now, I can *easily* be up by six.

Well, OK, maybe seven.

Anyway, as I said, unlike Charlene I can't afford to lose my job.

All four of us jump in a cab which drops Jo and me back to the dotey little townhouse we share and then takes the other two on to Charlene's mansion on Millionaires' Row, as we've all nicknamed it, in the poshest, leafiest and most exclusive part of town (a twenty-first birthday present from her father, no kidding). Jo and I stagger upstairs, drunkenly hug each other goodnight and five minutes later I'm tucked up in bed, out for the count.

Now, a wise man once said that the difference between fate and destiny is that while fate is the hand of cards we're all dealt at birth, destiny is the way you play them. In other words, everyone *always* has a choice. Call it free will if you like, but people like me can advise till the cows come home and say, 'OK, here's what's around you at the moment and here's what's likely to happen,' but at the end of the day, everyone has the option to jump on a flight to the Outer Hebrides and start a new life there in the morning, if they so choose.

That's why I have to be so careful. When I tell people what I see, I always stress that it's in everyone's power to change their own future, at the shake of a lamb's tail. Example: I had to choose whether to continue all-night partying with the others and I decided not to.

At four a.m., I shoot up in the bed, suddenly wide awake. I'm seeing what's happening in the Odessa, right now, as clearly as if I'm there. And I know with absolute certainty that what I'm seeing will alter the course of my life for ever ...

Chapter Two

THE TAROT DECK
THE TWO OF CUPS CARD

Signifies the happy couple. A new love will appear, possibly within the next two weeks. If you are single and looking for romance, this person could well turn out to be your soulmate.

On the downside, though, he might be involved with another, in which case you will have to spend the rest of your life knowing that the love of your life is with someone else and that, basically, it's your own tough luck, because, hey, she got there first . . .

One of the reasons why Jo and I live so well together (we've been sharing this house for four years now and still not a single cross word) is that we're both not just single, but serially, chronically single. I honestly don't know why in Jo's case, she's so smart and sharp and funny, except maybe that she feels it's not right even to think about getting into a deeply committed relationship until Third World debt has been cancelled. Put it like this: if someone with a social conscience along the lines of Bono/Bob Geldof/the newly single Paul McCartney were active on the Dublin dating scene, they'd be her perfect match.

My problem, surprise, surprise, is a tad more embarrassing.

I see the end coming, ages before it even happens and, in the interests of self-preservation and not having my heart smashed, usually choose to cut my losses and get out quick. It's a sad and sorry admission, but at the grand old age of twenty-eight, I honestly don't think I've ever really been in love. You know, like *movie* love. The kind of love that makes you finally get what James Blunt has been warbling on about all this time.

On the plus side, though, I have at least managed to stop seeing my single status as a big neon sign that I couldn't get it right and keep reminding myself that I just haven't met the right one . . . yet.

Don't think I haven't been a brave little tryer, though.

Take, for instance, the last guy I dated, all of a year ago. I was knickers mad about him and exhibited all three classic signs of a woman in love: (a) I couldn't eat, (b) I couldn't sleep and (c) I went out and bought all new underwear.

We hadn't been together all that long before we planned to go to Paris for a romantic, getaway weekend. I'll never forget it; I was rummaging around Charlene's fabulous walk-in closet (no kidding, it's so huge, you'd need an overnight sleeper just to get to Narnia), filching handbags and shoes for the trip, delighted to have got a special dispensation from her to actually borrow stuff. Suddenly I got one of my flashes. Clear as you like, I saw myself sitting on my suitcase at the Air France check-in desk, alone, bawling crying and clearly stood up.

Needless to say, that was the end of that. Nor could I even tell the guy the real reason why I wanted to break up with him ('I had a premonition and now I want out' just sounds so *made up*) so, in the end, I gave him a load of drivel about how I wanted to concentrate on my career and be on my own for a while and blah, blah, blah, none of which he even remotely believed, but I still figured anything would be better than ending up alone and crying and dumped at an airport.

Ho hum. Nothing for it then but to put a brave face on it, trot out my time-honoured, face-saving catch-phrase and just get on with life.

I never fancied him anyway.

Trust me, if you say it often enough, you eventually start to believe it.

Besides, as Jo pointed out at the time, when she was weighing up the cost/benefit analysis of him as a boy-friend (every best friend's unwritten duty) in retrospect, the guy had all the charm and charisma of a flesh-eating Ebola virus.

Bless her; I think she meant to cheer me up.

Then, before him, I briefly dated a guy I met at Marc with a C's gym, a gorgeous-looking Matthew McConaughey-type solicitor who texted me one night to say he was working late in his office with a client, only for me to get an immediate flash of him in a night-club, at that very moment, wrapped around the same very young, very pretty, very blonde 'client'.

Needless to say, very soon I found myself single again, but it was absolutely fine. I never fancied him anyway.

But there is a lesson here: never, ever, *ever* lie to a psychic. Really bad plan, on every level.

Then, before him, there was James. Alas, poor James. In the early days, I genuinely believed that my luck had changed and that I had finally, *finally* met a D.S.M. (decent single man). When I first met him, I'd just read an article in *Tattle* magazine about how, just before you go on a first date, you should tell yourself that you're not looking for a soulmate, only a potential friend.

Apparently this is supposed to take the pressure off and stop you from dwelling on the possibility of babies with the guy before the waiter has even had a chance to bring the pepper and parmesan.

Anyway, he invited me to his flat for dinner and, hey presto, my new attitude worked like a charm and we started seeing each other and I liked him and my friends liked him and even my mother liked him and it took me weeks to finally put my finger on what was wrong with him.

He never, ever, *ever* took me out in public. Or introduced me to his family and friends. I had become almost the girlfriend equivalent of a capsule wardrobe; kept on a hanger labelled 'for sex and fun', but always worn on my own and washed separately. On the rare occasions when we were walking down a street together, he'd behave almost like he was on the witness protection programme, and on one occasion, when I had the temerity to suggest going away for a weekend together, he looked at me as if I'd just fouled the pavement. I was always there for him, but always kept conveniently in the background. As far as he was concerned, I was as handy as Sky Plus. Or a ready meal. Or a wrap-over dress.

You get the picture. So, feeling completely and utterly fed up, I was just about to confront him with all of this, when, suddenly, I got a flash.

He had not one, not two but *three* other girlfriends

on the go, all at the same time. So, that was the end of that, natch, but I'll always remember Jo's final pearl of wisdom on the subject, brilliant dating wing woman that she is. 'Cassie, if you set the bar low enough, only a louse can crawl underneath.'

Anyway, it was fine and I was fine. I never fancied him anyway and only hope none of the other three girlfriends did either. Like I say, we all have the power to choose between fate and destiny and on all of those occasions, I chose to go down the heartache-avoidance route.

But after what I saw so clearly last night, this time I may not have any choice.

Where Jo and I live is close to the city centre, only a brisk twenty minutes from *Tattle* magazine's office on Fleet Street, and as it's a lovely, sunny October morning, I'm racing into work, cursing myself for being so disorganized and leaving my column to the very last minute.

Well, when I say 'morning', mid-morning would actually be more accurate; needless to say, my plan of having Prussian discipline and getting up at dawn came to nought.

With me, this is a regular occurrence; if you want star charts done, astrological compatibility grids, aura reading, dream interpretation or any kind of space/energy clearing, I'm your girl, but ask me to do a tax return, or stick to a set-in-stone deadline or . . . well, you know, be all organized and grown-up, then I'm beyond useless. None of this is helped (a) by the minging hangover I'm still nursing from last night and (b) worse, the fact that I'm frantically willing my mobile not to ring, when, on the principle that if you dread something enough, you'll attract it, of course, it does. *Shit. Shit, shit shit . . .*

I don't even have to look at the number to know who it is; more importantly, why she's calling; and, worst of all, what I'll then have to tell her.

If she asks, that is. Which, with a bit of luck, she mightn't . . .

Charlene: 'So, he's called Jack Hamilton and to save you the bother of asking . . . yes! I'm in lurrvve,' she says, sounding as hungover as a dog. 'He's a total hottie McHot from the Planet Hotland. You know, the kind of guy who knows how to make a girl feel like a woman. And then a woman feel like a big dirty slapper.'

She roars laughing and, immediately, the knot of tension that's been in the pit of my stomach worsens. Whenever Charlene really likes a guy, she goes to the bother of memorizing his last name, almost like she's practising to see what her Christian name will sound like with it.

'That's great, honey,' I say, trying as hard as I can to keep the nervous sense of foreboding out of my voice. Lucky for me, though, oversensitivity towards others has never been any failing of Charlene's.

'*And* I stayed over! Now, the only tiny blight on the horizon is that he's one of those perfect gentlemen types, who insisted on giving me his room while he crashed out on the sofa, but you know me, darling, baby steps. Oh sweetie, you should just see his apartment. I think the theme is "James Bond just won the Lotto, but failed to acquire taste". No kidding, it's got more boytoys than you can imagine, a giant plasma-screen TV, which, as we all know, is just sooooo last year, and a full-size snooker table, which I think he probably eats off. Or else he just eats out all the time. Never in my whole life have I seen anywhere so badly in need of gay-spray. Anyway, you just couldn't keep me from doing a mental redecoration and I honestly think the best thing all round is if he moves in with me.'

'Charlene! You only just met the guy! What about "baby steps"?'

'Will you relax? Obviously I don't mean straight away. I'm prepared to wait a month or so, if that's what it'll take. Don't judge me, Cassie, can I help it if I'm goal-driven? I have exactly one year and eleven months to "I do" so there's no time for arsing about.'

'OK, whatever you say, fruit of the *loon.*'

'Have you been paying any attention to my life of late? Next month I have to go through the public humiliation of attending Anna Regan's engagement party. Up until last night, all I had was a plan and a dress.

Now I have a plan and a man and a dress and if that's not making progress, I don't know what is. Whereabouts are you now?'

'On my way into work. Remember work? Remember the Dragon Lady?' Oh God, just the very thought of her makes me quicken my pace a bit.

'Ha bloody ha. I *really* need to talk to you, honey, can you meet me for a lightning quick coffee? Pleeeeease?'

'You mean you're not ringing me from bed? Don't tell me you're up and about at this ungodly hour of the morning?'

'I'm just doing the walk of shame from his apartment, which is in Temple Bar, and, crippled as I am in these shoes, I think I might just be about able to hobble as far as Café en Seine. I'm urgently in need of an espresso the size of a soccer ball.'

OK. Now, I know I've a mountain of work to get through and I know I should have been at my desk hours and hours ago, but then, a quickie coffee just sounds sooooo tempting. Sure I'll only be twenty minutes, and if I run into the Dragon Lady on my way in, well . . . well . . . I can just cross that bridge if/when I come to it, can't I? Great plan. Love it.

Besides, I always work miles better with a shot of caffeine inside me, so in a way, this is actually kind of productive and not just plain old-fashioned skiving off.

If you think about it.

'OK, you're on. Anything to help me through the morning. I'm not joking, my hangover's so bad, you could practically grate cheese on my tongue.'

'Cool, see you there in five, baby. Big, big news, I couldn't possibly tell you over the phone so don't even attempt to guess because I want to tell you myself. So BFN, bye for now.'

Right, that's it then. Charlene's my friend and if she asks me what I'm dreading she's going to ask, I'll just have to tell her straight out, honestly and directly. Simple as that. Oh God, this is the part about being a psychic that I really, really hate . . .

The one thing I have going in my favour, I think as I head down Dawson Street, is that Charlene never, ever asks me about her actual future with any of her boyfriends, on the grounds that she's superstitious and believes it brings dating bad luck.

This very happy arrangement dates back to her last serious romance (i.e., one that lasted longer than a boozy weekend) when she begged/cajoled/emotionally guilted me into working out her relationship compatibility with the guy in question. I was reluctant to, because I'd already seen the outcome and knew she'd be upset if I told her and there's nothing worse than having to give bad news, but what can I say, she insisted. So, one his 'n' hers astrological star chart later (both Western and Chinese

– well, in my business you have to be thorough), I told her what was on the cards.

The conversation went something along these lines:

CHARLENE: So will I marry him?

ME (*hesitating*): Well, if you remember that you're Aquarius and he's Virgo, so that's an air sign and an earth sign which isn't really ...

HER (*with rising impatience*): Cassie, just tell me straight out, is this guy my future husband?

ME (*humming and hawing*): Then there's the Chinese element to consider. You're an earth goat and he's a metal monkey and really earth and fire aren't exactly the most suited ...

HER: Not hearing a straight answer here!

ME (*playing for time*): Charlene, listen to me. I want you to be happy with the *right* man. Now, if this guy isn't for you ...

HER (*narky*): A simple yes or no will suffice, thank you very much.

ME (*mortified; I hate being the bearer of bad news*): Well ... umm, on a scale of one to ten, I'd have to give it a ...

HER (*hysterical*): A WHAT?!

ME (*thinking, Oh, what the hell, the game's up*): OK, don't shoot the messenger, but a minus four. Honey, you've about as much chance of marrying Pope Benedict the Sixteenth. Now, remember, that's not to say that things won't change ...

HER (*wailing*): So you're effectively telling me my crush is actually a crash? (*then screeching*) You've ruined my life, you insensitive cow, etc., etc., etc.

ME (*silently to myself*): Never, never again . . .

So, on the plus side, at least she's unlikely to ask about her future with him. But that's not what's worrying me . . .

When I eventually do get to Café en Seine, Charlene is right at the very back of the café, where it's shadowy and dark, wearing her 'sitting alone' armour, i.e., her Jackie O face-covering, limo-tinted sunglasses, with her mobile phone clamped to her ear, chatting to one of her trustafarian pals and (I'm not making this up) a copy of Dostoevsky's *Crime and Punishment* on the table in front of her. She keeps this in her handbag at all times, I should explain, so casual passers-by will think that she's really brainy and that this is her actual reading material. The irony is, in trying to be inconspicuous, she might as well be standing under a hot spotlight doing the cancan. You couldn't miss her, particularly as she was still wearing what she had on last night, a stunning Versace little red number with a matching red velvet coat.

'Hey, sweetie,' she says, hanging up the phone as she sees me, 'sorry for picking a table in such a crap part of the café, but look . . . eeeeek!' She tips up her glasses for a second, to flash the fact that she's not wearing any make-up. (Just to put this into perspective: for Charlene to venture out without make-up is akin to the rest of us going for a mountain hike without footwear.) 'Meet the new me,' she says dramatically. 'I've just made not one, but two life-alteringly huge decisions, one of which directly affects you, my darling.'

'What's that?' I ask as the waiter bounds over. Charlene hurriedly flips the shades back over her bloodshot eyes as we order a double espresso with hot soya milk on the side for her (and if you think she's fussy about ordering in a café, you want to see her inside a shoe shop) plus a plain, old-fashioned, big mug of black coffee for me.

'Number one, I have decided that from now on, disposable is for cameras and not for relationships. I'm officially taking my *Rules* book and flinging it out the window. No more reading faddish self-help books that advise me to sit back and wait for the guy to call or make the first move. Been there, done that and all with zero per cent success. So, meet the new, proactive me.'

OK, I think, she just wants to talk about her management skills. This is good. In fact, this is better than good. This, I can handle.

'Charlene, let's not rewrite history here,' I say, slightly teasing her, but then she's a good sport and takes a slagging. 'You were a *Rules* girl for about twenty minutes, two boyfriends ago, then you had a few too many in the

Ice Bar one drunken weekend and rang the poor guy so many times he ended up changing his phone number and, if memory serves me right, sending you a solicitor's letter.'

I don't like to remind her, but she was also a vegetarian for about twenty minutes (under Jo's influence) and smoked for about three-quarters of an hour. Charlene is more fun than anyone else you'll ever meet, but staying power isn't exactly her strong point.

'Ugh, thanks for the remind,' she groans. 'I rue the sad day I ever laid lips on that guy. Do you realize that he is now *engaged*? If that oddball can find a life-partner, so can I. Now you know how I haven't really been truly, madly, deeply in love since, oh, since, like, Riverdance played Broadway, but now I'm finally ready to lay to rest the ghost of relationships past. And let me tell you, there'll be no more sitting on my gorgeous ass waiting on the phone to ring. If I feel like calling Jack, then I will. Which I have done. Three times already since I left his flat this morning.'

'Emm, that's great.'

'So, aren't you just *dying* to know where you come in to all this?'

Oh God, here we go. Please don't let her ask, please, please, please.

'Your order, ladies,' says the waiter, sliding a linen-covered tray on to the table in front of us.

Phew, saved by the bell, I'm thinking as we bicker over whose turn it is to pay.

'No, I asked you, I'm getting this,' says Charlene, handing over a fifty and telling the stunned waiter to keep the change.

Now, as I always say, being psychic isn't something that's on tap, twenty-four hours a day, which is a right shame because I'd have loved some kind of early warning signal for what was coming next. (Charlene tends to talk stream of consciousness whenever she's a bit overexcited, so you'll just have to bear with me.)

'So anyway Jack is this, like, bigshot television producer on that morning TV show – oh, what the hell is it called? – oh yeah, the *Breakfast Club*, that's it, well, you know how absolutely *everyone* says it's really good but of course I've never seen it – you know me, sweetie, I'm never out of bed for it – so *naturellement*, I lied through my teeth and told Jack that it was right up there with *Desperate Housewives* on my list of absolute must-see television, and then I got to telling him about how I'd just lost my job which led us on to *Tattle* magazine which led us on to you and the way you just, like, see things and how *amazing* it is when you do it and how you're always, I mean *always*, right and he was just sooooo interested, we talked about you for, like, ages and then he asked did you have representation and I didn't have, like, the first clue what he meant and I was about to say no she's never

61

been in a beauty pageant that I know of, but it turned out it meant did you have an agent and right there and then I got this incredibly sudden *rush* of inspiration and I decided on the spot, yes, she bloody does . . . get this . . . and it's *me*! So do you need me to moon at you, Cassie? 'Cos you should be kissing my ass right now.'

'Sorry, what did you just say?' My head is spinning just from the effort of trying to keep up with her. It's hard enough at the best of times, but throw in a hangover . . .

'So meet your new agent. *Moi*. Yesterday I got fired, but then I took my personal pain and channelled it to joy, just like Oprah is always telling us to do. So aren't you proud of me?'

'Charlene, are you kidding me? It's a really sweet offer, but please understand, I don't want an agent, I don't need an agent—'

'If you want a television career, you do.'

'I don't want a television career.'

'You do now that I'm representing you.'

'Charlene!'

'Just ride the wave, honey, will you? The wonderful news for you is that I'm making you my brand-new pet project. I'm going to make it the focus of my remaining years to expand your brand and turn you into a global name. Would anyone have ever heard of U2 if Paul McGuinness hadn't been such a shit-hot manager? No, they'd probably be the resident wedding band now at some Holiday Inn beside Heathrow Airport.'

'Honey, don't get me wrong, I'm very flattered that you'd want to devote time to my career—'

'And your image, honey.'

'What's wrong with my image?'

'Nothing, if you want people to think you've got some boring office job.'

'These trousers are Joseph! You made me buy them at a discount sale and you told me they'd practically pay for themselves.'

'Oh darling, don't be cross with me when I've got such a filthy hangover. All I meant is that I want to get you out of all the city-chic gear and hippy-dippy you up a bit. You know, a bit less glamourella and a bit more Mystic Meg. Esoteric. We might even put you in a head-scarf and start calling you Madame Cassandra.'

'Thanks so much. Why don't you just drop a safe on my head while you're at it?'

'You're so pretty, darling, but I want to make you into a TV personality.'

'Why can't I help feeling that all your compliments are in fact thinly disguised blows to my self-esteem?'

'Oh, come on, I've been thinking about nothing else but the grand makeover – or should I say make-under? – I'm going to give you all morning. So you see? Unemployment pays.' Then her mobile rings. Marc with a C, dying to know what became of her after they parted company in Odessa the previous night.

'Do you mind if I take this, sweetie?' she coos at me. 'I need to feign gratitude to Marc with a C for disappearing as soon as I got chatting to my darling Jack, although, no kidding, I only had to invoke our dating code word about eighteen times just to get rid of him. What can I say? You know what he's like when he's a bit . . . well, you know, *gin-discreet*, and I didn't want him telling Jack any home truths about me at this early and highly critical stage— Hello? Marc with a C! How are you, my angel? How are you not working for the United Nations, you left so tactfully last night?'

I glance at my watch and realize that if I don't want to completely miss my deadline/lose my job, I'd better leg it at full speed to the *Tattle* magazine office.

This is not cowardice, you understand, this is not a case of me doing anything to avoid the conversation I'm going to have to have with Charlene at *some* point, this is just a case of I need my job, I love my job and I really, *really* don't want to get fired.

I make my excuses and leave, scarcely able to believe that I didn't have to tell her. Correction. That I didn't have to tell her yet.

'Spill it all out, right from the very start and omit no detail, however minute.'

Jo's so cool. Honest to God, I don't know what I'd do without her. We're both home much later that night, sharing a lovely bottle of Chianti and chatting about our respective days. It's one of those wild and windy autumny nights when you're just delighted *not* to be going out; i.e., lashing rain and freezing cold outside, but great TV on, the fire lit and our little sitting room all snug and cosy and smelling of the delicious incense that Jo brought back from her last trip to India.

'Oh Jo, this just seems so trivial compared with what you've been working on.'

'I don't care. Go for it, I could use the distraction.'

Jo, I should point out, has spent her whole day spearheading a campaign to stop the death penalty in China, where there's evidence to prove that high profits from organs taken for transplant from the unlawfully executed might be an incentive for the government to keep capital punishment in place. She's deeply concerned and is actually having sleepless nights about this. I, on the other hand, spent my day typing up my column, answering love queries from women (it's rarely guys, believe me, and I'd conservatively guess that about ninety per cent of the questions I get asked are all relationship-based).

Oh yeah. That and fielding calls from Charlene, demanding that I speak to her/shop with her/go afternoon boozing with her on the grounds that she's now my new agent. I tell Jo exactly what I'd seen the previous night, in glorious Technicolor. She's a fabulous listener, and the minute I'm finished rambling, she reaches for a notebook and pen.

'OK, let's make a list and then whittle away at what's worrying you, on a point–by–point basis.'

Lists, I should also tell you, figure very largely in Jo's highly organized life. She's always making them and I roar laughing at her, but she assures me it gives her a smug feeling of achievement every time she ticks something off, even if it's only 'Get up', 'Brush teeth', 'Remember to floss'. Lists and debates. Whenever there's a topic on the floor for discussion, she'll examine the pros and cons of each argument as forensically as Jeremy Paxman would on *Newsnight*. She's just one of those people.

'OK,' I say, taking another slug of lovely, nerve-calming wine. 'Jack Hamilton is – correction, could be – oh who am I kidding? – is, one hundred per cent . . . oh God . . .' I almost drop the wine glass, the mental picture I'm getting of him at this moment is so pin-sharp, I can practically smell his aftershave. It's almost like he's standing right in front of me.

He's tall, six feet, trim, jet-black hair and olive skin, but with deep green eyes, the most amazingly toned body I've ever seen on a man and a lovely, sexy, dimply smile that makes him look as if he's distantly related to Michael/Kirk Douglas. And I think he's in a car right now … I'm feeling him driving fast, but it's only a short journey …

'Jo, I haven't even met him and already the physical attraction I'm feeling for him is . . . what can I say? Up until now, I thought I'd be perfectly happy just to settle for a guy with normal social skills, but this man . . . oh my God, this man is like the heterosexual Holy Grail. Come to Mama.'

'Let's leave emotion out of the equation for the moment and concentrate on the facts. Point one. You think—'

'I *know* . . .'

'Sorry, you *know* that Jack Hamilton is probably—'

'Is *definitely* . . .'

'Is *definitely* the first true—'

'The first *real* true . . .'

'Sorry, the first *real* true love of your life.'

'Correct.'

'OK. Point two. Your predictions have never yet been known to be wrong, so if you are right in your assumptions, then that brings us neatly to point three . . .'

We say it in unison. 'He's going out with Charlene.'

I look at Jo hopelessly but she carries on undeterred.

'Point four. Much as we adore our dear friend Charlene, the Tipsy Queen herself, she has yet to have a relationship that lasts longer than her roots. Her boy-friends tend to have the same shelf life as a carton of milk.'

'This is different. She's deadly serious about this guy. I nearly gave myself an ulcer when I met her this morning, I was so terrified she'd ask me if I had any strong psychic feelings about him. Not about her and him as a couple, I mean, about just *him* as a person. I'd have had to tell her what I saw straight out. It's an absolute miracle that she didn't.'

'Point accepted; she's serious about him. Last week she was serious about giving up processed sugar. Next week, she'll have moved on to something else. I love the girl dearly, but let's just be searingly honest for a minute here. Focus and staying power are not exactly her strong suits.'

'Jo, she's so serious she went for a full Brazilian wax this afternoon. I had to hear all the gory graphic details when I was trying to work and believe you me, that is *not* a conversation you'd want me to repeat.'

'Ugh, please, do you mind? That image is so distressing I want to go and exfoliate my eyes. I'm sorry, but I happen to find the idea of putting yourself through physical pain for the sake of beauty just so *demeaning*. Do you ever see guys torturing themselves purely to look good for the opposite sex? When I meet someone, I'm sorry, but it'll be a case of love me, love my hairy legs.'

I choose not to get sidetracked into this particular discussion with her and top up our wine glasses instead. Not that I don't enjoy debating with Jo, it's just that right now I wouldn't really be up to that level of concentration.

'Well, I've barely been able to think about anything else all day. How I got my column delivered on time is nothing short of a miracle.'

'I just thought of point five,' says Jo crisply. 'We have lumps of cheese lying at the back of our fridge that have been around far longer than some of Charlene's boyfriends. Come on, Cassie, so she got there first. Big deal, fifty euro says she'll dump him by the end of the week, have forgotten him by the end of the month and by the end of the year, won't even care if you're having his baby. This, after all, is the woman who broke up with her last boyfriend because he had a hairy back and a car that failed its NCT.'

'I thought of that,' I say, staring blankly into the crackling fire, 'which brings me to my next question. Assuming that Charlene *does* dump him—'

'I'll take that bet,' Jo chips in.

'And assuming that free will doesn't come into play . . .'

'Explain?'

'You know, that he doesn't up sticks and move to the Outer Hebrides, then – Oh, how do I put this? – what is the statute of limitations on going out with a friend's ex-boyfriend?'

We look at each other blankly. It's virgin territory for both of us.

'Well, I'd have no problem with you going out with any of the sad parade of losers that I ever dated,' she says firmly. 'And while we're on the subject, can I just add that the thought of any of us clinging to the ghost of relationships past is completely abhorrent. That level of possessiveness over men, just because you used to go out with them, is just so demeaning to women. Don't you agree?'

'Of course,' I say, a bit worried now that this debate could go on into the wee small hours.

'My point is that if a guy exhibited the same obsessive control over an ex-girlfriend, society would label him a stalker,' Jo goes on, slowly warming to her theme. 'Equality works both ways. Agreed?'

'Agreed. My only concern is that none of my exes would be good enough for you.'

'But then you never fancied them anyway, did you?' she says, coming out of her Millie-Tant mode a bit and teasing me, which is a relief.

'The thing is, this is *Charlene* we're dealing with. You know what she's like if you even borrow her shoes.'

'Just thought of point six,' Jo says, scribbling away on her notepad.

'Shoot.'

'Well, it's obvious. You avoid contact with him at all costs. If you never meet him in the first place, then how can you fall for each other? Problem solved.'

'Could be tricky. Charlene will wonder why I'm dodging her new boyfriend. Suppose she has one of her posh dinner parties so we can all meet him. Don't you think she'll wonder why I'm a no-show? Nope, there's nothing else for it.'

'What?'

'I tell her out straight. Come clean. It'll be tough, but at least it'll all be out in the open. Now is the perfect time, before I've even met him.'

Jo is tapping her Biro against the notepad now, all of a sudden looking like she's miles away.

'What?' I ask. 'Don't you think that's the best thing all round?'

'Mmm,' she says absent-mindedly. 'I'm about to say an awful thing, but it would be on my conscience if I didn't.'

'Go on.'

'Well, I just can't help wondering if she'd do the same for you. How often have you thought there was a guy out there for you, Cassie? I'll tell you how often – *never*. Not once, in all the years I've known you. And now here you are, convinced that there actually could be some-one and what do you do? Walk away. You spend all day helping other people with their romantic problems and when the first smell of real love comes along, you run very fast in the opposite direction.'

There's a silence as I try to digest what she's just said.

And then my mobile rings.

Charlene.

Before answering, I let the phone ring in my hand for a moment, then turn to Jo. 'I'm a great believer in signs from the Universe and here's one right now. I'm going to tell her. Get it over with. Just stay here beside me in case it gets ugly.'

Jo just shakes her head as I answer.

'Sweetie!' Charlene trills. 'I thought you'd never pick up! Oh, do I have the most fantabulous news for you!'

'I'm really glad you rang,' I say, trying to sound all casual and normal, 'because there's something I really have to—'

A disapproving look from Jo, but Charlene doesn't let me get a word in.

'I'm here with Jack now. Say hello, darling.'

'Hi there!' I hear him distantly, as if he's driving and she's just put me on speakerphone. His voice is deep, sexy. Like I knew it would be. And he's Libra, I'm feeling, definitely Libra ...

'I've heard so much about you,' he says simply. 'Can't wait to meet you.'

'And you,' I say, trying to sound light and bright and

breezy and not like a stammering schoolgirl, which is exactly how I feel.

Then Charlene comes back on. 'As your brand-new agent, my darling, I've just got you your very first gig! Well, you know how Jack is from TV?' she asks, making it sound almost as if he's from another country. 'Anyway, he had a free slot on the *Breakfast Club* tomorrow morning, all because of some soap-opera star I never heard of having a last-minute scheduling problem, so guess what? You're the replacement!'

'*What* did you say?' My mouth is full of wine and I splurt some of it out, I'm so stunned.

'You, my darling, who has practically been screaming to be on TV for years now, are finally getting your big break!'

'Charlene, you have got to be joking, or let me re-phrase, YOU HAVE GOT TO BE JOKING!'

'Oh honey, there's nothing for you to worry about. It'll all be over in a few minutes, probably. And you won't be on till well after nine-thirty so only housewives and the unemployed will be watching— Oops! Sorry, Jack, I didn't mean that to come out like that, I'm sure you have a lovely audience made up of only the most discerning viewers.'

'We'd really love to have you on,' says Jack, coming on the phone again. Even at the sound of his voice, I swear my tummy is flipping somersaults. In my head,

I've already cast him as a Baldwin brother. Billy, or Alec, maybe, when he was pre-Kim Basinger. You know, young, hot and really, *really* sexy . . .

'It's nothing really, just a quick chat. Think of it a bit like the interview section on *Who Wants to Be a Millionaire?*, except stretched out to ten minutes.'

I can't help giggling. I knew he'd have a sense of humour, I just *knew* it . . .

Then Charlene comes back, putting on her best bossy schoolmarm voice. 'Now just listen to me, Cassandra, this is a wonderful opportunity and only the start of big things for you!'

'Charlene!' I say, suddenly nervous. 'I don't think I can do this. I don't know if I can go on television. There's a strong possibility I could end up being a laughing stock for years to come.'

'Too late, the deal's done: Jack's already put you into the programme schedule so there's no backing out now. I'll pick you up at eight!'

And, with a click, she's gone.

Chapter Three

THE TAROT DECK
THE ACE OF WANDS CARD, INVERTED

Symbolizes a new beginning. It could be a business venture, a new work project or some other fortuitous, unlooked-for opportunity. All going well, you should prosper and do very well at whatever it is, unless of course the card is inverted, in which case it heralds bad news. The ace of wands then becomes a card of warning and the exact opposite will apply.

In other words, God help you, because you're about to make a complete and utter show of yourself . . .

In the end, it's Jo who talks me into it.

I sleep it out (surprise, surprise) and she comes walloping on my bedroom door to haul me out of bed and into Charlene's car which, unbelievably, is waiting outside, punctual to the dot. (A limited edition Porsche GT, by the way, which she only drives when sober, invariably in the morning, before she heads off on one of her four-hour-long, girlie-boozy lunches.)

'Jo, I'll donate my entire next week's wages to Amnesty if you go down there and tell her I'm not doing it, I can't do it, I don't want to do it,' I say, groggily hauling myself up on to one elbow and squinting sleepily at Jo who, bless her, is plonking a lovely steaming mug of tea down on my bedside table.

'Too late to back out now, I'm afraid,' she says, sitting down on the edge of the bed. 'The Tipsy Queen herself is downstairs with an armful of the most horrible-looking flowery dresses she's brought for you to try on. God knows where she got them from. I wouldn't even sell them at Oxfam.'

'How horrible?'

'Hyacinth Bouquet horrible. Barbara Bush senior horrible.'

'Oh God, Jo, I sooooo don't want to go through with this,' I groan, slumping back against the pillow. 'And believe you me, Charlene and her cast-off outfits are the least of my worries.' Now that I'm fully awake, the

76

overwhelming nervousness I'm feeling is nauseatingly unreal.

'Oh come on, this could actually be a really good thing for you, Cassie. You've been given an amazing gift and it's your duty to help people with it, isn't it? So here's a chance to help them on a much wider scale. Why would you not want to do that?'

I try to take a gulp of tea but am afraid it'll make me throw up. 'I dunno. In no particular order, one: sheer, paralysing terror. I've never voluntarily got up in front of an audience in my life, apart from the time I was at that awful play with you—'

'Oh yeah, I'd totally blanked that out, the Reduced Shakespeare Company, wasn't it?'

'And there was audience participation and they dragged me up and made me be Ophelia.'

'And you threw up, got weak and then passed out, in that order.'

I shudder just at the memory. 'How I'm still not re-counting that God-awful night on some psychiatrist's couch somewhere is nothing short of a miracle. Number two, there's the very real fear that I could make a total eejit out of myself, live on national television—'

'You will NOT make an eejit of yourself.'

'Jo, I regularly make an eejit of myself. I've hit my humiliation limit so many times, I should have T-shirts printed and coasters made. Or even upgrade to business-class humiliation. And let's not forget point number three—'

'You *cannot* avoid Jack Hamilton for ever,' says Jo firmly, reading my thoughts with one-hundred-per-cent accuracy. 'Besides, you're the one who's always saying that everyone has the power to choose between fate and destiny. Can't you just decide *not* to fall for a guy?'

It's an interesting point and now I'm actually kind of hoping Jo might turn this into one of her great debates. Anything to buy me a bit of time.

'Mmm,' I say, rubbing my eyes, 'good one. Do we actually get to choose who we love—?'

'Well, I for one refuse to believe what chick-flicks are constantly peddling to us,' says Jo, not even letting me finish my sentence, but then, this particular subject is something of a well-worn hobby horse for her. And don't even dare get her started on the subject of the movies of Jennifer Aniston, her personal pet peeve. 'All romance *cannot* be predestined. It's just not possible.'

'It's not so much about predestination, it's just that if fate has something specific in store for you, it can sometimes be incredibly difficult to dodge. But then, on the other hand, not a week goes by when I don't write in the column that we're all human beings with free will, not farmyard animals.'

'There's the Dunkirk spirit,' says Jo, getting up briskly.

'Now, are you going to lie there all day philosophizing, or are you actually going to get up?'

'Yeah. Terrific. Great plan. That's the answer. I'll just keep telling myself over and over that if he's not available, then he's not available,' I say, staring at the ceiling, repeating it like a mantra and making no attempt whatsoever to physically get out of bed.

'Hmm. Not available for the moment. We'll just see how unavailable he is in a week or so,' says Jo, looking a bit disapproving. 'Now, out of bed and hop in the shower, missy. Charlene's in the kitchen downstairs and, I swear, it's worth getting up just to feast your eyes on the sight of her trying to use our coffee maker.'

One lightning-quick shower and by the time I get back to my room, Charlene and Jo are standing in front of my full-length mirror, bickering over a pile of clothes that are strewn all over the floor. Charlene's looking very businesslike today, with her mane of red curls tied back and wearing a beautifully cut Paul Costelloe trouser suit which I happen to know he gave her for free as a thank you, not only for being his bestest customer but for practically keeping him in business.

'Just try it on, that's all I'm asking,' Charlene is pleading to poor old Jo, waving a revolting, garish, flowery dress with (I'm *not* messing) a corsage sewn on to it in front of her.

'Charlene, if you don't stop trying to change my

image, I will go downstairs, open the oven door and personally shove your head in. I'm not a girlie girl and I never will be.'

'Don't be so ratty, you're the one who hasn't changed her look since we did the Leaving Cert,' says Charlene defensively. 'Here am I only trying to help and you're just so ungrateful. Honestly, Josephine, I feel like sticking my finger in your coffee only I'm afraid I'd lose an acrylic nail.'

'Yes, and I'm sure you must need those for climbing up trees and warding off predators.'

'You're only jealous, but surely you know me well enough to know that I take all forms of jealousy as inverted compliments. Oh, look, it's our resident TV star.' Charlene beams at me as she clocks me padding in behind them, still wrapped in a towel. 'Help me out, will you, sweetie? Here's our darling Jo, screaming for a makeover and all I'm getting is a torrent of dog's abuse.'

'Leave me out of your squabbling, girlies,' I plead, rummaging around in my wardrobe for my good Armani jeans and a crisp white Zara shirt that I'm pretty certain I washed last week. From bitter experience, I've learned to keep well out of the way when Jo and Charlene are at each other's throats. It's a very regular occurrence and I'm just not feeling well enough this morning to referee between the pair of them.

'Josephine, it's not often I compliment you,' says

Charlene imperiously, 'but it's just that underneath that' – she pokes at Jo's chunky-knit, bum-and-thigh-covering jumper – 'you have the rack of an angel and the waist of a fifteen-year-old just waiting to be unleashed. So why do you insist on going around dressed like a refugee?'

'Because I don't *care* about the way I look,' Jo almost shouts back at her. 'There are far more important things in this world than appearances. I'm actually comfortable in my own skin and I just wonder if you can say the same. Now can we please change the subject? This conversation demeans women.'

'I'm only trying to help. You're like the ultimate challenge for me to make over. I look on you kind of like the dowdy sister I never had.'

'One more crack like that and I'll drag you downstairs and wash your mouth out with cheap wine.'

'You'd have far more success with men if you re-invented a bit. Just look at me and learn by osmosis. May I point out that I am the only one in this room with a bona fide boyfriend?'

A hint of a glance from Jo, which only makes my tummy churn even more. Jesus, I think there's a very real chance I might be sick . . .

Charlene goes on: 'What I'm trying to say is that the only living person who changes their look more than me is Madonna.'

'The only reason you reinvent is to compensate for your short attention span,' says Jo. 'Now get that flowery thing away from me and throw it over there, in the suck pile.'

'Oh drama, drama, drama,' snaps Charlene, deeply put out and beginning to get a bit upset, 'and FYI? This dress is not some flowery thing, as you choose to call it. This happens to be vintage Versace.'

'Great. Well, can you donate it to Oxfam? I'll be sure to put it in our vintage *crap* section.'

'Jo . . .' But Jo's on a roll and there's no stopping her now.

'Where did you buy it, anyway? The same shop Jordan goes to for all her clothes? You know, where the more money you spend, the worse you end up looking?'

'Actually, that dress was Mum's,' Charlene says simply.

There's a long, long pause.

'I'm sorry,' Jo eventually says in a small voice, looking mortified.

'OK. You weren't to know.'

'It's, emm . . . Well, on second thoughts, it's not actually that bad. Emm, the dress, I mean.'

'Jo, please. You don't have to do this. It's fine. Really.'

'Oh come here, you daft lass,' says Jo softly, pulling Charlene to sit down on the bed beside her and hugging her tight. 'Sorry for being an insensitive cow.'

Charlene lets herself be hugged, looking absolutely tiny and frail and vulnerable. 'It's OK. I'm used to you.'

'Are we still buddies?'

'Course. Although there are times when I don't know why I hang around with you. The ingratitude . . .'

Charlene has a bit of a glint in her eye now, which Jo immediately picks up on and starts teasing her again, except more gently this time.

'You hang around with us because we keep you normal. Ish.'

'I know. Anyway, this conversation demeans my wardrobe, I suppose,' says Charlene, doing a very accurate impression of Jo at her most Millie-Tant.

A quick smile at each other and the tropical storm has blown over.

'So, Cassie, what do you think about wearing the Valentino skirt— Oh my God, honey, are you OK?'

The minute they notice me, like lightning they're both over to where I'm now slumped against a chair, head between my knees, frantically gulping for air.

'It's only nerves, that's all, I'll be fine in a minute,' I say, trying to convince myself as much as the pair of them.

'You're not a bit fine,' says Jo, really concerned, 'you're as white as a sheet. Stay right there and I'll grab you a glass of water.'

'Charlene, I'll make a deal with you,' I say, slowly feeling the blood coming back to my head.

'Whatever you say, hon,' she says, patting my wrists and loosening the top button on my shirt.

'What are you doing?'

'This is what they do on *ER*. Trust me, I watch a lot of medical dramas.'

'Look, I'll come in the car with you and go as far as the TV studios, but if I still feel like this when we get there, I'm chickening out. Deal?'

She mightn't look too happy about it, but then she doesn't exactly have a choice. 'Deal,' she eventually agrees, with a big bright smile. 'Hey, I'm your agent and you're my star. Got to keep the talent happy, don't I?'

Channel Seven isn't too far from our house, and by the time we get there I'm actually starting to feel a little better. This is mainly due to the fact that (a) while Charlene is busy on her mobile telling everyone she's ever met in her entire life that I'm about to go on TV, the one person she can't get hold of is Jack Hamilton. This makes me secretly hope against hope that I've hit the karmic jackpot and some eleventh-hour domestic/personal/medical crisis has kept him out of work for the day. Also, (b) I managed to root out a bottle of Rescue Remedy from the depths of my handbag and am now taking huge, calming gulps of it, dispensing with the dropper-thing altogether. If this isn't an emergency, I don't know what is.

We drive past security and, although there's loads of

parking, Charlene pulls up right in front of the main entrance, in a space clearly labelled 'Reserved for the Director General'.

'What are you doing?' I say. 'Actively *trying* to get clamped?'

'Don't be like that, you're still a bit weak and you need minding. Oh and besides, I'm in my favourite suede Manolos and there might be puddles. Like them, sweetie? On a cost-per-wear basis they practically paid for themselves, but I still can't walk in them.'

I'm just not up to arguing with her, so we park, hop out and head, or in Charlene's case, hobble, towards TV reception.

'Morning, ladies! Are you here for the *Breakfast Club*?' asks a smiling, friendly receptionist. 'If you want to pop up to the make-up room, I'll tell Lisa, the stage manager, to find you there. It's just upstairs, first on your right.'

And still no sign of Jack Hamilton, which is driving Charlene nuts, but helping me and my nerves considerably.

My phone beep-beeps as a text comes through. Marc with a C, wishing me luck, bless him.

HI MY LOVELY. B UR FAB SELF. HAVE THE TV ON IN THE GYM AND WE R ALL GLUED. HOW R THE BUTTERFLIES?

'Ugh, butterflies?' says Charlene, clinging to the banister rail as she limps upstairs. 'Butterflies in my tummy are always a tell-tale symptom that I'm afraid of losing a guy and, let me tell you, Jack's phone being off isn't exactly inspiring confidence right now.'

I'm actually beginning to breathe normally now. This mightn't be too bad. This, I might just be able to pull off . . .

We head into the make-up room, where a guy with orange fake-tan-gone-wrong and lime-green trousers that really shouldn't be seen either in daylight or outside of a dance floor bounds over to us.

'Oh my Gowwd, you must be Cassandra!' he says, waving a make-up brush with intent. 'I know I must sound like one of those losers that meet William Shatner at a Trekkie convention, but I am just sooooo thrilled to meet you!'

We all shake hands, he sits me down and immediately starts pampering me, which makes me feel even more relaxed, although I do wince slightly when Charlene refers to herself as my agent. It makes me feel a bit high-maintenance and I-go-nowhere-without-my-entourage-in-the-manner-of-Liza-Minnelli-ish, whereas all I really want to do is slip out of here, slink home, go straight back to bed and stay there, with my head well under the duvet, for the rest of the day.

'I just *love* your column,' says orange-fake-tan guy,

vigorously lashing foundation on me, 'you're the main reason I buy *Tattle* magazine these days. Well, apart from all those fabulous dish-the-dirt photos they have of celebrities walking the streets without make-up, looking like total crap. I get through my day so much better knowing that I'm marginally cuter than Matt Damon when he's caught off guard.'

'Oh, emm . . . thanks, that's good to hear.'

'First time on TV?'

'Yup. And to say I'm nervous would be a major understatement.'

'Walk in the park, baby. Oh, I am going to have you looking so *fabulous*. Wish everyone I had in my chair had your cheekbones, it would make my job so easy. Hey, Joanie!' he says, calling over to Joan Davis, a well-known newsreader I instantly recognize, who's sitting in the chair opposite me having her hair blow-dried. 'Honey, you won't believe who I have sitting here! Only Cassandra, you know, *the* Cassandra from *Tattle* magazine!'

'Oh wow! I'm such a big fan,' she says, waving at me and shouting over the dryer.

'Thanks so much,' I say, hardly able to believe that an actual celebrity has heard of me.

'Are you here for the *Breakfast Club*?'

'If I manage not to pass out or throw up first, yes.'

'You'll be absolutely brilliant. Best of luck.'

'Thanks. I hope you don't mind my asking, but you're leaving here to go over to the BBC soon, aren't you?'

She immediately gasps. 'Oh my God, can you see that in my aura?'

'Emm, no,' I mumble, a bit embarrassed. 'I read it in the *Star*.'

'Now, if you happen to see anything about me and my ex,' says fake-tan man, still all bright and bubbly, 'you will tell me, won't you? No pressure, but we've just broken up and you know how there's always, always, *always* a contest with any recent ex called "Who's the happiest and who looks the best", versus "Who's put on two stone and who's going to die alone and miserable".' He's laughing but there's something forced about it. 'Now, don't get me wrong, I'm fine about the break-up, absolutely tip top; I mean, it was very much a mutual decision, no question, but I just wondered . . .'

OK, I'm not actually sure whether he's protesting too much or if all his high-octane, in-your-face babbling sets me off, but before I know where I am, I get a flash.

It's him, fake-tan man, but, no, he's not a bit fine at all. Far from it. I can see him lying in an unmade bed alone, cradling himself, rocking from side to side, with an almost empty bottle of Jack Daniel's on the bedside table and an overflowing ashtray stuffed with butts. He looks hollow, baggy-eyed, thin and frail and the feeling

of absolute desolation I'm picking up from him is almost
overwhelming …

'Are you OK, love?' he asks. 'You've gone very quiet. Nerves, huh?'

Please let me see something good ahead for this guy, I'm thinking as he lashes the mascara on to me, still yapping away. Something, anything positive, please, please, please.

'Emm, yeah. Nerves. That's all.'

Shit, come on, Cassie, you must be able to pick up something.

Meanwhile, Charlene is punching impatiently at buttons on her mobile phone. 'Ugh, Jack, for the love of God, will you *please* turn your bloody phone on? Call yourself a producer and your phone's switched off?'

'Are you trying to call Jack Hamilton?' asks fake-tan guy in surprise. ''Cos, honey, you're wasting your time till we're off the air.'

'Well, do you think someone could take me to him?' says Charlene, effortlessly switching on her best little-girl-lost voice. 'Or maybe just let him know that his girlfriend is here? Please?'

No kidding, she uses the GF word without even batting an eyelid.

'Sure, I can do that for you, not a problem,' says a bright, bubbly girl who's just bounced into the make-up room, wearing a headset, combat jeans and a vest. She looks so young, you'd wonder if she's even left school and she introduces herself as Lisa, the stage manager. 'You must be Cassandra. Lovely to meet you,' she adds, warmly shaking hands.

'And you.'

'It's great to have you on. Nothing to worry about, you'll be fab.'

She waves over at Charlene, who's now gone on to another call, making an appointment for her personal eyebrow-waxing lady to call out to her house later. Charlene completely blanks her, but then politeness towards strangers isn't exactly her strong point.

'I try not to talk to the little people,' she once let slip, 'because before you know where you are, they're calling you by your first name and taking all sorts of liberties. That's how the French revolution started, you know.' She was pissed, but we haven't forgotten and regularly slag her about it. Jo nicknamed her Marie Antoinette after this and every now and then throws the odd French word in her direction to annoy her and makes loads of gags about letting people eat cake. It never fails to get a rise out of her.

'OK, our future TV star is good to go, hot to trot,' says fake-tan man, whipping the make-up gown off theatrically.

He's done an amazing job on me; it's done my

confidence the world of good and I really can't thank him enough.

'All down to good raw materials,' he says, cheerily waving us off. 'Now, the very best of luck and remember you've absolutely nothing to be nervous about!'

Lisa is just leading Charlene and me out of the door when suddenly, miracle of miracles, a flash comes.

'On a beach,' I tell him with absolute certainty, 'it's all going to happen for you on a beach.'

'What did you say?' says fake-tan man, all ears.

'Your next relationship will start on a beach. There's a party and everyone's wearing Hawaiian shirts and drinking cocktails. He's foreign, I think, olive skin, dark eyes, very athletic. It's going to happen soon too, within . . . about six weeks. I can see it. Trust me, your days of drinking home alone are numbered.'

Oh shit, did I just say that aloud? I wouldn't want him to think I'd seen, well, what I saw.

'Oh my *GAWD*, you're just amazing,' he says, bounding over to me and hugging me tight, really, genuinely touched. 'I'm getting straight on to that internet to book the cheapest foreign holiday I can find. Eeeeek!'

'Gotta move, people,' says Lisa, tapping her wristwatch.

'I'll let you know when it happens!' fake-tan man calls after us as we trundle downstairs, absolutely delighted with himself. 'I'll write to you care of the magazine!'

Amazingly, I'm actually feeling all right by the time we get to the studio door. Cooler, calmer. No nausea, which is always a plus. And still no sign of Jack Hamilton which is an A plus plus.

This is fine, this is . . . do-able.

'Just be yourself and you'll be grand,' Lisa says, squeezing my arm encouragingly and holding open the studio door for me.

I take a deep, calming breath and am about to step through when suddenly Charlene snaps her phone shut and seems to notice Lisa's presence for the first time.

'Oh, hi there,' she says, smiling angelically. 'So do you think maybe *now* you could take me up to wherever my boyfriend is? Please? I suffer from an incredibly low patience threshold.'

'First of all I need to get Cassandra settled,' Lisa replies curtly. 'Secondly, you need to switch your mobile off.'

'Oh, don't be cross. I absolutely *had* to make that call, it was a dire emergency. Do you think these eyebrows just wax themselves?'

'And lastly, I'm afraid you're just going to have to wait here. Apparently some idiot went and parked in the Director General's space and now I have to pop outside to troubleshoot.'

It's pitch dark when we go into studio and Lisa whispers to me to watch out for the cables strewn all over the floor. A sound man with headphones strapped to him comes at me from nowhere and clips a tiny microphone to my shirt, silently giving me the thumbs up as if to say, 'Good luck.'

'They're just wrapping up the last item, then we go to a quick commercial break, then you're on,' hisses Lisa, gently steering me over to a monitor so I can see what's happening.

Now, you mightn't believe it, but I have occasionally been out of bed in time to see the *Breakfast Club*. Well, it's kind of hard to avoid, as it goes out six days a week. Anyway, I'm able to recognize the two presenters immediately. One's called Mary and the other is Maura and they operate kind of like Tweedledum and Tweedledee. Good cop/bad cop, that type of thing.

Mary is comfortably settling into middle age, warm, welcoming and with an almost motherly manner, whereas Maura is younger, sharper, brittle and caustic, with a bone-dry sense of humour, usually at the poor hapless guest's expense. You wouldn't think it, but the combination of two such polar-opposite personality types actually works and the *Breakfast Club* is one of Channel Seven's biggest audience-pullers.

'So anyone watching who fancies giving their home a nice bit of an upgrade, just remember, it needn't cost the earth,' says Mary, beaming into the camera. 'And what do you call this lovely piece we have here?' she asks a tall, lanky guy with his hair in a ponytail, who I can only presume is an interior designer. He's proudly swaggering around what looks like the Tardis from *Doctor Who* in the middle of the studio floor, but it turns out to be one of those stand-alone shower cubicle thingies, perched precariously on a granite-stone dais.

'I call it *Flow*,' says the designer, shoving his glasses up his nose and managing to look both affected and a complete eejit at the same time. 'I'm trying to combine both yin and yang in terms of structure. I set out to create a concept where showering can become a uniquely spiritual experience.'

'Mmm,' says Maura, unimpressed, as she pokes her nose inside it. 'It's-raining-Zen-type vibe. That what you're trying to get at?'

'Lovely, lovely,' says Mary a bit unenthusiastically. 'Mind you, I have to confess I'm more of an Ikea woman myself. Have either of you seen this month's catalogue? The outdoor lighting is only to die for. And don't get me started on the sofas. Only beautiful. With machine-washable covers and all.' Then, at a wind-it-up-quick hand signal from the floor manager, she turns to beam beatifically at the camera. 'Well, thank you so much for coming along, and the best of luck with your . . . ehh . . . what did you call it again? Oh sorry, yes, with *Flow*.'

'Stay with us,' says Maura, looking bored and making no attempt to conceal it. 'We have a real live psychic in

studio with us this morning, which should be . . . emm
. . . illuminating. Back after the break.'

Before I know where I am, Lisa has ushered me on
to the set, which is like a big, colourful living room, and
plonked me down on a bright, canary-yellow, oversized
comfy sofa. Mary and Maura are sitting opposite me, but
only Mary introduces herself, shaking me warmly by
the hand and wishing me luck. She's just lovely close up,
looks a dead ringer for Maeve Binchy.

Maura just fiddles with her radio mike and completely
blanks me.

'No hard questions now,' I whisper, attempting to
make light of the situation.

'Ah, relax, sure you'll be fine,' says Mary, patting my
knee affectionately. 'It's only a bit of an aul' chat, that's
all.'

'We're going to have to talk to Jack about the calibre
of guests we're getting,' snaps Maura as a make-up girl
hastily dusts powder on her nose. 'That last guy could
have bored for Ireland at Olympic level. I was this close
to wrapping it up by saying, "OK, time to check out of
this yawn-fest." Frankly, it's just not good enough.'

All of a sudden I'm nervous again, not only at her
appalling rudeness, but at the mere mention of Jack
Hamilton's name . . .

Come on, Cassie, hold it together.

Anyway, before I even have time to dwell on it, the

studio goes deathly quiet and the floor manager is over. 'OK, ladies, we're back on in five, four, three, two, one . . .'

'And welcome back,' beams Mary. 'Now, we have a lovely treat for any readers of *Tattle* magazine who might be watching. Their resident psychic columnist is here with us this morning for a nice little chat. Cassandra, you're very welcome and thank you so much for coming along.'

'Emm . . . hi!' I say, trying my best to sound all chirpy and relaxed.

'Now, tell us, I understand that you were born with this very special *gift*,' Mary goes on, stressing the word 'gift' as if it were something that came wrapped in a big blue bow from Tiffany's.

'But then, it's a bit like the weather report, isn't it?' Maura chips in. 'I'm not interested in what today was like, tell me about tomorrow.'

There's an awkward pause as they both just look at me.

Shit. This must be the part where I'm expected to perform.

'Emm . . . well, you see,' I stammer, doing my very best to sound confident, 'as I always say, being psychic isn't something that's on tap twenty-four hours a day. I just sometimes get these very strong visions about things that haven't happened yet, but . . . you see . . . I can never actually tell when I'm going to get a flash.'

'Well, that's convenient,' snipes Maura and I swear to God I want to die.

Another silence. I can hear someone behind the camera coughing, loud and clear. Oh God, all this awful scene needs is tumbleweed rolling through it.

'So your gift is a sort of *force of nature*, then, is that what you mean?' Maura continues in a tone I can only describe as disparaging. 'Like Niagara Falls.'

'Yeah. Or a fifty-per-cent sale at H & M.' What the hell, she's being so rude I might as well try to lighten things up a bit.

I can see Lisa out of the corner of my eye sniggering beside a studio monitor and silently giving me the thumbs up, bless her.

'Mmm,' says Maura. 'OK, I accept that you may not perform to order, but you do go around calling yourself a psychic, don't you? So come on then, make a prediction.' She's glaring at me, almost challenging me and there's a very long, very awkward pause. Which probably only lasts for a minute, but, oh my God, it feels like half an hour. I must have been deranged to agree to do this. Never, ever again as long as I live . . .

Then Mary obviously gets a frantic instruction in her earpiece about filling in the silence because she starts twittering inanely, which only gives me a fresh bout of nerves. 'Well, maybe you could help me with this one, Cassandra. For the life of me I can't decide where to take my son on holiday after he's finished his college exams. He's turned Buddhist now and wants to go to Tibet, but I'd be more of a Lanzarote woman myself. So I said to him last night that if he worked hard and got good grades, maybe we could reach a compromise. Like Gran Canaria. Well, you can't go wrong in the Canaries, now can you?'

And then I get a flash.

It's a tabloid paper, with a grainy picture of Maura – yes, it's definitely Maura, I'd recognize that pinched-looking face a mile off. She's falling out of a nightclub, looking the worse for wear and kissing an older-looking man, with a banner headline that reads 'BREAKFAST CLUB STAR'S MARRIED LOVER' …

'So come on then,' says Maura, almost goading me. 'Are you seeing anything now, or is there some kind of roadblock in the cosmos this morning?'

Another flash. Another headline and Maura's still snapping at me. Bloody hell, this is unbelievable. It's like the more she talks and the ruder she gets, the more I'm seeing: 'TV STAR BRANDED HOMEWRECKER AS HER MARRIED BOYFRIEND'S WIFE SPEAKS OUT. BREAKFAST CLUB CONTRACT "UNDER REVIEW" SAYS CHANNEL SEVEN SOURCE.'

'Emm . . . no. Not really,' I say in a small voice.

'Sorry?'

'Nothing. At the moment. Sorry . . .'

Well, what am I supposed to say? Yes, I've seen the writing on the wall for your television career? What do you want me to do, I'm frantically thinking, announce it live to the nation? Oh hell, this is where I'd kill *not* to be psychic . . .

'So,' says Maura, who's gone back to looking bored again. 'How do I phrase this politely? Maybe your psychic powers aren't at their best first thing in the morning?'

By now, I'm starting to wish for either (a) a medical emergency or (b) some major international incident, like an assassination attempt or the collapse of a government, something that'll mean they have to go straight to a news bulletin and stay there for the rest of the day. Hopefully. With a bit of luck. Anything, and I really mean *anything*, just to get me out of here.

What's even worse is Maura's stony silence. She's glaring at me with an expression that manages to say both 'despicable con-artist' and 'chancer who has just been ruthlessly exposed in huge important *Breakfast Club* scoop' all at the same time. And then the miracle happens.

'What's that?' says Mary, nervously tapping her earpiece before turning back to camera. 'Oh, right, OK.

Ladies and gentlemen, a bit of good news, we have a caller on line one who'd like to ask Cassandra's advice, if that's OK?'

'Emm . . . yes, sure, I'm delighted to . . . emm . . . help . . .' Thank God, thank God, now please just let me be able to see something, anything . . .

A woman's voice immediately fills the studio. She sounds about as agitated as I feel and her voice is low, hushed. 'Ehh, hello? Am I through to Cassandra? *The* Cassandra?'

I'm dimly aware of Maura glowering at me, willing me to fall flat on my face (again) and I'm madly trying to tune out her negative energy – this caller really sounds like she needs help.

'Yes, I'm Cassandra. What's the problem?'

'Can you hear me? I have to whisper just in case anyone in my office overhears me. I'd die of embarrassment if anyone here copped on to what I'm at.'

'I understand,' I say, dropping my voice instinctively too, so it really feels like an intimate chat and that half the country isn't listening in.

'We were all having coffee in our office canteen and the TV was on and there you were and . . . I just HAD to ring you. I hope you don't mind?'

'Of course not. What's your name?'

'Emm, Jenny.'

She's lying, I instantly feel, but then, would you

100

blame her? Although her name begins with a G, I think.

'Emm, well, here's the thing. I'm . . . thirty-nine' – her voice is now a total whisper and I have to sit forward and really strain to hear her – 'next birthday and I'm still single and I *so* don't want to be. I mean, all my friends are getting married and engaged now and are dropping babies like you wouldn't believe and I can't even get arrested. So I went to' – another whisper – 'a speed-dating do last night—'

'Brave girl,' I say, hoping to calm her down a bit. Gina, that's it, that's her real name, but I better be careful not to mortify the poor girl by calling her that live to the nation.

'So there I was, all dressed up, hair done, nails done and probably looking like a right dog's dinner, but I really felt like I'd put in the effort, and you know how many guys ticked my box? None, not a single one. So there was a drinks do afterwards and I was on my own, as per bloody usual and, oh God, I'm so embarrassed to tell you what happened . . .'

'It's OK, emm, Jenny,' I say gently, coaxingly, 'none of us here is Judge Judy and executioner.'

I'm dimly aware of Mary and Maura both staring at me, unsure of whether I'll fall to pieces or not, but I'm suddenly filled with a huge surge of confidence. I can do this. I do this every day of the week. After all, ninety per cent of all the letters I get sent are from women and ninety per cent again all involve relationship queries, don't they?

The only thing that's making this different is that I'm being watched by thousands— No, banish that thought and keep concentrating on Gina. Sorry, Jenny.

'So, we were all in this very trendy cocktail bar after the speed dating wrapped up,' she's going on, 'and most of the women there are far younger and far, far hotter than me and then as the night wears on, everyone's starting to pair off with a few drinks in them, you know the way . . .'

'I do indeed. My flatmate's always saying that, with Irish fellas, alcohol is the only jump lead you'll ever need.'

There's laughter coming from behind the camera as Gina/Jenny keeps on talking, sounding a bit less wobbly now and a lot more self-assured.

'And then, oh Cassandra, I'm so embarrassed, I just stood at the bar, all on my own, and started feeling so miserable for myself . . . and I know all the self-help books tell you that you have to smile at the room brightly and confidently and trust that some guy will eventually come and chat you up, but no one did and then . . . Oh, it was just so *embarrassing* . . .'

'It's OK, you can tell me. Can't be anything worse than what I've done myself in the past.'

'Promise you won't judge me?'

'Cross my heart.'

'I burst into tears. In public. And not just a few snivels. I wailed, and I really mean *howled*, to the four walls. So everyone's looking at me thinking what a poor, sad spinny and they're probably right – I mean, how pathetic am I? It's one thing to have a bit of a bawl in the privacy of your own home, or in front of a girlfriend, but to let yourself down in front of a bar full of total strangers . . .'

'And you start looking like you're dangerously close to butterfly-net territory,' snipes Maura and without even being aware of what I'm doing, I find myself signalling at her to *shut up*.

Jenny/Gina mercifully doesn't hear and is now in full flow. 'So then the barman comes over to me, just to make sure I'm not about to open a vein or anything and, I'm not joking you, he's about half my age and the next thing he's escorting me to a taxi and . . . oh Cassandra, I just felt so completely and utterly alone that I ended up dragging him into the back of the cab with me, and then he came back to my place and I don't even have the excuse of being plastered because I was stone-cold sober but in my desperation I was thinking: He's way too young for me, I don't really fancy him all that much so he *can't* break my heart . . . hey, this could work! But of course when I woke up this morning he was gone and I can't tell you how sordid and cheap I felt, that I let a total stranger pick me up in a bar and now I'm frightened that I'll end up as one of those pathetic older women who go out with shiny guys called Brad who just use them for sex and never marry them and, Cassandra, the thing is I really, desperately want to have a child and, please God, a family and I'm so afraid it'll never happen for me . . . I mean is this really my life? Miserable and unhappy and phoning up a psychic on a TV show, desperate for some chink of hope?'

Thank God. *Thank you, God.* During her monologue, a flash comes.

Jenny/Gina's on a train, and it's lashing rain. I can see her clear as crystal. She's small, tiny, very pretty, with dark brown hair and big soulful brown eyes. She's laden down with files and folders and is looking very stressed and hassled, then . . .

'Sorry to interrupt you,' I say to her gently, afraid she'll hang up at any minute, 'but, by any chance, do you take a train to work every day?'

There's a stunned silence. 'Wow! Yes, I do. How did you know?'

Another flash.

A guy bumps into her, knocking over her stuff and instantly apologizes and helps her to pick it all up. He's older, maybe

*fifties, attractive, newly divorced with a grown-up daughter,
I think …*

'Gina . . . sorry, I mean Jenny, that's where romance
will come to you. Relax. Your days of standing on your
own in singles bars and regretting one-night stands will
soon be at an end. I'm certain of it.'

'Oh my God, that's astonishing!'

'Oh, this guy is so lovely,' I add for good measure.
Can't help myself, I just feel this so strongly. 'I really
think that he'll be good for you, and you for him.'

'Cassandra, I really can't thank you enough,' she says,
sounding a bit teary now, 'you're just *amazing.*'

Mary's in like a shot. 'Well now, isn't that lovely, just
lovely. If there's one thing I love it's a nice, happy ending,
all neatly wrapped up.'

'Of course, that's presuming you're not bluffing just
to get out of an awkward situation,' smiles Maura so
smugly that I swear I want to smack her across her
pinched little face. 'I mean, how are viewers supposed to
know whether or not that caller's love life will pan out
all neatly and tidily, just like you said?'

There's no time for me to answer her back though, as
Mary immediately takes over. 'Sorry, sorry to interrupt
you there, but we have another caller on line two. Hello?
Line two? Yes, you're through to Cassandra. Go right
ahead.'

'Ehh, hello? Am I through to Cassandra? *Tattle* magazine Cassandra?'

'Yes, here I am,' I say cheerily, mentally reminding myself to try and not sound like one of those cheesy radio phone-in psychiatrists that they have in the States.

'Cassandra, thank Jesus it's you. I've an emergency on my hands and if you can't help me, I am so dead.'

A woman's voice. She's middle-aged, stressed and . . . Nuala. That's it, that's her name. Definitely a Nuala. 'Go ahead, Nuala.' Please understand, I wasn't showing off or acting flashy for the sake of it, the name just slipped out.

'That's my name! How did you know?'

I shoot a glance over at Maura, who's rolling her eyes up to heaven. Like I'd staged this and got some hoaxer to ring up. As if.

'All part of the gig, Nuala,' I say, calmly. 'So, what's the problem?'

'It's my engagement ring. It's lost. And it's only worth a fortune. And if my husband finds out, I'm not joking, he'll divorce me. It's an antique ruby that's been in his family for generations. It was, like, the only thing his grandmother managed to salvage from their house before the Black and Tans burnt it to the ground. Believe me, I have searched high and low for it.'

An instant flash.

Gardening gloves, I'm seeing gardening gloves, thick, green ones. By a rose bush, I think, I'm pretty sure I can smell roses …

'Nuala, by any chance, do you have a garden?'

'Yes, yes, I do. Just had it landscaped last month. Why do you ask? Oh Lord, no … don't tell me … !'

'I think that you'll probably find—'

'I was only out there this morning doing the roses. Oh, how stupid am I! Will you stay on the phone till I go and check, Cassandra? Hang on a sec, now …' Her footsteps are clearly audible throughout the studio as she makes her way across what sounds like a tiled kitchen floor, then we hear a creaking back door, then the sound of her outdoors. 'Stay with me, Cassandra, there's a good girl.'

'The gloves,' I say, firmly, really feeling rock-solid certain. 'Check inside your gardening gloves.'

I can physically feel the bad vibes hopping from Maura and am doing my best to channel her out and just concentrate on the ring.

'I have them in my hand now,' says Nuala, puffing and panting, 'wait one sec till I see …'

I hold my nerve and even try to smile at the camera. It sounds weird, but right now, I'm actually starting to enjoy this whole experience. I feel on top of things. Confident. The way you do when you really think things are finally going your way.

There's a long pause, then, thank God, right on cue comes the unmistakable sound of something metallic hitting off a stone pathway.

Knew it. I just *knew* it.

'It's here! It's really here! I have it in my hand! Oh Cassandra, you have saved my life, you really have. Not to mention my marriage!'

'Be a bit more careful next time, Nuala,' says Mary, all motherly. 'Get the ring sized if you can, there's a good woman. That's what I'd do after an awful fright like that.'

I barely have time to breathe easy and relax before another call comes through. A man's voice, which is kind of unusual.

'Cassandra?' he says and instantly I can see him.

He has pale skin and is in his late forties, the type of man who gives off an image of being stand-offish and brusque but who actually has a lot of very deep sadness in his aura …

'Yes, go ahead.'

'Look, in a million years I'd never have phoned in to a show like this, but as I just said to your researcher, I couldn't believe the things you were seeing for those other two callers. I'm impressed. And I'm rarely impressed.'

'What's the trouble?' I ask as gently as I can, trying to keep him on the phone as much as anything. I have a strong feeling this guy could just hang up at any second.

'The trouble is it's almost ten a.m. and I'm sitting at home watching breakfast television, that's the trouble. I was made redundant from my last job and I can't get anything else. Nothing. Not unless I go abroad and I really don't want to do that for, well, for personal reasons.'

A flash.

He has an elderly mother, wheelchair bound, that he's taking care of. They live together and he's devoted to her. An only child too, I'm getting …

And another one.

His hands. Odd. Why am I seeing hands?

I go for it. 'Excuse me, I hope you don't mind me asking you, but—'

'Ask what you like. Why do you think I phoned in?'

'I don't mean to be rude, but, well, first of all I'm sensing a lot of unhappiness around where you used to work. An office job?'

'Computers. Boring as hell. Then, without warning, the company shut down and relocated to India. Two hundred staff laid off, just like that. And at my age it's hard to just walk into another job.'

The image of hands again, only this time with a strong feeling of deep peace and serenity …

'Are you some kind of painter? Or do you work with wood? As a hobby, I mean?'

'Yeah, bit of carpentry in my spare time. Why?'

'Ever think about doing it full-time?'

'*What?*'

'Because that's the way forward for you, I'm absolutely certain. You'll go into business on your own and be very successful. I'm sure of it.'

There's a stunned silence. 'Are you serious?'

'One hundred per cent. All you need do is trust yourself. Take the leap of faith. You can do it.'

'Thank you,' is all he says. 'I . . . never would have considered that . . . you know, as a career option, but, yeah, I'll certainly give it some thought. I'm glad I called you.'

I'm about to wish him the best of luck in the future, when Mary cuts in.

'Well, this is really turning into something very special, isn't it? The bad news is, ladies and gentlemen, that we'll have to wrap it up there for the morning— Oh sorry, what was that?' she says, tapping her earpiece. 'OK, one last and final caller on line four. Hello? You're through to Cassandra. Go ahead, please, but if you wouldn't mind keeping it short? We're almost out of time. I hope you don't mind taking this one last call?' she asks me.

Mind, I feel like saying, why would I mind? Amazingly, this is turning out to be *fun*!

A woman's voice comes through, about my own age. 'Cassandra?'

'That's me.'

'Oh thank God. I was ages trying to get through but the switchboard was jammers. You have got to help me. I'm getting married this Saturday coming and—

A flash.

She's blonde and a bit ditzy and has an S in her name … I can definitely see an S …

'Congratulations. What's your name?'

'Sabrina.'

Knew it. Ooh, this feels good.

'The thing is, Cassandra, I'm having serious cold feet and I need, like, *mega* psychic advice here. Now, I love my fiancé, don't get me wrong, and if you're watching, Hi baby! Don't forget to pick up the rings! I'm just panicking because my mother's driving me nuts with all this crap about centrepieces having to exactly tone in with the bridal colours and I'm wondering, well, basically, my worry is, are Paul Newman and Joanne Woodward the only couple alive who can make marriage work?'

Out of the corner of my eye I see Charlene, who's just

111

tiptoed into studio hanging on to . . . oh shit and double shit. It's him. It has to be.

Jack Hamilton. No mistake.

It's dark and shadowy where they're standing side by side at a monitor, watching me watching them. He's even better looking in the flesh. Tall, but with his head bent slightly forward as if he's embarrassed by his height and stoops to compensate. He's looking directly at me now and I swear I can feel myself blushing to the roots like some hormonal teenybopper.

Come on, Cassie, concentrate, focus. You're doing OK and you're nearly home and dry . . .

'We haven't even been seeing each other all that long,' Sabrina is chirping on, her voice filling the studio. 'We got engaged after, like, two months and no one could believe it. But then he's an actor and he always says dating an actor is kind of like dog years, you know? So really, two months is really seven times that, but . . . hey! Don't ask me to do sums.'

She giggles and I'm desperately trying to tune into her and her problem, but I'm breaking out into a sticky cold sweat and it's awful and worst of all – oh shit – I can't see anything. Nothing. *Nada*. Not one single bloody thing.

'I didn't even want to get engaged,' Sabrina's saying, although the whooshing noise in my ears is almost drowning her out, 'but he insisted. Said relationships either move forwards or backwards and he didn't particularly want to go backwards.'

Come on, Cassie. Get it together. Try and see something. Anything.

'So basically, what should I do?' asks Sabrina, sounding cool as a breeze, which is a million miles from how I'm feeling. 'And if I *do* call it off, can I still get to keep all the presents?'

A pause and I'm aware of everyone looking at me. Mary, Maura, the crew, cameramen, Lisa, Charlene and worst of all . . . Jack Hamilton.

Not a thing. Not a single sausage. Not even a *sense* of anything . . . Another pause and I swear I want to just rip off my radio mike and run out of there. My mouth must be opening and closing like a goldfish. This is awful, this is just so awful . . . it feels like a classic panic attack. Shortness of breath, dizziness, the works.

'Well,' says Maura, unable to keep the note of triumph out of her voice. 'On that note, we'll have to sign off for another morning. Bad luck, Cassandra, but then, I suppose you can't win them all, can you?'

I can't answer; I'm too busy trying to compose myself because now the theme music is blaring and everyone's moving briskly off in all directions, anxious to get out of there. I'm gutted, completely and utterly knocked for six.

Maura disappears; Mary shakes me by the hand and tells me not to worry, that up until then the piece was going great, which only makes me feel, if possible, even worse.

Then Charlene's over, squealing and hugging me tight. 'Oh babes, I am so *jazzed* just to be your friend! You were a-mazing! How good an agent am I?'

'Charlene, I couldn't see a thing. I completely blanked out.'

'Oh sweetie, are you kidding? After this, the sky is the limit for you! We could get you on *Big Brother*, get your picture in *Heat* magazine, you could start dating a footballer; the world is your Bacardi Breezer!'

'Charlene, listen to me. That last caller, I should have been able to see something, but I couldn't pick up a thing. One minute, I'm getting flashes all over the place, then nothing. Like turning off a tap. It was scary. It was terrifying. It's never happened to me before. Never.'

She's not paying even the slightest bit of attention. 'And what about that bitch Maura? Boy, she was harsh and so was the lighting. I'm going to have a serious word with Jack about her manner.'

Before I even have time to react, he's over.

'What can I say?' he says, shaking my hand warmly, firmly and making direct eye contact with me. 'A star is born.'

I'm still so shaken by the last, excruciating few minutes of my life that all I can do is stand there and smile, trying desperately to stay cool and calm and not come across like a dribbling eejit. He's unavailable, I remind myself sternly. The sexiest thing I've ever laid eyes on, yes, but *unavailable*.

It's out of the question, so stop ogling him.

Shit, I better say something first though, or else it'll look rude.

'Ehh . . . hi. It's . . . emm . . . nice to meet you.' OK, not exactly the Gettysburg address, but duty done and I can skedaddle. Now. Fast.

'I've been exec producing this show for a year now,' he says, smiling down at me, warm and friendly and kind of shyly, which only makes him even cuter. If that were possible. 'And I can't remember ever getting a response quite like this before. You have an amazing gift, Cassandra, or can I call you Cassie, like your friends do?'

'Ehh . . . yeah. Yes, I mean . . . umm . . .'

OK, here comes a comforting thought. Now that we've actually physically met, I've done my duty as a friend to Charlene, so after today I can avoid him like the Black Death, can't I?

Course I can.

Yes, love it, fantastic plan.

'The thing is, Cassie, if you were interested, I'd really like to offer you a permanent slot on the show.'

Oh shit.

Chapter Four

THE TAROT DECK
THE STAR CARD

A rare card, signifying great success. At long last, the Universe is conspiring to place you on your true path in life. A time of great abundance and joy, of finding and carving out your own personal niche. Believe it or not, you are actually being guided in the right direction. Finally, at long last, your time has come.

It's all about you, baby.

It just mightn't feel that way, that's all . . .

'At the risk of having a *Dawson's Creek* moment, I have to tell you, Cassie, you were so stupendously, awesomely stunning on that show that I feel like having a T-shirt printed saying, "My best friend just happens to be a super-cool mega TV star."'

'You're lying, but bless you anyway,' I say, mobile clamped to my ear. 'They should hurry up and perfect the cloning process just so that everyone can have a Jo in their life.' And I truly mean it from the bottom of my heart. It's times like this that really make me realize what a rare diamond she is. Unjudgemental, supportive and just . . . well, just my Jo.

I've *raced* out of Channel Seven, practically leaving a cloud of dust in my wake, I'm so anxious to put as much distance between me and Jack Hamilton/Charlene/ the whole bloody, icky situation as fast as possible. No kidding, I legged it out of there like a sprinter on steroids, jumped straight into a cab and am now en route into town and the *Tattle* office.

'So what did you say when he offered you the gig? Were you thrilled? I mean, come on, Cassie, talk about a major vote of confidence!'

'I was so shocked, I think my exact words might have been, "Eerrrhhh . . . umm . . . weeelll . . . eeeeehhhhh . . . sheeeeezzz," but I could be mistaken. It mightn't have been anything quite so logical or coherent.'

'Stop messing.'

'You think I could mess at a time like this? Jo, I must have sounded like I had all the intelligence, wit and vivacity of a Thermos flask.'

'Where is he now? Did you leave him and the Tipsy Queen back at the studio?'

'If memory serves, and believe me, the last twenty minutes have pretty much been one big blur, he invited both of us for brekkie, Charlene said something like, "What do you mean, eat? What, like, *food*?", and I made my escape while the going was good. Jo, I really need for you to tell me honestly. As my bestest pal, the one who gets to say all the hard stuff that I don't necessarily want to hear . . . on a scale of one to ten, how noticeable was it when I blanked out? When I couldn't see anything? Because I can tell you right now, I have never been so terrified in my entire life.'

She pauses to weigh up her answer and I know I won't necessarily like what's coming, but I'm actually pleased. Jo has never told an untruth in her entire life and, good or bad, I know she won't start now. For God's sake, this is the woman who told me, to my face, that my last haircut was less Cameron Diaz and more Myra Hindley. Ouch.

'OK, Cassie, you asked. I knew there was something up as soon as that last caller rang in. There was just this really weird look that came across your face.'

'Raw panic?'

'No, more like—'

'Like someone who mixes medications?'

'Will you let me answer? You looked like you'd had an epiphany, if that doesn't sound like something a television evangelist would come out with. Frightened, yes, rabbit-in-the-headlights, yes, but there was something else . . .'

For a second, I can't talk. Because she's hit the nail on the head. That's exactly what it felt like when I first locked eyes with Jack Hamilton. As if I'd just met something I'd been unconsciously searching for.

Oh hell, Jo's right. It does sound like the verbal equivalent of one of those John Hinde postcards; you know, the ones with donkeys carrying bales of turf on them and girls with red curly hair.

'Of course, that's if you happen to believe in pre-destined romance and all that malarkey, which, as you know, I don't,' she adds, bringing both of us right back down to earth with a big, unsubtle bang. 'It's utterly demeaning to presuppose that we're not rational beings with free will who make our own life choices, instead of being at the mercy of a random cosmos.'

'Well, it could have been worse, I suppose,' I say, desperately trying to see something positive about the situation. 'For a minute there, I thought you were going to tell me I looked like I had a dose of quadruple diarrhoea and that the nearest loo was in Kazakhstan.'

'Hmm, now I may not be psychic, but—'

'I may not be either after this morning. I'm so afraid

I'm losing it, Jo. What will I do if I can't see things any more? I'll lose my column, I'll be unemployed, I won't be able to pay our rent—'

'Oh, come on, you had one tiny blip, you stage-panicked yourself into a spin and now you've put two and two together and come up with forty million. Honestly, we should nickname you Hector Projector. In another minute you'll be visualizing yourself on the side of the road in a cardboard box living off parish relief. Who do you think you are, Heather Mills?'

'Sorry, hon. That's what panic attacks do to me. Oh Jo, I wish I knew what happened to me back there. Why couldn't I see anything? *Why?*'

'That, I cannot say. However, I'm sensing we need to discuss this further. Meet me for lunch?'

'Defo.'

'Usual place?'

'You got it.'

'Should I bring valium/alcohol/max-strength rhinoceros tranquillizers?'

'Ha, ha, very funny.'

'Keep the head. Stay cool and I'll see you later!'

She's probably right. It was only one blip. One small, barely noticeable, teeny-weeny blip. Perceptible only to the select few who know me intimately. Hopefully. With a bit of luck.

I'm sure it was just my nerves playing up and that I'll

be back to normal and getting my usual hit rate of flashes in no time. And no, I won't end up jobless, unemployed and sleeping rough under a bridge with a cardboard sign saying, 'I used to be psychic but mysteriously lost it all, please give generously.'

Come on, Cassie, pull it together. If you imagine the worst, then that's what you'll create.

Right. Nice, deep, soothing breath.

I hang up the phone and turn to the taxi driver. *Brainwave.* I'll get him talking and see if I can see anything about his life. Dublin taxi drivers are well known for loving the chat, aren't they? I mean, I've had times when a ten-minute taxi ride ends up taking half an hour because I'd get into such a deep conversation with the driver; they end up telling me their innermost secrets and I get flashes to beat the band. And the last time I got into a big conversation with one, I accurately predicted that he'd get five numbers on the Lotto that Saturday night. He even sent me a bunch of flowers care of the magazine as a thank you and I was only raging that I didn't think of asking him what the numbers actually were, so I could have made a few extra quid on the side myself.

'Ehh, sorry about that. Had to take that call,' I say, smiling encouragingly at him and sitting forward, all set for a good chin-wag.

'No worries, love.'

'So. How are things with you then?'

'Grand.'

'Busy?'

'Yeah.'

'Are you married then? With . . . emm . . . kids, maybe?'

'Ehh . . . no.'

'Oh, right.'

A pause.

'So, no holidays planned or anything?'

'No. Sorry.'

OK, now he's looking at me through the rear-view mirror as if I'm some sort of pathetic saddo that's desperately trying to pick him up. We drive the rest of the way in total silence.

Shit, shit, shit. Just my luck to land the only non-talkative taxi driver in the whole of the greater Dublin area.

When I finally get to the office, I grab the lift, jump out at the fifth floor, Arts and Features (yes, I know a psychic column doesn't strictly fall into either category, but that's just where my desk happens to be), and – you won't believe this – get a big round of applause from everyone who's there.

'Heartiest congratulations on a sterling performance, Cassandra my dear,' says Bob Thornton, the social diarist, coming over and pecking me elegantly on each cheek. 'Caught the show on the old telly-box just now and may

I just say, you were the absolute epitome of grace under pressure.'

'Oh, thanks . . . emm . . . Bob,' I mutter, mortified at everyone looking at me and feeling, as I always do, cheeky for even calling him by his first name.

Bob, I should point out, is actually Sir Bob, although he doesn't use his full title as he considers it vulgar ever since, as he puts it, the Queen started knighting supermarket barons and soap stars. He's wearing a beautifully cut, slightly crumpled white linen suit today, with a pink hankie just peeping out of the top of his breast pocket. In short, he looks as if he just stepped off the set of a Merchant Ivory movie and is having a nice little breather before he goes back to governing India with the rest of his pals from the Raj. All the girls in the office think he's adorably sweet and cuddly, which, as we all know, is girl-code for: 'Hmm, very nice guy, absolutely lovely, but let's face it, probably gay.'

'May I offer you a refreshing cup of peppermint tea after your ordeal, my dear? I've just infused some.'

That's the other thing about Sir Bob – sorry, I mean Bob. He categorically refuses to go to Starbucks downstairs like the rest of us because he feels it's tasteless and crude to drink out of paper cups with bits of cardboard wrapped around them. Instead he brings his own cups and saucers to work, on the grounds that the correct way to drink herbal tea is out of posh china and nothing else.

I wouldn't mind, but he can't be any more than about thirty.

'Oh thanks, Bob, you read my thoughts,' I say. 'I'd love one.'

'Cassie! I'm so bloody *proud* of you!' squeals Sandra Kelly, coming over to give me one of her trademark bear-hugs. Sandra is the magazine's restaurant critic and for a split second I have to squint hard to recognize her; not that I'm losing my marbles, at least not entirely, you understand, it's just that today she's resplendent in a jet-black, bobbed wig with a huge, face-covering pair of wraparound sunglasses. Sandra, who's known and feared throughout the restaurant community, once read about a critic in New York who disguised herself every time she went out to eat, on the grounds that this meant she was treated exactly the same way as any other punter, for better or for worse. Worse, usually. Sandra's reviews have been known to make or break a kitchen and one well-known restaurateur has even nicknamed her Foodzilla of Fleet Street.

'Saw the *Breakfast Club* and you were a total wow,' she squeals, thumping me on the back. 'When you saw yer one's engagement ring inside her gardening gloves, you should have seen that snotty presenter glaring daggers at you. What's her name? The one with a face like a beaten tambourine?'

'Oh, you mean Maura,' I say, gratefully taking a nice

cuppa from good old Sir Bob. Sorry, sorry, I mean Bob. 'Love the new wig, by the way. Very . . . lemme think . . . Dorothy Parker.'

'You're on the money, honey. Exactly the look I'm going for. I'm having lunch today at that new place in town—'

Just then Lucy from Features shrieks over from the window, 'Look out, everyone! Piranha in the tank! Just getting out of a taxi! Now!'

There's instant panic as people scatter to the four winds, racing back to their desks; Sandra disappears into a lift and immediately a library-like hush descends on the whole office, broken only by the tap-tapping sound of fingernails busily clickety-clacking off keyboards. The only person who looks and behaves exactly as before is Sir Bob, who strolls back to his desk, cool and unflappable, sipping tea from the good china with his little finger up in the air, looking like he's a guest in the royal enclosure at Ascot.

I should explain. 'Piranha in the tank' is the *Tattle* office code word for when our esteemed editor is on her way in. Yes, the Dragon Lady herself. And believe me, you know neither the day nor the hour when she'll appear. Her actual name is Amanda Crotty and for a while there she was nicknamed Snotty Crotty, but somehow the Dragon Lady just stuck. Honestly, it sums up her personality a helluva lot better.

Here is a vox pop of how we all feel about her, in no particular order.

ME: No kidding, the woman is about as cuddly as a diamond-cutter.

CHARLENE (*before she got fired*): The Dragon Lady is actually a man in drag who shaves with a cut-throat razor every first Friday of the month. I have proof.

SANDRA: She's like a female Gordon Ramsay, except with even worse language.

SIR BOB: That ghastly woman is snappier than a crocodile handbag with a pair of matching shoes.

LUCY FROM FEATURES: I'm not saying for definite that she's gay; all I'm saying is that she goes around in flat shoes dressed like a prison warden, she never wears make-up, the hair is cropped like k. d. lang and I have yet to see the woman wearing a bra. Go figure.

Secretly, I once had a flash about the Dragon Lady that she'd find love on a gay-and-lesbian mountain hike, but I didn't dare tell her for fear she'd throw me out of the window. I have a very highly developed sense of self-preservation, as you see.

Anyway, it's gone as quiet as a tomb in here and I take advantage of the silence to start wading through the mountain of letters waiting for me for next week's column. I've got to see something; I just have to.

OK, focus.

I'm running my fingers over my letters pile, as if I'm some kind of human metal detector or divining rod, willing something to jump out at me and grab my attention, when whaddya know, it does.

It's handwritten, in spidery writing that I'd swear looks almost tear-splodged. Perfect. A good, juicy relationship dilemma, with a bit of luck. I rip it open.

Not to put too much pressure on myself or anything, but my entire future livelihood depends on what, if anything, I can see here.

Dear Cassandra,

I wouldn't be writing to you at all, only I'm at my wits' end here and I really don't know who else I can turn to. Freud once said that we are never so helplessly unhappy as when we lose love and that's exactly the position I find myself in.

The thing is, Cassandra, what do you do when your ex moves on and you don't? It's barely five months since our break-up and I just found out he's got engaged to his latest. ENGAGED. No matter what way you look at it, this is meant to be his transitional person; she's not, under any circumstances, supposed to be The One. I've been phoning and texting him and when we first went our separate ways, he would always get back to me and even though we'd broken up, at least we'd still talk, but now he doesn't even return calls. All my friends say I should look through the relationship rear-view mirror and try to focus only on the negative things about our time together. I presume they mean this as a sort of cheer-up-you're-so-much-better-off-without-him exercise, but the thing is, I can't do it.

I'm still in love with him. And now he's with someone else and he's happy and it's just killing me. Cassandra, I'm almost thirty-five years old and of course, as everyone around me says, the sensible thing is for me to forget about this guy, get back out there again and try to meet someone else but I just can't bring myself to, mainly because I really do believe that this is the man for me. It just mightn't look that way, that's all. So now I find myself cast in the incredibly embarrassing role of 'needy and desperate ex who just won't let go', and I can just envisage him physically shuddering every time he sees my number coming up on his phone, before he shuts it off. Which he does, every time, unfailingly.

Please understand, Cassandra, I'm neither needy nor desperate; this is purely and simply the way this guy makes me behave. I just can't believe I've turned into this Glenn-Close-from-*Fatal-Attraction* type. For God's sake, I live in a house where my curtains match the duvet covers. I have wooden floors and underfloor heating. This is NOT me. All I want is for this man to re-evaluate me and for us to get back together.

Help me. Please help me.

Barbara in Dublin

Oh God, I suddenly feel so achingly sorry for her. I mean, we've all been there, haven't we? The amount of times I've been devastated over a guy and then, after some time has passed, looked at him and thought: 'This man put my heart through the wringer and all the while I barely made the tiniest little foothold in his.'

Now, normally I'd do my level best to bounce back and try to save face by claiming I never fancied him anyway, but somehow, I feel that kind of advice just isn't good enough for this poor woman.

OK, Cassie, you're on, hop to it.

I sit and finger the paper, madly trying to get a picture of her as she wrote me this heartbreaking letter with such searing honesty.

Nothing.

OK. I try not to get panicky and instead focus on how intelligent and articulate she comes across in her letter.

Still nothing.

Shit, you wouldn't exactly have to be psychic to come to that conclusion about her character, now would you? Come on! The silence in the office is almost like a mortuary at this stage and you'd think that would help me concentrate, but it doesn't.

Oh hell, now I'm really in trouble.

I'm frantically racking my brains, trying to pick up something, anything, a feeling, a face, an initial, a star sign . . .

Still nothing.

Right, now I've bypassed panic and am starting to feel terror, real terror. This could really be it. This could spell the end of my career. My palms are starting to sweat, my mouth is all dry and I've barely even noticed the Dragon Lady stepping out of the lift and into the main office.

Keep the head, Cassie, keep the head. You can do this.

Another deep, soothing breath. I remind myself that an awful lot of the advice that I give readers is just plain, practical common sense.

Right then, good start. What would I say if it was one of my pals in this position? Charlene, for example? Oh God, we'd all give her a dog's abuse. I can just hear Marc with a C slagging her off and saying things like: 'Isn't it such a shame that we don't live in a universe where needy and desperate are turn-ons?'

I pick a pen and paper and start drafting a rough response. Really rough.

Dear Barbara,

I felt so sorry for you, reading your letter. We've all been in that awful, post-break-up dark place where it's nigh on impossible to see the wood for the trees. And anyone who says they've never got in-text-icated and sent a few messages they shouldn't have, particularly after a few glasses of wine, is a dirty big liar. But then, it's only when you come up for air that you really get true relationship perspective and think: What was I doing? You really should listen to your friends and even though it probably feels like medieval torture, try to get yourself back out there again. You're only mid-thirties and, sure, that's nothing. You could try joining a book club or a gym. My friend Marc with a C says the fitness centre he works at is a total pick-up joint and that if they turned the lights down a bit lower and put Barcardi Breezers in the water coolers instead of Volvic, there'd be more mad coupling going on there than in Lillie's Bordello, any night of the week.

I stop for a sec, reread what I've written, scrunch it up and throw it in the bin. Total crap; my granny could have come up with that gem of advice. To get over a guy you should try joining a gym? Ugh, vomit. Can't believe I even bothered writing that.

'Morning Cassandra. Having difficulties readjusting to your day job after all the glamour of television?'

Oh shit, I don't believe this. It's the Dragon Lady herself, standing over my desk and glowering down at me, all five feet ten of her. Just when I thought my day couldn't get any worse.

'Oh hi, emm, morning . . . emm' – at this point I'm frantically racking my brains to remind myself to call her by her real name – 'Amanda.' I beam, trying to sound all cheery and confident and upbeat, as if she comes over to talk to me every day.

Which she doesn't ever, to anyone. Not unless you're in *really, really* majorly big trouble. Like the last time I missed my deadline and there was blue murder.

It was through no fault of my own, you understand. I just left everything till the last minute, as per usual, but I had a watertight schedule all worked out in my head – I was going to get up at four a.m. on the morning my column was due – but then something urgent came up and I ended up delivering it late. Very late. Flirting with disaster late. Can't even remember what it was that delayed me now . . . Oh yeah. Charlene threw a surprise party for herself (to mark the fact that it was exactly six months to the day between her last birthday and her next birthday). I'm not joking, there were guests still wandering around her house/mansion three days later, which in Charlene-land is the mark of a triumphantly successful night.

Anyway, I knew I had a very good reason for being so – ahem – eleventh hour.

That time.

'Earth to Cassandra?'

Oh shit. She's still here, still standing in front of me, and now I'm dimly aware that most of the office is looking over. Nor can I blame them; whenever the Dragon Lady decides to tear strips off any of us, you're pretty much guaranteed a highly entertaining side-show.

'If your head hasn't been completely turned by your fifteen minutes of fame, perhaps you'd step into my office for a minute?'

And with that the old Nazi in nylons strides off, at her usual two steps at a time, leaving me to trail behind her in my little kitten heels with what feels like the whole office staring at me. I'm not joking, it's just like in that film, *Dead Man Walking*.

As the Dragon Lady makes for her office/torture chamber, Lucy from Features has the misfortune to look up and catch her eye. 'Morning, Amanda,' she chirrups brightly.

Whereupon the Dragon Lady barks back at her: 'Nothing to see here, dearie, so why don't you just go back to flicking through your Gary Larson desktop calendar and saying, "I don't get it, I don't get it," over and over again.'

Jesus, she's really in a firing humour this morning.

Poor Lucy looks really shaken at her sheer rudeness and I give her a weak smile as I walk past her.

Lucy's only been here a few weeks, I should point out. No one who's worked here for a long time would ever dream of trying to exchange pleasantries with the Dragon Lady. Complete waste of time trying to be sycophantic with her.

Everyone's looking at me and everyone, myself included, is thinking the same thing. There's really only one reason why you get hauled into that office and it begins with 'F' and ends with me standing at the back of the dole queue.

So, trying really hard not to throw up with nerves, I step into the lair of the she-wolf, she bangs the door tightly behind me and I'm immediately struck by the sheer horribleness of her workspace. It's sparse and clinical, a bit like a doctor's surgery, with not as much as one item that would personalize the place and – I dunno – humanize the Dragon Lady a bit more. Like a family photo or a novelty mouse mat. Or even a mug that says 'World's most terrifying boss'. Something. Anything. This place is about as close to a prison cell as you can get. There are two empty seats across from her desk and as I make to sit down on one of them, her mobile rings.

'Not there,' she growls at me before answering her call. 'Do you mind? That seat is reserved for my bad mood.'

Oh help, I must really be for it.

I do my best to keep a cool head as I slither into the

chair furthest away from her while she snaps away at some poor eejit down the phone.

'Well, I sincerely hope, for your sake, that this is a phone call of apology,' she's snarling and, I swear to God, she sounds just like a female version of Alan Sugar or Donald Trump or one of those I-eat-your-type-for-breakfast types. If you know what I mean. Anyway, while she's verbally savaging away, my mind races.

OK. I can think of two possible reasons why she wants to see me and, let's face it, neither one of them will have me coming up smelling like guest-room soap.

1. The old gizzard saw me on TV this morning and somehow, without even knowing it, I've inadvertently broken some clause in my contract with *Tattle* that says, 'Thou shalt not ever go on the telly without obtaining prior permission from thine editor, signed in blood on a full moon on Halloween night with bloodhounds baying in the background for dramatic effect.' Or something like that.

   OK, this one isn't actually too bad, this I might just conceivably be able to blag my way out of. I'll plead complete and total ignorance. Brilliant. Which is the truth. I mean, everyone knows you just sign work contracts and wait for your pay cheque to roll in and that's the end of that. No one actually *reads* all the tiny little small print – do they?

2. She's had it with the way I'm always late with deadlines

and me going on the TV this morning was the final straw and now she's firing me. For not being a model of efficiency and getting through the *mound* of letters I get sent every day.

Can this really be happening to me? In a single morning, I lose my job, my psychic ability and my livelihood? Oh God, this is a living nightmare. I'll have no money, Jo earns even less than I do so she won't be able to support me so I'll have to move back in with my parents and be twenty-eight and pathetic with no career, and I'll have to go and stack the shelves part-time in our local Tesco and every time I get sent by the dole office to a proper job interview, I'll tell them I used to be psychic but completely lost it and they'll all roar laughing at me.

Sing, fat lady, sing, my career is almost at an end . . .

OK, there's nothing else for it. I'll just have to beg/ grovel/plead to hang on to my column with the added condition thrown in that I will never, ever, as long as I live, miss any deadline *ever* again. Really, truly, cross my heart.

If I can just get my gift back and hang on to my job, I will become a model employee. I will never disappear off for long chats and cups of leaf tea with Sir Bob, sorry Bob. I will stop using *Tattle* magazine time to surf the net looking for cheapie flights/holidays/discount sample sales. I faithfully promise.

And if the Universe lets me cut a deal and sees fit to give me my life back, I will start helping Jo out in the charity shop at weekends. And not moan about it, like I normally do. And generally become a much better, kinder, more philanthropic member of society who gives free psychic readings in old folks' homes in my spare time . . .

Oh for God's sake, who am I kidding? I can't just cut a deal; this is the Universe, not the Mafia, I'm dealing with.

'Surely after all these years I don't need to explain to you how valuable my time is?' The Dragon Lady is still ranting down the phone. 'Are you seriously telling me that you think it's OK to keep me waiting for *twenty-five minutes*? When, as you well know, I have zero tolerance for unpunctuality in any form?'

Must be her accountant or her bank manager, I'm thinking, God help them. Although a tiny part of me wishes I could be as assertive as that next time I'm looking for an extension on my overdraft.

I come back down to earth as she winds up her call.

'Right. Well, thanks for nothing, Mum, and I'll see you for lunch on Sunday as usual.'

Bloody hell.

OK, deep breath and remember, I'll do my level best to plead with her but if I am for the chop, I'm determined at least to leave here with my dignity intact. I will *not* let her bully me or reduce me to tears, if it's the last bloody thing I do. I'll save my tears for the dole queue.

'So, Cassandra,' she says, kicking off her horrible, chunky, sensible shoes and putting her feet up on the desk. I attempt a watery smile. 'It's very hard for me to compliment you on your television performance this morning since, as you are no doubt aware, your column personifies everything I resent in the print media.'

Now, although this is fabulously rude, it doesn't actually come as a surprise, mainly because, for as long as I've worked for the Dragon Lady, which is . . . oh, years now, she has always told me straight to my face that astrology, palmistry, clairvoyance and basically everything that I write about are a complete load of dog poo. In her opinion.

(She *would* think that, though, because I happen to know she's Virgo with Saturn as her ruling planet, which means she was bound to end up really cynical and disbelieving about anything remotely spiritual or other-worldly.)

'However, I do know about selling magazines and for whatever dim-witted reason, readers seem to actually enjoy "Ask Cassandra".'

'Emm . . . well, emm . . . thanks. I suppose.'

'Normally I tell my journalists what to write about, but with you I can't. You're an unknown quantity and I don't particularly relish dealing in unknown quantities.

However, people buy *Tattle* to read you and although personally I don't get it, I can't argue with it either.'

Am I hearing things or did that actually sound like a backhanded compliment? From the Dragon Lady? No, I must need my ears testing . . .

'So all I'll say about your TV debut this morning is, the duck took to water.'

I'm not imagining things. That actually sounded . . . OK. Quite nice, in fact. Didn't it?

'Oh right. Ehh, thanks. So, emm . . . I'm not in any kind of trouble then, am I?'

She looks at me as if I'm a few coupons short of a special offer. 'Oh please, where do you think you are, boot camp? All I'm saying is, I know the media and how it works and, based on your performance this morning, I'd be astonishingly surprised if they don't want to have you back on that show.'

Bloody hell, she should be the psychic, not me . . .

'So. Am I right? Cassandra? Hello? Are you still in the room? Not having some out-of-body experience, or anything, I trust?'

'Oh sorry . . . Well, actually . . . emm . . . well, you see, the producer *did* mention something about that, but I didn't say yes or no . . . In fact, I didn't give him any kind of answer . . .'

'So here's my question. Are you deserting us for the bright lights of television? Or to put it more bluntly, do

I need to go out there and start hiring another psychic? Because if it's a question of matching an offer that a TV company is making you, you need to let me know. *Tattle* magazine will not want to lose Cassandra.'

I'm actually beginning to feel a bit dizzy now. This is unbelievable. Not only am I *not* fired, I might even end up getting a pay rise out of this? Incredible. 'Thanks so much . . . emm . . . Amanda, I really appreciate the . . . ehh . . . vote of confidence. As I said, though, I haven't accepted any other offer, and to be honest with you . . .'

Bloody hell, good luck finishing that sentence, Cassie.

What am I supposed to say? To be honest with you, oh mighty Dragon Lady, I don't think I'm in any position to accept any career offers seeing as how, in the last couple of hours, my gift seems to have completely deserted me?

'You could do both, you know,' she interrupts. 'I see no reason why you can't continue with your column as normal and do the odd TV appearance. Publicity for the magazine, publicity for you, a decent TV slot for them. Just think about it.'

Her phone rings again and I take this as my cue to leave.

'Let me know what you decide,' she barks at me, 'and I'll square things with the publisher. Shouldn't envisage any problem with you appearing as "*Tattle* magazine's

Cassandra", though. This seems to be one of those rare situations where everyone's a winner.'

'Emm ... thanks, thanks very much, emm ... Amanda,' I stammer as I try to stand up. Which is easier said than done, as my legs have completely gone to jelly underneath me.

And then the miracle happens. The woman in my letter. I'm on my way out of the door when I get a clear flash.

She's going to write a self-help book describing what she's been through and how she coped with her awful break-up. It's going to be a bestseller, a publishing phenomenon, a sort of bible for any woman who's ever loved too much. It'll be snapped up. Oh for God's sake, this is amazing! I can even see the book's title.

'*I Love You, But Don't Push Your Luck,*' I blurt, accidentally out loud, on my way out the door.

'What did you say?' says her royal Dragon-ness, looking at me in that way she has, which makes me feel as if I should be committed.

'Oops, ehh ... sorry about that, just a letter I've been working on, that's all.'

She rolls her eyes, goes back to her phone call and, I swear, I practically float back to my desk on clouds of sheer, unadulterated *relief*. Everything's going to be just fine. I'm not unemployed and I'm not unemployable. I can still see things. Gift intact.

Sir Bob saunters over to me, looking a tad concerned. 'Everything all right, old thing?'

'Couldn't be better, Bob.' I beam back at him, fishing around my desk for the letter so I can scribble out my reply. Quickly, while I still remember what I saw. After what happened this morning, I'm not taking any chances.

'Jolly good, glad to hear it,' he says, smiling back at me and really looking reassured on my behalf, bless him. 'Oh, before I forget, my dear, I took a telephone message for you while you were, shall we say, otherwise engaged. From reception downstairs. Apparently there's someone waiting to see you so I said you might pop down as soon as you were free.'

'Thanks, Bob,' I say, half wondering who it could be. Jo? No, it's too early for lunch; besides, I've already arranged to meet her at the vegetarian place we always go to, which is about the only place she'll actually pay to eat in. Otherwise she just makes tofu sandwiches and we'll eat them sitting on a park bench. Charlene? No, Charlene waits for no one; she'd just barge up here unannounced. Marc with a C is definitely doing fitness assessments, two divorcees this morning, I distinctly remember him telling me.

'I wrote the name down for you, somewhere, oh yes,

here we are,' says Bob, handing me a slip of his mono-grammed notepaper, covered in his beautiful copper-plate handwriting.

I almost fall over.

'11.30. Message for Cassandra. Gentleman waiting to see her downstairs. A Mr Jack Hamilton.'

Chapter Five

THE TAROT DECK
THE KNIGHT OF CUPS CARD, INVERTED

Well, woop-di-doo for you. A handsome man will appear, possibly with an intriguing offer, which, initially, will dazzle you. This man could well be the total package, a warm-hearted soul, charismatic, deeply talented – oh, and did I mention incredibly good-looking? He brings joy and fun and will have you holding your sides laughing at some of the things he'll come out with. For a single gal to pick this card signifies that he could well become a lover in time.

If you're lucky and the card is the right way up, that is.

However, if the card is inverted, then it becomes a card of warning. Tread carefully. You might just look back on this guy and realize he was about as welcome as a fungus. Basically, he's out of your league, honey; he's out of bounds and you'd be well advised to move on and not get sucked into this particular Vietnam . . .

Just as well I haven't got a lip gloss in my bag, I think as I stand nervously sandwiched into the back of the crowded lift as it shoots downstairs. I mean, I don't want to look like I made any kind of effort. Why would I do that? He's probably just popped by to . . . to what? Say thanks for this morning? To find out why I legged it out of there like a scalded cat? To (gulp) talk about the offer he made me?

OK, it is absolutely essential that I stay very cool and calm and remember at all times that Charlene is my friend. End of story. If he wants to talk business with me, fine, grand, I will be an absolute model of professionalism. The main thing is (a) I haven't lost my column and (b) it was a close call, but, thank God, I can still see things and am not about to be propelled to the back of a dole queue.

Deep, calming breath.

The lift door glides open and there he is, sitting at reception flicking through a newspaper, looking all relaxed and casual. He spots me immediately and is straight over, shaking me warmly by the hand and making direct eye contact in that way he has which is just so magnetic and warm and . . . *appealing.*

'Hi, Cassie,' he says, a bit shyly.

'Hi . . . emm . . . Jack.'

'I hope you don't mind me dropping by your office? Please don't think I'm stalking you or anything. I just wondered if we could have a quick chat? If you have time, that is.'

'Ehh . . . yeah. That would be . . . emm . . . fine.'

Oh, well done, what a fab response. God, I should have been a speechwriter at the White House or somewhere really big and important. My witty dialogue would completely change people . . . from awake to asleep, that is.

'It's just that you left the station in such a rush, we never got a chance to talk properly. You practically left a glass slipper lying on the steps behind you.' He smiles kindly. 'All we were short of was a clock chiming midnight and a squashed pumpkin in the car park to complete the picture, you know.'

'Oh . . . ehh, yes, well, I'm very sorry about that, but . . . I had to get back to work as quickly as possible. Meet an important deadline, you know?' I say, trying my best to sound all serene and professional. As if meeting deadlines is a perfectly normal feature of my day, ahem, ahem.

'Great, good for you. Oh, is it OK if we go to Starbucks?' he asks politely. 'It's just that after a show I'm always in need of a caffeine hit the approximate size of Mount Rushmore.'

'Lovely.'

Just stay nice and cool. Just remember that I'm not only über-confident, I'm also deeply relaxed and calm. Zen-like, you might almost say.

We head inside the coffee shop and lo and behold, there's a free table by the window which I grab while he goes up to order.

OK, Jack Hamilton. So, you're cute but you're not that cute. Yes, in fairness, I freely admit that the body is fantastic, but you just walk past any building site in the city and you'll see biceps just as tanned and toned on any builder. Oh, you know the type, the sort of guys who think vests should be worn as outerwear.

Come off it, Cassie, who do you think you're kidding?

This guy could be a body double for Alec Baldwin, easy.

Nice cleansing breath.

I'll be absolutely grand just as long as I keep reminding myself that he's Charlene's boyfriend. And Charlene is my friend. My great friend. My friend who I've been through thick and thin with.

Right, great, good plan. I'll just keep repeating that like a mantra and I won't go too far wrong. I'll keep introducing her name into the conversation every chance I get, just so he's aware of how close she and I are.

In no time at all he's back, plonking two yummy frothy cappuccinos down and sitting right opposite me, doing his direct-eye-contact, you-are-the-only-woman-in-the-room thing. And I'm not joking; the eyes really are the colour of pure green emeralds.

Come on, cop yourself on, Cassie. Repeat your mantra . . .

'Look,' he says, smiling warmly, 'first things first. Everyone back at Channel Seven has been raving about how amazingly well you did this morning. My God, you were like some sort of psychic caped crusader.'

I take a sip of coffee and giggle.

'You should be out there fighting crime. The last time I saw our phone lines hopping like that was the time we gave away two free tickets to the World Cup final.'

'Thanks . . . emm . . . So where's Charlene?'

He looks at me, a bit taken aback at my . . . well, bluntness. 'Charlene? Oh, her car got clamped and she said she was late for a very important meeting . . .'

With her eyebrow-waxing lady, I'm thinking, although, out of loyalty to my pal, I say nothing out loud.

'. . . so I suggested she grab a bus but she refused to. She said something about how she never uses public transport because it should be like the way it is in *Brief Encounter* but never is.'

'I know, isn't she fab?' I say staunchly. 'I managed to get her on to a bus once and she said the last time she'd been on one, there were actual conductors.'

'I did ask her what she was up to for the rest of the day and she said breaking in her new Manolo Blahniks.'

I gamely laugh at this, as if Charlene was only winding him up, although if the truth be known, she was probably being deadly serious. 'Isn't she hilarious? I just love her. She's *so* amazing. I often think there's no one in the world quite like our Charlene.'

I manage to stop myself short of coming out with, 'It'll be a lucky man who gets her,' on the grounds that they have only known each other for a few short days and let's face it, I've a rash on my arm I've had for longer.

Jack just smiles and gets straight back to the point. 'Look, the thing is, I'll be the first here to admit that—'

'Do you know that Charlene and I have been friends since we were six years old? We met in primary school. And she hasn't changed a day, you know, in spite of everything the poor girl has been through.'

OK, you need to shut that big mouth of yours right now, Cassie. It's early days, so why would she have mentioned anything about family skeletons to Jack? If you're going to yak on, then concentrate on her other wonderful qualities, quick . . .

'Anyway, what I mean is, she's still the same warm, wonderful person that she always was . . .' I trail off, hoping he doesn't pick up on my awful indiscretion. Which, luckily, he doesn't.

'Oh. That's great to hear. But you see I really wanted to talk to you about—'

'And she's such great fun to be around. Don't you agree? I mean, isn't she just great, *great* fun? Even sitting in the back of a taxi with her is an adventure, I always think. She's one of those rare people that the more you get to know her, the more you love her. Dunno what I'd do without that girl.'

OK, maybe now you need to tone it down a bit, you're start-ing to sound like some crazed Jehovah's Witness. Or maybe he's thinking that you're gay and have a long-standing secret lust for Charlene yourself.

'Ehh, Cassie?' Jack says, looking at me like I'm only an olive short of a pizza.

'Yes?'

'I'm aware of the fact that you and Charlene are good buddies, but I'm actually trying to offer you a contract here.'

'Oh. Right. Sorry, I'll shut up,' I say in a small voice, thinking, did he just say 'contract'?

'Anyway,' he goes on, still smiling, 'as I was saying, when it comes to anything remotely, you know, mind/body/spirit, the best thing I can do is admit that I know what I don't know – which is pretty much, well, nothing.' A pause. 'Well, no, actually, that's not strictly true,' he corrects himself, taking a sip of coffee. 'I would have heard of the Dalai Lama by way of Richard Gere and past life experiences by way of Shirley MacLaine.'

I giggle and have to consciously order myself not to keep staring at the dimple on his chin which is just the cutest thing . . .

'But I couldn't tell you what my star sign is.'

Libra, I'm silently betting. 'When's your birthday?'

'October the fifteenth.'

'Oh, then you're a Libra.' I smile.

OK, so Libra is my five-star perfect astrological match in Western astrology, but that doesn't necessarily mean anything, does it? Our Chinese animals could be diametrically opposed . . . 'What year were you born?' I ask innocently. 'If it's not too personal a question.'

'Don't laugh. Nineteen seventy-four. I know, I look older, but that's what the stress of a TV career does to you. As you'll find out in due course. I hope.'

Seventy-four, seventy-four, seventy-four . . . oh *shit* and *double shit*. Only the bloody Chinese year of the Tiger. My astrological equivalent of six numbers on the National Lottery. My perfect, perfect five-star match.

OK. Time to repeat my mantra: Charlene is my friend and he's going out with her . . .

'Look, Cassie, we really want to have you back on

the show. On a regular basis, maybe starting next week,' he says hopefully. 'You just name your terms. Whatever day you want, whatever time slot, you just let me know what suits. I want the *Breakfast Club* to be the first TV show with its very own resident psychic and can I just say one thing to you?' He leans forward, locking eyes with me, and I swear my tummy does an Olympic-gold-medal-standard backward somersault. 'You have a fantastic personality which practically jumps off the TV screen, you look stunning and, based on this morning, the audience seem to love you. You've tapped a vein, you really have. Up until now, I would have had an image of anyone remotely mystical as being . . . well, no offence, but a lot older than you, and a lot greyer with, emm, maybe a crystal ball, a few teeth missing and an outstretched hand saying, "Cross my palm with silver." Not a super-hot babe like you. So in short, Cassandra, you are the answer to my prayers.'

I just sit there for a moment, stunned, the romantic part of my brain saying, *My God, did he really just say that?* Then the practical part of my brain (which, let's face it, I don't hear from all that often) kicks in. *Don't be ridiculous, cop yourself on, he's talking professionally, not personally, you big roaring eejit.*

Right, in that case I need to be just as businesslike right back at him. Think. What would I normally do in this situation?

Shit, shit, shit . . . how do I know? I've never been made an offer like this in my life before, bar the time *Tattle* magazine hired me and that was mainly because I hassled the Dragon Lady so much that she eventually did give me a shot, probably to get a bit of peace as much as anything else. And there's something else slowly formulating at the back of my mind that's worrying me, something an awful lot more serious . . . But I'll put it aside till later, when I can think straight.

OK, Cassie, this pause is starting to get awkward, you're going to have to say something. Anything. Deep, soothing breath. Bright confident smile. 'Emm . . . Jack, I'm really flattered by your offer, but you see . . . the thing is . . .'

'Yes?'

'Can I . . . emm . . . can I get back to you?'

Brilliant, Cassie, just wonderful, my, what a huge loss you were to the business world.

'Sure. I'll give you my card, on the condition that you call me any time.'

'Of course.'

'I'm worried now I might have scared you off by being a bit over-zealous in my quest to win you over. I promise you, I'm not normally the type to go around twirling a moustache and tying blonde maidens to the train tracks, just to get my wicked way.'

I'm laughing at him so much that some coffee actually dribbles down my chin. God, I must look so attractive.

'But if I've failed to hypnotize you with my Svengali-like powers,' he goes on, putting on a scary Vincent Price voice and making me laugh again, 'then let me leave you with one thought.'

'Yeah?'

'I've just hit on the perfect pitch for all the press coverage which your slot cannot fail to generate.'

Now he's looking at me so persuasively I find myself wondering: has anyone said no to this man, ever? Once in his life? 'And what's that?' I ask, trying to come across as very cool and, you know, not too glued to my seat with anticipation.

'I want you to imagine the TV guide section of the paper,' he says, spreading his hands expressively in front of him. 'Now, imagine your picture, with you looking as amazing as you do, with your name in block capitals above. Now, imagine a tag line: "Live and exclusive. Only on the *Breakfast Club*. For those who believe, no explanation is necessary. For those who don't, no explanation is possible."'

Bloody hell, this guy is good . . .

OK. I have finally figured out what it is that's been worrying me all day. It wasn't easy, as I had a lot of distractions from the gang later this afternoon, which can be summarized pretty much as follows:

CHARLENE (*over the phone as I'm sitting at my desk actually trying to work and not just looking like I'm working while I'm actually surfing the net, as I normally do. This is the new, ultra-professional, post-stay-of-execution Cassandra, you understand*): Now, Cassie, you just listen to me. I am starting to develop stress lines about this situation and, as we all know, those lines don't go away. You have got to take up Jack's offer and that's all there is to it. You have to promise me faithfully, as your fabulous agent who has already done *sooooo* much for you. And you needn't think this is like a wedding vow or something, this promise actually *matters*. I just don't think I'll be up to escorting you into the studio again as, let's face it, it's just too bloody early. All right, sweetie, I have to say cheery-bye for now, I'm so haggard-looking because I had to haul myself out of beddy-byes at the crack of dawn this morning that I'm off for a chemical peel. You know, one of those super-duper industrial-strength ones, where by the time I'm done, you'll practically be able to see my kidneys. Oh, drama, drama, drama! Chat later! Love you, missing you already!

JO (*over lunch, a tad more sympathetically, but then Jo actually listens to what you're saying, as opposed to monologuing at you like Charlene . . . Sorry, scrap that disloyal thought immediately. Of course I meant to say, 'Like some people that I could mention'*): Cassie, what exactly is the problem? I think it's amazing that you've made such a successful living out of being psychic, so isn't TV the next logical progression? OK, so you had a bit of a wobbly moment this morning, but it was more than likely down to nerves, that's all. Give it a go. After all, what's the worst that can happen? And for the record, it would be on my conscience if I didn't say that our day-to-day problems here in the West are a trip to Disneyland compared with what's happening in other parts of the world. Do you realize that the Australian government has just announced the harshest proposal for legislation I've *ever* had to fight, which, if it's passed by parliament, means they're going to start punishing asylum-seekers who arrive by boat? Honestly, Cassie, you think you have problems. Even our giving so much airtime to this is demeaning to what's happening globally. I'm going to be up all night writing letters for our campaign . . .

This, I have to tell you, acts as a major reality check and temporarily shuts me up. Well, until Marc with a C calls me later in the afternoon, that is.

MARC WITH A C: Well, babe, how are you getting on with your oh-will-I-be-a-major-TV-star/household-name dilemma or will I spend the rest of my days basking in obscurity working for the bitch troll/Princess of Darkness/Dragon Lady or whatever it is you call her. I think Jack Hamilton has made you a fabulous offer and I take my Calvin Klein knickers off to you. Although I do have to say that I'm kind of getting bored with the way all I'm hearing about from you and Charlene is Jack this, Jack that, Jack the other. Not that I'm insecure or anything, but I just need reassurance that I'm better-looking than him, that's all. Ooh, while we're on the subject, may I share one piece of wisdom?

ME: Please. The state of mind I'm in, all words of wisdom are gratefully received.

MARC WITH A C: Right, wait for it. 'Failure is never half as frightening as regret.'

ME AGAIN: Oh honey, that's such an amazing quote! Where did you come across it?

MARC WITH A C: Promise you won't guffaw? Inspirational toilet roll.

OK, time for me to hit the nail on the head. Here's what's been gnawing away at me and making my tummy churn over with sheer worry all day. Yes, I have just been made a wonderful offer and yes, of course, technically I should be dancing on the tables with joy. But, here's the biggie.

This morning, I came closer than I ever have, *ever*, to having an on-air cardiac arrest. When I blanked out on TV, without exaggeration, it was probably the single most frightening thing that's ever, *ever* happened to me. As if a safety net I've had comfortably under me my whole life, which I completely took for granted, was, suddenly and without warning, pulled out from underneath me. And it could happen again. Easily. I'm not out of the woods.

Yes, I had a flash in the Dragon Lady's office, but the whole time I was with Jack, nothing, *nada*, not a single thing. Which isn't like me. Not at all, not by a long shot. It's not like I have an average daily flash rate or anything, you know, every hour on the hour, like Sky News, but this is just plain *weird*.

So could you just imagine if I go ahead and accept a big, glamorous TV contract and then dry? On air? Broadcasting live to the entire nation? Not to mention my mother's living room?

In this game (if you could call it that), the minute you lose your nerve, then your confidence is next out of the window and then, sorry, but you're pretty much finished. I shudder again, just thinking about how dangerously close I am to that dole queue. OK, I really need to remain calm and positive here.

Brainwave. Got it. I'll ask for a sign from the Universe. One absolutely clear-cut signal that will leave me in no doubt that this is the right course of action for me to follow.

Fab idea. Right then.

I'm just about to get back to the mound of letters waiting for me on my desk, when some tiny, barely perceptible little voice inside me urges me to check my emails.

Come on, Cassie, you know the golden rule: follow your instincts at all times.

I bring up my inbox and there are, no kidding, twenty-seven new messages waiting for me. Bloody hell, I'll be here all night.

No, banish that negative thought, focus and regroup. I'm looking for a sign here.

The first email I click on is from my mum, who got a computer for her birthday and has taken to the life of a silver surfer like a duck to water. I'm not joking, there're days when I get six emails from her, not to mention all the rubbishy attachments she sends telling me about how I can save ten per cent on industrial-strength binliners if I buy online, you know the kind of thing.

From: mothership@hotmail.com
To: Cassandra@tattlemagazine.com
Subject: So proud of you!

Hello darling,

Your father and I just wanted to let you know how thrilled we were to see our little princess on the telly this morning. Now, I always liked that nice Mary who presents the *Breakfast Club* but as for that other one, Maura, she's a right piece of work. As contrary as a bag of weasels, your dad was just saying. Margaret from next door popped in to watch the show with us, and she reckoned Maura was mad jealous of you and that's why she gave you such a hard time. Or maybe she caught a glimpse of her own reflection in a spoon or something and that's what had her so narky. Otherwise, it was absolutely great and you were a credit to us all, although you know I do prefer your hair a bit longer, love.

Hope you and Jo will still come for Sunday lunch this weekend. Tell Jo I went to Iceland and bought nice veggie burgers especially for her. And of course Charlene is welcome too, although I know perfectly well she sniggers whenever I mention my friends from the amateur musical society and how we're all getting on at rehearsals. (*The Sound Of Music* this year, darling, the last Saturday in October, don't forget to put it in your diary.) And your father and I still remember last Christmas when she referred to my marzipan holy family as '*überkitsch*', whatever that means. Oh yes, and will you be sure to tell Marc that we'd love to have him too. No ulterior motive or anything, but you remember Margaret's youngest daughter is home from college for the holidays and the last time she met Marc, she thought he was very handsome. Just like a young Simon Cowell, she said. But you needn't let on I'm matchmaking, love. I wouldn't want to scare the poor fella away.

Take care and don't worry. Your dad taped the *Breakfast Club* for you and we can all watch it again on Sunday after lunch, please God.

Mum xxx

PS: Margaret just stuck her head round the garden door looking for a quick favour. She's finally going into hospital to have her varicose veins done next week and she just wanted to ask you if you'd had any flashes about how she'd get on. She's a bit nervous, God love her. You remember what she was like the time she had that ingrown toenail but this surgery is so much worse, whatever way you look at it. She says to tell you she's Aquarius with Taurus rising, just in case that makes any difference.

Don't get me wrong; it's great to hear from Mum, but this is hardly what you might call a clear-cut sign from above, now is it? Anyway, I'm just about to reply to her, when another email catches my eye. Well, not so much the email itself as what's written in the subject box.

From:	tanyaod@eircom.net
To:	Cassandra@tattlemagazine.com
Subject:	If you only get around to answering one letter this week, then please, please, for the love of GOD, let it be this one

Now, how could I ignore a message like that? I read on ...

Dear Cassandra,

You may not remember, but I wrote to you last year looking
for some career advice and you were absolutely 100% on the
money then, as I hope you will be now. I'm a thirty-three-year-
old professional and here's my dilemma.

Firstly, I have a fantastic job. I'm a finance lawyer in
CarthySimpson and the only reason I'm even mentioning this
is because when I applied to the firm, you were the one who
encouraged me to go for it and who assured me that I'd get the
job – and you were right. So now here I am: fabulous friends,
a penthouse apartment in town and a six-figure annual salary.
I'm up for partnership in a few months' time and regularly put
in one-hundred-hour weeks. Theoretically, life is good. I work
hard, I play hard, I make big decisions all day long and then I
come home. To my boyfriend. Who has taken a year off work
to see if he can make it as an actor. An ACTOR. I know, it's
the most ridiculous thing I ever heard, too. What's especially
irritating is that he did actually have a very successful career,
with a terrific salary (he's an investment banker) and has given
all that up . . . for what?

So far, he's appeared in one detergent commercial (he's
the 'before' man wearing a filthy shirt just before his TV wife
washes it in new Daz Ultra-Brite) and one incredibly boring
play, in one of those God-awful black box studio spaces,

where at one point (and I really wish I were joking here)
most of the cast crawled around the stage pretending to be
chickens, for which they were paid the princely sum of 140
euros a week. Cassandra, I don't want to sound in any way
unsupportive, but I really question anyone who considers
clucking like a chicken in front of all their friends and family
to be a valid career move. I wouldn't mind, but I even took
my parents to see the show, telling them it would be cutting
edge, experimental and cool, and was left very red-faced
afterwards.

So now the state of play is this: I'm effectively supporting
my boyfriend and yet, when I come home exhausted at the
end of a fourteen-hour day, he's done absolutely nothing
around the flat. Whenever I ask (gently, in a non-nagging
tone of voice, naturally) what exactly his contribution to the
household has been, he tells me he spent the entire day doing
voice exercises, which, as far as I can see, involve him going
'ummmmmmm' over and over again with *Richard and Judy* on
in the background. Not a cup washed, not a shirt ironed, no
groceries bought, NOTHING.

I do love him, Cassandra, but my patience is wearing very
thin. Do you see any future for him in showbiz? If he got cast
in a major motion picture and became the next Colin Farrell,
making vast seven-figure sums, then, maybe, MAYBE I could
just about deal with this.

I appreciate your time.

With thanks,
Tanya in Temple Bar

It's late afternoon and the office is buzzing and busy, but I do my level best to tune out all distractions and really, really concentrate . . .

Yes! Brilliant! Success! I'm getting a very clear picture of the boyfriend Tanya's on about: tall, fair, ruggedly good-looking, very posh accent.

Oh bugger. It's not a flash at all. I just remember seeing him in the Daz ad.

OK, come on, I can do this. Correction: I *have* to do this.

Just then, Sir Bob wafts past, clutching a copy of an evening paper. 'I say, Cassie, old thing,' he says, briefly pausing at my desk, 'just wondered if you'd seen this? Thought it might be of interest. After all your adventures this morning, I mean.' With that he plonks the paper in front of me and I almost fall over.

It's a front-page picture of Maura from the *Breakfast Club*, looking a bit the worse for wear, staggering out of a nightclub wrapped around a much older-looking man and bending upwards, as if to kiss him. The picture is grainy and God only knows when it was taken, but there's no mistaking that it's her. The headline reads:

'*BREAKFAST CLUB* STAR'S MARRIED LOVER.' Underneath: 'TV STAR BRANDED HOMEWRECKER AS HER MARRIED BOY-FRIEND'S WIFE SPEAKS OUT'.

I stare at the paper in deep, total shock. I saw this. Only this morning. Word for word, clear as crystal.

'All right, my dear?' asks Sir Bob, looking at me, a tad concerned.

'Oh . . . sorry, Bob, I'm just a bit . . . emm . . . dis-tracted.'

He nods and moves off, totally used to, shall we say, my odd little ways. And then another flash hits like a ton of lead.

It's Tanya from Temple Bar's boyfriend, the Daz-ad man himself, and he's been cast in a soap opera. As a villain, one of those J.R. Ewing-type characters that audiences love to hate. I see big success for him, a regular job and a steady income, but as for Tanya . . . Oh God, this just gets better and better. I can see Tanya as clearly as if she's standing right in front of me. She's petite with dark bobbed hair and glasses. And . . . yes! She's met someone new, someone so much more suited to her. I see her with this new man, hand-in-hand outside a neo-classical-looking building . . . I'm seeing pillars, stone columns, steps . . .

The High Court. Yes, definitely the High Court. I've seen it on the six o'clock news loads of times. And the man she's with is wearing a wig – oh, I've got it, he's a barrister. A top one too, the type who takes on all the big, high-profile cases. And she's happy. I'm certain of it. I feel a deep sense of peace and happiness and security emanating from all around her . . .

YESSSSS!
SUCCESSSSS!

For the first time today, I feel like hopping up on my desk and dancing a jig. I can do this. I'm absolutely back in the game. Gift restored. All well.

Jack gave me his business card with strict instructions that I call him the minute I come to a decision.

I don't hesitate for a single moment longer. I pick up the phone and dial.

Chapter Six

THE TAROT DECK
THE HIGH PRIESTESS CARD

Signifies that a wise woman of keen intelligence and understanding will be close at hand, counselling you, advising you, looking out for you. She is more than likely to be an old soul, deep and conscientious, with a rare talent for understanding people and their motives. This amazing woman is in your corner, one hundred per cent behind you, with no other purpose than to guide and steer you away from trouble.

So you'd better make bloody sure that you listen to her . . .

'No pressure on anyone, it's all going to be very relaxed and informal, just a typical, normal evening in the mansion. A typical *black tie* normal evening, that is. And, of course, a sit-down dinner. I think you're all aware that I'm allergic to buffets.'

It's only lunchtime on Saturday and already Charlene has gone into introduce-the-new-boyfriend-to-everyone-I-ever-met-in-my-entire-life overdrive.

'Anyway,' she goes on, 'tonight's the night when Jack will realize that I have an undisputed reputation as a CH.'

'Celebrated hostess,' Marc with a C chips in, correctly interpreting our blank expressions, as we all finish up brunch, or our bi-monthly bitch-brunch as he insists on calling it.

'Hold on one second,' Jo thunders across the table at her. 'Does Jack Hamilton actually *realize* that he's going to be centre stage in some sort of sick parade ring for the night, with everyone gawping at him? Or maybe you're actually physically trying to drive the poor guy away? Could that be your cunning master plan?'

'Josephine, I'll have you know I'm operating a watertight schedule here. If I want to be married by thirty, then I need to get engaged this Christmas, because, number one, I want to be a fiancée for as long as I can. I mean, everyone knows all they do is have parties thrown in their honour whilst getting showered with fabbie-dabbie gifts. And number two, it takes a minimum of two years to book a wedding – at least, the kind of five-day extravaganza that I'll be hosting, Liz Hurley eat your heart out. Try to keep up, will you, sweetie? This is hardly advanced maths.' Charlene smiles sweetly back at her.

'My God, you're like some kind of heat-seeking romance missile. And how, might I ask, does Jack feel about a fancy, posh dinner party being thrown in his honour barely a week after you even met him?'

Charlene looks a tiny bit shifty and her freshly ex-foliated face starts to blush a bit, which eagle-eyed Jo instantly picks up on.

'Oh, I *do not* believe you. You haven't even told him, have you?'

'Now don't be cross, but you see, the thing is . . . well, I didn't want to scare him off. He thinks he's popping in for a glass of wine and a slice of pizza on his way home from work.'

'Poor Jack Hamilton,' says Jo, shaking her head in disbelief. 'I never would have thought it possible that I'd feel this sorry for someone I haven't even met yet. We'll be lucky if he doesn't have a heart attack on the floor of your one-hundred-thousand-euro conservatory.'

'Besides, can I remind you that you're still only twenty-eight?' I say, munching on a Danish and, if the truth be told, hoping we can get off this subject, which is starting to make me feel a bit queasy. Fat chance, though, as Jack has pretty much been Charlene's sole topic of conversation for the past few days. It's almost as if, now that she doesn't have the bothersome distraction of a job to go to, she's channelling all of her considerable energies into her quest to become a bride. And I'm going to have to go to this bloody dinner tonight whether I like it or not. There's just no way out of it.

That is, not unless I think of something, very, *very* fast . . .

'Quite apart from the fact that you've only just met him, what's the mad rush?' I add lamely.

'I'm one hundred per cent with the girlies on this one,' says Marc with a C, who's looking very fetching today in a black Lycra Spandex all-in-one gym suit, which leaves next to nothing to the imagination.

'Please, not girlies, *women*,' Jo interrupts him. 'Do you mind?'

'Sorry, Millie-Tant. Excuse me for breathing. Of course I meant to say *women*. Anyway, let's face it, Charlene, I've seen you let good men go and bad men stay. And the ones in the middle, you've been mean to. So can I just be frank here, please?'

'Only if it ends up with me getting what I want,' says Charlene, looking angelic.

'Will you please tell me what's so special about this

one? What makes you think that Jack Hamilton is a keeper?'

Jo shoots me a tiny, barely perceptible look.

Needless to say, neither of us has breathed a word to Marc with a C about the flash I had/the whole Jack Hamilton situation. We jointly decided that, in this case, discretion is most *definitely* the better form of valour, mainly because, much as we love Marc with a C dearly, he's genetically incapable of keeping anything to himself. Even labelling something as 'highly confidential' is absolutely no use; that just means he'll only tell one person at a time.

'Because I'm a romantic,' Charlene says a bit defensively, 'and he just *is*, that's all there is to it. And when the happy day comes when each of you meets THE ONE, you'll know just the way I do. A woman's instinct is never wrong.'

'Would that be the same instinct that chose those shoes?' says Jo.

'Shut up, you. Look, so far, of all my friends, Jack has only met Cassie and look how well that turned out for all concerned. When I called him last night all he could talk about was Cassie this, Cassie that. All his big plans for her TV slot, which as we know, is largely down to me.'

Another glance from Jo, which only makes me redden even more.

'But I want him to meet you guys as well as my other, shall we say, less economically challenged friends,' Charlene goes on, luckily not noticing that I've turned the colour of gazpacho. 'And I want him to see my humble abode slash mansion. The theme of the night, people, will be L.A.M.B.'

'L.A.M.B.?' we all chant in unison.

'Yeah. Look at my billions.'

Jo shakes her head in disbelief. 'Charlene, I know the cornerstone of your whole belief system is that there's very little money can't buy, but *a husband*?'

'Jo has a point, babes,' says Marc with a C, nodding in agreement. 'Apart from the night you met, and the morning you took Cassie into the TV studio, may I point out that not only have you not slept with him, you've only been on one date. Which was a quick drink, entirely arranged by you, so that doesn't really add up to much, now does it?'

'Kindly clarify, please?' says Charlene, playing with a long Titian coil of her hair. It's a characteristic gesture of hers, whenever she feels the rest of us are ganging up on her and she knows, deep down, that she's in the wrong.

Marc with a C sighs as if he's trying to explain quantum physics to a six-year-old. 'Everyone knows that one dinner date equals three drink dates, which in turn equal half a dozen coffee dates. So you do the maths, sweetie.'

'If I give you money, will you stop talking?'

'Now, don't get angry with me, babes,' says Marc with a C, cool as a breeze. 'You look older when you're angry.'

'My Lycra-clad friend here has a point,' says Jo, with just the teeniest glance in my direction.

'Not Lycra, on a point of order, this is Spandex actually,' he replies, snapping the fabric off his thigh. 'And if we ever manage to get off the everlasting subject of Jack Hamilton, I need you all to tell me honestly whether or not you think I'm gaining weight. I feel beaten into this like a blood sausage. Why oh why can't I be manorexic?'

'Sorry to have to spell it out to you,' says Jo, completely ignoring him, 'but let's be brutally honest here. Jack isn't exactly jumping in feet first like you are, now is he?'

'Thanks so much for that, moment-stealer,' says Charlene, making a winced-up face at the direction this conversation is taking. 'Could you back me up here, please, Cassie? Seeing as how you're the only one who's actually met my boyfriend?'

Shit. I've got to think of something fast. Something that won't upset her but at the same time sounds vague and non-committal and might, just might, get her to cancel or at least postpone tonight . . .

Yes. Got it.

'Well . . . emm . . . what's wrong with taking things nice and easy?' I say, doing my best to sound supportive in a casual, disinterested way, if you know what I mean. Bloody hell, it's like walking a tightrope. Over a minefield. During an earthquake. 'After all, you don't want to put pressure on the guy, do you? He gets enough of that in work, I'd say. Why not have this big, scary, formal dinner another time? Down the line, I mean, maybe in a few months, you know, when you know each other a bit better.'

Charlene looks at me a bit funnily. 'You're not getting any flashes about Jack, are you?' she asks me directly and I swear I want to crawl under the table and die.

There's a horrible pause and they're all looking at me and I just catch Jo's eye and see her shaking her head and silently mouthing 'no'.

'Because, if you are,' Charlene goes on slowly, 'under no circumstances are you to tell me. I don't want to know. Number one, it brings dating bad luck and number two, you're the one who's always saying we choose between fate and destiny, aren't you? So Jack Hamilton is my destiny and I've chosen him, whether the Universe likes it or not.'

There's another pause while it sinks into the rest of us. Shit. She's serious. Deadly serious.

But that's just fine, I hastily remind myself. After all, what have I done wrong? Nothing. All I'll be doing is

working with him. That's it. All above board with absolutely no hidden agenda. Yes, he's attractive, but then so
are loads of other fellas. We all have control of our own
fortunes and, while wishing Charlene the very best of
luck, I choose to stay as far away from this icky situation
as I possibly can.

Great. All I need to do is keep saying that over and
over and I'll be absolutely grand. Now if there was only
some way I could get out of going to this God-awful
dinner tonight . . .

'OK, darlings,' says Marc with a C, 'time for me to say
BFN, bye for now.'

'But you can't just leave, sweetie,' says Charlene plead-
ingly. 'I absolutely, positively *need* you to come back to
the mansion and help me for this evening. I'm totally
relying on you.'

'Help you?' says Jo incredulously. 'Charlene, you have
a maid, a housekeeper, a full-time cook and a butler. And
on top of that, you're probably hiring caterers in for the
night. What help could you possibly need?'

'I need help getting into my outfit,' she replies, not
looking even vaguely embarrassed about it. 'It's a basque.
Vintage Vivienne Westwood. And besides, my staff never
tell me the real truth about how I look, like you guys do.
And I'm tired of relying on digital cameras all the time.'

Jo rolls her eyes to heaven but says nothing.

'Oh, come on, pleeeeese?' says Charlene, batting the

eyelids at Marc with a C. 'I mean, otherwise, what's the point of having a gay best friend if you won't help dress me?'

'OK, OK, you emotionally guilted me into it,' he says, getting up to go. 'I'll call round early and be your personal dresser, if that's what it takes for you to get a husband, O girlfriend with an agenda. One condition, though: after I've finished kitting you out, I'll need enough time to dash back home and put on my Tanfastic. Last time I went out without my false tan on, some smartarse asked me how much I charged to haunt a house.'

'Where are you off to in such a rush?' I ask him, faux-casual, as he gathers up his stuff to leave, hoping against hope that we can talk about something other than Jack Hamilton. Middle East politics, the price of oil, the state of Brad Pitt and Angelina Jolie's relationship, for the love of God, *anything*. 'You haven't even told us your week's news yet.'

'I'm taking my granny to the beauty salon for a wash and blow dry.'

'Marc with a C, I am *so* proud of you,' says Jo, beaming. 'I always knew there was a caring, civic-minded, upright member of the community inside you, just bursting to get out. Maybe when you're done at the hairdresser's, you'd like to pop in to help me at Oxfam for the afternoon? I could always do with an extra pair of hands.'

'Ehh . . . bit of a crossed wire here, Jo,' he says, looking a bit embarrassed. 'It's just that there's a hot hot hottie from the gym who takes his granny to the salon every Saturday too and I was kind of hoping to bump into him. And you know how I'm still healing from my last disastrous liaison, so as I always say, if you wanna get over someone, get under someone.'

'Come on, Jo, I'll give you a hand,' I say, taking a last gulp of coffee and reminding myself of the soul contract I made with the Universe that if I got my gift back, I'd help her out every Saturday and *not moan*.

'Good girl,' Jo says appreciatively as she throws us all our bags and coats, which are strewn around the table under us.

'Sweetie, do you mind not manhandling my bag?' Charlene says to her. 'That's a limited edition Hermès Birkin. I had to go on a waiting list for it.'

'Oh, for God's sake, it's a handbag, not a hospital bed,' says Jo, dumping it unceremoniously on the table in front of her.

'Right then,' sighs Charlene, slinging it over her shoulder, 'I'm off to meet Anna Regan for a snipe of fizz. I want a second opinion about Jack from someone who tells me what I want to hear. And to work out a table plan for this evening, *naturellement*.'

Marc with a C, Jo and I all shoot panicky glances at each other. There's an awkward pause. It's a known fact that none of us can *stand* Anna Regan, who is probably the richest, snottiest and most spoilt of all Charlene's trust-fund-babe pals. And that, believe me, is really saying something.

'*She's* going to be there?' says Marc with a C dismally.

'Of course, why wouldn't she be?' asks Charlene innocently. 'And her . . . *fiancé*.' She's barely able to get the word out. 'And all of her gang.'

'So why are you asking us then?' Jo demands. 'You know how we feel about her and you know the way she looks down her nose at us. Are we part of some poor-friends outreach programme you're running or something?'

Then it hits me. Finally. The one amazingly simple, clear-cut way to get all of us off all hooks. Especially, if I'm being really honest, me.

OK, so maybe not a brainwave worthy of Stephen Hawking, but it's the best I can come up with under pressure.

'You know, Charlene,' I say, 'none of us will take the slightest offence if you want to keep tonight just, ehh, wealthy pals. You know, friends who can talk about their limited-edition sports cars and ski trips and houses that cost millions, all of that stuff. It might be better all round. I mean, Jack can meet up with us any time, can't he? For a coffee or a drink or . . . something a bit less formal. More relaxed and low key. Not to mention cheap. None of us will take the slightest offence if you want to leave us out. Honestly.'

Brilliant. I'm officially a genius. Why didn't I think of this earlier?

'Fab idea, love it, great, let's do that,' Jo and Marc with a C almost sing together, both looking at me very gratefully.

'Sorry, honey, too late,' says Charlene firmly, getting up to go. 'I've already given a final guest list to my housekeeper. Besides, I think you're all aware of the lengths I'll go to for even seating.'

'I really couldn't feel sorrier for Jack Hamilton,' Jo says for about the tenth time, as she, Marc with a C and I share a taxi on our way to Charlene's that evening. 'Anyone care to place a bet on how long the poor unfortunate will last tonight?'

'No takers, honey,' I answer dismally, absolutely dreading the night ahead and only hoping the three of us can leave as early as possible without it seeming rude. Like the minute the dessert course is over or something – that would be OK, wouldn't it?

Oh hell, who am I kidding? It'll be midnight at the earliest before we can scarper. Last time Charlene had one of her excruciating dinner parties, the guests arrived so late it was well after eleven before the main course was even served. And, just for the record, by 'main course' I mean yet more champagne, which is mostly what her pals seem to live off. Charlene, in her defence, is well able to put away a burger and chips with the best of us, but her friends appear to survive solely on weeny bits of lettuce with shavings of cheese. Apparently all you're allowed to eat if you're a bona-fide trust-fund babe.

Besides, I remind myself, let's face it, I am going to be working with Jack for the foreseeable future. So I'd better start getting used to nights like this, hadn't I?

'Can I please get something off my chest? Something that sounds incredibly disloyal, but would be on my conscience if I didn't say it aloud?' Jo says slowly.

'Go ahead,' says Marc with a C. 'I'll try not to judge you. Besides, every time I do, you all remind me that I used to work out to Milli Vanilli.'

'I know Charlene is our friend,' says Jo, ignoring him and looking deadly serious. 'But, Jesus, at times like this she really, and I mean *really*, drives me nuts. I can put up with all her superficiality, I can put up with her complete and total self-absorption, all I'm saying is that there are times when she *really* pushes it a bridge too far. Viz, tonight.'

'I know just how you feel, sweetie,' says Marc with a C, patting her knee, 'and you all know there's nothing I love more than a good old-fashioned bitch-fest, but friends love each other unconditionally and that's what we all have to remember.'

'Besides, she does have a heart of gold,' I add. 'If you scratch deep enough.'

'I know, I know,' Jo sighs. 'If you scratch deep enough, you can see her . . . right the way down to the surface.'

'Remember the time I broke up with Greg from the gym because he didn't call me for three weeks and then when we did meet, he reintroduced himself as if he didn't even remember who I was, and to save face in front of everyone I had to say, "Oh yes, Greg. I seem to remember an answering machine that went by that name," just to avoid the public humiliation?' says Marc with a C. 'She was such a support to me after that. Flying me to the Bahamas in her dad's private plane and everything. You know, so I could heal my wounded heart and get a tan at the same time.'

'You're only using that as an example because you ended up dating the co-pilot,' says Jo wearily. 'You big rebounder.'

'Don't get narky with me just because I bounce back quickly. OK, rebound, if you will.'

'Then there was the time you and I had flu,' I remind Jo, 'and Charlene came round with homemade vegetarian soup for the two of us. Remember?'

'Cassie, you have a highly selective memory. She came round with her personal chef who rustled up the soup for us. While she sat on the edge of my bed slagging off my swollen glands and calling me, if memory serves, the Elephant Woman.'

'Anyway,' I repeat firmly, 'you can't deny it. The girl

does have a heart of gold. What about all that money she gives to charity? Remember the time you were stuck for sponsorship so she completely financed the entire Amnesty team to run the city marathon? You were over the moon with her then. Not to mention the fact that Oxfam practically survive on all the designer clothes and bags and shoes she donates. And she's never even worn most of the stuff.'

'I wholeheartedly agree,' says Marc with a C. 'There are bag ladies who shop at Oxfam walking the streets in haute couture entirely because of Charlene. When the chips are down, there's no one like her. And let's face it, the high-maintenance carry-on just makes her all the more adorable. My love for her is just like my appendix scar. Ugly, but permanent.'

'I know, I know,' says Jo, still staring out of the window. 'I just had some irritation/anger issues that I needed to express, that's all. I do love the girl as well, you know. It's just that, right now, I love her like a cold sore.'

'I don't know what you're getting so het up about anyway,' he goes on. 'This is hardly like the time you caught her wearing real fur.'

Jo shoots a daggers look at him, clearly illuminated by the lights of a passing car. Animal fur and the people who wear it are strictly taboo subjects with her. At all times, always.

'NOT REMOTELY funny,' she practically growls at him.

'Oops, sorry, hon.'

'Oh, it's OK. All out of my system now. Don't worry, guys, I'll go in there and beam at them all and be perfectly false all night.'

'I just have one thing to add and then I'll shut up,' says Marc with a C. 'Now, I may not have been in a serious relationship for a long time, but I do read a lot of chicklit and I would confidently like to venture a prediction for what lies ahead.'

'Go on,' says Jo dully.

'It's little short of a racing certainty that when Jack Hamilton sees what our darling little Tipsy Queen has laid on for him, he'll run for the hills and she'll have a seizure. Mark my words: there will be bloodshed in the mansion before the night is out. On a carpeted area, possibly, you know, for added drama. What do you think, Cassie?'

But I'm hardly listening to him as the taxi has just pulled through the enormous gates of Charlene's house and my jaw has almost dropped. She's had lanterns tastefully arranged all up the stone steps that lead to the front door and has dotted the immaculate front garden with, literally, dozens and dozens of twinkly fairy lights. I'm not joking; there are runways at Heathrow less brightly lit than this.

'Wow,' I say, stunned. I mean, we all knew Charlene always goes to trouble when she entertains, but *bloody hell* . . .

'I'll see your wow and I'll raise you a wowee,' says Marc with a C, equally knocked for six.

The only one of us who's acting completely normally is Jo, bless her. 'Right then,' she says as we pay the driver and hop out of the taxi. 'How much do you dare me to go in there and ask the butler for a lump of cheese string and a can of Bulmers?'

The house is buzzing. There's a roaring fire lit in the huge marble hallway and Charlene's housekeeper is busy circulating around guests, carrying a silver tray loaded down with champagne. No sign of our hostess, no sign of Jack and no sign of the awful Anna Regan (thank God) but as the three of us all shed coats and bags we unexpectedly bump into Charlene's father.

Shit.

He's obviously flown back at the last minute from his tax-exiled hillside paradise in Monaco to check up on his only child, something he's prone to springing on her without any prior warning.

Did I tell you about Charlene's father? His whole life is almost like something you'd see on the Biography channel: the eldest of ten kids, he left school at fourteen to support his family, got a job as a window cleaner, worked his way up to the top, eventually buying the company, then bought a hardware company, then invented and patented a new type of water-resistant shower-curtain ring, and the rest is history. The kind of history you can read in the *Financial Times*, that is. In person, he's tall, imposing and peers down at you through those very scary-looking half-moon glasses which, behind his back, we all reckon he doesn't actually need at all, but only wears to intimidate people.

That's the other thing about him. Like a lot of business people who scale the heights, in manner he can be tough, uncompromising and cutting, occasionally to the point of rudeness. Particularly with Charlene. He gives her an unbelievably miserable time over just about everything: her chronic overspending, lack of career focus, lack of motivation, complete inability to live within a budget, you name it. Honestly, there are times when you really have to feel sorry for the poor girl.

'Hello, Mr Ferguson.' We all smile lamely at him, trying to act pleased to see him. Even though we've known him for so long, there's no question of ever calling him by his first name, like everyone does with my dad. Trust me, you just wouldn't dare.

'Evening.' He nods curtly before looking around in that cold-eyed, calculating way that he has. 'So what do you all make of this? How much is tonight costing, is what I'd very much like to know. I come home to see

Charlene and discover that not only has she lost a job which I had to pull a lot of strings to get for her, she's also wantonly throwing my money down the toilet on pointless, extravagant soirées like this. You still working at *Tattle*?' he fires at me, catching me off-guard.

God, I feel like I'm a contestant on *The Apprentice* who's about to be fired. 'Emm . . . yes, Mr Ferguson.'

'How much are you making then?'

If it was anyone else, you'd tell them where to go for asking such a personal question, but Charlene's dad makes all of us regress a bit and, right now, I'm stammering like the fifteen-year-old who once talked Charlene into climbing over the back wall late at night and going to a school disco to meet boys, when we were meant to be having an innocent sleepover at her house. When Mr Ferguson found out (we were caught on security camera, so he had actual videotaped evidence of our shenanigans), the consequences were terrible and, for a time, all contact between us was banned. Well, until my parents intervened and calmed him down a bit, that is. 'Emm . . . well, my job isn't really about money; I have enough, thank God,' I stammer. 'The way I see it, my column is more about helping people . . .'

He just nods, a bit disapprovingly. Money, I should point out, is the beginning, middle and end of Mr Ferguson's day and I think he can't quite see the point of Jo and me and our total lack of ambition to go forth and earn six-figure salaries, like he was doing at our age. He turns to Jo. 'And what about you?'

'Same answer,' she shrugs. 'Money is *not* a motivator for me either, I'm afraid. Never was, never will be.'

God, Jo's brave. She'll be hitting him for a good tax-deductible donation to Amnesty International next.

'So, making much in the fitness game?' Mr Ferguson says to Marc with a C. 'Boom industry at the moment. Boom economy. You should be doing well.'

'Not enough to keep me in those,' says Marc with a C, very cheekily indicating Mr Ferguson's Salvatore Ferragamo shirt with the solid gold cufflinks. 'Besides, my job is kind of more about meeting people, dating people, seeing sweaty guys work out in tight Lycra. It's all about the perks, if you catch my drift.'

Marc with a C, I should point out, hasn't known Mr Ferguson as long as Jo and I have and is therefore that bit more fearless around him. 'Now, would you all excuse me if I run to the bathroom?' he throws in for good measure. 'I've spotted a cute guy and you know me! I can never flirt on a full bladder.'

'Hey, I'll come with you!' says Jo, dying to make her escape, and the pair of them scarper, practically leaving a trail of dust in their wake. Luckily, I'm rescued by Mr Ferguson's long-term girlfriend, Marilyn, who spots me and immediately comes over, giving me a big warm hug.

'Hey, Cassie, I caught you on the TV the other day – you were so *fab*! I see huge, and by that I really mean *huge*, things for you, honey. You're so televisual.'

'Wow, thanks, Marilyn,' I say, gratefully hugging her right back.

I've always liked Marilyn. She's maybe fortyish, but closer in age to us than to Mr Ferguson; an ex-model (most of his girlfriends are) who now works as a highly successful casting director on movies and commercials.

She's actually lovely to be around but it's very hard on Charlene, as you can imagine, not helped by the fact that Mr Ferguson keeps holding Marilyn up as a role model of the perfect career girl who's gone out there and made something of herself, whilst being fiercely critical of Charlene for her general 'lack of direction in life', as he sees it. Charlene, who's a great one for using humour as a defence mechanism whenever she's *really* hurting, has retaliated by nicknaming Marilyn 'the Diva in a D-cup'. She also claims (a bit unfairly) that Marilyn both looks and dresses like a drag queen and she keeps saying, 'So who knew Mae West had children?' at the top of her voice whenever she's around. Honest to God, this family would make the Osbournes look sane and functional.

'So what about this guy that Charlene's seeing, then?' Marilyn asks me, grabbing my arm and thankfully steering me well away from Mr Ferguson. 'Jack something, isn't it? Come on, Cassie, spill the beans. What's he like? Have you met him?'

OK, here we go. Just stay nice and calm. Cool and dignified win the day. And loyalty towards my friend, of course.

Oh yeah, and please remember to stop blushing and being so bloody adolescent; you're behaving like a schoolgirl with a full-blown crush every time Jack's name is even mentioned, you big eejit.

'Yup, he's . . . that is, he seems . . . emm . . . lovely. Big hot-shot producer. I think Charlene really, *really* likes him.'

That sounded OK, didn't it? As if I'm really happy for Charlene and that I hope things work out for her, romance-wise? Which, of course, I do, just with the right person, that's all . . .

'Hmm, so I see,' says Marilyn, looking around and taking everything in: the perfect flower arrangements; the trays of champagne; the formidable guests; everything. No kidding, this would make the court of Versailles look like a free-for-all. 'So, are you getting any flashes about this guy?' she asks me straight out and I immediately go bright red.

'Well . . . emm . . . you see, Charlene always feels it's bad luck for me to tell her if . . . you know, if I have any feelings about guys she's involved with.'

'None at all? Absolutely nothing?' says Marilyn,

looking at me keenly. 'I hope you don't mind me stating the obvious, but that's not really like you, now is it?'

And then, suddenly, I get one. Clear as crystal. Except it's not about Charlene. At least, not directly. Oh my God.

I see Marilyn and Mr Ferguson sitting in a doctor's waiting room. I'm not sure why or what exactly is going on, but there's a real feeling of tense nervousness practically hopping off the pair of them. Then I see an older, twinkly-eyed doctor opening the surgery door and calling them both inside …

Now I see Marilyn looking very white-faced and clinging on to Mr Ferguson's hand, almost in a vice-grip, as they go into the surgery. He doesn't look too good either. On the surface he's as cool as ever, but I can see that he's sweating and twiddling with his cufflinks anxiously.

'Please, take a seat,' the doctor says gently, closing the door behind them.

Oh God, now the feeling of sheer terror I'm picking up from the pair of them is almost making me weak …

'Well now, Marilyn,' says the doctor, sitting in his swivel chair behind his desk and pulling out a huge sheaf of notes. 'Your test results have just come back from the lab. Have it all here, bloods, everything.'

There's a horrible pause and poor Marilyn honestly looks as if she might pass out.

'Oh, nothing to worry about, all good news,' says the doctor. 'Congratulations,' he says warmly to both of them, stretching across his desk to shake each of them by the hand. 'You're about to become parents.'

'Cassie, what is it?' says Marilyn, looking at me with real concern. 'What are you seeing? You've gone as white as a sheet, you poor thing. Here, have a seat.'

'No, no, I'm fine. It's absolutely fine, honestly,' I say, taking a very welcome glug of champagne from my glass.

'Did you just get a flash? Ooh . . . I bet it was something about Charlene's new fella. Am I right?'

Bloody hell. What do I tell her? Would this be good news or bad news? Good news for Marilyn, of course, but for Charlene and her already strained relations with her father . . . I'm feeling, well, to put it mildly, this would sure as hell take her a lot of getting used to . . .

Oh shit, here is a classic example of the moral and ethical dilemmas faced on a daily basis by anyone with a sixth sense. To tell or not to tell, that is the question.

Phew. I'm saved from having to say anything at all by the arrival of our hostess, looking absolutely breathtaking in the Vivienne Westwood basque worn with a huge, neo-Victorian, full-length, voluminous black skirt. I'm not joking; there are so many ruffles and frills all over it that I'm almost afraid if she stands near the fire, she'll go up like a torch.

Anyway, you get the picture; Charlene is looking a million dollars tonight. Apart from her expression, that is, which, to put it mildly, would stop a clock.

'Wow, you look amazing,' I say, kissing her. 'Everything OK?'

'No,' she says in a tiny voice and I can immediately see that she's on the verge of tears. 'Will you do something for me? Would you find Jo and meet me in the library? I really, badly need a private word with you guys and if I go searching for Jo, Dad will only collar me and demand to know in front of everyone how much my outfit cost. Dire emergency.'

Five minutes later, the three of us are alone in the library, which is just to the left of the entrance hall. It's a fab room, brand spanking new, but made to look old, and covered with shelf after shelf of leather-bound first editions. None of which Charlene has ever read, of course. In fact, we slag her something rotten about the fact that the only reading she ever does in her custom-built library is to occasionally glance through *Tattle* magazine, counting up how many people she knows on the society pages versus how many times she appears herself.

'So what's up?' I ask her, half dreading the answer. 'Is it your dad?'

'Yeah,' says Jo sympathetically, 'what a bummer, him just turning up tonight of all nights. Will there be hell to pay when he finds out how much all this is costing him?' Jo's actually being very gentle to Charlene, almost as if she's on a guilt trip for having given out about her in the taxi earlier. But then, the sight of Mr Ferguson tends to have that effect on all of us.

'Least of my worries. Right now, *this* is what's upsetting me,' Charlene almost wails, shoving her mobile phone under our noses. There's a short, curt text message.

HI. AM STILL DELAYED AT CHANNEL SEVEN. PRODUCTION MEETING ONGOING. SORRY TO LET U DOWN. ENJOY UR PIZZA AND I'LL TRY MY BEST TO SEE YOU LATER. JACK.

So now he mightn't be coming at all, my mind races. He mightn't turn up. Tonight could just be about bearable . . .

'So,' says Charlene. 'Any bright ideas? Apart from the fact that there'll be hell to pay from Dad in the morning, now all of my friends have gathered here to meet my new boyfriend, who may or may not even arrive. Any second now, Anna Regan could waltz in here, flashing her Tiffany-cut engagement ring under my nose, and here I am, dateless, hopeless and *furious.*'

193

'Well, I guess this is what happens when you're not straight with people,' says Jo coolly. 'If you'd just been upfront with Jack in the first place and told him what he was in for, then he'd either have chickened out or shown up on time.'

'Y.P.B.?' says Charlene, really starting to get upset now.

'Y.P.B.? What does that mean?' Jo asks.

'Your point being?'

'My point is, he'd have given you a straight yes or no answer and at least you wouldn't be in this mess. Charlene, get a grip, will you? I've never seen you like this before.'

'Not pretty, is it?'

Oh dear. Now the tears have started. It was only ever a matter of time before this happened, I know, but you should just see her. The girl looks – there's no other word for it – *crumpled*.

'All I wanted was for him to meet you. My real friends, I mean. You guys. And I went to so much trouble—' She breaks off, genuinely upset, and Jo and I look at each other. 'And he won't even return my calls. What is the *problem* with me? Why am I so fundamentally undateable? Or is Dad right and am I just a useless, pointless member of society?'

This is the thing about Charlene. One minute, she's completely exasperating, driving you up the walls; the next, she's so tiny and vulnerable and upset that, well, you just want to hug her. Which we both do.

'OK, OK, the way I see it, this is not necessarily a mess,' I interject, bravely trying to introduce a positive note.

'Explain,' sniffs Charlene, a bit more hopefully now.

'So Jack got a bit delayed. Jo's right; if you'd told him he was about to walk on to the set of *The Great Gatsby*, then I'm sure he'd either have cancelled or postponed his meeting. But, in fairness, you can hardly beat the guy up for not knowing he was to be the guest of honour here tonight. For God's sake, all he expected was a tin of Coke and a slice of pepperoni.'

'So what do I do? Any psychic flashes right now would be gratefully received.'

I take a deep breath. Tonight could possibly, conceivably work out really well for all concerned.

'No psychic flashes necessary. It's obvious what you do,' I say, feeling calm for the first time all evening. 'You just go out there and apologize on Jack's behalf; say he's a TV producer and this is the downside of his job. They work twenty-four/seven. Just tell them all an emergency's come up and he'll do his best to be here but go ahead and start without him anyway. You're only telling the truth.'

'Brilliant,' says Charlene, clicking her fingers and looking a bit calmer. 'Just brilliant. I knew you'd come up with something, sweetie. I'll just act like none of this bothers me at all . . . the *bastard*.'

Jo and I exchange glances, but say nothing.

'Right then, come on, back into the fray,' Charlene says, brightening up, linking me and Jo as we head back to the main hall, the tears forgotten as if they never were. 'Oh, and by the way, what were you talking to Marilyn about for so long? You looked like you were having a flash.'

Shit and double shit. Now is not the time to tell Charlene she may be getting a new baby half-brother or sister.

'Oh, you know. This and that.'

'Doesn't she look a mess? God, that dress she's wearing would make some drag queen somewhere very happy. And don't even get me started on the supermarket make-up.'

In fact, scrap that. NEVER might be a good time for this particular piece of news . . .

'OK, here I go, wish me luck,' says Charlene, taking a deep breath and forcing a bright grin before she drifts off. 'Remember the mantra: my smile is my umbrella and I'll deal with Dad in the morning. I'm just thanking my lucky stars he has a business dinner tonight so I won't have to put up with him criticizing me in front of my friends. At times like this, small mercies really do go a long way.'

Jo squeezes my arm. 'So what *did* you see in store for Marilyn?'

'Long story. Tell you later.'

It goes without saying that the dinner is beyond excruciating.

Marc with a C is in ratty humour because the one cute guy he targeted was, shall we say, not of his persuasion. 'I really, really hate it when straight guys look like that,' he hisses to me between courses. 'Simon Cowell has a lot to answer for.'

'What are you talking about? For inventing *The X Factor*?'

'No, dopey. For inventing the concept of the meterosexual.'

Charlene is completely distracted throughout the whole meal and when she's not checking her mobile phone every two minutes, she's almost jumping out of her seat whenever someone comes in or out of the dining-room door, then getting upset with them for not being Jack.

The good news for me is that I'm sitting across from Jo; the bad news is that I'm right beside Anna Regan. The beyond-awful Anna Regan. And her fiancé, Timmy. And her famous Tiffany-cut engagement ring. And the same story, told over and over again, about how rich he is and how he proposed to her on top of the Eiffel Tower and how *stunned* she was and how rich he is and how he went down on bended knee, oh . . . and did I remember to mention how *rich* he is?

To give you an idea just how agonizing the whole conversation is, purely to get a breather I suggest to Jo and Marc with a C that we slip outside to the garden between courses for cigarette breaks. None of us actually smokes, but we're hoping that's a detail no one will notice. It's also freezing, but none of us cares much about that either.

'Stroke of genius thinking of that, Cassie,' says Marc with a C as the three of us plonk down on to an elegant Louis XVI wrought-iron bench on the terrace. 'I humbly thank you from the heart of my bottom.'

'Anna Regan's fiancé is the most boring, geekiest-looking yoke I have *ever* come across,' says Jo, dismally. 'What can she possibly see in him? Or, more to the point, what can he possibly see in her?'

'Apart from the fifty million, you mean?' I say. 'Oh God, she's only been engaged five minutes and already she's turned into Bridezilla. I really don't know how much more of her I can listen to.'

And it's only half-nine. On the plus side though, there's still no sign of Jack.

Jack, my new boss, I remind myself. Jack, who I'll be working with very regularly from next week onwards. Jack, who I'm just going to have to bloody well get used to being around, whether I like it or not.

'So it's all going to be very informal and low-key,' Anna Regan is still chirruping on as we're dragged back inside for yet another course. 'Just your typical, normal, two-hundred-thousand-euro wedding, you know. There you are, Cassie!' she says, spotting me and patting imperiously on the empty seat beside her. 'No pressure, but what do you see about our astrological compatibility? I'm Taurus and Timmy here is Aries. Oh, and I was wondering if you had any psychic episodes, or flashes or whatever it is you call them, about next July for a wedding? If I go for the strapless Vera Wang with the twelve-foot train and then it rains, I'll look *sooooo* ridiculous.'

'Well, long-range weather forecasting wouldn't really be my thing, Anna,' I say, mortified.

She always, unfailingly, does this whenever I'm in her company; treats me like some kind of freak show/performing monkey, at her beck and call to play soothsayer for the night. It *really* drives me nuts.

'Oh, and in Chinese astrology, I was born in the year of the Monkey! I know, nineteen eighty! Can you just believe that I'm only twenty-six and I'll be the first of the gang to get married!'

I'm not kidding; this really is how she goes on. I've never met anyone like her; Anna Regan actually does speak in exclamation marks.

'Ooh, and do you see anything in my lifeline about how long I'll live for?' she says, shoving her hand under my nose. As if I've suddenly turned into a fortune-teller at a circus or something. Jesus, she'll be crossing my palm with silver in a minute. 'I hate to sound ghoulish, but when I die, I want it to be at the exact same moment as Timmy, so neither of us ever has to be alone again, not even for a single second. I strongly believe in mating for life. You know, kind of like penguins.'

I look over at Jo and am relieved to see that I'm not the only one fit to throw up at this.

'Ooh, how fab! Is Cassandra doing predictions?' says a blonde-haired girl from the other side of the table, who I think is called Ayesha, although Marc with a C keeps drunkenly referring to her as 'Eyeshadow'. 'Can you see anything in the future for me?' she's pleading with me. 'My love life is just such a natural disaster. Kind of like Julia Roberts's hair, you know.'

It's almost like some kind of floodgate has been opened and they're all acting as if they've just been waiting for this the entire night and now it's open season for freebie predictions.

'Me next! My go!' says the girl beside her, who has bright red hair and a trout-pout. 'Do you think this is a good time for me to get a job, like my mother is always telling me to? A boob-job, that is.'

'Leave Cassie alone, you big thunder-stealer,' says Anna. 'She's dealing with me first. So, who should I ask to be my chief bridesmaid? I love everyone here dearly, but I think we all know there can only be one clear winner! Oh, and do you think I'll lose a few pounds before the big day? It would be so cool if you saw me down to a size two. That would be my absolute thinspiration.'

'But can I ask just one teeny thing?' says a deep-voiced, dark-haired girl on the other side of Anna, who's hardly said a single word all night. 'Do you think that I'm destined to repeat patterns in my love life over and over again, like my analyst keeps telling me? She says I'm like a magnet for emotionally unavailable men. She also says I need to live in the now, but as far as I can see, women who do that tend to die alone and penniless and single. Which, I suppose, is why we turn to psychics.'

'Yes, but you're *better* at being single than some of us,' says red-haired girl again. 'What about the guy I'm seeing at the moment? Because I think his idea of fidelity is not to flirt with other women until the end of the evening. Is that a bad sign, do you think? I really need guidance here, Cassandra, and I'd be far too embarrassed to write to you care of your magazine.'

'Ha! You think that's bad?' says the girl who Marc with a C keeps calling Eyeshadow, and now, forever-more, that'll be her name in my head. 'Do you realize a guy rang my mobile number by accident and we got chatting and it turned out to be probably the best conversation with a single man that I've had in months? A wrong number. I'm not kidding, girls, squirrels get more action than me. Everyone keeps telling me to get a cat, just to alleviate the sheer loneliness, but my problem is, I distrust anything that loves me that unconditionally.'

You've no idea what this all sounds like. A cacophony of relationship problems is being hurled at me from all different directions and I'm beginning to feel like some kind of freak show.

And then, quite unexpectedly, the flashes start. A load of them, like an avalanche, all at once. I'm seeing things and I haven't got the first clue what they mean, or what they signify.

I see Anna Regan, sitting at an immaculate kitchen table, looking like a cross between a Stepford wife and something out of a 1950s' Doris Day movie, wearing a Cath Kidston apron with her hair freshly blow-dried and immaculately applied lipstick. There's a strong smell of burning coming from her oven and the clock on the wall says it's eleven at night. And it's pitch dark outside and she's alone and there's no sign of her husband. Everything around her is absolutely pristine and gleaming, right down to the granite work surfaces and the Villeroy and Boch china, all beautifully laid out for dinner. For two.

But the feeling of utter desolation and despair I'm getting from her is almost overwhelming.

Then I see her pouring herself a very large brandy and knocking it back in a single gulp …

'Cassie? Are you OK? Can you hear me?' I can hear Jo's voice dimly in the background, but it's almost as if I'm in the deepest sleep you could imagine and can't quite bring myself to wake up.

'Maybe she's not actually seeing things,' I can hear Charlene saying, concerned. 'Maybe it's just an ice-cream headache.'

'Don't be so ridiculous. Will you just look at her? She's shaking like a paint-mixer.'

Then I see Eyeshadow. At least I think it's her. It's hard to tell as she's wearing a ski-suit and is all muffled up in a huge scarf. Thank God, I'm glad to say this is a much happier flash: she's strolling hand-in-hand with someone, also in ski gear, and they're having fun, relaxed, in love. It's all just so romantic, it's twilight and there's deep snow on the ground, chalets in the distance, and I'd swear they were in Austria, or somewhere near the Alps.

Then she impulsively turns round to kiss her partner and, at the same time, they both pull their hoods down a bit and … I don't believe it, it's a woman. The partner is a woman. Definitely. She's older, more mature, very attractive, and the two of them look as if they're absolutely mad about each other; they're just so loved-up, it's adorable … This is it, this is for ever, I just feel it …

'Is she OK? Should I get her some water?'

Oh God, it's Jack's voice. I'm certain. I'd know that voice anywhere. Shit. He came then.

I open my eyes and he's standing right in front of me, looking really worried. Oh, and very sexy, too, by the way. Charlene is beside him, hands on hips, and Jo is patting my hand and looking matronly, just like you see the nurses doing on *Grey's Anatomy*.

'Sorry,' I say in a tiny voice, 'I think I might have got a bit weak.'

'Hey, I hope there's nothing wrong with my TV star,' Jack says, smiling kindly down at me. 'I don't want you cancelling on me next week. There'll be a public outcry. People will start demanding their licence fees back.'

I smile and so, I notice sneakily, does Jo. Good. That means she likes him.

'So where were you all evening then, Jack?' Charlene asks, tugging on his arm.

'Big drama at work. I don't know if you've seen the papers today, but—'

'I only ever read the gossip pages and the horoscopes,' says Charlene innocently.

'Oh right,' he says, looking at her, a bit puzzled, as if he's wondering whether or not she's actually being serious. (She is.) 'Anyway, there was a lot of, shall we say, very negative press coverage about one of the *Breakfast Club* presenters—'

'Maura,' I say, gratefully taking a sip of water.

'That's it,' he goes on. 'Anyway, to make a long story short, we had an emergency production meeting to discuss her future with the show and . . . I'll let you read all about it in tomorrow's papers,' he trails off, a bit embarrassed. 'It was the Director General's call in the end and not a popular decision, but, well, put it this way, Cassie, I think you'll only have one person interviewing you on the show next week. I'm really sorry about this. Circumstances way beyond my control, I'm afraid.'

'That's fine,' I say, knowing exactly what he means and exactly what happened to Maura. Bloody hell.

'Come on,' says Jo, gripping me tightly. 'I'm putting you into a taxi and I'm taking you home.'

'Can I give you ladies a lift?' asks Jack politely.

'*What* did you say?' says Charlene, looking panicky, then stops, remembers herself and beams angelically. 'I mean, you have to stay and have something to eat, Jack. Dinner is finished but maybe you'll have some dessert? There's loads left over.'

'That's really nice,' he says, looking mortified, 'but I had no idea you were having company. And such posh company too. I wouldn't have dreamt of barging in like this if I'd known you were entertaining. I should really leave. I'm sure I'm the last person you want to see.'

Poor guy, if only he knew . . .

Now Charlene looks really flustered, but Jo rescues her.

'It's fine, thanks,' she says firmly. 'You stay and have a drink, Jack. I can take Cassie home from here.'

'Right then,' he says, looking a bit, well, snookered. 'If you're sure, that is.'

'Certain, thanks. By the way, it's really nice to meet you.' And I can tell by looking at her that she means it.

It's only when we get into a taxi on our way home that she tells me what she really thinks. 'Don't you get it?' she says to me. 'It's so obvious what's happening.'

'Ehh, couldn't make it a bit more obvious, could you?'

'Why did none of us see this before?'

'Jo! See what?'

'There you were, seeing things, getting flashes all over the place the whole evening, being amazing, until the minute Jack walked into the room. It's just like what happened to you in that TV studio. It might as well have been a repeat performance.'

'Jo, what are you talking about?'

'You have a gift, this incredible gift. Which goes completely out the window whenever he's in the room. It wasn't *nerves* that made you dry in that TV studio, it was *him*. Don't you understand?'

My stomach starts to feel a bit sick: that awful, nauseous feeling you get when you hear something you'd far rather not and you know it's the truth, whether you like it or not. And then I think about next week.

And the contract I've just signed with the *Breakfast Club*.
And how there is absolutely no way of getting out of it.
   Absolutely none . . .
   In the end, Jo says it out loud. 'Cassie, I don't mean to
alarm you, but, unless we come up with a plan, and *fast*,
I think you could be in really big trouble here.'

Chapter Seven

THE TAROT DECK
THE HANGED MAN CARD

Oh dear. Probably the most feared card in the whole deck. Generally people who pick this card should think about what they're going to do, then not do it and then run very, very fast in the opposite direction.

This card generally symbolizes bad news and worse news. The bad news is that you may well find yourself in a situation you really, and I mean *really*, would rather not be in. The worse news is there is absolutely no way out of it. Unless a miracle happens, that is, but how likely is that?

Sorry to be the bearer of bad news, but fore-warned is forearmed . . .

'And now, ladies and gentlemen, a very special treat for all our viewers this morning. You may remember last week we had Cassandra, the resident psychic from *Tattle* magazine, with us. And wasn't she just wonderful? The phone lines hopped for days afterwards with everyone *demanding* to know when she was coming back to us. Quite honestly, I've never seen anything like it. So now, the goods news is that, from today, she's going to join us for a regular guest appearance, so please will you give a big, warm *Breakfast Club* welcome to . . . Cassandra!'

And I'm on.

And I don't really have a clue how I managed it without (a) passing out or (b) throwing up with nerves, but, for better or for worse, here I am.

As Jo pointed out about a thousand times yesterday, welcome to the wonderful world of got-no-choice. Bless her, she even did one of her lists for me, to stop my obsessive worrying, on the long drive down to my parents' house for a big Mammy Sunday lunch. Needless to say, it ended up being just the two of us who actually made the visit down. Charlene was forced to cancel and instead endure a lengthy lecture from her father about the excesses of the previous night and the fact that she has yet to hold down a stable career, start making something of her life and do something, anything, that might actually impress him. 'Wait till you see, he'll go through my credit card statements next,' she groaned down the phone to me, 'and I wouldn't mind, but I've got such a thumping hangover, all I'm really fit for is a home visit from my masseuse followed by a carb-heavy dinner, but just try telling that to Daddy Dearest.'

Marc with a C chickened out too, claiming he had a fitness assessment he'd clean forgotten about. But he's no actor, and I think being as hungover as a dog, coupled with getting to bed at six a.m. following the party, might just have had something to do with it as well.

Anyway, as I say, Jo wrote out one of her super-duper, über-organized lists for me and it went something along these lines:

Reasons for Cassie to be cheerful, optimistic and positive instead of getting herself into a right tizzy, like last time, about the TV show

1. The small matter of a signed, sealed contract. So unless I actually *want* to be sued and end up bankrupt and homeless, I'm going on. (Jo made this particular argument very forcefully, pointing out the laughing stock I'd be and the field day the papers would have. You know, headlines like 'DAFT PSYCHIC FAILS TO

PREDICT OWN DRAMATIC DOWNFALL'. Ugh.) So, a TV slot beckons, whether I like it or not.

2. If I'm being honest, half of me does like it, very much. I hasten to remind myself that up until I blanked out the last time I was on, I was really enjoying the whole experience. It was actually *fun*. Seeing things and helping people. I mean, isn't that what I do for a living? Course it is. Jo's absolutely right, time for me to toughen up a bit. Get practical.

3. On these grounds, I have therefore made an executive decision that the whole Jack Hamilton situation is a force completely and utterly beyond my control. You know, much like a hurricane or a tsunami, there's pretty much feck all that I can do about it, so I might as well not sacrifice my whole career for the sake of a silly infatuation, based on one single late-night flash I had about him. We're not one hundred per cent sure exactly what the state of play is between him and Charlene; all she told us before her father yelled at her to get off the phone is that he stayed in the mansion for a quick drink after we skedaddled on Saturday, then made his excuses and left not too long after us.

'I only hope I didn't go too far in my tipsy haze?' she said before our conversation was rudely interrupted. 'The plan was that I'd come at him from a position of strength, i.e., wealth, but I'm not sure that my strategy was an entire triumph. He said he needed to talk to me and that he'd call soon. So in boy language that means probably Saturday fortnight.' She's still sticking to her daft.com engagement schedule, though, and is making plans to cajole him into going away on a weekend break the minute her father and Marilyn have gone back to their paradise villa in Monaco. To my knowledge, Jack is blissfully unaware of any of this. Not that it's any of my business really. Is it?

4. The stroke of genius, which I wish I could claim credit for but it's all down to Jo's laser-like thinking. (Honestly, she'd have made a brilliant military strategist, except that she's fundamentally opposed to all warfare of any description.) Given that I can see bugger all whenever Jack is within a ten-foot radius of me, now proven beyond all reasonable doubt, here's my one-hundred-per-cent foolproof strategy to extricate myself gracefully from that one.

Plan a: should I bump into Jack before we go on air

I walk right up to him, coolly and very calmly, and say something along these lines. 'Jack. Being psychic isn't an exact science. No offence, but I strongly suspect that when you're around, my energy is being blocked. Of course, this isn't your fault and I'm not in any way suggesting you're doing it on purpose or anything, I just think that I'd work a whole lot better if you weren't in the studio when I'm doing the slot.'

That sounds OK, doesn't it? Not too, emm, rude, or anything? I mean, 'My energy is being blocked . . .' Does it sound like the kind of emergency you'd ring a plumber for? Or am I comparing myself to a sewage pipe unnecessarily?

Plan b: should Jack walk into studio while I'm on air, which, let's face it, he is entitled to do, given that he is the producer and it is actually his show

This is a tad more embarrassing, but unavoidable. As Jo says, needs must when the devil drives. In this event, the plan is, I turn calmly to Mary, say I'm having a problem seeing things and request that we go to a commercial break. During this time, I then hop out of my seat, approach Jack and repeat the above speech (see Plan A, the blocked energy/sewage pipe speech).

So there you have it. Nothing like being prepared, is there?

Anyway, here I am back in the studio, feeling as if I've never been away and I haven't so much as laid eyes on Jack yet, which is beyond fab. According to fake-tan man in the make-up room (who I've since discovered is called Damien and who I'll really have to stop referring to as fake-tan man), he normally stays well out of the way up in the production box until after the show, as is the norm for any producer apparently (not that I'd know). And Lisa, the lovely stage manager, never even mentioned his name, not once.

Phew. So far, so good.

Mary is interviewing me on her own this morning, which is great because she's just so relaxed and informal, you almost feel as if you're sitting down for a nice cuppa with a favourite auntie. And if she's missing having the awful Maura co-presenting with her, she's certainly not letting it show. In fact, I'm so chilled out I'm almost inclined to forget there's a camera pointing at me. This will be just fine. No, this will be better than fine. Confidence and serenity will win the day.

I take a deep breath and make a silent vow that I'm going to try to *enjoy* myself. And, of course, the calmer I am, the more I'll see . . .

'Well now, Cassandra, I know there's already a list of callers all dying to talk to you, so without further ado, let's go straight to line one. To . . . what was that? Oh sorry, yes. We have Joan here for you. Hello? Yes, good morning, Joan, you're through to Cassandra.'

A thumbs-up sign from the floor manager telling me I'm good to go.

'Hello? Is that Cassandra?'

'Certainly is. Hi there, Joan. How are you today?'

'How *am* I? I'll tell you exactly how I am, lovey. I'm here at home trying to get through a mountain of laundry and ironing, you know, all the normal morning jobs, and I have a layabout husband in the living room next door who thinks it's absolutely acceptable behaviour to sit around in a dressing gown till nine in the morning— Oh, hang on there, will you, just one sec . . . WILL YOU PLEASE USE A PLATE! AND A COASTER! IF IT'S NOT ASKING TOO MUCH! Sorry about that, Cassandra. I am hoarse telling him that the coffee table in the good room is solid mahogany and that a hot mug will leave a ring, but I might as well be talking to the wall. Now he says that I nag him so much it's very difficult for him to zone in on which are the really *important* nags, as if that's any kind of excuse . . .'

She chats on and I get an immediate flash. Thank God.

I see Joan, clear as day. She's maybe sixtyish and has her hair permed so tightly it almost looks like someone has poured a tin of beans on top of her head. Her house is absolutely pristine, so spotlessly clean you could most probably perform surgery on her kitchen surfaces. The smell of bleach I'm picking up is almost making me cough. The husband is a bit older and looks exhausted, really worn out: his skin is grey and his hair is white, and for some reason I feel chest pain coming from him – tension, as if there's a great weight pressing down on him . . .

'DO I SMELL CIGARETTE SMOKE COMING FROM IN THERE?' Joan is shrieking at him, nearly taking the ear off me, clearly audible to everyone in the studio and live to the nation. 'DON'T TAKE ME OVER TO YOU, I'M WARNING YOU! Sorry, Cassandra, but at least you can see for yourself just what I have to deal with here. I'm not a nag, you know, but I swear to God, that man is slowly turning me into one.'

Another flash. Except this time I'm seeing her husband. Oh no, this isn't so good ... I'm getting the most awful feeling from him of desolation, of emptiness, of someone who's worked so hard all his life and now doesn't know what to do with himself and who's being shouted at all day and who's just sitting there, quietly taking it and hating every second of it ...

'He was made redundant five weeks ago,' Joan is going on. 'Five weeks and four days, to be exact. Anyway, ever since ...'

Now I'm seeing him again, but this time he's wearing overalls and covered in oil, in what looks like – could it be an airport hangar? I'm hearing an awful lot of noise, engines roaring, bustle, mechanics rushing around ...

'... now I don't want to say the name of the company

that George worked for, because quite frankly, after the way they treated him, I'd rather not give them the free publicity . . .'

Yes, it's an airline. For definite. I can see the huge, distinctive shamrock logo on a parked Boeing 747 . . .

'. . . let's just say he worked in maintenance for a large semi-state body out at the airport. So, after forty years of having the house to myself all day every day, now all of a sudden I don't. Not that I'm complaining, I'm not a moaning type, you understand, it's just been quite a bit of a readjustment for me, Cassandra. It was one thing when he was coming home at seven in the evening, like a normal husband, but now he's under my feet all day every day, from morning till night.'

Oh God. Now an awful flash . . .

'It's just that George is finding it very difficult to get other work, all to do with his age, you know. So my question is: do you see anything in the future for him? Not to sound impatient, but sooner rather than later? Because I really don't know how much more of this I can take . . . NO, NOT THOSE COASTERS, THE OTHER ONES. THE ONES WITH THE FAMILY CREST ON THEM AND IF THAT'S THE SOUND OF YOU PUTTING YOUR FEET UP ON

THE SOFA, THEN GOD HELP ME, I WON'T BE RESPONSIBLE.'

And I'm off again. Oh no, no, no. This is unbelievable. This is where being psychic is the greatest curse you could ever possibly be landed with.

I see Joan again, except this time she's dressed head to toe in black. She's outside a church and it's packed. People are coming up to her shaking her hand and sympathizing with her, saying how tragic it was. To be taken so suddenly. So comparatively young. And just as he was settling down into a nice, cosy retirement too, with the rest of his life to look forward to. And who even knew he had heart trouble?

Behind Joan, I can see a hearse with a coffin, covered in flowers, about to be taken off to its final resting place.

I can even see that the flowers are spelling out a name in big red and white letters: one single word, George.

'Now, Cassandra, of course I do realize that George has worked hard all his life. He's the one who went out there and paid off our mortgage, but this has been a big readjustment for me as well, you know. I mean, take this morning, for example. I've had to cancel a lovely coffee morning I had planned with the girls because George was supposed to do a job on the front garden but instead spent the entire day yesterday lying in front of the TV watching a repeat of Manchester playing Sunderland.

One simple little thing I asked him to do, one simple, little thing. ARE YOU HAVING A GOOD LISTEN TO THIS IN THERE, GEORGE? I can hardly entertain with the front driveway covered in leaves and weeds, can I? I'd be mortified. So what do you think, Cassandra? Do you see any light at the end of the tunnel for me at all?'

There's an awful silence. Oh God, what am I going to say to her? I can't tell her what I really see, it would be too horrible, just awful.

Think, think, think . . .

I'm dimly aware that the studio has gone eerily quiet and everyone's looking at me. The cameraman, sound man, Lisa the stage manager, Mary, everyone is looking at me, just waiting for me to come out with something. But what? Shit and double shit . . .

Eventually Mary leans forward. 'Ehh . . . Cassandra?' she says gently. 'If you're not seeing anything, sure don't worry. There's a load of other callers dying to talk to you. Maybe you'd like to move on to someone else?'

I must look like a goldfish, with my mouth opening and closing every two seconds. I'm frantically racking my brains for some wise words, but for the life of me, I just can't come up with any. This is just so excruciating. There must be something I can do or say, not to warn Joan, but in some way to give her an inkling of what lies ahead . . .

'Cassandra?' Mary is saying, looking at me, very concerned. 'Would you like a glass of water, love? You've gone very pale.'

Come on, come on, say something . . . 'Emm, no, thanks . . . can I just . . . it's . . . well, you see . . .'

Brilliant, Cassie, just brilliant. Come on, get it together, try to remember you are on LIVE TELEVISION . . .

I take a deep breath, clear my throat and go for it. 'Joan? Are you still on the line?'

'Yes, still here. Oh, hang on a sec, our paper's just been delivered. GEORGE? IF YOU COULD JUST PEEL YOURSELF OFF THAT SOFA FOR TWO SECONDS AND HAVE A LOOK AT THE JOBS SECTION OF *THE TIMES*? IT DOES EXIST, YOU KNOW, YOU'LL FIND IT RIGHT THERE IN BLACK AND WHITE, BESIDE THE RACING PAGES. Sorry, Cassandra, you were saying?'

'I'm getting a very strong feeling that—' Oh hell, how do I phrase this tactfully?

OK, got it. At least, I think I've got it. 'What I'm trying to say, Joan, is that this time with George could turn out to be very precious. Umm . . . for both of you. I think.'

'Sorry?' Joan sounds incredulous.

'So instead of focusing on the negatives, maybe you should both try to enjoy it. Do things together. Go for long walks. See a movie in the afternoon. Maybe even try to take a holiday?'

'A holiday? Cassandra, my husband is *unemployed*.' Her tone is clear: have you even been listening to a word I've been saying?

'All I'm suggesting is that you cherish this . . . emm . . . phase in your lives. You might very well look back on this time together as a kind of gift.'

'Excuse me, did you say a *gift*?'

'Yes. I mean, how often do we get to spend *real* quality time with our loved ones? I don't think you'll regret it.'

Now everyone in the studio, including kind-hearted Mary, is looking at me as if I've completely lost it. That I can't see a thing and am just trotting out inconsequential dribbles of superficial advice that anyone with a grain of sense could tell you.

'Right. Is that it then?' Joan is asking me, a bit impatiently. 'You don't see any lucrative job offers coming George's way? Nothing at all? Not even anything part-time? At this stage I'd settle for him working on the check-out in Tesco's.'

As she's talking, or rather giving out, I get another flash.

This time, Joan's sitting at her kitchen table with three other women, all drinking sherry, giggling and laughing. Spread out on the table is a pile of luxury cruise brochures, all glittering blue seas and ships that promise loads of light entertainment, Céline Dion/ Liza Minnelli impersonators, bingo, bridge nights and a guaranteed seat at the captain's table – that type of cruise holiday. And she's happy. It sounds awful, but I'm really feeling that the life of a widow is agreeing with her ... maybe even far more than the life of a wife ever did ...

Right. Tactful phrasing required. Quick. 'I see a lot of travel for you, Joan. For pleasure. Things may be tough in the short-term, but there are definitely happier times ahead.'

Even as I say the words, I'm aware of how twee it sounds, as if I'm bluffing, making it up as I go along. All I can think is anyone watching this who's remotely sceptical about what people like me do for a living must be having a field day. I'm coming across as nothing more than a glorified chancer. But what else can I do? Say: 'Yes, Joan, there are happier times ahead for you, spending your late husband's life insurance?'

Sometimes I really, really *hate* being able to see things . . .

Joan doesn't even thank me, she just clicks off the phone and whaddya know, before I even have time to get my head together, we're straight on to another caller.

Please, please, Cosmos, let this be a nice easy one where I can see clearly, preferably information which I can actually communicate: a relationship problem, a teenager waiting on exam results; an answer I'd be happy to broadcast live to the nation . . .

'And now we're going over to line two,' says Mary, looking at me a bit – well, worriedly, actually. If she were a cartoon, there'd be a thought bubble coming out of her head right now, saying, 'Be prepared to go straight to a commercial break if this con-artist lets us all down again.'

'We have Julia here for you. Hello, Julia! You're through to Cassandra. Go right ahead.'

'Hi, Julia,' I say, trying to sound confident. Bright. On top of things.

'Hello, is that really Cassandra? Can you hear me?'

A woman. She's maybe . . . early thirties. I'm seeing strawberry-blond hair and I think she's calling me from a big, open-plan office . . .

'Yes, hi, Julia! How can I help you?' God, now I sound as if I work behind the customer-service desk in Marks and Spencer.

'Can you hear me? I have to keep my voice down.'

'Yes, loud and clear.'

'I'm ringing you from my office. I'm on my own, but the partition is paper-thin and I'd die a thousand deaths if anyone overheard me. Anyway, I'll come straight to the point. I've been in a relationship for nearly three years with my boyfriend and the trouble is that I'm the one who has to make all the decisions and I'm beginning to get bloody sick of it.'

'Do you mean little things or big things?' Please, please let me see some happy news ahead for this girl, because so far, I'm not picking up anything, good or bad . . .

'Define little things.'

'Oh, you know, like deciding what movie you'll go to see or where to eat if you're going out, that kind of thing.'

'Yes, Cassandra, I make all of those decisions for him and more. Apart from letting him ask me out, which only really happened because I was heavily influenced by that *Rules* book we were all reading at the time, I have pretty much been the driving force behind this entire relationship. And it's *really* starting to wear me down. I decided two years ago that the time was right for us to move in together, which we did, into *my* apartment.' Nope, still not seeing anything yet, but on she goes. 'I make more money than he does, so invariably I end up deciding where we go on holiday. And paying for it too, I might add. And now all of our other friends who are in couples seem to be moving on, getting engaged, getting married, starting families, and here I am, night after night, looking across the dinner table at this man who I do love, very much by the way. I'm just getting sick and tired of wondering when it's going to be my turn. Where's the romance, Cassandra? I mean, I can't very well propose to him, now can I?'

Suddenly, I get a flash. Oh no. Please no, don't let me be seeing this. If I thought what I saw for Joan was bad . . .

I can see Julia, so clearly. She's very pretty, with an air of crisp, no-nonsense efficiency about her. She's wearing a dark-coloured business suit and carrying a briefcase. I can just see a BlackBerry peeking out of the top of her soft black Gucci handbag. She's in her apartment building, stepping out of the lift, fiddling about for her door keys. She's humming to herself, bubbly, in good form. Then she opens the apartment door.

There are piles of cardboard boxes neatly placed in the tiny hallway, all stuffed full to the brim.

Now Julia is moving towards the bedroom, suspicious, not quite knowing what's going on, for a split second wondering if her cleaning lady has completely lost the run of herself. Or if she's been burgled by incredibly tidy burglars.

The door's already open. On the bed, strewn messily all over the place, is a big pile of men's clothes. Two packed-to-capacity suitcases are lying on the floor. A load of books are gone from the bookshelf by the bed, leaving gaping holes, like missing teeth.

Now she moves over to the wardrobe and, I swear, I can physically feel her disbelief slowly turning to shock. It's empty. His half of the wardrobe has been totally cleared out. I can even hear the sound of the empty wire hangers rattling away as she just stares, completely and utterly knocked for six …

'I mean, Cassandra, I can tell you this because you're a single woman too and you'll understand. I've already jettisoned so much for this relationship to work. Romance has given way to reality. I've pretty much abandoned all hope of being whisked off my feet and proposed to and I've accepted that if things are to progress, then I'm the one that'll have to do all the running. As per bloody usual. There are times when I feel more like his mother than his girlfriend, which is not exactly red roses and champagne, but that's the way it is. So I just wondered what you saw in my future, Cassandra? Basically what I need to know is: if I ask him to marry me, will he say yes?'

Jesus, now this flash is getting even worse.

He's left a note. The cowardly bastard left her a note. I can see her picking it up and I can feel her disbelief as the poor girl slumps down on the bed to read it. It's full of all the usual clichés, the it's-not-you-it's-me type. I can even make out that particular old chestnut: 'You're a wonderful person, I just really need to be alone for a while.'

Vomit city.

'Cassandra, are you still on the line?'

'Ehh . . . yeah . . . I mean yes, I'm here, sorry. Go on.'

'Well, that's it really, I've pretty much spelt it out to you. I'm absolutely certain this is the man I'll spend the rest of my life with; all I need from you is the where and when. When should I ask and where will I marry him?'

Her tone sounds weary and resigned, a woman who's decided this is it, this is my destiny. OK, it may not be the fairy tale but it's the best on offer so I may as well just get on with it because, frankly, the thought of getting back out there again and doing the whole clubby/pubby scene is just too *exhausting*.

Right. So what in the name of God do I tell her?

Another terrible silence fills the studio and I can see Mary looking at me, wondering whether or not she'll need to jump in and rescue what could turn out to be the single most boring slot they've ever had on the show.

'Cassandra?' says Julia, and I get the most awful feeling that she's beginning to cop on. 'You don't see anything bad, do you?'

I can't even answer her. I'm too busy trying to work out what the hell I'll say.

'You . . . would tell me if what you see isn't good, wouldn't you?'

Shit. Right, nothing for it but to try and let the poor girl down as gently as possible.

'Cassandra? All I'm looking for is a simple yes or no here. If I ask him, will he say yes?'

Bloody hell, this is one direct lady. Think, think, think. 'Em . . . well . . . the thing is . . . I can't see whether—'

'Can't see or can't say? Which is it?'

Nothing for it. I'll just have to be equally direct. At least, as direct as I can be on national television without scarring this poor woman for life. I take the plunge. Deep breath. 'Julia, you sound like a highly efficient, organized person. And no doubt you're very successful at what you do.'

'Yes, yes?' Now she's starting to sound a bit impatient.

'What I'm trying to say is, well, sometimes the worst thing that happens to you can turn out to be the best thing. You mustn't cling too tightly to the idea that this man is the one who'll make you happy. After all, there's a whole world of guys out there . . .' Oh God, that sounds like a line straight out of *Dawson's Creek*.

'So what exactly are you advising me, Cassandra? Is this your way of telling me that I'm not going to marry this man? A simple, straight answer would be really useful here.'

Trust me, I want to say to her, a simple, straight answer would be impossible . . .

'Um, Julia, all I'm advising is that you trust in the Universe. Relax and know that the right thing will happen. Maybe not in the short term, but you may look back on this period in your life and . . . and . . .' I just stop myself short at saying, 'And thank your stars for a lucky escape.'

'Right. Well, if that's all you have to say on the subject, then I really have to go.' A short beep-beep and she's gone. Not even a thank you, nothing. Not that I really blame her; 'trust in the Universe' is most definitely not what she was hoping to hear and now half the nation is probably watching me thinking what a load of dog poo being a TV psychic is.

Even Mary is looking at me like I'm an out-and-out fraudster. Only a degree away from the kind of fortune-tellers you see at church fêtes, you know, the ones who tell everyone the same generic thing. 'You may or may not take a holiday within the next year. You may cross water. You may change hairstyle, but that mightn't happen for at least five years. Thanks very much, that'll be fifty euro, please.'

I shudder and look to the floor manager, hoping and praying I can redeem both myself and my tattered repu-tation with the next phone call.

But then I clock Mary making a slightly pleading can-we-wind-this-up-for-the-love-of-God-please face at the floor manager. He glances at his watch and seems to be making a cut-to-a-commercial-break signal back at Mary (honest to God, you'd need a degree in semaphore) when suddenly she starts tapping on her earpiece. 'What was that? Oh right, well, only if you're sure then,' she says in a low voice, which immediately makes me think she's talking to Jack, up in the production box.

At least, I hope he's up in the production box. Bloody hell, as if I didn't have enough to sweat about.

'OK, ladies and gentlemen, it seems we're going to take one final caller.'

Now written all over her face is 'although I can't for the life of me see why', and I swear, I want to bolt for the hills.

Although . . . my instinct is telling me something different. I'm feeling Jack's hand behind this, giving me another chance, another stab at winning the audience over, maybe even realizing that the crap I came out with for the last two callers was for a very good reason?

No, come on, get a grip, Cassie; let's not hold out for miracles . . .

Anyway. A man's voice fills the studio, which is also a surprise, given the ratio of women to men who contact me is approximately ninety-nine to one. Ish.

'Cassandra? That you?'

Ooh, he sounds lovely. I'm immediately picking up a strong West of Ireland accent, although you wouldn't need to be psychic for that.

So, absolutely no different to the rest of this morning then.

'Yes, hi, it's Cassandra here.'

'Jaypurs, you're not really having too good a day of it today, are you, pet? I hope I bring you better luck.'

Ooh, he's just adorable! I see him straight off: he's tall, well built, handsome in an unkempt kind of way, maybe ... oh rats, this is hard ... yes. Early thirties, I think. Pisces, plays soccer ... very outgoing, I feel; I can see him surrounded by loads of friends in a pub with a brilliant atmosphere, laughing, all having great crack ...

'Cassandra, are you there? You haven't hung up on me?'

'Oh, no! I'm still here, I'm just trying to ...'

I'm trying to pick up his name actually, and I can't. Although I'm feeling it's something really unusual, with a V. Vivien? No ... Vincent?

'You have a very uncommon name,' I say, slowly, 'beginning with V ...' Shit, what is it?

'You won't believe this,' he says laughing and I get a strong feeling that this is a guy who laughs quite a lot. Who enjoys life. Popular, loves horse racing too. 'Now do you promise not to laugh?'

'I promise,' I say, grinning.

'It's Valentine. I know, I know, probably the greatest

irony you've ever heard; a fella like me who can't get arrested when it comes to women, lumbered with a name like Valentine.'

He sounds so jovial and good-hearted that I can't help warming to him, you just couldn't. I sneak a quick glance over at Mary and see that she's smiling too. Good sign. Maybe, just maybe, I can turn the whole horror of this slot around . . .

'Thing is, Cassandra,' he says, and he sounds so friendly and open, I almost feel like we're chatting over a drink in a cosy, quiet country pub. 'I caught a bit of the show and, to be honest with you, I thought the male race weren't coming out of it too well after listening to your last two callers. To put it mildly. We're not all layabouts and some of us are very romantic, you know. Here's me, single when all I really want is to be with the right girl. I'm thirty-three; I have my own business and a grand house by the sea. Now, I may not be George Clooney in the looks department, but all I'm looking for is a good-natured, easy-going girl that will want a nice fella to spoil her rotten, take her to all the fancy places, wine her and dine her and treat her like a princess. No kidding, Cassandra, I would put any woman who would go out with me up on a pedestal . . .'

The more he talks the more I see. Well, well, well, this is certainly one for the books.

*I almost think Valentine can barely believe it himself.
As a direct result of this programme, he's become a bit
like a cult figure in his own right. He's been offered his
own column in an upmarket magazine, chronicling the
life of a hopelessly romantic bachelor looking for love
and marriage, the whole package, instead of the normal,
stereotypical lad on the town, wanting nothing more
fulfilling than meaningless flings with as many different
hot babes as possible.*

'Don't get me wrong, Cassandra,' he's saying, 'I'm not
exactly the stay-at-home type, if you're with me. I've a
great bunch of lads I hang around with, but we're after
very different things. They all want to meet up in the
pub on a Sunday after soccer training and brag about
this one they were with the night before and that one
they'd like to be with tonight. But that's not where I'm
coming from at all. I'm not looking for someone to go
to bed with, Cassandra, I'm looking for someone to
wake up with.'

There's a big 'awwwww' from Mary on the sofa beside
me and I can practically see the thought balloon coming
out of Lisa: 'How cute. I wonder if he'd date me?'

*This is incredible. Now I see a TV camera following
him around on a date, almost documentary style. It's some
time from now and Valentine is still single, still looking*

for love, but by God, he's having the time of his life while he's waiting for it to come along. Women are practically throwing themselves at him; everywhere he goes, he's besieged...

'This is no joke, Cassandra; the last girl I took out jumped out of a moving vehicle to get away from me.' He's laughing as he's telling the story against himself, which is only making him, if possible, even more endearing.

Now I see him singing for charity on one of those celebrity X Factor-type shows and the audience is largely full of women, all screaming, as if he's some kind of a rock god. He's singing that Queen song, 'Somebody To Love', and every woman in the audience is going bananas over him. This is amazing; I even see the name of his column, which I blurt out by accident.

'"Valentine's Day".'

'Sorry, pet, what was that?' asks Valentine politely.

'Nothing,' I laugh. 'I just hope you're ready for fame and fortune, that's all.'

'Ah, pull the other one.'

'No kidding. Valentine, you will be a household name within six months. I guarantee it. I just hope you're ready for all the hot dates you'll be going on.'

'Ah, that is just great news, so it is. And do you mind me asking, do you see a special lady out there for me? Or do you hear the sound of wedding bells, even?'

I have to be honest with him. I've no choice. But unlike my other two callers, at least this story has a happy ending, of sorts. 'Valentine, I feel that in time . . . yes, yes . . . I think . . . you *will* marry, but while you're waiting, your life is going to take you in a direction you've never even dreamt of. I see nothing but fun and laughter ahead; great nights out, a string of beautiful women all asking *you* out, for a change. You'll play the field, like you never have before. I mean, what man alive wouldn't kill for that Hugh Hefner lifestyle?'

If Marc with a C is watching, he's probably thrown up by now. He gets very jealous of anyone of any persuasion who multiple-dates, mainly because it's the kind of life he actively covets for himself.

Now I see the floor manager making a wrap-it-up-we're-out-of-time signal, so I go for it. 'Valentine, you're a very lucky guy. While you're waiting for Miss Right, I don't see just one special lady out there for you, I see literally dozens.'

'Right, well, thank you so much for that, Cassandra,' says Mary, expertly taking over. 'And good luck, Valentine! Maybe you'll call again and let us know how you're getting on?'

'Will do and thanks again!' he says cheerily down the

phone, sounding all delighted with life. 'And if I'm ever up in Dublin, sure I'll be in touch!'

'Well now,' says Mary direct to camera, 'I'm afraid that's all we have time for this morning. Don't forget to tune in tomorrow, same time, same place, when we've a very special feature to mark the beginning of Fashion Week.' Then she taps her earpiece again. 'Oh yes, and anyone who said patterned tights have had their day will be sadly mistaken, or so I'm told. Thank you very much for watching and it's goodbye from me!'

I'm so euphoric after being able to see such good things for Valentine that I almost have to stop myself from saying, 'And it's goodbye from her!' Like *The Two Ronnies*.

There's an eerie feeling in the studio after the show has wrapped. After all the nerves and tension and bright lights shining in your face, Gestapo-style, suddenly the place goes deathly quiet, as cameramen, sound men and crew bolt for the door. God love them, presumably they're all dying for a big, yummy, well-earned brekkie. No one comes near me or says a word to me – not even 'That was good, bad or indifferent.' Which kind of makes me a bit nervy. I mean, yes, the first two callers were a disaster, but that wasn't exactly my fault, was it? And then the chat with lovely Valentine went OK . . . didn't it? I mean, I'm back in the game . . . aren't I?

Anyway, I'm just about to unhook the tiny microphone

that's neatly clipped to my T-shirt when Lisa bounds over. 'Hey, Cassandra! Boy, I'd say you're glad that's over.'

'You said it. Do you think . . . well, do you think it went OK?'

'Yeah! Yeah, definitely!' she says, a bit too quickly. The 'yeah' makes me relax a bit, the 'definitely' makes me think I was complete and total crap. 'Look, do you have a minute?' she adds. 'You're not rushing back to the magazine or anything?'

'No, I'm not in a rush. What's up?'

'It's just that Jack asked if he could have a word with you before you left. Upstairs in the production office. I can take you there right now, if that's OK with you.'

Oh right. Well, that can't be a good sign then, can it?

As ever, my psychic abilities completely disappear out of the window whenever they'd actually come in handy. Like now, for instance. I honestly have no idea what Jack wants me for.

My mind races as I follow Lisa to the back of the studio floor, being careful not to trip over all the wires and cables strewn all over the place.

I may as well face up to it. There can only be one reason I'm being hauled up to the production office. Jack wants to say something along the lines of: 'Yeah, very sorry, you did well the first time we had you on the show, but you seem to have mysteriously lost whatever it was you had in the first place, so, basically, your contract's terminated, goodbye, good luck, and kindly don't bawl crying on the carpet on your way out.'

Shit. He probably wants Lisa there as a witness in case I turn nasty.

She leads me up a flight of steps and into the control booth, which, no kidding, is the nearest thing to Cape Canaveral I've ever seen; all mini-TV screens and desks and a bird's-eye view of the studio below. It's deserted but still boiling hot and sticky, probably from the whole production team sweating blood during my slot. There're half-drunk cups of still-warm coffee lying all over the place. God, it's almost like being on the *Mary Celeste.*

'There's always a mass exodus to the canteen the minute the show wraps,' Lisa explains, leading me on through another door, then into the *Breakfast Club* office itself, which, thankfully, is deserted too. Before I know where I am, Lisa is knocking on another door, a kind of inner sanctum, and ushering me inside. 'She's all yours, Jack!' she says cheerily. 'See you at brekkie!'

Right, here I go. As Charlene always says, when the going gets tough, let your smile be your umbrella, so I step inside with what I hope isn't a deranged grin on my face.

'Hey, good to see you,' says Jack, leaping up from behind his desk and giving me a bear-hug. God, he looks divine today; crisp denim shirt and really cool-looking chinos, as if he should be on a billboard in Times Square doing Gap ads. He smells yummy too and boy, I really, *really* needed that hug.

Anyway. I decide to get my spoke in first. 'Hi, Jack. Look, I just wanted to say that . . . well, the thing is that I saw trouble ahead for the first two women who rang in . . . you know, and I didn't want to give bad news . . . not on live TV . . . so I just thought, the best . . . and by the best I mean, you know, the *kindest* thing—'

'Look, Cassie, I actually brought you up here because there's someone who'd very much like to meet you,' he says, gently cutting me off in mid-ramble.

For the first time, I notice there's someone else in the room with us. He's sitting in a leather chair with his back to me and swivels round, James Bond baddie-style. Young. Hot. Fair-haired. And kind of familiar, some-how.

'This is Oliver Hall,' Jack says as we shake hands. 'Oliver is a producer and a presenter too.'

'Oh, hi there,' I say, as if I've been part of the team for years and not just a complete blow-in. Who may or may not be on the verge of being 'let go' at any moment.

'Hi, Cassandra, good to meet you,' he says with a flashy, television-friendly grin. There's almost an American twang in his accent, as though he's lived there for years. This is driving me nuts; where do I know him from?

'You might recognize Oliver from his TV reports?' Jack chips in, politely filling in the silence and correctly interpreting my bewildered expression. 'He's come to us all the way from our Washington office. We're very excited to have him back here at Channel Seven, although I'm afraid it's not for much longer. He's about to join the competition over at TV1, if you don't mind. Did that sound bitter?' he adds, messing. 'I am thrilled for you, Oliver, but if I find out you're getting paid more than me, it'll be a completely different story.'

That's it, of course. Not that I'm a huge fan of news reports (well, in fairness, they always seem to clash with my soaps) but Jo would have them on all night if she could, and that's where I know him from. He's a reporter on one of those exposé-type programmes; you know, the sort where they put a hidden camera in the toilets of McDonald's and then scandalize the nation with stories about how the employees don't wash their hands properly. Sensationalist stuff that always gets followed up in the tabloids. Ooh, now I remember another one where he exposed all these airline pilots getting plastered drunk and partying all night on a lay-over in Dubai or somewhere, then secretly filmed them getting behind the controls of a 747 early the next morning, not just with alcohol in their blood, but with blood in their alcohol.

'Wow, great to meet you,' I say, wondering if he's single.

No wedding ring, good. This could be a lovely guy

for Charlene, is my logic. You know, glamorous, tabloid journalist type. And cute. Except that . . . she's not exactly single, now, is she? Ho, hum, back to the drawing board.

'That was quite an interesting slot you had,' he says to me.

Shit, I almost forgot about that. 'Ooh, ehh . . . yes, that . . .' I mumble. 'Well . . . yes, I admit, I have had better days, but the thing is—'

'No, I found it very . . . interesting,' he says in the American drawl. 'In fact, I was just saying to Jack, your performance gave me a really great idea for a freelance report I'm hoping to shoot before I leave.'

Chapter Eight

THE TAROT DECK
THE TOWER CARD

Symbolizes that a disaster is about to strike. Maybe for you, or perhaps for someone close to you, who you will then be called on to help and support in their hour of dire need. The Tower can often signify an event or experience which, quite literally, will strike like a 'bolt of lightning'.

Sorry, but that's what it's going to feel like and that's what you must prepare for. It can often be interpreted as a radical life overhaul that's looming or perhaps even the end of a relationship. So, no,

**it won't be an easy time, but if you resist going
with the tide, remember, you're only making it
worse for yourself in the long run.**

**In other words, this is a time just to roll with
the punches, honey . . .**

The thunderbolt hits that night.

It's about eight in the evening and Jo and I are both
home, bickering over the TV remote control. (She wants
to watch *The Political Day in Review,* live and unedited
from Washington, DC, her fave show, whereas I was kind
of hoping to catch up on *EastEnders*.) A taxi pulls up
outside, there's a loud banging on our front door and
in comes a tear-streaked, very shaken-looking Charlene.
She looks so pale and shocked, I almost get a fright as I
let her in and usher her into our snug little sitting room.
Fire roaring, candles burning; you couldn't ask for a
better, more soothing environment to blurt out troubles.
Particularly for someone like our Charlene, whose
personal belief system is that there's no problem in the
whole world that can't be solved with a nice pedicure
and a blow-dry.

'What's the matter, honey?' I ask her, instinctively
pouring her a glass of wine, which she almost grabs off
me to down a huge big gulp. 'What's up?'

'Oh girlies,' she says, slumping down into an armchair.
'Girlies, I . . . I know . . .'

'Shh, it's OK,' I say as soothingly as I can. 'Come on, deep breath, whatever it is you can tell us.'

She gives me a weak smile and squeezes my hand gratefully. 'OK, here's the thing. As you're both aware, I never exactly' – sniff – 'expected my life to turn out like a Jackie Collins novel, but ... but ...' The tears start welling up in her big saucery eyes and now I'm slowly starting to get an incredibly strong feeling about what she's going to say.

No, scrap that. *Two* incredibly strong feelings.

'In the interests of saving time, just tell me, at the end of this sentence, will I roll my eyes?' Jo says, a bit unsympathetically.

'Two – no, not two, *three* disasters have hit me simultaneously,' Charlene sniffs, whipping a monogrammed hanky from up her sleeve and dabbing her eyes. 'And you're my best friends in the whole world and I honestly have no one else to turn to.'

OK, two of her disasters I can see, but not the third. Shit. And I'm not picking anything up either, which is odd.

'Broken fingernail? Bad leg wax?' says Jo, barely looking up from the screen.

I grab the remote from her, firmly switch the TV off and throw her a look which I hope conveys 'This is not Charlene's normal histrionics; she's actually genuinely upset, so just be a friend, shut up and listen.

OK?' All that in a single glance. Jesus, why wasn't I an actress?

'You always say that bad things come in threes, Cassie, and, as usual, you're bloody well right,' says Charlene, taking another slug from her wine glass. As ever, when excited or upset, she talks stream of consciousness, so Jo and I end up really having to concentrate just to keep up with her. 'Well, first of all, my maid wakes me up this morning, at the crack of lunch, with Earl Grey tea instead of Japanese, so I had to get up—'

'Sorry, just let me guess, could this possibly be the first bad thing?' says Jo.

I glare at her to shush her up, but Charlene keeps on yakking regardless.

'So I had no choice but to haul my ass out of bed and come downstairs and there's Dad and Marilyn sitting at the kitchen table looking like a pair of ghosts. I went to turn on my heel and get the hell out of their way, but he told me to sit down, that he had some big news for me, which I might find a bit shocking. Well, you both know how scary he can be, so I did what I was told.'

OK, right. I think I might already know how this story is going to pan out, but I say nothing. I never told Jo about the flash I had the night of Charlene's dinner party and, boy, is she about to get the surprise of her life.

'So, then . . . then . . .' Charlene pauses here to dab her

eyes again. 'Dad said that, for a while now, they'd been a little bit worried about Marilyn and how she'd been looking and feeling over the past few weeks and I was on the verge of saying, "Oh, I wouldn't worry about her, I'm sure she spends vast amounts of your money to end up looking that cheap," but something told me to shut up. Then Dad said that one of the reasons they came back to Ireland was so Marilyn could have some medical tests done here and so apparently they spent a full day at Blackrock Clinic, and then her test results came back and . . . and . . .' Another sniff.

'What? Tell us!' says Jo, really concerned now and on the edge of her seat, with a look on her face that says she's thinking the absolute worst. Jo's quite fond of Marilyn, as am I. As is everyone who meets her really, except Charlene.

'She's . . . she's . . . *pregnant*,' says Charlene.

There's a stunned silence and Jo looks over at me, with her jaw somewhere around her collarbone, and I have to remind myself to look shocked too, as if I'd never seen this coming, so I end up smacking my hand off my cheek like some ham actress in a daytime soap opera.

Jo is utterly speechless, which Charlene takes as her cue to keep on talking.

'If you can believe that. I barely can myself; I mean, the woman must be pushing fifty if she's a day—'

'She's forty-one,' I say. 'You know, these days that's

practically a spring chicken, fertility-wise. Look at Holly Hunter. She had twins at forty-seven.'

Oh dear. No sooner have the words left my mouth than I regret them; poor Charlene's eyes well up again and she starts to bawl. God love her, I could shoot my mouth off for being so tactless. Like me, she's an only child, which is probably why we initially bonded so much back in school. Only children tend to get just as close to their friends as they would to siblings. So to be suddenly faced with a new baby in the family . . .

'Well, there's nothing to do but be happy for Marilyn,' Jo says a bit more kindly, 'and for your dad. I mean, it's not as if she's some kind of fling or one-night stand; they've been together for years. So isn't this good news? New life and all that?'

Then I chip in: 'I know this comes like a bolt from the blue, honey, but there are some positives about the situation.' But this only starts her off again, even worse.

'And wh-what p-p-*pooooositives* would those be?' she almost wails at me.

It's really hard to understand her when she's this upset, but at least I think that's what she said. Mind you, it could also have been 'My life is ruined.'

'Well, come on, I mean it's not as if you're going to be asked to . . . emm . . . change nappies or anything, is it?' I say, my heart almost breaking at how *stricken* she is.

'Or, you know, babysit,' says Jo, who looks as if she's scarcely able to believe it herself.

'Or . . . emm . . .' Jo and I are frantically looking at each other, trying to think of things to say, which is particularly hard given that neither of us would know one end of a baby from the other.

'Do night feeds or burp the baby,' says Jo helpfully.

'Or take it for walks in one of those buggy thingies.'

'Or have to get rid of your Porsche and get a four-wheel drive so you can get a baby seat in the back of it . . .' Jo trails off, seeing the real devastation on Charlene's face. 'And those cars are complete rubbish for the environment too, you know,' she adds lamely.

'Girlies, I know you both mean well, but let's face it, babies eat, sleep and poo. My God, I'd kill for that life.'

'You *have* that life,' says Jo without thinking. She shuts up, though, when she sees the crushed look on Charlene's tear-streaked face. 'Sorry. I didn't mean that to come out how it sounded.'

'Anyway, Charlene, the thing to focus on is that you'll have a brand-new half-brother or -sister,' I say, in a vain attempt to lift this awful cloud of depression that's hanging over the room.

'Who are you telling? That's the thing I'm trying very hard *not* to focus on. Yet another memory for me to suppress,' she sniffs. 'Can I please just go on with telling? That, believe you me, was only the warm-up story.'

'There's *more*?' says Jo incredulously.

'There's more. Darling, I have generated enough scandal today to keep Max Clifford on a retainer.'

We both look at her blankly and away she goes again, stream of consciousness.

'So I'm there, reeling with shock, and I try to get up to leave the room, but Dad barks at me to sit back down again. Then he launches into this big speech about how this is a new start for all of us as a family and I want to scream at him: "A family? When were we ever a family?" but I'm too much of a coward so I just sit there and say nothing. Anyway, I think he must have taken my silence as a sign that I was OK with this because he goes on to say . . .'

'Yes?' says Jo.

'That . . . that . . . he feels that . . .'

'Go on.'

'That it's only right that he and Marilyn should . . . should . . .' She breaks down here and, I swear, Jo and I are almost on the edge of our seats.

'Shh, shh,' says Jo gently, 'come on, whatever it is, you can tell us.'

Charlene takes a deep breath and wipes her eyes. 'They're getting married.'

Oh my God. In a million years I'd never have seen that coming and clearly neither did Jo, who's looking about as shocked as I feel.

'I know,' says poor Charlene, seeing the look on our faces. 'I can't believe it either. Remember Mum's anniversary last month? He never even called me, nothing. He pays for the upkeep of her grave, but that's it. Typical him, throw money at a problem and just walk away.'

There's a stunned silence as Jo and I try to digest all this.

'I don't blame either of you for looking so stunned,' says Charlene. 'It's a lot to take in. So I got up and Dad practically yelled at me to sit back down again, but I couldn't, I just couldn't take any more. I staggered as far as the library to phone my boyfriend and tell him to drop whatever it is he's doing, come quickly and bring vodka, except that he's not answering his phone, so I leave a message, which he doesn't reply to, so then I figure he probably never got it so I leave six other messages just to be on the safe side.'

'And did he get back to you?' asks Jo.

'No, he bloody well didn't. Honestly, girls, I did my very best not to sound like a complete desperado. I just said that the minute he listened into his voicemail, he was under starter's orders to call me *immediately* so we could arrange to meet up, that I needed him urgently. So I waited patiently for a full twenty minutes and still no call, so then I got really upset and Dad and that bloody praying mantis kept thumping on the door to make sure

I wasn't opening a vein or anything and then I decided I just had to put as much distance between me and them as possible so I got dressed, jumped in a cab and went straight round to Anna Regan's but she wasn't a bit sympathetic at all, not like . . . not like . . . you guys . . .' She has to break off the monologue here, she's crying so hard, and both Jo and I hug her tight. In all my years, I've only ever once seen Charlene quite this shattered about anything.

'Go on,' Jo says, looking genuinely concerned about her.

'What would I do without my two best girlies?' Charlene says, hugging us both right back. 'So, anyway, I told Anna everything but all she can talk about is her big engagement party and here's me and I can't even get my so-called boyfriend to return a simple phone call, so then I got even more upset and I practically left a trail of dust I ran out of her house so fast—'

'Oh honey, why didn't you call one of us?' I ask. 'We'd have dropped everything and come round.'

'Well, first I went to Marc with a C's gym to talk to him, but he couldn't really give me his undivided attention, on account of he was giving a spinning class, so in total desperation I went round to Channel Seven and at reception I asked for Jack and they said he was in a production meeting but he was nearly finished and would I like to wait, so I did for, like, ages, and all the while Dad and Marilyn both keep phoning and texting and I keep snapping off my phone, because I'm just not in a place where I can talk to either of them right now.' She breaks off, seeing the look on both our faces. 'Oh girls, I know you're both probably thinking that I'm practically stalking Jack, but all I want is to be happily married and have a *normal* family life, you know, about as different to what I come from as possible. Is that so terrible?'

'No, of course it's not,' Jo and I chorus sympathetically.

'So eventually Jack does come downstairs, looking all gorgeous the way he always does and he says he's actually glad I dropped by because he really needs to talk to me too . . .'

Oh shit. I think I have a fair idea of what's coming next.

'And by now I'm thinking, OK, at least he's not avoiding me like the Black Death, this is good, everything is fine, if nothing else at least my relationship may still be salvageable. So we get into his car and we drive to a bar that's close by which he says is really quiet and he sits me down in, like, only the most secluded part of the whole place and I'm just so bloody grateful to him that I burst into tears and he's all, like, "Oh what's wrong?" and so I tell him everything and he's just . . . he's just . . . he's so unbelievably *nice* about the whole awful thing . . .'

Another chorus of tears here and it takes a few minutes and a lot more wine for Jo and me to calm her down again.

'So he insists on buying me a stiff gin and tonic which I knock back, I'm that shaken, and then it's like there's an alarm bell starting to ring at the back of my head so I ask him what it was he wanted to talk to me about.'

I brace myself. Here it comes. Deep breath and have the Kleenex at hand, ready for the fallout.

'And what did he say?' asks Jo a bit suspiciously. I think she can guess what's coming too. Let's face it, you wouldn't exactly need to be psychic for this one, now would you? Jack hasn't exactly been behaving like a model boyfriend towards Charlene these past couple of days. In fact, as Jo put it, he hasn't been behaving like a boyfriend at all. No calls, no invitations out, plus the way he stayed for a polite drink at her dinner party then left as soon as he reasonably could without seeming rude: he's doing all the things guys do when they're trying to put as much distance between them and an unwanted relationship, or in this case an unwanted non-relationship entirely driven by Charlene. This has been coming from a mile off. You could have seen the signs from space, but then, as Oscar Wilde once said, women can discover absolutely everything except the obvious. Sometimes the hardest thing is to see what's staring everyone else in the face. Oh God, this is going to be so awful for her and on today of all days . . .

Charlene takes a long pause to wipe her eyes again, but she only ends up smudging her mascara all over her face, so now she looks like a tiny, vulnerable baby panda, the kind that always used to make headline news on John Craven's *Newsround*.

'He . . . he . . . he said . . . he said that . . .'

Even though I know what's coming next, my heart constricts a bit.

'Go on,' says Jo, slowly and gently, sounding as if she's equally certain of what's on the way.

'He said that it wasn't anything for me to worry about, that this wasn't the time and that he would always be there for me . . . as a friend.'

OK, that I did *not* see coming. I honestly thought he was going to finish things with her, to give her the old it's-not-you-it's-me speech, but now . . . I actually kind of *like* that he didn't. It would have been bordering on cruel for him to have dumped her when she was this upset, wouldn't it?

'Obviously, I was a tiny bit put out by the "friend" reference,' Charlene continues, still doing her stream-of-consciousness thing, 'but he was just so sweet and supportive and then he really had to go back to his office so he offered to drive me home first and I said OK. I tried to get him to come in for a drink, but he said he'd better not, which I didn't really like either, but I figured he's been so compassionate and lovely I shouldn't really give him a hard time over not coming in, although I really could have done with a cuddle. But he did say he was only on the other end of the phone if I needed to talk and I think he may have used the friend reference again, but I can't remember. Or I might have just blanked it out.'

'So are we up to the third bad thing yet?' asks Jo gingerly.

'Nearly. Bear with me. Anyway, I go back into the house and Dad and Marilyn call me into the drawing room and the pair of them are sitting there staring at me and it's *awful*, just awful. Then Dad says that he and Marilyn are very upset at the way I've been behaving and they did their best to break the news to me as gently as they could and he knew I was a bit shocked but couldn't I just be happy for them? Then he started going on about how good he'd been to me over the years and that all they wanted was for me to be involved with the new baby and be happy that I was going to have a new stepmother and that's when I lost it. I just totally lost it.'

'What, what did you say?' Jo and I say together, unable to shut up and just let her tell her story.

'I turned to Marilyn and – oh girls, I couldn't control myself – I said, "Has anyone bothered to tell you about your predecessor? And what happened to her?"'

Oh God, I can hardly believe this.

'And Dad says, "Your mother passed away well over thirteen years ago and can't we just let go of the past?" So I shout back at him, "Yeah, like you let go, barely three months after she died, when you were shacked up in Monaco with someone new." Then Dad yells at me, and you know how scary he can be, telling me I need to move on and get over it myself – so that's when I do it.'

'*What?*'

'I turn to Marilyn and I tell her everything. All the family skeletons come tumbling out of the closet in one go. About how devastated Mum had been about the divorce and how everyone said it was a freak boating accident and that she should never have gone sailing on her own, particularly as she wasn't a strong swimmer, and then how we had that awful wait for the autopsy results . . .'

At this point both Jo and I are starting to well up too. I remember that awful time as if it were yesterday. How could I forget? We were only in school, barely fifteen, when the nuns took Charlene out of class to break the terrible news to her.

I had a flash, though. One of the worst ones I ever had. I saw the whole thing so clearly that for years afterwards I had nightmares about what had happened. And about the aftermath too.

'And it came out that Mum had taken barbiturates,

that her stomach was full of them; the autopsy report said death by misadventure but we all knew exactly what she was going through and how this was her way out. Everyone tried to say how terrible, that Mum had quietly been suffering from depression all this time and told no one, but she *wasn't*. I *know* she wasn't. This was the only way she felt she could cope with the awful pain she was going through, that *he* had put her through.'

Jo and I can barely speak.

'Then Dad told me to shut up, that I'd said quite enough, and I started getting really upset all over again. I think I may have said that I didn't particularly like misery and disaster but it had a really annoying habit of following me around and then Dad got really mad and said, "You better explain yourself." I'm not kidding, he may even have used the phrase "young lady". So I gave it to him straight. I told him that he'd never been much of a father to me and that his idea of parenting was to come home, wreak havoc and then leave, just as he's doing right now.'

'Brave, brave girl,' says Jo, shaking her head.

'Oh, that was only the warm-up, once I got going there was no stopping me. I told him he was pathetic and going through a mid-life crisis and that I never really understood the misery poor Stella McCartney must have gone through when her dad came home with Heather

Mills until this moment and then Dad really, really lost it and told me that I was insulting the woman he loved and if I didn't keep a civil tongue in my head, he'd stop supporting me and I was just so angry, I said . . .'

'WHAT?'

'I said, "Yeah, right, Father, if you could call fifty thousand euro a month *support*," and he was white with fury, I've never seen him like that before. Then he went this ghostly shade and said that if that's the way I felt then, fine, I could just try living without his money for a change, that it would do me some good to learn how to rough it a bit, like he had to at my age and that my problems were just so middle class. So then I said, "May I remind you that you are in my home and now I'd like the pair of you to leave." That they'd grossly overstayed their welcome and would they please pack their bags and he refused to budge, saying that he'd bought the house for me as a present but it was technically in his name so he and Marilyn were staying put. And then he said that I was – if you can believe this – nothing but a spoilt princess who'd never amount to anything in the world. So I looked him straight in the eye and said, "I hope for this baby's sake you do a better job at parenting than you did on me." Then I said to Marilyn, and I'm bawling by now, that at eighteen I was given a house, a car and a credit card and his only idea of being a good father is to appear every six months or so and criticize me and run me into the ground until I can't take it any more.'

Jo and I are both too gobsmacked even to speak. I almost feel like switching on the Weather Channel just to see if hell has, in fact, frozen over.

'So . . . my allowance is gone!' she sniffs, reaching for the Kleenex. 'As of right now, this minute. What am I going to do – without money, I mean? I've nothing to live off, *nothing*.'

'Shh, shh, shh,' says Jo soothingly. 'It's not the end of the world, you know. You could get a proper job; start earning your own living, making your own way in the world.'

'She's right,' I say. 'And, in time, your dad would be so proud of you for standing on your own two feet.'

'And it's not as if you don't have a roof over your head,' says Jo.

'Good point,' I add, trying to sound helpful and confident, as if this is a completely solvable problem.

'OK, so he and Marilyn are staying put for the moment, but it's not like this is their only home. They're hardly going to stay there for ever,' says Jo, which is actually a terrific point and I only wish I'd thought of it first.

Mr Ferguson has an incredible portfolio of trophy homes all over the world. Well, the part of the world that's tax-exiled, that is. Stunning, palatial-type residences, the kind that estate agents must drool over in their sleep. He even keeps an apartment in that giant floating hotel/cruise-ship, *The World*, which Charlene and Marc with a C once took a trip on, but they both got bored after a few days, saying they thought it would be like *Titanic* but it wasn't. (By that I think they meant it would be stuffed full with Leonardo DiCaprio types, but it turned out to be all elderly, rich, retired couples who wanted to sip sherry and play bridge all day.)

'Anyway,' Jo goes on, 'what I'm trying to say is that a bit of distance and space from each other might give all of you a chance to get your heads around everything.'

'Oh, come on, Jo, you know what Dad is like when he's dug his heels in,' says Charlene, whiter than a sheet by now. 'He said they weren't budging and, believe me, he meant it. So I looked him in the eye and said, "Fine. If that's how you want to play it, that's cool by me. If you're staying, then I'm going." And Dad said, "Right, best of luck," and he was looking at me as if he expected me to crumble, as if I was bluffing, but I thought: No, I'll show you what I'm made of, so I held my head high and said, "I'm moving out, have the place to your bloody selves and may it fall on your bastard heads some night for causing me such misery." Then he said, "You won't last a wet day in the real world without cash and credit cards," and I said, "You just see if I don't," and – Oh girlies, you'd have been so proud of me – I drew myself up to my full five feet two and said, "This is the last you'll ever see of me." And I went out through the hall, banged the door behind me and came straight round here.'

Jo whistles. 'You are one incredibly strong girl, I'll give you that,' she says as we both hug her again. 'So where are you going to stay until it all blows over?'

Charlene looks at Jo, puzzled. 'What do you mean, "until it all blows over?" I told you, I've completely cut all ties with those people. That's it. *Finito*. I've deadheaded them and that's all there is to it. I share DNA with my father, which entitles him to either bone marrow or possibly a kidney, but from now on, that's it.'

'You're too upset to make any big decisions now.'

'I'm not upset.' Huge sniff.

'So . . . what's the next step?' says Jo.

'Well, it's obvious,' says Charlene. 'I'm going to prove to that shower that I'm well capable of standing on my own two feet. I'm going to become a huge success and I'm going to do it without Dad and without his blood money.'

'Bravo,' I say proudly. 'Good girl.'

'Oh, and there's just one other, tiny thing I forgot to mention,' she adds.

'What's that?' Jo and I say together.

'I'm moving in here. With the two of you. My loyal and true friends.'

There's a stunned silence as Jo and I try to digest this.

All I can think is: I call myself a psychic but in a million years, I never saw this coming.

'So can I have your room, Jo?' says Charlene, pouring herself another large glass of wine. 'You know it's bad for my chakras to sleep in a north-facing room. And most of your stuff is in the spare room anyway. Girlies, why have you both gone so quiet? I assume this isn't a problem?'

Chapter Nine

THE TAROT DECK
THE THREE OF CUPS CARD

Signifies three women. Three women, possibly living together. Three women sharing one bathroom, one remote control and, even more testingly, one shower. Pictured on this card are three lovely ladies, all young and carefree, one blonde, one dark and one red-haired, kind of like Charlie's Angels. In fact, if this was America, they'd probably be out on the streets of LA fighting crime. However, the warning this card carries is that a test of friendship could well be looming.

In other words, this is a time to be patient and tolerant with your pals, even if they persist in borrowing your favourite shoes, lashing on your really posh, expensive La Prairie face cream as if it was aftersun lotion, using every last drop of available hot water and generally driving you nuts. Because, hey, isn't that what friends are for?

The following morning, the three of us come to a non-negotiable arrangement. Given that Charlene is now, shall we say, short of funds and completely determined to forge her way in the big bad world without going cap in hand to her father, here's the deal.

Jo and I have agreed that she can stay with us, rent-free, for as long as she likes, on the condition that she keeps the place tidy in return. And that's pretty much it.

We both feel that we can't really ask her to do any more as (a) she's been so inordinately generous to all of us over the years, it just wouldn't seem right somehow; (b) this is a woman whose proudest boast is that the only supermarket she's ever set foot inside is Harrods' food hall; but most of all (c) the fact is that she's never cooked anything, not even a piece of toast, in her entire life and there's a very real chance that if we ask her to put on a nice, straightforward bit of pasta for us all later, we could well come home to the charred remains of our house.

I even remember one Christmas when I presented her

with Nigella Lawson's *Domestic Goddess* book and she handed it straight back with ill-concealed disappointment, saying 'Oh look, a gift gag. So where's my *real* pressie then?'

Anyway, we make the deal, both Jo and Charlene look at me just to double-check that I'm not getting any flashes along the lines that our house goes up in flames and we all end up visiting Charlene in a hospital burn-victims unit, which I'm not. I am, however, getting a very clear flash that Marilyn will call me later on, but more about that anon . . .

After the tears and drama of last night, Charlene, amazingly, comes out full of fighting spirit this morning, brave heart that she is. Jo fishes out a pair of yellow Marigolds and hands them to her and she immediately puts them on and starts strutting around the kitchen saying, 'Look at me! I feel like I'm in a play!' So off to work we go, with Charlene squealing down the driveway after us, 'Doesn't this just feel like the nineteen fifties, starring me as the stay-at-home wifey? If I knew a Doris Day song, I'd sing it right now!'

'Stepford wife, more like,' Jo quips to me as we both hop into my car.

'Don't be like that,' I say defensively, 'this is a really good thing we're doing, you know. Speaking for myself, I've never felt so noble in my entire life. I feel like I'm all profile.'

265

Anyway, I drop Jo off, make it into the *Tattle* office, head for my desk and get stuck right into the stack of letters that's waiting for me. (Is it my imagination, or am I getting sent even more than usual ever since I started going on TV? Hmm, the plot thickens . . .) And, miraculously, for once I'm not late for my deadline.

Well, not all that late. My deadline is tomorrow morning and it's not as if I don't have the whole day ahead of me. Ah sure, I'll be grand, won't I? I mean, it's only half-nine and if I chain myself to the desk, work right through lunch and everything and don't get stuck into major long gossips with Sir Bob, and stay here until really, really late tonight, honour will be saved.

'Hello there, old thing,' Sir Bob, the man himself, interrupts me. 'How's the life of a telly-box star treating you, then?'

'Morning, Sir— oops, sorry, I mean Bob,' I answer cheerily.

'Fancy a spot of tea? I've got such a lot of delicious scandal to impart.'

'Ooh, what are you waiting for, then? Stick that kettle on this minute.' What the hell. Sure, I'm only having a teeny, weeny little tea break. Five minutes of chat, then back to work. Promise.

'Goodness, what a veritable mountain of letters you've received, my dear,' he says, rifling through my pile and picking a few up at random.

'I know. Course, they're not all going to get published but I do try to get around to answering as many as I can.'

'Jolly nice of you too, old thing. Golly, just look at this one.'

'I think I'm in love with my dead husband's brother. Please can you contact said late husband in the spirit world to see if he'd approve,' I read over his shoulder. 'Bloody hell, I'll have my work cut out with that one.'

'No, no dear, I meant this one,' he says, leafing through the pile.

'I married for a passport then fell in love?' I ask him, singling out another one and instantly getting a feeling that it was written by someone Russian.

I'm suddenly seeing a tall, brown-eyed woman with long blond hair and short black roots. From Moscow, I think. Sagittarius …

Oops, sorry, I was getting so caught up in my flash I almost forgot Sir Bob is standing right in front of me. 'That's mild compared to some of them, believe you me.'

'No, you goose, this one here,' he says, handing one over to me. 'It was the red pen on top of it that caught one's attention. Now, I do hope you don't think it's terribly rude of me to read it, but then it is about to receive national publication, is it not? I think the laws of privacy can be waived a little here, don't you?'

I grab the letter from him and groan. Oh shit and double shit, how could I have forgotten? This letter must have been sitting on my desk for ages now and I know that I must have had a flash about it, because I've scribbled across the top of it in red Biro, as I always do whenever I see something, so that I'll actually remember that it's done and dealt with and not end up just shoving it into yet another pile at the back of my desk. As I obviously did with this one. 'Writer desperately worried about the house she's just moved into. Real fear at play here. Poor woman genuinely terrified.'

That's not what's making me bang my head off my forehead in frustration, though. It's this: 'Memo to self: must phone her to arrange suitable time to call to house and possibly do an energy clearing. Important. Discretion required. Her husband sounds like a right bully. Do not shove at back of desk and forget about.'

Rats, rats, rats, why am I so bloody *scatty*? Story of my life. It's like the Erma Bombeck principle, which clearly states that the supermarket queue you're *not* in is always the one that will move the fastest. Same with me. The more important and critical a job is, the more likely I am to clean forget all about it.

OK, nothing for it but to ring this poor woman now and put her out of her misery. Right now, before I forget all about it again. Except I can't because Sir Bob's still here.

'Shall I toss you a sneak preview of last night's salacious news, my dear?'

Oh, what the hell, that woman has already waited over a week to hear back from me. Sure, what's another five minutes?

'That you even need to ask that question shows just how little you know me,' I reply, dying to hear all. God, I just love Sir Bob. Well, you couldn't not. He's so full of all the juiciest, grade-A gossip. He's also a brilliant mimic, so when he's dishing the dirt on some minor celeb, you almost feel as if they're in the room with you.

'Well, I had to attend the dreariest launch party yesterday evening, one of those ghastly soirées where one comes home and says to oneself, "Thank you, Satan." Thing is, though, while I was there I did happen on the most amusing anecdote, concerning a certain acerbic breakfast telly-box presenter with whom, I believe, you were once acquainted, my dear?'

I look at him blankly, a bit like early man being taught the meaning of fire.

'Who, shall we say, enjoyed a dalliance with a gentleman who was married? Contract not renewed? Am I ringing any bells, my dear?'

My eyes immediately light up. 'Ooh, yes!' Then I mouth a single word at him, silently. 'Maura?'

Sir Bob just taps his index finger sagely against his nose and nods like bookies do in their secret sign language at the races. No kidding, he's getting more and more like John McCririck every day. 'Well, she was, in polite parlance, three sheets to the wind last night and she practically assailed a certain ruggedly good-looking member of a rather popular Irish boy band, who seem intent upon world domination . . .'

Ooh, yes, I know exactly who he means. Howard Woodward. Huge with pre-teens. His poster is probably hanging on the bedroom wall of every ten-year-old in the country. Oh yes, and a while ago, he went into one of those super-posh rehab clinics like the Priory to wean himself off what's politely described as his very trendy 'addiction to prescription painkillers'.

'And she told him he'd never amount to anything because his name sounded like a dog farting in the bath.'

I'm guffawing so much I have to stuff a tissue in my mouth.

'To which he replied, in psychobabble of the highest order, "Excuse me, are you trying to derail my self-esteem train?"'

'Oh Bob, you couldn't make it up. Are you going to write about it?'

'All in the line of duty, my dear. Do you wish to answer that?'

Damn, my mobile's ringing and I never know how to react when that happens around Sir Bob. Not that he minds, it's just that he's probably the only journalist in the country who absolutely refuses to use a mobile and has all these rules and regulations about the correct etiquette involved with them. When to take a call, when it's impolite to, the general rudeness bordering on thuggery of people who insist on answering them in restaurants and don't even get him started on phones that go off at the theatre . . . I'm telling you, it's a social minefield.

'Do you mind?' I say, figuring it's probably OK, given that I am in an office with phones ringing all around us. Plus, I have an overriding instinct that this call is important.

Sir Bob nods and wafts off, hanky in hand, looking as if he's off to tea at Buckingham Palace, as he normally does, and I answer.

And thank God that I did. It's the Dragon Lady, calling me from somewhere really noisy. I really have to strain to hear her. And then I get a flash.

She's at the airport, on her way to . . . somewhere mountainous. I can see green hills and pathways and a gorgeous chalet in the background . . . Austria. That's it, got it. I knew it looked like the set of The Sound Of Music. *All that's missing is the von Trapp children running around wearing the curtains and singing 'Do-Re-Mi'.*

'Cassandra? It's me.'

I recognize her voice instantly but, as usual, I have to rack my brains to come up with her proper name. Shit . . . 'Hi . . . emm . . .' Come on, *think*. 'Emm . . . Amanda.'

'Can you hear me? I'm at the airport.'

Knew it. Bugger, why is she ringing me? Must be something really important. No, I'm not picking up a single thing, nothing. Rats. All I can see is a pair of hiking boots and thick woolly socks, which, come to think of it, she could very well be wearing right now. This is not exactly a woman who's known and lauded for her dress sense and ability to accessorize. 'Yeah, I can hear you . . . Amanda.'

'Look, I'll keep this short and snappy because I'm on my way to a *very* important work conference in London.'

Oh, you dirty big liar, I'm thinking. You're on your way to Salzburg for . . . it's coming to me . . . yes, got it: for a mountain hiking trip. I've said it before and I'll say it again: why do people bother fibbing to psychics? Such a waste of time, on every level.

'That guy who rang into your *Breakfast Club* slot yesterday, do you remember? The one who couldn't get a date for love nor money?'

I remember immediately. Well, it's not exactly a name you could forget in a rush, now is it? 'Yes, Valentine, wasn't he just so sweet and cuddly and adorable?'

No sooner are the words out of my mouth than I instantly regret them. Note to self: the Dragon Lady does *not* do girlie talk, ever, ever, *ever*.

'Ugh, please don't start a puke fest with me,' she snaps back. 'I'm a bad enough flyer without your teenage imagery going through my head.'

Serves you right, Cassie, you should have known better.

'So here's the deal. I want to offer that guy a weekly column, chronicling his adventures in the dating world. *Sex and the City*, except written from a man's point of view, in a society where they're in a buyer's market.'

God, she's good, I'm thinking. Fantastic idea. I'm already hooked and dying to read it. In fact, I had a flash live on TV that this would happen. I just didn't think it would happen on my own magazine, that's all. Bloody hell . . .

Anyway, Valentine really sounded lovely and this is great news for him. Ooh, added bonus: all the single gals in the office will get to meet him. Myself included.

Well, aren't I a single girl? Course I am . . .

'Cassandra, are you still on the line?' the Dragon Lady barks at me.

'Yes, still here. So . . . did you want me to get his contact details from the *Breakfast Club* for you?'

'Precisely. You can email them to me and I'll pick them up on my BlackBerry. And you can tell everyone in that office, your best buddy Sir Bob included, to get straight back to work. Fortune does not favour the bone idle.'

'Ehh . . . yup, will do. So, safe trip and enjoy Salzburg!'

What can I say? The words are out of my mouth before I even get a chance to think. There's a tiny, barely perceptible silence before she hangs up.

Cassandra's new and improved time-management skills in action

Doddle, really. Easy peasy.

My God, I should really be at some management institute, giving seminars, lecturing accountants and whiz-kid business types on how to extract the most out of each day. And all I had to do was not talk to anyone, skip lunch, switch off my mobile, not answer my office phone and limit my chatting time with Sir Bob to precisely five minutes. On the plus side, though, I've got through most of my letters pile, my column's almost finished and all I have to do is write everything up. Which I can easily do at home, later on tonight. Great idea. Fab. Only one more call to make and then I can skive off for the rest of the day with a clear conscience.

Well, a clearish conscience.

I pick up the letter Sir Bob drew my attention to earlier, check the phone number scrawled at the bottom and dial. It rings and is answered almost immediately. A man's voice, gruff, impatient.

'Yes?' With a single word, I swear, he almost takes the nose off me.

'Emm, hello, I wondered if I could speak to . . .'

Oh hell, what do I say now? The letter is signed 'Worried in Rathgar' and I can hardly ask to speak to Mrs Worried, now can I?

Got it. God, I'm so smart. 'I wondered if I might speak to your wife, please.'

'In connection with?'

Shit. His manner is bordering on rude and now I'm starting to feel like some kind of nuisance telesales caller. I also have a strong feeling that if I tell him the real reason for my call ('Hi there, I'm a psychic and am ringing about a letter I got from your wife, where she tells me she's really concerned that there may be some kind of energy disturbance in the beautiful house you've only just bought') he'll bang the phone down on me and call the nearest mental hospital to check they've no escaped patients wandering the streets. People who don't believe in psychic phenomena tend to treat you like a cross between a weirdo and a con-artist and something is telling me that this man is most definitely a non-believer.

'I'm calling in connection with a letter she sent me recently.' There, did that sound OK? Crisp and business-like is what I'm going for here.

'Very well. Hold the line,' he barks at me. 'LIZ?

PHONE CALL FOR YOU IN MY STUDY.' Heavy footsteps, a door slamming, then lighter, more rushed footsteps, then his voice again, only a bit muffled this time, as if he has his hand over the receiver. 'Who's this complete stranger ringing you?'

'I don't know. How can I know until I speak to them? A friend, maybe?'

'You don't have any friends.'

'Well, maybe one of the old neighbours. I really don't know. Now please, Gerry, can I just have the phone?' A disagreeable grunt, then her voice again. 'Hello? This is Liz Henderson speaking.' She sounds timid, a bit nervous. 'Who is this, please?'

I explain who I am and why I'm calling and all of a sudden it's as if I'm on a hotline to the KGB.

'Just one moment, please.' Then the sounds get a bit muffled again, but I do hear her say, 'Gerry? I wonder if you'd mind keeping an eye on the potatoes I have on the stove? Please? I may be a few minutes on the phone and you know how much you hate them when they get floury.'

'You haven't told me exactly who it is on the phone.'

'Oh, it's just . . . emm . . . a thing for a magazine.'

'Why would a magazine possibly want to speak to you?'

God, he sounds awful. 'It's a survey,' I hiss at her. 'Say you're taking part in a survey.'

'Oh, thank you, it's . . . emm . . . a survey about . . . leisure activities for the over sixty-fives.'

'Yes, so you said. It still doesn't explain why they'd want to speak to *you*. And how did a magazine get this number?'

'Please, Gerry, the potatoes will be ruined.'

A grunt, then heavy footsteps, a door slamming, then I think he's gone. Bloody hell, it's almost like listening into a radio play. Now Liz's voice again, but speaking a bit less nervously this time.

'Cassandra, I'm so mortified about that, I don't know where to start apologizing to you.'

'Don't worry, it's no problem, really.'

'If Gerry knew I'd written to you about the goings-on in this house, he'd hit the ceiling. And things have got so bad here, you wouldn't believe it. Only yesterday, I came home to find the fridge door ajar, vegetables strewn all over the floor, the cupboard doors wide open and bleach spilt everywhere. Gerry nearly went mad and kept blaming me, saying it was somehow all my fault. And that's the very least of it. We have a lovely bedroom upstairs that's an absolute no-go zone. I'm at my wits' end here, Cassandra, and if you can't help me, I honestly don't know who can.'

'Mrs Henderson, you mustn't worry. I'm not quite sure what the problem is, but maybe I could come by tomorrow? I promise I'll do my best to help.'

'Oh Cassandra, you absolute lifesaver. Let me know whatever time suits and I'll try to think of something to get Gerry out of the house. Say a prayer it's a fine day because then, with luck, he'll go out playing golf. And that'll tie him up for hours too. We'll be quite safe from him.'

Which is an odd thing to say about your husband, I'm thinking as we say our goodbyes. The image I'm getting of Gerry is – well, put it this way: he's starting to make the Dragon Lady look like a Relate counsellor. Anyway, I'm absolutely certain about one thing. I have to go there. I'm *meant* to go there. All in the line of duty.

So, that done and feeling deliciously organized and on top of things (a rarity for me, you understand), I switch my mobile back on. Two missed calls. The first one's from Marilyn, sounding, well, a bit wobbly and speaking so low that I almost have to strain to hear her.

'Cassie? Hi, it's me, Marilyn. I'm sure you've heard the news by now; I mean about' – an even more hushed whisper – 'the baby and getting married and everything. Have to keep my voice down 'cos no one in work suspects a thing. Look, the thing is, we know Charlene is staying with you and maybe – huge favour here – if you think there's any chance that she might come round, would you call me? We all know what she and her father are like when they dig their heels in, but, personally, I'm holding out for the miracle. Perhaps you and I could meet up? I'm in castings all day, but text and I'll get straight back to you. I'm really worried about her. It was a horrific row and, well, a lot of things were said that can't be taken back. This is such a shock, but at the same time, we're all the family she has in this world and we're both anxious to build bridges with her.'

Beep.

Second message. Charlene, sounding in a panic.

'Hi, it's me. OK, OK, this may not exactly be my finest hour, but the thing is I was trying to clean the kitchen floor with that stinky stuff – whaddya call it? Oh yeah, bleach – and anyway, it brought out all my allergies. Well, you know what I'm like around cheap perfume and this is, like, a *thousand* times worse, so I didn't know what to do so I fished out the Yellow Pages and got a contract cleaner to come and sort out the mess and she did and she was Polish, I think, just brilliant, did the insides of the windows, ironing, everything, while I caught up with my magazines. I never bother eating lunch, you know, mainly because I always figure that *Vogue* nourishes me far, *far* more, but now you see the awful thing is that I have to pay the cleaner and it's really embarrassing because she doesn't speak any English, well, apart from the odd word like Hoover and Mr Sheen, who I thought might have been relatives of hers, but anyhow, I don't have any cash and she doesn't take Visa, if you can believe that in this day and age, and now she's starting to glower at me and is saying something about calling her three brothers, who apparently are all professional weightlifters, to get her money for her. Can you come home soon, sweetie, and make all of this go away? Pleeeeease?'

I race home to find Marc with a C and Jo already in before me, troubleshooting and soothing irate Polish feathers.

'OK, so maybe I made a poor judgement call,' Charlene is squealing from the kitchen.

'You call this a poor judgement call?' Jo is yelling back at her. 'You wanted to pay an honest, hard-working economic migrant who has slaved all afternoon in this house with a *credit card*?'

'Your point being?'

'My point being that if you don't start to make some kind of effort in the real world, then I am going to force you to do voluntary work for me at Amnesty.'

'I did make an effort. I decided that from now on, today is going to be called Champagne Tuesday. I'm thinking of making it permanent. You know, a bit like daylight saving time.'

'Oh, for God's sake, what is that, Charlene-onomics?'

'Don't you raise your eyebrow at me, Josephine. May I remind you that I'm going through a terrible family trauma. So instead of trying to make *me* your pet project, why don't you just go and, I dunno, adopt a cat, or something?'

'Ladies, ladies, ladies, let's just keep our powder dry here, shall we?' Marc with a C is saying, but then he's always great at refereeing. He'd have been amazing as a hostage negotiator in the Middle East. 'Charlene, my sweet darling innocent, I have a teeny question for you. How do you normally pay for your credit card?'

'I don't. I send the bill to Dad's head office in Switzerland.'

'And who do you think foots the bill there?'

'I don't know. Never gave it much thought. It goes to accountants and then it goes to more accountants and then they write it off as expenses and that's pretty much the end of my involvement in the matter. It's an arrangement which has always suited me fairly well.'

'Oh, my poor short-sighted girl, with you living in this house, who needs soap opera? If you're determined to plough ahead with this whole I'm-financially-independent thing, then the credit card has to go. Because, let me enlighten you, it is ultimately paid for by your dad, if that doesn't come as too much of a shock to you.'

'I know, I know, I know *eventually* it has to be, but I thought, just this once? I just don't know if I'm up to credit-card cold turkey. And by the way, you didn't see the Diane von Furstenberg silk wrap-over dress in Harvey Nicks that I *didn't* buy today. You should have seen me on the ready-to-wear couture floor. I was like some kind of Tibetan monk. An absolute model of discipline.'

Marc with a C sighs so deeply, it's almost as if it's causing him physical pain. 'I'm sorry to be the bearer of bad news, babes, but it's time for you to pursue gainful employment.'

'I don't need a job, I already have one.'

On cue I walk through the kitchen door.

'And what *job* would that be?' Jo asks dryly as I greet everyone.

'You can just drop that tone right now and stop speaking in italics,' sniffs Charlene, looking close to tears. 'Look at me. In the space of twenty-four hours I've gone from having the world at my feet to the world at my throat and do you hear one single complaint out of me? I've spent all evening cooking for you guys, even though you said I didn't have to, just so I could be useful, and do I hear a single word of thanks?'

But now an alarm bell is ringing in my head. 'Sorry, Charlene, go back to the bit where you said you had a job?' I ask, almost dreading the answer.

'Well, I'm still your agent, sweetie, aren't I? Oh, and by the way, I took a message for you earlier. Some guy rang from Channel Seven and says you're to call him back.'

Shit, I'm thinking. I thought she'd got bored and moved on from that idea ages ago.

'Speaking for myself, I honestly can't say what I'm

more shocked by,' says Marc with a C as I head out
to the hall to return the call. 'That you didn't buy the
Diane von Furstenberg, or that you actually cooked. Oh
and Jo, dearie? You owe me five euro. I just won a bet
that the three of you wouldn't last twenty-four hours
living under the same roof.'

'Just out of idle curiosity,' says Jo slowly, 'what did you
cook?'

'Duck à la marmalade,' she says proudly. 'From the
Nigella book. It's meant to be duck à l'orange but we
didn't have any, so I just used Chivers from the back of
the fridge instead. Like, there's a difference?'

'Charlene, you are aware that I'm a strict vegetarian?'

'Well, yeah . . . but I did go to loads of trouble and I
thought, maybe, just this once?'

'My conscience does *not* take a day off.'

'What else was I supposed to do?'

'Haven't you ever heard of tofu?'

'You mean that's an actual *ingredient*? I thought it was
a small country in Africa.'

Double shit, I think, closing the kitchen door so they
can't be heard sniping at each other while I'm on the
phone. It's going to be a long, long night.

I pick up our gas bill which has a message scrawled on
the back of it. 'Cassie, some bloke called Oliver called.
Here's his number . . .'

Oliver, Oliver, Oliver: I'm racking my brains to think

where I've heard that name recently . . . Got it. He's the guy I met in Jack's office. The cute guy. Hmm.

As I'm dialling his number, I'm trying to figure out what he could want me for. To slag me off for being such total crap on yesterday's show? Unlikely.

He answers after only two rings.

'Hi, Oliver? It's Cassandra here, from the *Breakfast Club*?'

'Cassandra, hi! Great, yeah, good, thanks so much for getting back to me.' He talks really fast, as if he's thinking aloud, and it sounds like he's pacing up and down a room. I can almost sense him waving his hands in front of his face, expressively, the way highly intelligent people in Mensa are supposed to do. And, of course, there's the American twang. 'Now, of course, I'm only throwing this at you, it's just a pitch, but do have a think, won't you? Basically, your performance on TV gave me an idea. I'm putting a documentary together at the moment, freelance, you know, and after seeing you, I thought about maybe looking into the whole psychic phenomenon and how popular it is, particularly among single people.'

'Oh. Wow.'

'Just the reaction I'd hoped for. So I just wondered, first of all, if you'd be interested in taking part and secondly if you might have anything coming up that I could shoot. I'm seeing maybe you doing a psychic reading for a punter, I'm seeing maybe you sitting in your dressing room getting flashes, I'm seeing maybe you advising people on relationship problems – that really seems to be your strong suit. Except face to face, instead of over the phone in a studio. I really want us to delve into the psyche of a person who's looking for romance; you know, the type of women out there who aren't just dating anyone, they're dating *everyone*. And then, to balance the documentary, we'd talk to guys who see these women and are terrified and think, My God, there are cannibals out there less man-hungry.'

He pauses to draw breath and I'm left thinking: Did he really say that? Did he really just compare single women to man-hungry cannibals?

'I'm speaking metaphorically, of course,' he adds apologetically, almost reading my thoughts. 'It's just that this is what the light entertainment market really seems to want and, based on what I've seen, you are the *Breakfast Club*'s very own resident psychic relationship coach. Just wondered where you stood on this, that's all. Any thoughts? Anything coming up that we might be able to talk about?'

Before I even have a chance to draw breath, he's off again.

'OK, now I'm seeing maybe you watching a monitor with a live feed from a bar or a nightclub, so we can see guy chatting up girl and then cut to you telling us, when he says X, this is actually what he really means and when she says Y here's what she really means. So you'd be a sort of psychic dating detective, if you're with me.'

Wow, that's a lot to digest. A lot of rubbish to digest, if I'm being honest. I have to think for a sec before answering.

'Cassandra? Are you still there? I hope I'm not scaring you off?'

'Ehh, no, it's just that, well, you see . . .' Oh shit, what'll I say to him? I've only just got my foot in the door at Channel Seven and I don't want to appear uncooperative to a big famous senior TV journalist, but at the same time I don't want to get myself in too deep over my head. I mean, come on, a psychic dating detective? I think I'd rather have my toenails pulled out by a trained badger. The potential for humiliation is so monumental and, boy, if anyone knows about humiliation, I do.

And then I remember. Something nice and straight-forward that's all lined up anyway. And it makes me look cooperative and interested in taking part in a big documentary and being a team player, without the awkwardness of actually having to turn down any of his awful pitches. 'Well, there is something, emm, Oliver, if you're interested.'

'Yeah, shoot, go for it.'

Now he's beginning to sound like one of those high-energy executives you see on TV shows like *The*

Apprentice. Except this guy would be the type to do the actual hiring and firing, not one of the poor eejits sitting opposite at a boardroom table, sweating and stressing and waiting to see who's for the chop, as I probably would be.

'Right. Now don't laugh.'

'Would I?'

'It's just that I've arranged to call at a house tomorrow to see if I can help a very worried lady who wrote to me about some disturbances there.'

'Brilliant! A haunted house, love it!'

'I did *not* say that it was haunted, I don't know what's going on and I won't know until I get there.' Rats, why did I have to open my big mouth? But now he's run away with the idea, almost as if he's trying to create a story out of nothing.

'Already I'm seeing a darkened room, candles, you looking fabulous all dressed in black at the head of a table touching hands with this woman and saying stuff like, "Is there anyone out there? Knock once for yes and twice for no."'

'Oliver, I have to stop you right there. I'm just having a look-see, that's all. Maybe a possible energy-clearing. Most definitely *not* a séance.' Shit. He sounds like he's expecting a dramatic re-enactment of a scene from *Blithe Spirit*.

'Hey, just kidding,' he says, although half of me thinks

he wasn't. 'OK, now I'm seeing us shooting you on a night camera. Maybe we'll find out a bit about the history of the haunted house – you know, whether Mary Queen of Scots ever stayed there. Audiences love that kind of thing.'

'It's a housing estate in Rathgar. I'd be astonished if Mary Queen of Scots was ever passing through.'

'Just kidding. OK, now I'm seeing a dusty attic. Maybe we'll get an actress to dress up as one of the Brontës in a white sheet or something. LISA? CAN YOU PUT A CALL IN TO WARDROBE?'

'The Brontës? In a dormer bungalow in the middle of Dublin?'

'Hey, just kidding. Although I do see you coming slowly into the frame telling the viewer about how you're identifying with this spirit so much. God, this will make show-stopping television. I can practically smell the BAFTA . . .'

OK, that's quite enough. Foot down, now. And, while it may sound rude, I think this is someone you need to spell things out to, in bullet-point form so there's absolutely no grey area or misunderstanding. 'Oliver. Will you listen for one minute, please? Number one, yes, I am very happy to take part in your documentary. Number two, yes, you are very welcome to come along to this house tomorrow. Number three, the lady I'm going to see is, well, let's just say a very private person and it's highly unlikely she'll give permission for her home to be filmed. So if you can respect that, we'll all get along.'

'Absolutely,' says Oliver, smoothly. 'You know, I am a professional and under no circumstances would I ask you to do anything you weren't happy or comfortable with. OK?'

'OK.'

We hang up and although outwardly everything seems fine, my instinct is saying something different. Something very different.

Sweet baby Jesus and the orphans. What have I let myself in for?

Chapter Ten

THE TAROT DECK
THE MAGICIAN CARD

Wow, and I really mean WOW. The Magician can do anything, go anywhere, be anything his or her mystical, magical qualities can conjure. Wealth, power, fame, prestige, glory and success are within your grasp. Anything you desire is yours for the asking.

Just maybe not the fella you fancy, but then you can't have everything, can you? It is, after all, only a tarot card we're talking about, not a magic wand . . .

Before carrying out an energy-clearing, as any psychic worth their salt will tell you, it's advisable to go to a place of calm and serenity, empty your mind, breathe deeply and allow yourself to get in touch with your inner voice.

This morning, I, on the other hand, have to put up with the following:

CHARLENE (*screeching from the bottom of our stairs and, even though my bedroom door is closed tight, she sounds as loud as a Hezbollah rocket attack*): Jo? Cassie? Come on down! You'll never guess what I made – brekkie!

JO (*shouting back at her from our bathroom, but again, clearly audible*): Hang on one second. For you to be up and about at this hour can only mean one thing. You WANT something.

CHARLENE (*deeply miffed or, at least, sounding as if she is*): Oh, welcome to cynical land. Population: YOU.

Must tune out all distractions. Must focus on task ahead, a bit like the way Zen masters are supposed to. Must not get sucked into domestic squabbles. Breathe, breathe and breathe again . . .

JO (*to the sound of a flushing toilet*): So why don't you save us all a lot of time and energy and just tell us what it is you're after?

CHARLENE: OK, well, seeing as you've asked, I do need money, just to tide me over, just a few euro, just for now. Seeing as how you've all banned me from doing what I normally would. Taking my platinum card and charging myself happy.

JO (*her voice and my blood pressure rising*): On principle, NO. What happened to all your big notions of standing on your own two feet?

CHARLENE (*defensively*): It's only to get me though a bit of a cash-flow crisis, until I really start making it as Cassie's agent. I have a primal, basic need to shop, you know.

JO: Oh, for God's sake, if this is about dresses by Diane von Carlsberg or whatever it is she calls herself —

CHARLENE (*as though her religion has just been insulted, which, in a way, it has*): That's Diane von FURSTENBERG and FYI, Mrs Big Fat Scroogie-pants, the reason I need dosh is to buy household . . . emm . . . whaddya call them? Oh yeah, appliances. I happened to notice that Harvey Nicks have a sale in, you know, essential housey things like, emm, loo roll and . . . after dinner mints and . . . hand lotion . . .'

Deep breath, focus on reaching a cool and detached state of Tibetan monk-like calm, must connect with my inner voice and block out all exterior distractions/discussions about loo roll, hand lotion, etc. . . .

JO (*almost spluttering*): Are you seriously suggesting that you do the grocery shopping at Harvey Nichols? Charlene, even the royal family doesn't do that.

CHARLENE (*almost apologetically*): Don't be cross with me, sweetie, I am trying, you know.

JO (*coming back down to earth a bit*): Hmm. Very trying.

Anyway, kind-hearted old Jo is obviously reminding herself of the huge upheaval Charlene has been through and feeling a bit guilty for snapping the head off her, because when she comes out of the bathroom and goes downstairs, she says to her, in far more conciliatory tones, 'OK, OK, you guilted me into it. I can give you exactly one hundred euro. It's not a lend, it's for keeps, but you have to promise to pay it forward to an aid organization of my choosing. Not one of your trendy, glamorous save-the-lesser-spotted-whale charities. OK?'

CHARLENE (*playing down her victory*): Thank you. You're very kind. Oh, and one more teeny favour?

JO: Go on.

CHARLENE (*OK, slightly pushing her luck now*): Well, it's just that I'm going to need clothes, aren't I? And handbags. And don't even get me started on shoes. And all my stuff is back at the house. And you can hardly expect me to go round there and collect everything, now can you?

There's a silence and I swear I can practically hear the sound of Jo's eyes rolling.

JO: Right, we'll get Marc with a C on to it. After all, he's our resident expert on conflict resolution.

CHARLENE (*meekly*): You're so good to me, sweetie. (*Sound of dozens of air-kisses.*) OK, now come on, hurry up, I want you to eat your brekkie. Bang on Cassie's door, will you? I'd say she's still asleep and we have a big day ahead of us.

JO (*suspiciously*): When you say 'I made brekkie' what exactly do you mean? Because if it involves bacon or sausages, frankly I'd rather eat a Travelodge pillow.

CHARLENE: Oh, keep your vegetarian smug-brella up. Especially for you, I opened a tin of pineapple chunks I found in the back of a cupboard.

A full hour later, Jo's long gone to work and I'm still waiting for Charlene to decide on what she's going to wear. She's standing in front of my wardrobe in her nightie, filching through my stuff with a 'discard' pile at her feet that's mounting higher and higher by the second.

'You don't have to come with me, you know, I won't be offended in the least,' I say for about the thousandth time, in the vain hope that she'll take the hint. 'You'd be bored, it's no fun and with any luck it'll all be over in an hour or so.'

She's barely even listening to me. 'What is it with you and the colour pink?' she mutters, flinging my last year's, really expensive, investment-buy cashmere cardigan into the 'discard' pile with abandon. 'With my hair colour, it makes me look like a marshmallow.'

'Charlene, we're going to do an energy-clearing. It's not like there's a dress code. Besides, my stuff doesn't even fit you properly.'

'Welcome to my wonderful world of "Got no choice". I need clean clothes. Supposing Jack is there?'

'*What* did you say?' Oh shit and double shit. Never even thought of that. Suppose he is?

No, he wouldn't be . . . would he?

'Well, you never know, sweetie. I mean, he's the one who introduced you to Oliver in the first place, they're both producers at Channel Seven, so who's to say he won't come along too?'

Oh, bugger, bugger, bugger, she's right. What'll I do? I won't be able to see a thing, I'll be beyond useless, I'll let everyone down and, worse than all that, I'll have to tell Charlene.

And won't that just sound lovely?

Yes, Charlene, my old friend, I fully appreciate that you're going through a personal crisis at the moment, but, by the way, I think I fancy your fella, in the full knowledge that nothing can ever happen between us. However, the more immediate issue at hand is that whenever he's in the room, my psychic gifts seem to fly out of the bleeding window.

Yeah, great, best of luck with that speech, Cassie.

Think, think, think . . .

'But won't Jack still be shooting the *Breakfast Club*?'

'Should be finished by now. Can you believe it's almost ten? How long *exactly* does it take you to get ready, Cassie?'

I can't even answer her back, I'm too busy racking my brains.

Hang on. Oliver wants to film me this morning for – what did he say again? For a freelance documentary he's putting together, wasn't that it? Yup, sounds right. Which is brilliant. This is nothing to do with either Channel Seven or the *Breakfast Club* then. I hope. And nothing to do with Jack. Theoretically. And therefore there's no actual, cast-iron *reason* for him to be there.

Shit. Unless Charlene goes and invites him. That would just be my bloody luck, wouldn't it?

On cue, the phone rings and Charlene races downstairs to get it. Now, I'm only hearing one side of the conversation, but it goes something along these lines.

'Hello? Sweetie! You *called*! I'm so pleased! But why didn't you call my mobile? Oh, right. You want to speak to her now? Yeah, she's here, upstairs, taking ages to decide what to wear. Yes, OK, relax, I'll get her. So, when am I going to see you? Not until *then*? Meetings, meetings, meetings, is that all you producers do? Well, how long do your bloody meetings go on for, anyway? No, no, *au contraire*, I *do* understand. I'm just not feeling very prioritized in your life right now. Frankly, this kind of treatment is a relationship weapon of mass destruction.' Long pause. 'Right, fine, I'll see you then. I suppose. Well, thanks for fitting me into your action-packed schedule; much appreciated. Oh, and just so you're aware? Right now, you're being obnoxious at a level not even acceptable in show business. CASSIE! PHONE!'

Another instance where you don't need to be psychic to know who it is. I come down and she practically flings the phone at me before flouncing back upstairs again.

'Cassie? Hi, it's Jack here.' He sounds frazzled, stressed.

'Hi. Emm . . . how are things?'

There's a pause and I can hear pandemonium in the background. Phones ringing, voices chattering, doors slamming. 'Oh, just the normal post-broadcast chaos. Look, the thing is, Oliver Hall just mentioned that he's planning on doing an EFP shoot with you this morning—'

'Excuse me, a what?'

'Sorry,' he says and I swear I can almost hear the smile. 'Technical term for a location shoot. EFP stands for Electronic Field Production, or the way I'm feeling this morning, Extra F★★king Pressure.'

We both laugh and then I remember that Charlene's upstairs and I shut up.

'Anyway,' he goes on, 'I just wanted to make sure that this was absolutely OK with you, that's all. I know . . . well, put it like this, I know how persuasive Oliver can be. For God's sake, he's a TV journalist, the guy could probably talk the Dalai Lama into coming out with something risqué and inflammatory.'

I laugh again, can't help it.

'So you're all right with this? Sure?'

'Yes, of course, it's absolutely fine,' I say brightly, as if I go around the place with TV cameras trailing after me every day of the week, like, I dunno, George Bush or Paris Hilton or somebody.

Then I remember it's not fine, it's absolutely not fine, it's the exact opposite. Oh bugger, how will I phrase this delicately?

Another phone starts ringing in the background and I can sense he's a bit distracted. 'Great, well, technically, Oliver is doing this as a freelance gig, but you should just know that you're doing the *Breakfast Club* a huge favour, publicity-wise,' he says, in an I'm-not-being-rude-it's-just-I'm-in-work-and-have-to-go tone of voice.

Right, nothing for it, I have to jump in feet first. 'Jack? Before you go?'

'Yup?'

'Are you planning on coming to the shoot too?'

There's just the tiniest pause. 'What do you mean, did you want me to be there?'

'No, no, no, I mean, yes, I mean, I'm not telling you your job, I just ... err ... wondered, that's all.' Great, now I sound as if I fancy him. Which ... let's be honest, I do.

And Charlene's upstairs.

OK, I am officially the most horrible person in the world.

He laughs it off. Luckily, *very* luckily for me. 'Cassie, while there is nothing in the world I'd enjoy more than a day's location shoot in your sparkling company, unfortunately I'm going to be stuck in budgeting meetings for the rest of the day, most likely.'

'Oh, OK then. Well ... enjoy, I suppose.'

Yes, yes, I am fully aware that sounded teenagery and pathetic, but what was I supposed to say? I mean, what do I know about budgeting meetings?

'Enjoy?' Jack says, sounding a bit more like himself now. 'Believe you me, there are Samuel Beckett plays that are more gripping and move faster than our quarterly financial meetings.'

I snort with laughter, then realize how unattractive it sounds, then remember Charlene upstairs, still rummaging through my wardrobe, then I instantly shut up.

'So, best of luck, Cassie, you're in safe hands, but do call me if, well, if there's anything you're not one hundred per cent happy with. Deal?'

'Deal.' I smile, feeling all safe and minded.

'Oh, and will you tell Charlene I'll call her as soon

as I get out of here so we can . . . well, so we can . . . emm . . .' Another phone rings in the background and suddenly the production office he's calling from sounds like Grand Central and I couldn't quite catch the end of his sentence. But I think I can guess what he meant. I think at this stage the dogs on the street could pretty much guess what's coming.

Yet another one you don't need to be psychic for.

OK, so now I've gone from being the most horrible person in the world to the most hateful person who ever lived. Worse than Pol Pot, worse than Hitler and right up there with the worst relationship-sabotaging cow ever to grace the screen of a daytime soap opera.

This, however, makes me an awful lot nicer and a helluva lot more patient with Charlene in the car. 'I mean, what is it about Jack Hamilton, would you please mind telling me?' she rants to me as I try to navigate my way to the Hendersons' house in Rathgar. 'On the rare occasions when he actually *does* want to see me – and I might add that getting a date with him is like pulling teeth – it's only ever in the daytime. This makes him either (a) married, or (b) a vampire.'

'Honey,' I say as I attempt to reverse the car out of a cul-de-sac after taking yet another wrong turn, 'I want you to be blissfully happy with the right guy. I'll repeat that for further emphasis: the *right guy*. Someone who will love and adore you and treat you like a princess.'

Did that sound OK? Gentle but firm is what I'm going for here. And honest. This *is* what I want for her. For all of us. I'm not sure she's even listening to me, though; from the corner of my eye I catch her staring at her reflection in the wing mirror.

'Charlene? Have I lost you? Are you drifting?'

She doesn't answer. Which is odd. Normally you have a job shutting her up, particularly whenever the conversation revolves around fellas.

'Are you maybe fantasizing about this month's *Vogue*?' What the hell, I might as well make a joke of it.

'Something's up, Cassie,' she eventually says, slowly turning to face me, the big blue eyes swimming with wobbly tears. 'With Jack, I mean.' And she's not acting, this is for real. She smells what's coming, same as we all do.

'Oh honey, are you OK?' I ask as soothingly as I can. God love her, I think, feeling if possible even lousier than I did earlier. Bad enough that she's going through a family crisis but now this . . .

'Cassie, I think you know me well enough to know that I'm beyond looking for a boyfriend. I'm auditioning for a *husband*. And to be perfectly honest, I smell a dumping in the air. And what's even worse, I'm going to be the dumpee. Oh, to hell with bloody Jack Hamilton anyway, that's all I can say. Stupid bastard just bought me about five more years on my analyst's couch.'

For once I find myself wishing for a miracle to happen. Not for me, you understand, for Charlene.

Years and years ago, when I was just out of college, wondering what to do with my life and still coming to terms with being psychic, I went to (and I swear I'm not messing here) a white witches' convention in Hastings, England, centre of all sorcery activity in Europe.

Now, I stress that I only went for the laugh and because I thought I'd fit in. But guess what, I didn't. They all looked down their noses at me for being psychic and for (a) telling people who came to me the flashes I saw about their futures and (b) daring to even think about accepting a job writing a column in a magazine, which in white witch circles is the equivalent of selling out and becoming a door-to-door encyclopaedia saleswoman. For my part, I thought they were a shower of headcases who never, ever washed and somehow always smelt of hash.

Anyway, while I was there, I met the head of all white witches, leader of the coven, who we had to address by his proper title – Kevin. Kevin was in his sixties, white-haired and sprightly, and if you didn't know, you'd almost think he was an assistant bank manager. He would throw his broomstick into the back of his Nissan Micra and cheerfully head off to do energy-clearings and chanting and maybe the odd spell. It was a confused time in my life and the only reason I even mention Kevin now is that he always used to say this. Or at least, this is the gist of it: if you wish something unselfishly for someone else, for good, with goodness in your heart and for the greater good of mankind ('good' and 'evil' feature an awful lot in the white witch community. Honestly, it's like something out of *Harry Potter*), and if the Universe is in very good form that day, and all other things being equal, then it will come to pass.

It might well sound like tosh, but I find myself doing it right now. It's worth a try.

I wish some knight in shining Armani would magically appear out of nowhere and sweep Charlene off her feet. Give her everything she wants and make all her dreams come true. She's a good soul and she really, truly deserves it. It's all she's ever wanted out of life and, given her family background, it's not really that hard to understand why she so desperately craves a normal family of her own. It's not much to ask, and can I just add that if ever she should meet someone, now is the perfect, perfect time.

Anyway, I finally find the Hendersons' house, which is very posh, with a long sweeping driveway up to it. We scrunch the car up, pulling in behind a very swish-looking Mercedes, brand new, almost in showroom condition. The driver's door opens and, with a spring in his step, out steps Oliver.

Chapter Eleven

THE TAROT DECK
THE ACE OF CUPS CARD

The card of impulse and intuition. Signifies that you must trust yourself and be guided by your sixth sense. If you do follow your gut instinct and stay in close contact with your inner voice, all will be well. If you chose not to, then, sorry, but I'm afraid that's a whole other story. Don't, however, come back crying and say that you weren't warned . . .

OK. We've only been here for half an hour and already Oliver is driving me *mental*. First of all, when we meet

Mrs Henderson (who is lovely, by the way, tall, pale, gracious and welcoming. She immediately puts me at ease by assuring me her awful husband is out for the day – phew), he launches into the hard sell to try and persuade her to participate in his documentary.

'I'm seeing you reading out the letter you wrote to Cassandra,' he says, oblivious to the stressed look on the poor woman's tired face. 'Then maybe we can cut to you walking around the house, inspecting all the damage that's been done by whatever unseen force is at work here. The place is looking a bit too tidy; maybe we'll mess it up a bit, you know, make it look more like a bomb hit it.'

'Well, I don't know if I'd be quite comfortable with that,' says Mrs Henderson timidly. 'You see, I don't think my husband would be very happy for me to appear on TV.'

'Oh come on, this could be for primetime broadcast,' says Oliver, flashing his gluey professional grin. 'Just think about the exposure.'

'That *was* what I was thinking about.'

'Would you like me to have a word with your husband?'

Now Mrs Henderson looks completely panic-stricken and it's at this point I step in, unable to witness any more of his shameless pushiness. 'Oliver,' I say crisply in my very best won't-take-no-for-an-answer tone of voice.

Claudia Carroll

'I need a word. Outside. Now. Please excuse us for a minute, Mrs Henderson.' I step into the front garden and take a breath of nice, soothing, cool air. Honestly, at times like this I really, really wish that I smoked.

He's hot on my heels like a bad smell. 'So? Everything all right with my beautiful star? Not getting cold feet on me, I hope?'

Unfortunately for him, the TV-friendly cheesy grin doesn't work on me. God, even the faux-American accent is really starting to irritate me now. 'Oliver, I don't mean to be rude, but you have got to back *right off*. Mrs Henderson clearly doesn't want to take part, so why can't you just leave her alone?'

'Hey, no need to get excited.'

'I cannot do an energy-clearing with you buzzing around like you're trying to direct *War and Peace*. It's just not possible. Now, I hate to sound insistent, but what I'm about to do requires calm and quiet and serenity so I can *hopefully*, with a bit of luck, and I'm making no promises here, tap into the energies around and actually help this woman—'

He doesn't even let me finish, just interrupts me with a pained look on his face that might as well say, 'I sure as hell don't want a ticket to whatever planet you're living on.' Jesus, I could strangle him.

'Cassandra, you may know a lot about the occult—'

'I DO NOT dabble in the occult.'

306

'But you have to admit, you know diddly squat about what makes great TV.' Another flash of the practised smile. 'Now, I've been making documentaries for years and years . . .'

Which have brought pleasure to fives of tens of people, I'm silently thinking, still smouldering.

'. . . and I instinctively know what will work here. You have to trust me. OK, so maybe I won't be able to talk Mrs Henderson round, but I'm seeing you marching purposefully up the driveway, I'm seeing you dressed like a sort of spiritual spring-cleaner . . .'

Oh my God, it just gets worse and worse. Did he really just say that? I'll be lucky if he doesn't play in the theme tune from *Ghostbusters*. But he's not even finished.

'. . . then I'm seeing you drifting into a trance and maybe even speaking in tongues.'

'OLIVER!'

'Don't worry, I can dub in the voices later in editing.'

I try my best to keep my voice cool, calm and measured, although what I'm actually thinking is, Kill me now, for the love of God. 'At the risk of sounding like a prima donna,' I say, slowly, slowly, slowly, 'if you want this clearing to be successful you are going to have to *back off* and let me do it my way. And just so we're absolutely clear, that means no voiceovers, no theme tune from *The Omen* and most definitely no extras floating by looking

307

like rejects from the set of *Jane Eyre*. It basically means you just let me get on with it. OK?

'Hey, if that's what you want, that's not a problem.' Again he beams the faux I-really-think-you're-great-and-I-love-love-*love*-working-with-you grin, which is utterly wasted on me. 'Although, a word to the wise: I wouldn't use the prima donna phrase in front of the cameraman if I were you. I mean, after all, you're the one who brought your agent here with you today.'

Well, colour me moody, I think furiously as he goes back inside the house. I didn't think it physically possible but this whole 'Hey! Fab idea! Let's film Cassandra doing a clearing' both sucks *and* blows. If Oily Oliver had only played his cards right, I might even have attempted, in time, to fix him up with Charlene, but right now he has a Hindu's chance in heaven of that ever happening. Oh well, his loss. No kidding, this man puts the noxious into obnoxious. Anyway, lucky escape for Charlene, if you ask me. I suppose the lesson for me here is be very, very careful what you wish for . . .

Anyway, Charlene is still in the car, in a deep chat on the mobile with Marc with a C. The good news is that she and 'Orrible Oliver have barely looked twice at each other since we got here; she's too upset, God love her, and he's too busy trying to be the next Ang Lee. Best of luck to him.

'I'm point-blank refusing to get out of the car,' she

shouts out of the window at me, covering the phone with her hand. 'It's starting to drizzle and I don't want to end up looking like Bigfoot's sister, Bighair.'

Suits me fine, I think to myself, trying to cool down a bit and focus on the job ahead. I take a few deep, soothing breaths, regroup and remind myself of why I'm here in the first place.

No one's around, not Mrs Henderson and most importantly not the dreaded Oliver going 'I'm seeing this and I'm seeing that'. Wonder if he sees the kick up the arse that's on its way to him before this day is out?

Come on, Cassie, banish all negative thoughts.

Now, I have done energy-clearings before, but it's not like there're aerobics classes you can do to brush up on your skills . . . Focus.

Concentrate.

I stand outside the hall door, go to a quiet place in my head, close my eyes and really try to *feel*.

Often, buildings with a 'bad' energy about them are built on ley lines, which is another word for the energy lines that cover the whole surface of the globe. Usually, where two ley lines cross over each other, you'll find there's a church, which is absolutely as it should be in the greater scheme of things. Intersecting ley lines bring huge energy, they impact on our feelings and emotions in the most colossal way and a place of worship is the perfect outlet for that.

In many cases, though, you can find yourself in a building that just has an 'ick' feel to it. An unlucky building. We've all been in one; you know, a place where things go wrong and keep going wrong and no one really knows why. People are constantly getting sick. Rows and arguments happen far more frequently than, by the law of averages, they should.

When we were in school, Charlene often blamed ley lines for not having her homework done or else used them as an excuse to get out of class early. 'I have to go, miss, the ley lines are killing me.' Lame as it sounds, it sure as hell beat my regular excuse: 'Miss, can I please be excused gym class today? My third eye is in ribbons.'

Scientists would call places like this 'geopathically stressed'; people like me know that it's usually because of ley lines. But I'm not feeling anything from outside this house. Nothing. Which is good. It makes my job a helluva lot simpler.

I move inside very slowly and trust that I'll be drawn to whatever room needs my help.

I get a strong feeling that this is not a happy home, not by a long shot, which unwittingly creates the perfect space for any negative psychic disturbances.

No one even notices me as I tiptoe upstairs. I don't know why, but for some reason, I'm feeling the strongest need to go upstairs. It's deathly silent as I reach the upstairs landing. Which is good too: above all, this job needs quiet.

The Hendersons' is a large house, and there're about six doors leading off the upstairs passageway, with one huge, diamond-paned window opposite me, bathing the whole area in light. On the windowsill there's a gorgeous black and white cat, all snuggled up in his basket, enjoying a toasty warm ray of sunshine that's beaming directly on to him. Instinctively, I go over to where he's sleeping and stroke him gently. He purrs and looks at me, as if to say, 'Who are you and what the hell are you doing on my territory?' Suddenly, there's a loud pounding noise from one of the bedrooms, shattering the quiet; the sound of a door banging heavily, a wardrobe maybe?

But there's no one else upstairs.

Tentatively, I move towards the door where the sound came from and slowly turn the handle. There's a quick rustling sound from the windowsill and I turn around to see that the cat's done a runner.

Interesting. Animals are incredibly sensitive to any sort of paranormal activity, so this immediately makes me think that I'm on the right track. One of the first signs that any living space has, shall we say, an unwanted guest is if family pets refuse to go near it.

The room is cluttered and untidy, unlike the rest of the house, which is pristine. It's almost as if the Hendersons realized there was something amiss here

311

and just gave up on it. They might as well have put yellow and black stripy plastic tape across the door saying, 'Ghostly occurrences within, do not cross line', a bit like they do with crime scenes in police dramas. It must have been used as a bedroom at one point, because there's a big double bed here, a wardrobe and a dresser, but there're also piles of books scattered all over the floor and, bizarrely, some gym equipment over against the wall: a rowing machine and a cross trainer. (Not that I'd recognize one bit of gym gear from another, it's just Charlene has a private gym in her house and used to let us play on the machines whenever we were all drunk enough and bored enough.)

Come on, concentrate, Cassie, really concentrate . . .

There's no doubt about it, I'm feeling a huge energy surge in the room. And it's definitely got colder; there's been a marked temperature drop; I'm shivering now and pull my cardigan closer to me for extra warmth.

Right then, to work.

I open my bag and fish about for some candles I brought with me. Only cheapie little tea lights, but they do the trick. I light four of them, place them carefully on the floor, one to the north, south, east and west and gently, slowly, sit down beside them.

Easy does it, Cassie, easy does it.

I have to empty my mind and think only peaceful, loving thoughts . . .

There's a loud tapping at the window pane and I look up. For a split second, I wonder if it's just the wind blowing the branches of a tree against the window, but when I look outside, there's nothing. No tree; not even a puff of wind. Thank God I don't scare easily.

And then I get a flash. OK, stay very calm.

There's a boy standing across the room from me, I can see him clear as you like over by the window, with a baseball bat in his little hand, hitting it against the glass, only he's not strong enough to smash it. The poor kid can't be any more than about six or seven, he's blond and blue-eyed, wearing jeans with a Manchester United strip and a baseball cap. He looks angry and frustrated, and what's more I'm pretty certain that he sees me too. He's looking directly at me, unflinching, as if he's trying to figure out whether I'm friend or foe. And I know, with absolute certainty, that he's a little spirit that's already passed on – only I don't think he knows it yet. Oh God, I feel so sorry for him.

Everything suddenly falls into place. I get the strongest feeling that this used to be *his* house, this was *his* room, except all his toys are gone and he doesn't know why. He's not being bold on purpose, he just doesn't know what's going on, who these new people are, where all his belongings are and, most importantly of all, where his mum is . . .

I know I have to try to make contact with him, but I'm nervous. I'm not frightened, it's just that my gift has always been more channelled towards the living and I'm not quite sure what to do. He's still looking at me.

Come on, Cassie, say something, anything . . .

Now, it's not that I'm completely useless at dealing with kids, it's just that I don't really know any. But I've no choice here, I'll just have to give this a go without talking down to him or, even worse, being patronizing.

'Hello,' I say, smiling and deliberately keeping my voice low. 'What's your name?'

He doesn't answer, doesn't even move. Just stares at me, as if he can't believe that I can actually see him. I get the feeling no one has spoken to this little boy in a long, long time.

'So you like Manchester United then?' I say softly, gently.

A sullen nod.

'Doesn't David Beckham play for them?' I know next to nothing about football either, apart from what I read in *Heat* magazine about the WAGs and all their fashion disasters. I just want to get him to trust me, that's all.

He gives me a furious glare and kicks the dresser beside him, then wallops it with his baseball bat. A revolting china ornament perched precariously on top of it falls to the ground and smashes to smithereens.

'Oh, I'm so sorry,' I say, suddenly remembering. 'He went to America, didn't he?'

Another nod.

Thank God for the gossip magazines. I only knew that because I'd seen photos of Posh Spice coming out of the Vuitton shop on Rodeo Drive, the time she'd cut her hair and went bright blonde.

'So, do you like . . . emm . . .'

Think, think, think, Cassie, come on, who do you remember reading about during the last World Cup? Yes, got it. 'Wayne Rooney?'

Bingo, jackpot. I'm rewarded with a huge grin. Oh, he's adorable, this little boy; his two front teeth are missing and if you dressed him up in a cowboy outfit, he'd almost be a dead ringer for the Milky Bar Kid. He's closer to me now, watching me intently and I feel I'm slowly gaining his confidence.

'Were you in an accident?' I ask. I'm not even sure where that came from; all I'm doing is following my gut.

He doesn't say anything, just lifts up the Man U jersey and shows me a huge red scar on his little chest. An impact scar. Suddenly I think I know what happened to him. It was quick, it was sudden and it claimed more that one life – a woman, I'm seeing a young woman . . .

Oh my God, now it all fits.

'Ooh, you poor pet, I'd say that hurt. Did you feel anything? When the other car hit you?'

He shakes his head and looks all brave, the way little boys do when they're showing off a bit.

'You know what I think?' I ask as gently as I can.

He's almost beside me now, looking directly at me, unflinching.

'I think that your mummy misses you so much. There's nothing she'd love more than to see you again.'

I don't say anything for a bit, I just let that much sink in.

He's staring straight ahead now, frowning, looking all serious.

Suddenly he turns back to me and I swear I can see his eyes welling up a bit. His little nose must be runny too because he wipes it against the back of his sleeve.

Then I go for it. 'Would you like to see her? I could take you to her, but only if you want me to.'

I can see him thinking about it, but I'm pretty sure I know what the answer will be. He looks up at me and the hope in his eyes would almost break your heart. 'You've been stuck here for ages, haven't you?' I ask and he nods. 'And it must be getting kind of boring for you. Maybe it's time to move on. Would you like that? I could help you, if you'd let me.'

He doesn't react, but I take that as a good sign.

'All you need to do is sit down here beside me and be

very still and quiet for me. That's all. I promise. Can you do that for me?'

He nods, and suddenly I feel an ice-cold sensation against my hand. I look down. Oh my God, he's holding my hand. He's actually holding my hand. He trusts me, he really trusts me and he wants my help.

OK, Cassie, you can't let this poor little lost soul down now.

'Shh, shh.' I half whisper to him. 'It's going to be fine.' I close my eyes. I visualize a giant white staircase, with the spirits looking down, protecting this child from harm, willing and wanting him to come home.

'In love and light,' I murmur, 'in love and light and without disturbing the eternal peace of those who have passed, I call on this child's mother to help him into the light.'

The icy feeling on my hand gets colder and I look down to see that he's gripping it tightly now.

'Nothing scary.' I smile back down at him, 'Nothing to worry about. It's just like when they go to sorcery class in *Harry Potter*, that's all.'

He smiles that cute toothless grin. I think he knows he's on his way home. And that's when I start to get a sense of her. I can't see her, but I feel that she's beautiful, she's young; she's all dressed in white, with long fair hair and her arms outstretched, reaching out for her little boy who she hasn't had a chance to cuddle in the longest time. 'I think she's there,' I say to him. 'Can you see her?'

He nods and stands up, ready to go, ready to move on, wanting his mum.

'Go to her,' I whisper, 'pass through the light. That's all you have to do. It won't hurt, I promise you.'

Next thing, I feel that they're together. I just feel it; she's scooping him up in her arms and kissing the face off him and he's beaming and crying at the same time. It's as if neither of them can quite believe that this has happened, that they found each other again after all this time.

I wave and I feel that she's smiling at me and, without even being aware that I'm crying, I feel tears start running down my cheeks.

Next thing, I almost jump out of my skin. I can feel an icy lump pressing against my chest like a hard cold rock.

I look down, not sure what's happening. Oh my God. He's hugging me. He came back to give me a hug.

OK, now I ask for a sign, some tiny sign just so I'm sure that poor troubled little soul has finally moved on and is now, finally, at peace. I need to know that this worked. I *have* to know.

I'm not quite sure how much time passes, but after a while, the same cat I'd seen earlier squeezes through the door and comes straight into the room, makes for the bed and curls up into a snug, tight little ball. I close my eyes, say a silent 'thank you' and blow out all the candles.

It's just the weirdest thing. I pack up my bag, leave the room, and head back downstairs again. No, I'm definitely not imagining it, the whole atmosphere has changed. The place is warmer, mellower; where there was a cold, austere feel to this house, now it feels like a proper home again.

I hear voices laughing from the kitchen. Two women's voices. Which is odd.

I tap gently on the door and Mrs Henderson says to come in. There's another woman here, about the same age, sitting having a cup of tea at the kitchen table. I'm really happy to see it; I get a feeling that Mrs Henderson is a lady who hasn't had female companionship in a very long time.

Oh, and 'Orrible Oliver's here too, but then you can't have everything, can you?

'Cassandra, dear, sit down and let me get you some tea,' says Mrs Henderson, kindly pulling out a chair for me. 'You were up there for ages, wasn't she, Louise? At least an hour. Everything all right now, do you think?'

'Yes, Mrs Henderson, I think so,' I say simply, not wanting to go into too much detail, not when she has company.

319

Was I really there for that long? Bloody hell.

'Oh, let me introduce my new neighbour, who I've only just met myself. Louise, this is Cassandra. You know, *Tattle* magazine Cassandra.'

'Oh, it's so lovely to meet you,' says Louise, warmly shaking my hand. 'I'm a big fan, you know. In fact, you're the only reason I buy that awful magazine at all these days as quite frankly it's really gone down the tubes lately, all that malarkey about how celebrities stay rake thin and those "What's hot and what's not" lists. Honestly, as if your average reader cared about whether or not it's now uncool to be seen drinking double tall iced mocha frappucinos or whatever it is they're calling an old-fashioned cup of coffee now. Would you agree, Mrs Henderson?'

'Oh absolutely.'

'*Tattle* magazine used to have lovely knitting patterns and very easy-to-follow recipes in my day, but now Cassandra's column is the only thing worth reading at all. Am I right or am I right?'

'Completely. And please, call me Liz.'

'Liz.' The two of them beam at each other and it's lovely to see.

'So you live near by, Louise?' I ask, gratefully taking a mouthful of tea.

She nods. 'Right next door. I was just saying, it's very remiss of me not to have paid a visit earlier, but, it's a terrible thing to admit, I didn't really feel comfortable calling here after the awful tragedy that happened.'

'I'm sorry, what was that? What did you say?' says Oliver, suddenly all ears.

'They were a lovely family, you know,' Louise goes on. 'I remember them so well. The Jordans. She was absolutely delightful. Arty type – Oh, you know the sort, Liz, she used to go around without a bra. She was a painter and her little boy can't have been more than about six when that terrible car accident happened. Ethan was his name, a right little scamp, always in trouble, but you could never be angry with him because he was just so adorable.'

'What happened?' asks Oliver, being his usual persistent self. I say nothing, though I'm actually dying to know myself.

'Car accident. It happened on Christmas Eve; I'll never forget it. It was the lead item on the six o'clock news. Hit by a drunken driver, God love them; sure they never stood a chance. The poor husband was only heartbroken, you never saw grief like it. I think he had this house on the market first thing that January. Must be coming up to two years ago now.'

I say a silent prayer, just to say thank you that the poor woman and her lovely little boy, Ethan, are now, finally, at rest.

'And then it was just the strangest thing,' Louise goes

on. 'There I was, passing by your house this morning and, after all this time, I just got the strongest urge to pop in and introduce myself. I really hope you don't mind, Liz.'

'Of course not. I'm absolutely delighted to meet you. Call in any time.'

I'm not joking, Mrs Henderson actually looks as if a physical weight has been lifted from her shoulders and I'm just thinking how pleased I am to have been able to help her, when suddenly I get a flash. Ooh, it's a nice one.

I see Liz and Louise, bosom buddies now, at the airport on their way to New York for some Christmas shopping. The pair of them are happy as sandboys, especially Liz, who is just looking so delighted to have finally made one good, true pal. An ally, someone she can have a bit of fun with. And after everything she's put up with over the years, no one deserves it more. The pair of them are chatting and laughing away, planning all the discount stores they're going to hit and the Broadway shows they're going to see, all delighted with life, when suddenly Liz's mobile rings.

It's Gerry, her husband. I can see her looking at the number coming up, smiling quietly to herself and switching her phone off.

Hours and hours later, when I'm tucked up in bed, absolutely wrecked tired for some reason, my mobile gives a beep-beep noise to let me know there's a text coming through. 'Shit,' I say sleepily, hauling myself up and staggering over to wherever I dumped the phone. Forgot to recharge it, as usual.

I don't believe it: it's from Jack. Why is he texting me?

HEY. SORRY TO DISTURB U SO LATE. HOPE TODAY WENT OK. OLIVER WANTS TO USE SOME BREAKFAST CLUB FOOTAGE FOR HIS DOC, BUT I WON'T GIVE HIM THE GO AHEAD UNLESS U R HAPPY.

OK. Fine.
Right then.
He's just being professional, I know, I know, I know. It's my own stupid bloody eejit fault that this very busi-nesslike message is making my heart race.

I hop back into bed, remembering that Charlene is only in the bedroom right next door. Nothing else to do, really, is there? I delete the text, switch off my phone and fall straight back into a deep, deep sleep.

Chapter Twelve

THE TAROT DECK
THE DEATH CARD

OK, first of all, don't panic. Technically, yes, this card symbolizes an ending, but on the plus side it's also the card of renewal and transformation. A major event may unfold either in your life or in that of a close friend. It may feel traumatic, but in the long run the old lifestyle just wasn't valid any more. It wasn't working and a change was long overdue.

A time to let go of who- or whatever is holding you back and to embrace the new, looking forward confidently to the future. Even though things may be rough in the short term, remember that life can only get better. Think positive and don't give the past a backward glance.

In other words, sometimes what seems like the worst thing that could possibly happen often turns out to be the best. Honest.

From: lennoxamy@hotmail.com

To: Cassandra@tattlemagazine.com

Subject: From Hero to Zero

Dear Cassandra,

I've been a fan of your column for so long now that there was a certain sort of fated inevitability that I would one day contact you looking for advice.

OK, here goes. I'm old enough to wonder why I'm not married, young enough still to have kids (I hope) and am now in the throes of what feels like a mid-life crisis. I've even given myself a nickname: the One before the One.

At this point, it's almost like a self-fulfilling prophecy, Cassandra; every time I get seriously involved with a guy, he will inevitably end up marrying the one who comes along next. Every, every time. This has now happened so often that my friends are starting to ask me if I've been going after some kind of Olympic recognition all this time. Take my most recent ex, and you can publish the bastard's name for all I care and I only hope he reads this and is suitably mortified, it's Tom Kirwan of 28 Avondale Terrace, Bray, Co. Wicklow. There, I said it. Good enough for him. When I first met this guy, his idea of long-term faithfulness was to bed only one woman at a time and his contribution to a cleaner, greener environment was to make the same pair of underpants last four days. So, what did I do? What all the women's magazines, yours included, are constantly telling us never, ever works. I nabbed him, dragged him home and spent the best part of two years sanding down all his rough edges, scrubbing and polishing him until I had successfully moulded him into the image of my perfect life-partner. If this were a production of *My Fair Lady*, I'd be Henry Higgins and he'd be the Eliza Doolittle character.

And then, the curse of the One before the One strikes yet again. He breaks up with me and before I even have time to go through our CD/DVD collection to figure out what belongs to who, he's moved on to someone else. Who, subsequently, after a disgracefully short length of time, he marries. *Of course* the next woman who came along grabbed him for herself while the going was good; I had already done all the hard work for her. I had broken him in, housetrained him, if you will, and now all she has to do is sit back and enjoy the foot rubs and back massages which I taught him how to do. From pig to *Pygmalion.* I should go into business.

My question is this, O mighty Cassandra who everyone I know reads and raves about. When, when, oh when, will the curse be broken?

Yours in single-woman solidarity,
Amy Lennox, officially the unluckiest woman in Ireland

The office is deadly quiet and I'm really able to concentrate. It's not quiet because I'm at my desk at some ungodly hour of the morning, you understand, it's just that the Dragon Lady is in residence and the place is a humming hive of activity. Until lunchtime that is, when, with a bit of luck, she'll bugger off for a few hours and let us all get back to messing, chatting and having a bit of crack like we normally do.

Lately, the Dragon Lady has taken to having very long lunches and the highly overactive *Tattle* magazine rumour mill has it that she's seeing someone. Romantically, that is. All very new, all very hush-hush, but everyone keeps turning to me wanting gory details, as if I'm some kind of psychic private detective. I, however, have decided for once in my life that discretion is the better part of valour and that I've a far better chance of hanging on to my job by keeping my mouth shut. Plus, it's never really a good idea to 'out' your boss before he or she is ready, really, now is it?

Sir Bob wafts in and instantly cops on that she's here.

Mind you, the stone-cold silence *is* a bit of a giveaway. Normally at this hour of the morning we'd all be fruitfully employed watching TV, reading out each other's horoscopes and having our mid-morning contest to see who can eat a doughnut without actually licking their lips.

'Have some rather juicy gossip from last night, my dear,' he says to me in a low voice, drifting past my desk, 'but I'll tell you when we have a chance for a proper natter. My goodness me, the effect that dreadful Dragon Lady has on this establishment. Really, we should consider hoisting a flag outside the building so we can all be warned when she's in residence. Just as the royal standard is flown whenever Her Majesty is at Buckingham Palace, you know.'

I don't actually have the first clue what he's talking about, but I nod and smile anyway out of politeness and mentally remind myself to tell him about my adventures with Obnoxious Oliver when, suddenly, without warning, I get a flash.

Ooh, for once it's a lovely one. This is the kind of news I adore giving people.

It's Amy, the lady from the letter, and she's hand in hand with a guy on a beach ... somewhere in Ireland, I think, because it's freezing cold and drizzling rain ... but the sense of love and romance I'm getting is just palpable. Then – yes! He's

producing a ring box from his jacket pocket ... she's looking
stunned ... Oh my God, this is it, he's proposing! And the
funny thing is, I feel they know each other from a long, long
time ago ... I don't believe it! He's one of her exes. But not the
guy she wrote to me about, a different one, from her distant
past. And I feel he loved her doing a Henry Higgins number
on him, as she calls it, and missed her all the long years they
were apart and now he wants to spend the rest of his life
with her ...

There's nothing like a storybook ending, is there?
Can't beat it. Only wish I was heading for one myself.
I'm just about to scribble down my notes while it's all
fresh in my head when I get a scary sense that someone's
standing over my shoulder.

Oh shit.

The Dragon Lady. Looking very smart, actually, in
a black trouser suit; I'd almost swear she was wearing
tinted moisturizer and are they *heels* she has on?

'Cassandra, remember I asked you to get me the
contact details of that guy who phoned into your
Breakfast Club slot?'

There's never a preamble or, God forbid, a hello, good
morning, how are you, with her, just straight to the
point, direct as a missile.

'Emm, ehh . . .' I mumble, like a schoolkid who hasn't
done her homework, all the time thinking, What the hell

is she talking about? Bugger, bugger, bugger . . . Then I remember. Valentine. The guy who phoned into the *Breakfast Club* because he couldn't get a date. Who I got flashes of being pursued by scores of gorgeous women, a bit like in a Benny Hill high-speed chase sequence. Who I predicted would get his own column.

OK, so I didn't exactly see that it was with *Tattle* magazine but, bloody hell, I was close enough. I really will have to start writing things down.

'It's on my "to do" list, emm' – shit, why can I never remember her real name? – 'Amanda.' I smile, as brightly and confidently as I can. 'I'm just going to work my way through all of these,' I add, indicating the huge mound of unopened letters all marked 'Cassandra. *Tattle* Magazine', as if to remind her that I haven't exactly been sitting here scratching my head all morning. 'And then I'm straight on to it.'

'I want it done by the time I get back,' she says in such a tone that you can almost hear the unspoken 'dear'. She must be in pretty good form, though. Time was you'd have had the head chewed off you and found yourself threatened with the back of the dole queue for less, far, far less. 'Well, carry on, then,' she says, rapping her fingers on my pile of letters as she moves away.

Well, I'll be. She's even had a manicure.

OK, nothing for it then. I pick up the phone and dial directly through to the *Breakfast Club*'s production office.

Half-eleven. Great, they'll be off the air and, with a bit of luck, someone, somewhere will still have Valentine's contact details. His last name, for instance, would be a start.

The phone rings. 'Good morning, the *Breakfast Club*, Lisa speaking.'

'Hi, Lisa, it's Cassie here.'

'Cassie! Oh my GAWD! It's total serendipity that you're ringing just now! Wait till I tell you – Oh, do you have time for this? What the hell, I'll just tell you anyway while I have you there. So, I was in Lillie's Bordello till five a.m. this morning, came straight from there into work, and I met the most gorgeous guy. He's a quantity surveyor or something really boring like that, but hey, nobody's perfect, as I always say. Anyway, do you see anything in my future? With this fella, I mean? 'Cos I've been single for so long that I'm almost starting to wonder if dating is any different now and' – sounding a bit muffled now, as if she's put her hand over the receiver – 'no Jack, *I'm* talking to her, go away. This is important, you know, how often do I meet a nice suitable fella? OK, all right then, but don't hang up, you're to put Cassie straight back on to me. I'm in the throes of a dilemma here, I'll have you know.'

I barely even have time to take a deep breath before he's on the phone.

'Hi, Cassie, how are you? Did you get my text

message?' He sounds relaxed, at ease, much less stressed out than last time we spoke.

'Hi . . . yeah . . . yes, I did.'

'So how did you survive a day's shoot with Oliver, then? Prime Ministers have been reduced to gibbering wrecks. Bill Clinton has never been the same since, so they say.'

I giggle. 'It was . . . emm . . . It went well, but I don't know that Oliver got quite what he was looking for. The woman who owns the house we visited was a bit reluctant to have it filmed, you see.' The truth actually is, Oliver ended up not shooting anything at all. He stayed on after I left, chatting away to Liz and Louise, but that was about the height of it.

'You didn't answer my question. Did you survive?'

'Oliver was a bit . . . emm . . . how do I phrase this . . .'

'It's OK, you can tell me.'

Shit, what do I answer here? They could be best of friends for all I know. 'He's . . . well . . . he's very work focused, isn't he? I think he wanted it to be a little more . . . dramatic than it turned out to be.'

'Say no more. I get the impression he was looking for something along the lines of *Scary Movie* all right. But as long as you're happy about him filming you for his documentary, that's my main concern. He's asked to use some footage from the *Breakfast Club* and I just wanted to ask you if you're OK with that.'

There's a pause and I'm thinking, He's so sweet. I'm rarely asked how I feel about anything. People are always telling me how they feel about everything, but no one ever asks *me*. This is all new, very new.

'The thing is, Oliver is a very trusted reporter. He's a pro, Cassie. I think the piece is in pretty safe hands. Just say the word and I'll tell him you're fine with it and that he can continue with his documentary. Your wish is my command.'

I can't help smiling. God, I could stay all day on the phone to this guy. He's just so easy to chat to. It's a struggle, but, as ever, I have to keep reminding myself that he's unavailable, untouchable.

But that's OK. I don't fancy him anyway.

I never fancied him anyway . . .

No. No use. My multi-purpose catchphrase just won't work with this guy.

'So how's your day?' he asks, making me feel as if he's all the time in the world to chat.

Bugger, I almost forgot. 'Jack, can I ask a favour?'

'The answer is yes, what is the question?'

'Remember Valentine? The guy who phoned in?'

'Do I remember him? I don't think the phone lines here have stopped hopping since. All women looking for blind dates with him. Clever bastard, whoever he is, if you ask me.'

'My editor wants his contact number, if you'd have it.'

'By when?'

'By . . . emm . . . last Tuesday.'

There's a pause and I swear I can practically *feel* him grinning. 'Cassie, were you supposed to do this ages ago and you forgot?'

'Ehh . . . well, maybe. I am a very busy lady, I'll have you know,' I say primly. 'Just listen to this.' I pick up a bunch of letters, hold them to the phone and flick my fingers through them. 'They won't answer themselves, you know.'

He whistles. 'Very impressive. And your deadline is when?'

'Don't ask.'

'Don't worry, busy lady, I'll get Lisa on to it for you. By the way, I've a meeting later with the Director General to try and wheedle a bigger production budget out of him, so any psychic predictions on the outcome would be greatly appreciated . . . Oh, here we go, here comes trouble, she's back. Lisa, *I'm* talking to her. Your turn to go away.' *There's a muffled hand-over-the-receiver sound.* 'What? Downstairs?' I'd swear I can almost hear him sigh. 'OK, I'm on the way. Cassie, you still there?'

'Yeah, are you OK?'

'Looks like Charlene is waiting to see me downstairs. Look, I'll talk to you again. I really have to go.' He puts me back on to Lisa and is gone. And his tone completely changed too.

Much later in the afternoon, I get a message from Marc with a C, whose text messages sometimes run the length of one-act radio plays, as you'll see.

S.O.S. CHARLENE HAS OFFICIALLY BEEN DUMPED BY JACK. WE'RE IN RON BLACK'S BAR GETTING V. DRUNK. A STICKY-FLOORED DIVE BAR, I KNOW, BUT SHE WANTS TO AVOID MEETING ANYONE SHE KNOWS, NATCH. UR PRESENCE ISN'T SO MUCH URGENTLY REQUIRED AS DEMANDED. OH AND PLEASE BRING CASH. WE R SMASHED BROKE. SORRY. XXX

Shit.

Even though it hardly comes as a surprise, I still really feel for her. Anyway. Charlene is my friend and she's hurting and I should be there for her. I abandon my desk and the groaning pile of letters that's waiting for next week's column and I'm there in ten minutes.

The bar is dark and a bit dingy, but I immediately spot the pair of them, sitting on bar stools with a line of tequila shots in front of them, like in a saloon in the Wild West. No kidding, all this scene is missing is tinny piano music playing in the background, gunshots going off every few minutes and a blowsy chorus girl straight from Central Casting, with a name like Lottie-May, saying, 'Come up and see me sometime.'

'Hi, baby, thanks for coming,' says Charlene dully as I hug them both.

'So, how are you?'

'How *am* I? OK, part of me is crushed. Part of me is in mourning. But most of me is drunk. I have to face up to the sad fact that even Pamela Anderson makes better choices about her men than I do.'

'I have a new nickname for Jack Hamilton,' says Marc with a C, slurring his words slightly, but then he's super-fit, on a macrobiotic diet and therefore rubbish at holding his alcohol. 'Assanova. Whaddya think, Cassie? Do you like it? We've decided we all hate him now, although . . . ooh . . . I've just had a rare thought. Maybe he's gay. Or questioning. Did that ever occur to you?'

'Definitely not gay, sorry to disappoint,' I say, hauling myself up on to an incredibly uncomfortable bar stool beside them and ordering another round. 'Where's Jo?'

'Working late, on her way.'

'Will one of you please tell me' – Charlene's starting to blubber a bit. 'Why do I have this tendency/habit/compulsion to ruin my fabulous life?'

'Oh, come on, sweetie,' says Marc with a C. 'You have to admit that it was, at best, a blocked U-bend of a relationship. May I point out that you have spent the last few days bashing a square peg into a round hole. Fruitless and pointless. Don't throw good time after bad, baby. You're not getting any younger.'

'Shut up,' she snaps miserably at him. 'Don't you know the old adage: people in last year's Helmut Lang shouldn't throw stones.'

'Come on, hon,' I say, putting my arm around her comfortingly. 'We've all been there and we're all here for you. But remember you're not mourning the loss of a boyfriend, you're mourning the loss of how you thought your life would be. You have to stop beating yourself up. If it wasn't to be, it wasn't to be.'

What I really mean is, yes, it's awful, yes, it's painful, but trust me, even if she and Jack had actually been a proper item, it would never, ever in a million years have worked out. Lovely and fanciable and all that Jack is, Charlene is looking for someone who will plonk her on top of a pedestal and idolize her. No, scrap that, she actively *needs* someone who'll worship the ground she walks on. And ground her. And give her the one thing she craves more than anything, which the rest of us completely take for granted: a normal family life.

'Agreed,' says Marc with a C, taking another slug of tequila. 'What you're putting yourself through right now is like a brand-new form of torture the Geneva Convention should look at.'

'Do you know what he said to me?' says Charlene.

'That I was a lovely person but we were fundamentally unsuited.'

'Ugh, snap,' says Marc with a C. 'I got that speech too, about three . . . no, four exes ago. Bastard dropped me quicker than ten kilos of excess flab.'

'Remind me again who that was?' I ask, genuinely puzzled. In my defence, though, it's very hard to keep up with all of Marc with a C's ex files.

'Oh you remember, sweetie, he was in a band. Said he couldn't commit to me because he wanted to stay focused on the music.'

'Lousy excuse.'

'I know. I heard the music.'

'Can you please stop making this all about you?' Charlene snaps at him. 'Why does every little thing always have to be about you?'

I'm about to point out the irony of that statement to her, when I catch her looking at me funnily.

'Hang on, I just had a horrible thought. You don't think that Jack has met someone else, do you, Cassie?'

Thank God I'm not drinking because I'd have spluttered it out. Luckily enough, though, she doesn't let me answer.

'Because I'd scratch the bloody bitch's eyes out and that's not a threat. The only thing that's making this misery bearable is that while we both agreed we would officially part, we would still remain completely committed to each other. OK, so he didn't exactly agree and I may not have put it exactly like that, but one thing's for certain: I'm going to have a man on my arm to flash in front of him faster than a Britney Spears divorce.'

'Writ me baby one more time,' sings Marc with a C.

'Come on, guys, I need a man here and I need him *now*. What are my options?'

A long pause.

'Well, there's a speed-dating night at the gym next Saturday,' Marc with a C says helpfully.

'Thanks, but I think I'll just choose to pretend that I never heard you or your crap lonely heart suggestions. Do you even *realize* how much is wrong with that sentence? For God's sake, speed dating? Why can't I just meet someone the way normal people do? Through friends?'

'What's so awful about being on your own for a bit?' I ask hopefully. 'You've had a tough time of it lately, what with your father and Marilyn, I mean—'

'Subject change imminent,' Marc with a C interrupts. 'But our fabulously tactless friend here does make a point of sorts, Charlene. I mean, ricocheting from one guy to another is just going to look like a pathetic attempt to bolster up your shattered self-esteem.'

'So what are you suggesting? That I become a nun?'

'No, sweetie, you'd never be able to get your roots retouched.'

'And I wouldn't mind but Anna Regan's engagement party is looming like a giant iceberg in the shipping lane of my life, may she gag on a length of Cath Kidston ribbon.'

God, at times like this, I really wish Jo was here. She'd give Charlene all the tough love, relationship perspective and hard-headed advice she needs. And there's a chance Charlene might actually pay attention to her. Frankly, I'm beginning to feel as if I might as well be talking to the wall for all the progress I'm making in calming her down a bit or making her see sense.

Anyway, hours later, Marc with a C and I end up dragging a very drunk Charlene into a taxi and somehow getting her back to our house and into our kitchen, still in one piece. Marc with a C even manages to find a bottle of Baileys at the back of a cupboard, which is only ever produced in cases of dire emergency, and pours out a full, home-measured, tumbler-sized glass for her.

It's late, well after ten, before Jo eventually does get home and boy am I delighted to see her. 'Welcome to an episode of *The Jerry Springer Show*, broadcasting live from our kitchen,' I say, going out to the front door to let her in. We hug, both utterly exhausted.

'Is this my destiny?' Charlene is wailing from inside, clearly audible even though the kitchen door is shut tight. 'To live out a life of loveless, hopeless spinster-hood?'

'That bad, huh?' says Jo, taking off her coat and scarf and dumping a wad of files on the hall table.

'Listen for yourself.'

'And to think I can't even go to Harvey Nicks and charge myself happy, as I normally would. You know how much spending soothes my battered soul?' Charlene is bawling from inside, plastered and almost bordering on hysteria by now.

'Mmm,' says Marc with a C, hiccupping, completely and utterly smashed.

'I wish . . . do you know what I wish? I wish that I could just leave my body and become emotionally dead,' Charlene continues their duologue of pain. 'I mean, how much easier would life be?'

'Oh, for God's sake,' sighs Jo wearily. 'Things sure have changed here on Walton's mountain. So come on, Cassie, where do you stand on this, the biggest overreaction to the greatest non-relationship of the century?'

I just look at her, not sure what to say. Not even sure what I think. It's as if I haven't even allowed myself to think the thought.

'OK, let me offer a Jack Hamilton-related thought,' Jo says, cool as you like. 'You like him, he seems to like you. You're single and now, guess what, so is he. There was one insuperable barrier between you which has now, conveniently, been removed.'

'Jo! Number one, she just broke up with him and

number two, will you shut up? She's just inside. She'll hear you!'

'I haven't finished. So here's the biggie, here's what you have to go figure. When is it OK to date a friend's ex? And in a target-poor environment, with so many hot women and so few single men to date them, what is the statute of limitations on dating a friend's ex anyway?' She's warming to her theme and might even have started one of her great debates about this topic when the kitchen door bursts open and there's Charlene, swaying in the door frame.

'What are you two in cahoots about here?'

'Knitting patterns, what do you think?' says Jo, cool as a fish's fart. 'Is that Baileys you pair are drinking? Bloody hell, bad sign. That stuff only gets dragged out when you're really, really locked.'

Charlene ignores that. 'Girlies, my dearest friends, a thought has just struck me,' she says, swaying so much I actually think she might be in danger of falling over. 'I've just thought of the absolute, perfect shove-this-up-your-ass-Jack-Hamilton revenge guy for me to go out with next. Staring me in the face. Dunno why I didn't think of him before.'

Oh no, now I'm starting to get a sick feeling in my stomach.

'Oliver,' she says brightly. 'Remember? From yesterday,' she adds, as if I could ever forget him, the oily, smarmy git. 'Come on, Cassie, I know I didn't exactly take pains to get to know him, but that can easily be rectified. Can you find out discreetly if he's seeing someone? I mean, he's blond, overbearing and a pain in the arse. Just my type, if you ask me.'

Chapter Thirteen

THE TAROT DECK
THE KNIGHT OF SWORDS CARD, INVERTED

A good-looking guy, über-confident and ready for action. He's ambitious, single-minded and capable of ruthlessness to get exactly what he wants. You know, the type of man who'd be perfect in politics. He's also quite attractive to women and is well able to make them swoon over him. Half the time, he barely even notices, though, he's too focused on climbing the next rung of the career ladder. This is a man who stops for nothing and for no one.

If the card is inverted, then the querient must

be extra wary, particularly if she is female. Protect yourself, and if your heart and your head start screaming that you actually like this guy then mark these words: remember the card's warning and run very, very fast in the opposite direction . . .

'Hi, is that Cassandra? Am I really through to you?'

'Yes, go right ahead. What's your name?'

'Ehh, tell you what, seeing as how this is live TV, why don't you just call me . . . emm . . . Jane. Although I stress my actual name is something considerably more exotic.' South Dublin accent. Nasal twang.

'OK, Jane, go right ahead.'

Well, fair play to her, I'm thinking. At least she didn't bother to lie.

I can hardly believe they've invited me back so soon, so much has happened since I was here last. But here I am, over-made-up, primped and preened with my hair curled from here to France, sitting on the *Breakfast Club* canary-yellow sofa, match-fit and ready for action.

Long story, but basically the make-up guy with orange fake tan on his face, Damien, who I met on my first day here, is just back from a few days' holiday in Greece, where he met someone really cute and interesting and foreign, with biceps like a hod-carrier, or so it seems. Anyway, he was particularly anxious to tell me the whole story, because he'd just come through a rotten break-up and apparently I predicted a happy outcome for him, so he said if he put me in rollers and backcombed my hair a bit, then we could prolong our chat. We had a great aul' gossip and a laugh. The only tiny drawback of having sat in a make-up chair for so long is that now my hair is so absurdly sculpted, it looks a bit like a six-year-old's drawing of a ski slope.

Anyway, back to work. This is, I think, the fifth call of the morning and I'm getting flashes all over the place. I feel great, I feel confident and really on top of my game. And no sign of Jack so far, which always helps.

Well, which always helps if I want to see anything and actually do what I'm being paid for, that is.

And Charlene was way too wrecked and hungover after the excesses of last night even to think about physically leaving the house and coming into Channel Seven with me this morning, which is helping even more considerably.

With a bit of luck, she wasn't serious about making a play for Oily Oliver. It was just drink talking, that's all. She probably won't even remember. When she sobers up, that is.

'Solpadeine? That's all you have, *Solpadeine*?' she growled at me as she fished through our bathroom cabinet at the crack of dawn this morning with a pink furry sleep mask on her forehead that says 'Total

Princess'. (What else?) I was trying to get organized for work and instead of rolling over for her second sleep, as she normally would, she followed me into the bathroom in search of pain relief.

'Trust me, just take two,' I said, whispering, so as not to wake Jo. 'You only got to bed about an hour ago so your hangover mightn't even have kicked in yet. And keep your voice down.'

'Why are you shouting at me?' she wailed at me.

'SHH!'

'There, you're doing it again. Rule one in the ten commandments of being a friend. Thou shalt have something stronger than these' – she waved the Solpadeine threateningly under my nose – 'in your medicine cabinet for guests who may have over-imbibed just the teeniest bit the previous night. Jesus, I might as well eat a box of Tic Tacs.'

'Will you please *shut up*,' I whispered hoarsely. 'Jo may not have superpowers but she can still hear you. Now, if you have a problem with what's in our bathroom, I suggest you take it up with your pharmacist.'

Anyway, back to studio.

'Hello, hello, hello, anyone there? Cassandra? Can you hear me OK?' Jane is saying and I can hear the wind whistling down her mobile phone, as if she's calling me from . . . a rooftop? Could that be right?

'Yes, I can just about hear you, go ahead.' I have to stop

myself from saying, 'I'm listening,' like a radio phone-in shrink. Like Doctor Ruth.

'Right. Now, I had to pretend to everyone in the office that I was going outside for a cigarette break. So if I hang up suddenly, it doesn't necessarily mean that I've lost interest in whatever you say, it just means that someone else came out here and I don't want them to know that I'm speaking to you.'

OK, a direct woman. Fine, this I can handle. 'So what's bothering you, Jane?'

'Can I ask you a question? Do you ever get fed up with women ringing you to moan about men? Or maybe you're businesslike about it and look on it much the way I would. Single women and their relationship dilemmas are probably what's keeping you in Prada dresses and Hermès handbags, whilst me and all the rest of humanity have to suffer the indignity of going on waiting lists to get our paws on anything "must have", in the true A-list sense of the word. I mean, honestly, waiting for handbags. How Soviet.'

I look across the sofa to Mary and Mary looks back to me and we both smile weakly at the camera. There's no answer to that one – well, at least nothing that won't insult half the nation.

'I'm more of an M and S woman myself,' says Mary, a bit feebly.

'And the only label I'm wearing today is drip dry,' I

add, trailing off lamely. God, this one is beginning to sound almost . . . rude.

'OK, Cassandra, time is money so I'll cut straight to the chase. Three essential details I can give you about my character, whilst observing the need to protect my own privacy. One. I work as an investment banker in the Financial Services Centre and am therefore both rich and eligible. Two. I'm a size eight by inclination rather than by girth, but my therapist tells me I would still be considered very attractive by men, if a little high-maintenance. Three. I recently celebrated a very significant birthday, which I won't elaborate on, at least not over the national airwaves.'

Forty, I think. You just turned forty.

'And the man that I've been seeing came to the dinner party I was hosting for a small, very select group of friends, clients and well-wishers and he presented me with – now wait for it – *nothing*. Big Fat Nothing. My therapist says that any guy who has the sheer brass neck to turn up at my dinner party empty-handed, knowing full well what day it was and knowing the potential embarrassment this would cause, has clearly lost all interest in me. And I wouldn't mind, but the financial director of Deutsche Bank was there to witness my humiliation. Anyway, the theory seems to be that if a so-called boyfriend ignores either Valentine's Day or your birthday for whatever pathetic reason, then get out at once.'

OK, now I'm beginning to see a potential problem ahead with this caller.

'So, to distil my query down to its bare essentials. As a banker I would instinctively always weigh up investment versus return. Having invested three full months in this relationship, apart from some particularly non-memorable meals out and some frankly boring evenings in, my return has been, in short, niggardly. So, when do I decide to cut my losses and move on?'

Potentially a *huge* problem.

'I should say that, ordinarily, Cassandra, I would be the last person alive ever to debase myself by phoning a psychic on some housewives' choice TV show. Is that middle-aged frumpy one still presenting it? God, has that woman ever met a flowery-patterned dress she didn't like?'

Now I can sense poor Mary's feathers starting to ruffle. And, honestly, would you blame her?

'It's just that I've heard some of the girls in my office reading your column and giving quite glowing reports of you, Cassandra. Mind you, none of them is actual *office* staff – well, apart from one receptionist who seems to do nothing all day except read *OK* magazine and surf the net. No, I'm referring to the canteen staff and the cleaners. You know, as you say in television, lowest-common-denominator types. But I suppose they're your target market really, are they not?'

OK, here it is. Not only is being psychic not something that's on tap, twenty-four/seven, there's something else. Something that's a little harder to put into words. There are rare occasions, very rare I hasten to add, where someone will come to me looking for advice or wanting a particular question answered and I can't do it, I just can't. I can be polite about it and put my complete failure to see anything down to any number of things – that I'm having a bad day, say, or I'm just a bit fuzzy about what lies ahead – but it's really all just a little white lie to cover up the awful, painful truth: if I take a strong dislike to someone, I can't see a blessed thing for them. Absolutely nothing.

Now, as I say, thankfully this doesn't happen too often, but I'm only human and I'm unable to work around negativity. Simple as that. Thankfully it hasn't happened to me in a long, long time, but by God it's happening this morning . . .

'Cassandra?' says Bossy Cow, her voice ringing around the studio floor, almost squeaky with impatience. 'Are you still there? Hello? Earth to Cassandra?'

OK, now I actually want to smack her. How *dare* she speak to me or anyone like this? Even patient, kind-hearted Mary is starting to make who-exactly-does-this-one-think-she-is? faces across the comfy sofa at me.

Right, deep breath. Invoke my emergency escape clause. 'Jane, I'm very sorry about that.'

'I've heard of a ten-second delay in live broadcasting, but never one that drags on for a full minute. I'm going to need an answer here, Cassandra. I'm out on a blustery rooftop in my good Versace silk shirt, freezing my ass off, and it's starting to drizzle.'

'Jane? I hate to tell you, but I'm afraid I can't help. I can't see anything. Sorry, but there it is.'

There. Said it. Did that sound firm and clear, without a trace of the unspoken 'because I've taken an instant dislike to you and I couldn't really give a shite about you or your love life, I'm just thankful that I don't know you socially, or, worse, that I have the misfortune to work for you'? I hope it did but I'm afraid not.

Mary is looking at me in shock and so, I notice, is the floor manager. There's a horrible pause. Then Jane's voice reverberates around the studio. 'Nothing? Did you say you can't see *anything*?'

'Yes, I'm afraid so.'

'Not a wedding ring, not even an engagement ring? A pregnancy? Even an unplanned one?'

'Jane, I can't help you. I'm sorry but that's all there is to it.' I glance imploringly over to our floor manager, hoping he'll cut to a commercial break, but Jane's not done with me yet, or so it seems.

'Look, Cassandra, I contacted you in good faith, mainly because of the positive word of mouth I've heard about you, but how can you sit there and have the

CHEEK to refer to yourself as some kind of twenty-first century soothsayer, when— Oh hi, James!' My God, in a nanosecond her tone has totally changed from snarl to simper. No kidding, this one is wasted in the Financial Services Centre when her true vocation is clearly on-stage in the Abbey Theatre. 'Yes, just came outside for a quick puff! So how *are* you? You look *absoluuuuutely* terrific, have you been working out?' Then a beep–beep sound. Then she's gone.

She hung up on me. I do *not* believe it. The rude cow just hung up.

This time there's an embarrassed pause, but Mary's on the ball, and thank God one of us is.

'Stay with us, we'll be right back with more from Cassandra after the break,' she says smiling to camera. 'Don't go away!' And we're out.

'Everything OK?' says the floor manager, coming over to me, finger on his headpiece as if he's just been talking to the production box. 'Jack says if you want to leave it at that for today, there's no problem. He says to tell you we have a particularly gripping outdoor piece on an environmentalist who lives in a self-contained eco-friendly pod that we can cut to, so we're not stuck for time.'

Great, now Jack thinks I've totally lost it. An eco-friendly *what*?

'Sorry, what's that?' the floor manager asks, talking into

his earpiece. 'Jack is asking if you'd like him to come on to the floor, just to see that you're OK.'

'NO! Sorry, I mean, no, no, please tell him not to bother. I mean ... emm ... I'm grand, could you tell him I'll see him later, if that's OK.'

'No prob, he just wants to make sure everything's fine with you,' he says, relaying the message back to his headset.

'Thanks. Promise, I'll be grand for the next call.'

'No worries.' Then he comes right over to the sofa I'm perched on and whispers to me. 'You know, I may not be psychic, but if you ask me, I think Jack likes you. Normally you can't drag him out of that production box during a transmission for love nor money.'

I try not to blush, reminding myself that I am (a) a grown adult with (b) a camera pointing directly into my face *which he can see me on*.

'Well, that Jane one wasn't a very pleasant lady at all, was she?' says Mary, still smarting from the 'frump' comment, poor thing.

'That's putting it mildly.'

'Cassie, can I ask you something? Did you see something really awful in store for her? Is that why you decided to say nothing again, love? Did you not want to upset her, live to the nation? Very nice of you, I'm sure. I'd gladly have taken that little madam down a peg or two. Imagine her calling me middle-aged. And I wouldn't mind but I'm only forty-seven. Since when is that middle-aged, I'd like to know?'

'Can you keep a secret?' I ask, smiling at her.

'No, but go on anyway.'

I drop my voice to a whisper. 'When I don't like someone, I blank out. Completely.'

'Really?'

'Doesn't happen often, but when it does, I'm worse than useless. Now, I could have sat here and told that one a load of drivel like, ooh, I dunno, some kind of needlepoint philosophy like "When you meet the right man for you, you'll just know", or "Trust to fate and destiny", but I resorted to plan B. Just apologize, tell the truth and say, "Sorry, as far as your future is concerned, I'm blind as a bat".'

Mary laughs. 'I don't know how you didn't tell her where to go. Though that's the trouble with live telly, isn't it? Do you know, I'm almost twenty years at it and I'm still regularly surprised by people and what they come out with. Amazed, more often than not. Ooh, looks like we're back.'

I look over my shoulder at a floor monitor, just in time to see the *Breakfast Club* logo reappearing on screen: a steamy, frothy, half-drunk mug of cappuccino and a croissant with a big nibble taken out of it, all shot against a bright yellow and red background, cartoon-animation style. And then ... Oh shit, no ... Am I seeing things?

Squinting through the darkness, beyond the camera and towards the back of the studio, I can just about make out Oily Oliver. And he seems to be filming everything that's going on, good luck to him.

But that's not what's bothering me. Standing right beside him, looking fabulous and not hungover as a dog as rightfully she should be, as she did not two hours ago, is Charlene. I barely have time to react before we're back on air.

'Thank you, welcome back,' Mary is glowing to camera, 'and I think we just have time for one more call, if that's all right with you, Cassandra love?'

I nod, dumbly. What the hell is she doing here?

No, no, she can't have been serious about what she said last night, about Oliver being just her type, that was just drink talking . . . wasn't it?

Wasn't it?

'Yes, we have Emily on line four. Good morning, Emily, you're through to Cassandra.'

Come on, Cassie, eye on the crisis.

I have a hunk of credibility to regain after that last disastrous call. Plenty of time for Charlene and whatever mini-drama she's playing out when we're off the air.

'Hello, is that Cass–Cass–Cassandra?'

Oh my God, it's a little girl's voice. Definitely. I can see her straight away. She's wearing glittery jeans and a fleecy pink tracksuit top with a big 'E' pendant around

356

her neck. And I'm picking up an overwhelming feeling of sadness.

'Hi, Emily.'

'I like your name, Cassandra.'

'You have a pretty name too. How old are you, sweet-heart?'

Treat her like a grown-up, Cassie, kids respond better to that.

At least, I think they do . . .

'I'm eight and three-quarters.'

I whistle. 'Birthday soon?'

'Yeah. And I'm getting my ears pierced and heelies.'

'Why aren't you at school, Emily?' Mary asks, all worried, and I can't believe I never thought of asking the child that question myself. Spot the non-parent.

'I'm sick. I couldn't sleep all night and today my throat hurts.'

'Emily,' I say slowly, 'does your mummy know that you're calling me?'

'She's in work.'

'And your dad?'

'He doesn't live with us any more. Though I see him sometimes and he always buys me treats.'

'So who's there with you?'

'Ulrika.'

'Who's that?'

'My minder. She was watching you on TV and she

says that you can do magic. She's upstairs now talking to her boyfriend on her mobile so that's why I'm ringing you. She's always on the phone to her boyfriend. All the time.'

Mary and I just look at each other.

'Is everything OK, Emily?' I ask, gently as I can.

'No.'

'Is there something that's making you a little bit sad?'

'Mmm.'

'Will you tell me?'

'OK. It's just . . . I'm a bit scared.'

'Scared of what, sweetheart?'

'Well . . . you see, there's a bogeyman in my bedroom and I hate our new house that me and my mummy live in now. I want to go back to our old house where Daddy is so they can be together and I can have my old room and there's no bogeyman under the bed but I told Mummy when I was scared last night and she said I was silly and that we're not going back. She said, "No way, we have to stay here." But I don't like it here. I want to go home.'

OK, I may not be a child psychologist, but I think I can figure out what's happening here.

Go easy, Cassie, remember she's only a kid – who might just be having a tough time dealing with her parents' separation.

'Emily, can I let you into a little secret?'

'Yeah. I like secrets.'

'Are you listening?'

'Mmm.'

I lean as close to my radio mike as I can. 'There is no such thing as the bogeyman. He doesn't exist.'

'What about ghosts?'

'Anyone who believes in ghosts is a big silly pants.'

'Do you promise me?' comes the little voice, sounding a little bit stronger now. 'Pinkie promise?'

'I pinkie promise.' Whatever that is. 'New houses can just be a bit scary in the beginning, Emily, that's all, pet. Once you get used to it, you'll be just fine. Hey, and I'll bet you'll make loads of new friends really soon. Wait till they all see you going up and down the road on the fab new heelies you're getting!'

'Thank you,' she says in her little voice and, honest to God, I just want to hug her.

'No more bogeyman?'

'No. Can I go out and play now? My sore throat is all better.'

'Course you can, sweetheart. You take care now!'

'Well, I'm sorry to interrupt, Cassandra, but I'm afraid that's all we have time for today,' says Mary, on a wrap-it-up hand signal from the floor manager. 'Thanks so much for tuning in and see you all tomorrow, bright and early!'

And we're out.

I say my goodbyes to Mary and all the rest of the

crew and look down to the back of the studio where Charlene is flirting her ass off with Oliver. I do not believe her; she's even wearing my good Karen Millen strappy evening shoes. At ten in the morning.

I unclip my radio mike and stride down to her.

'Hey, sweetie, here comes my favourite client. Well, OK, my only client, but, hey, I'm working on it. You were so fab! Wasn't that little kid who rang in just so adorable? Hey, I wonder if the dad is single?'

I, however, am not really in the form for pleasantries.

'Great, great slot, love it, went really well,' Oliver simpers at me in the awful American accent, and I give him a curt nod. It did *not* go really well and he's a lying toady git.

'Wanna know some hot gossip?' says Charlene. 'Oliver has very kindly agreed to come to Anna Regan's engagement party with me! I just asked him and he said yes! So are you stunned? I hope you don't expect too much now, Oliver,' she says, turning back to him in full-on flirtation mode, and I'm not kidding, her breasts are pushed up all the way from here to Ontario. 'It'll just be your average one-hundred-thousand-euro-soirée in the ballroom of the Four Seasons, that's all.'

'It's my pleasure. Hey, can't wait.' He smirks at her. 'Say, do you mind if I . . .' He indicates the camera beside him and carries on filming whatever the hell it is he's filming.

I don't know and I don't care.

Keep the head, Cassie, just stay cool . . .

I ask Charlene to walk me to my car, couching it in such a way that she can't say no. I really need to get the hell out of Dodge before Jack appears and I find myself stuck in whatever warped daytime soap-opera plot she has up her sleeve. Jesus, at times like this, I *really* could kill her.

I walk and she totters behind me all the way down the long corridor which leads to reception and on outside to the car park. We're almost at my car before I can even bring myself to speak to her. I do my best to keep my tone calm and measured, mainly because this always works better with her. And by that I mean you've a fifty per cent better chance of getting through to her.

'Charlene, please would you mind telling me what is going on with you? Why are you here?'

'Honey, I'm your agent. Didn't I promise you that by the time I'm finished revamping your career, you'll be so famous you'll end up as the centre square in *Celebrity Squares*?'

'*Charlene?*'

'OK, OK, don't get so narky. Let's all just be really grateful that this time I bounced back as quickly as I did from heartache. Thank God I'm an Aquarius, that's all I can say. You know how it normally takes me months and months to heal from the pain of broken relationships.'

'Name one occasion where that happened.'

'Well . . . emm . . . ehh . . . Oh, leave me alone. I will not belittle this with tawdry examples.'

'Please tell me that you're not doing what I think you're doing.'

'If getting a date for Anna Regan's big engagement night makes me some kind of monster then guilty as charged. I have downgraded my pain at being so unceremoniously dumped from "No man will ever love me" to "Ooh I think I'll put on Mac eyeliner and face the day", and you should be *proud* of me. Why are you being such a headgirl about this, anyway?'

'Because you're embarrassing yourself. And you're embarrassing me.'

'Oh, *listen* to you.'

'Are you honestly telling me that this was the only place you could go to in the entire metropolis, surfing for a date?' And stinking of booze, I could add, but I choose not to be bitchy.

'There's only one reason why you're being like this about the whole thing,' she snaps back.

'Enlighten me.'

'Well, this will make *two* of your colleagues I've dated now. And you're still Little Miss Can't-get-arrested-hasn't-had-a-date-in-a-year. Little Miss Oh-I-never-fancied-him-anyway.'

OK, now I really wish I had hit her with the stale booze line. That hurt. That really stung.

However, I take a deep breath and do my best to keep cool. 'Charlene, frankly you can bring a gibbon monkey with you to the engagement party for all I care. My problem is that you've asked *Oliver*. And he's awful. And he works with Jack and that's the only reason you're even doing this in the first place. Teenagers in Wesley would blush to be seen carrying on like this. What – do you think, in the warped parallel universe you're living in, that this will somehow make Jack jealous? That he'll be hit with a road-to-Damascus moment and suddenly want to be with you? What are you, headless?' I'm raising my voice now and I can't help it. I'm out-and-out furious with her now.

'Aren't you at least thankful that I've bounced back? Do you realize that I told that bastard Jack Hamilton not to call me and, damn him, he hasn't?'

'Charlene, this isn't something I get to say very often, but Oliver is not good enough for you. You yourself called him a pain in the arse, only last night.'

Yes, I know I did wish him for her, but . . . well, that was before I found out what he was really like and . . . well . . . that just comes under the heading: We all make mistakes, don't we?

'Oliver is single and he has a job. So, therefore, he passes the Charlene test. Why am I even talking to you, anyway? You're not my target audience.'

'Will you just *listen*? I'm getting a bad vibe from that guy and it's not just that he's so bloody irritating. It's more. Much more. He's just . . . I can't put it into words, he's . . . not what he seems.'

'Fab, even better. Naughty boys need love too, you know.'

Oh shit, there's no point in even talking to her. She'll just go her own sweet way no matter what I do or say.

'OK, Charlene, fine. Flirt your ass off with him. Go out with him if that's what you want. Whatever blows your skirt up.'

'Glad you finally see it my way.'

I'm just about to get into my car but she follows me to the driver's door.

'Oh, and one final tip for you, honey: this is happening whether you like it or not. Suck it up.'

That's the other thing about Charlene. She is always expert at getting the last word in.

Chapter Fourteen

THE TAROT DECK
THE PAGE OF CUPS CARD

A youngish person, usually male. He's good humoured and happy-go-lucky, invariably in top form, one of those people who just always seem to be delighted with life, whatever it may throw at them. This guy may be on the brink of starting a new career, which will be garlanded with great success. For a woman to draw this card means that you're about to make a new best friend. He's definitely in the friend category, this is not a lover, but he'll be just lovely, everything you could wish

**for in a mate; he's full of fun, and together you'll
have such a laugh.**

**This card symbolizes that a lucky man will
enter your life. And as the old saying goes, better
born lucky than born rich . . .**

For once I'm actually delighted to get into the office
and put Charlene and her antics behind me. I make a
mental note to phone Jo and arrange to meet her for
lunch, mainly so I can let off steam before we get back
to the house and face into yet more histrionics. Bloody
hell. This sure as hell feels like a high karmic price to pay
for fancying her ex.

Anyway, onwards and upwards. Have to put her out of
my head. I've a full day's work to get through.

The minute I step out of the lift and head into the
office, I immediately sense that there's something up.
God, the place is really buzzing, Sir Bob is here, Lucy
from Features and Sandra Kelly, our resident restaurant
critic (ringlety red wig today, which makes her look
very Nicole Kidman in her Tom Cruise days, by way of
Little Red Riding Hood). Anyway, the gang of them are
all clustered around the desk beside mine, over by the
window.

'And here's our resident televisual star,' says Sir Bob, in
that cute way he has of making it sound as if television
was only invented yesterday. God only knows how he

ever came to terms with the internet or mobile phones or the three-pin plug. 'Come over, dear, there's someone we'd like you to meet.'

They part like the Red Sea and there he is.

'Cassandra, this is Valentine. Valentine, meet Cassandra.'

Ooh, here we go . . .

Now I see what all the fuss is about. OK, so he may not be good-looking in a movie-star way, more cuddly in an introduce-him-to-your-mammy way, but he's incredibly attractive, really tall, light brown hair, twinkly blue eyes and a lovely warm smile.

'Ah, now, the famous Cassandra,' he says, standing up to shake my hand and making direct eye contact – and it's for real and not a put-on act, like some people do. (Well, when I say some people, I'm really referring to the professional slick-ass type of guy that's out there, namely Oliver. *Ugh.*)

'Sure, if it wasn't for you, I wouldn't even be here in the first place.' Valentine smiles warmly at me. 'You're like my lucky star, so you are.'

I laugh, instantly liking him and his gorgeous soft West of Ireland accent. You know how sometimes you meet new people and you feel as if you've known them for years and years? There's a theory that when this does happen, it's usually because your paths *have* actually crossed somewhere before, in a past life. Well, I dunno, who's to say? Maybe Valentine and I were slaves manacled together in ancient Egypt building the pyramids or something. Frankly, who cares. He seems like a lovely guy, I get a great feeling about him and – let's be honest – sweethearts like him are fairly thin on the ground in this city.

'Welcome to the wonderful world of *Tattle*,' I say, grinning at him. 'It sucks; you're going to love it.'

'And if there's anything we can help you with, *please* let me know,' Lucy purrs at him, eyelashes batting like butterfly shutters on a digital camera. She might as well have a thought balloon coming out of her head, like you see on cartoons, that says, 'Let me pinch you; you're not real!'

'Hey, maybe we could take you out after work?' says Sandra hopefully. 'You know, just to celebrate your first day here. I know a great Italian place, Dunne and Crecenzi's, *the* best arrabiata in town, without question, no dress code, very relaxed ambience—'

'Or else I just got an invitation to a fashion show this evening,' says Lucy, determined not to be outdone. 'It's in CHQ, which is like this wayyyyy cool venue and there's an after-show party . . .' She trails off and this time her thought balloon is saying, 'Wait up, hang on, get smart; if it's a fashion show there will be models there, models equal competition; do I really want to introduce this hunk of West of Ireland gorgeousness to other attractive women?'

'Or we could take you to a rather interesting gallery opening I've been asked to tonight,' says Sir Bob, and I'm thinking, *Et tu*? God, if you're a single man in this city, all you really have to do is pick and choose. Gay, straight, whatever your preference really.

Anyway, I don't have any glamorous invitations to throw into the mix – well, apart from coming back to the madhouse I live in to chance his arm with Charlene's cooking. Plus the cat fight we'll most likely have later on. No, not a very tempting offer.

'Ah, you're awful good,' says Valentine, smiling his big twinkly-eyed grin at them all. 'But, sure, would you look at the amount of yokes I'm after getting asked to just this evening alone.' He picks up just one invitation from a groaning pile on the desk and reads it aloud. '"You are cordially invited to an event to mark the launch of AROMATHERAPEE, our stunning new range of bathroom fragrances, for him and for her. Clarence Hotel, six p.m"'.

'Goodness me,' says Sir Bob, 'bathroom fragrances, what on earth can that be?'

'Posh word for air freshener?' says Sandra helpfully.

'Or toilet bleach?' I offer.

'Then I've to go to speed dating at eight,' says Valentine, wading through yet more gilt-edged invites, 'and I'm supposed to be at the Comedy Cellar at eleven to see a comedy improvisation troupe or something.

Apparently the girls that perform in it are all single too. Honest to God, lads, I don't know how I'll last the pace. And Ireland are playing Cyprus tonight and all, so I'll have to fit that in somewhere too. Jaypurs, I'll be lucky if I'm still standing by the end of the night.'

'Soccer? Really, how interesting,' says Sir Bob, smiling politely but (I sense) losing all interest in the conversation.

'Piranha in the tank!' Lucy squeals as a text message comes through from the receptionist at her desk outside by the lift to let us know the Dragon Lady is on her way in. 'Quick, back to work!'

We all scatter to the four winds and poor Valentine is left looking a bit lost.

'I'll explain to you later,' I whisper, plonking down at my desk and whipping off my jacket to make it look as if I've been hard at work for ages. 'Nothing to worry about. Just our editor on her way in. She'll probably go easy on you 'cos it's your first day.' I almost have to laugh at how bewildered he looks.

'Piranha in the tank?' he asks me.

'Yeah, it's our code word for "Get back to your desk and look as if you're actually doing something for a change." Kind of like those early-warning systems they have in military bases. Of course, normally she would send ahead her team of flying monkeys.'

'Oh right.'

'Valentine! I'm messing!' Aw, I'm thinking, you should just see him. He looks so adorably cute when he's thrown in at the deep end like this: one of those guys who just brings out the nurturing side in women. Honestly, all you want to do is bring him home and feed him a big meat and potato dinner.

Anyway, in bursts the Dragon Lady, in a very fetching bright red Chanel-type jacket, the first time I think I've ever seen her actually wearing a colour and not head-to-toe in black. She spots him instantly with that radar she has and is over like a bullet.

'You must be Valentine. Come this way,' she says, walking right past him without stopping. He looks imploringly at me and I make a face that he should follow her into her inner office/lair of the she-wolf/torture chamber, and off he goes, with every female eye in the office following after him.

The oestrogen level in the office drops considerably the minute he's out of sight, and the silence helps me think. OK, so I know I saw tons of single women all hurling themselves at Valentine like brickbats and, yes, that's still most definitely on the cards. For the foreseeable future. In the short term. But I can't help wondering if, further down the line, he might just turn out to be a nice fella for our Jo . . . Mmm, the plot thickens . . .

Anyway. To work. You should just see the amount of

letters waiting for me. And not only that, but there's a yellow Post-it sticker from the lads down in the dispatch department that says, 'Cassandra, this represents only about 40 per cent of the letters that arrived for you. Can't fit the rest of them on your desk.'

Bloody hell. That's not even including the emails. Ho hum, that's the power of television for you.

Right, concentrate. OK, computer on. I will remember that I'm a serious focused working professional and will resist the temptation to check out my favourite website: www.lastminuteholidays.com

I do not believe this. Fifty-seven emails waiting for me. *Fifty-seven*. I seriously do not get paid enough and will definitely ask the Dragon Lady for a pay rise next time I'm feeling (a) kamikaze enough or (b) am just slaughtered drunk and will do just about anything.

I randomly click on one from my mum, which was just sent this morning.

From: mothership@hotmail.com
To: Cassandra@tattlemagazine.com
Subject: Opening night!

Hello darling,

You were great on the telly this morning; although I had my heart in my throat when you told that rude caller you couldn't see anything. Margaret was here and she said it served her right. By the way, she says to tell you the operation on her veins was 100% successful and to thank you so much for telling her she'd be grand. She's here beside me now telling me you were dead right, the surgeon was a Pisces with dark eyes and from Ghana.

Anyway, love, just to remind you that the opening night of the musical society show is the weekend after next, on Sunday. I'll put you down for four tickets, for you and all your friends. It's *The Sound of Music* this year, you'll remember, and I'm playing two parts, third nun and elegant lady at the von Trapps' party. We had to get a professional singer to play Maria, you know yourself, because unfortunately that character holds the whole show together really, and you've no idea how difficult it is to find someone who not only looks right but who can sing and dance AND act. Triple threat, as our director Mrs Nugent says.

Margaret feels very strongly about this, though, because she IS a trained soprano and feels she would have been absolutely perfect in the part. Sure, under stage lights and in that hall where the front row is miles away from you, anyone can look early twenties if you ask me.

Anyway, I'm going back to make the costumes. The nuns' habits are a doddle but we're having a nightmare with the Nazi uniforms. Much love to our little princess and I'll see you at the show!

Mum xxx

Thank God she emailed to remind me. I had *totally* forgotten. Memo to self: be less scatty and remember to prioritize family commitments.

Then another email catches my eye but for very different reasons.

From: thenationalghostconvention@aol.com
To: Cassandra@tattlemagazine.com
Subject: Guest speaker

Dear Cassandra,

Firstly please excuse my writing to you care of the magazine you work for, but unfortunately I didn't know how else to contact you. As a like-minded person, it is my great pleasure to invite you to our inaugural 'Ghost Convention', this Halloween, October 31.

At this point I have to stop and rub my eyes in disbelief. There's a National Ghost Convention?

We've chosen the eerie Kilmainham Jail in Dublin as the

ideal venue because of the number of reported sightings, which have included nineteenth-century prisoners and guards mingling with the tourists. In what promises to be a highly 'spirited' affair, guest speakers – including witches, wizards, psychics such as yourself and academics – will gather we hope to swap ghost stories and, as the song lyric goes, 'break on through to the other side.'

We're particularly excited as, to mark our convention, we have been asked to nominate a guest for a Halloween special on television. The *Late Night Talk* show, to be exact. Dear Cassandra, we would be deeply honoured if you would consider appearing on our behalf. You already have such a wonderful television profile, which would be a huge asset to us.

May I add on a personal note that through your highly successful *Breakfast Club* appearances you have done a huge amount to dispel once and for all the myth that psychics and clairvoyants are mere charlatans, unscrupulously cashing in on a gullible public, hungry for answers. Gone for ever is the image of a gnarled spinster cradling a cat with one hand whilst stirring a cauldron with the other, casting wicked spells, when we have a beautiful, glowing young lady such as yourself speaking such sense and wisdom about all things spiritual and making such accurate predictions on television every week.

As I always say, spirits are our next-door neighbours. We are all going where they are some day and, in my experience, they're never here to cause us harm. In fact, invariably the opposite is the case.

Many thanks again, Cassandra, and I look forward to hearing from you,

Richard Bryan
Acting President, the National Ghost Convention

Wow. I immediately click on the 'Reply' key to accept the invitation. The convention sounds fun, somewhere full of, as he says, like-minded people. And then to be asked to go on *Late Night Talk*? Way-hey, what an honour!

Late Night Talk, I should explain, is a hugely popular chat show, very prestigious, almost like a national institution. It's completely unique as a programme because, in the space of a single show, you could have Bill Clinton plugging his new book, followed by a hot movie star, followed by a debate about the rise in the price of stamps in which the audience are allowed to join in and, well, things can get very heated. You get the picture.

Put it this way, my mother will be boasting about this to Margaret and the entire cast of *The Sound of Music* from now till opening night.

And yes, he did give me a sweet compliment in his email but somehow the picture I'm getting of Richard Bryan is . . . yup, there he is, I see him. Seventies, but looks trim and fit, white-haired with deep blue eyes.

Oh shit, is that him I'm seeing or Ian McKellan as Gandalf in *Lord of the Rings*? Nope, definitely Richard.

I don't even have to make a decision. I email back my acceptance, adding how thrilled I am that they'd want me to represent them on *Late Night Talk*, and make a mental note to try not to forget about it.

In no time, poor old Valentine's back, looking, there's no other word for it, pole-axed.

'So? How'd it go?' I ask encouragingly as he plonks down at the desk beside mine.

'Well now, Amanda is a very . . . how would I put this in a gentlemanly way? . . . a very highly strung woman, no doubt about that.'

Should have seen her before she found love in her own locker room, I'm thinking. This is the new, improved, fluffy-bunny, cuddly Dragon Lady that you just met. But I say nothing aloud.

'Anyway, she wants to call my column "Valentine's Day". Does that sound all right to you, Cassandra?'

'Please, call me Cassie.'

'She said she wanted it to be like *Sex and the City* except from a guy's point of view, and I'm not joking, I didn't have a clue what she was talking about. Sure, I didn't know what to say to her, I've never sat through a single episode of *Sex and the City* in my life. The lads back home would give me a right slagging, so they would.'

'Relax, I have the DVD box set at home. I'll lend them all to you.'

'Ah, you're just great, so you are. Then she said something about trying to get an insight into the psyche of the single male on the prowl around the city. Jaypurs, you'd swear we were all animals or something. Apparently there's some village in Cumbria where there were so few single women that the local fellas all got together to advertise, to get girls to go and live there, like. So she wants me to write about where I'm from as if that's the way things are down there too and that's why I was driven to the city, looking for love. But that's not true, Cassie. The girls down home are all brilliant, so they are, just none of them were right for me, that's all. I couldn't go making stuff up for my column, it wouldn't be fair. I told her that and she laughed at my innocence and said journalists make stuff up all the time. So I said she was kidding me and she said that with the possible exception of Dominick Dunne on *Vanity Fair*, they were all scum.'

'Vintage Dragon Lady, I wouldn't worry about it.'

'I was nearly afraid to say "Who's Dominick Dunne?" and "What's *Vanity Fair*?" Then she asked me if I ever read the gossip pages in the papers and magazines, so I'd have an idea who was who when I'm out and about, you know yourself. I said, "Gossip pages? First thing I throw out with my Sunday papers so I can get to the sports section that bit quicker." Couldn't help myself, Cassie. The words were just out of my mouth.'

I laugh. I love that he has a sense of humour and I think I know someone else who might appreciate it too. 'You just be true to yourself, Valentine, and you won't go far wrong. Trust me.'

Then out of nowhere, I get a flash about him.

Yup, there he is. I'm seeing scores of women, all vying for his phone number, with him dating one after another until he's completely fed up and worn out from playing the field and he eventually settles down with the right one. I can't see who she is, but I do see him in a morning suit, top hat and tails, on his way to church ... Ooh, I can even see a headline: 'IRELAND'S MOST ELIGIBLE BACHELOR TO TIE THE KNOT TODAY'. *There's a phalanx of press photographers following him too, all dying to get a glimpse of his bride-to-be. As am I, I just can't bloody well see her ...*

'Cassie, all I'm looking for is a lovely lady that'll be happy to be with me, that's all.'

OK, Jo, my dearest, oldest friend, I think tonight might just be your lucky night.

Why not? It's worth a try, isn't it? I mean, stranger things have happened. Plus, this has the added bonus of distracting attention away from the blazing row/screaming match that's hovering like a storm cloud over me and the Tipsy Queen.

'Valentine, did you say you wanted to see the big Ireland match on TV tonight? Because you know you're more than welcome to come round to our house and watch it from there.'

Chapter Fifteen

THE TAROT DECK
THE LOVERS CARD

Probably the single most powerful card in the whole deck. If you're unattached, you're now being guided towards that special someone who's destined to leave an indelible mark on your heart for ever. This card could herald you finally hooking up with your soulmate. Yes, him, the one you've been waiting for, the one true love of your life. So you'd just better make sure that you're ready, baby.

If you're already in a relationship or if the object of your affections is for some reason out of

bounds, then the overwhelming attraction that's coming to you may cause trouble. Big trouble. That's the downside of drawing the lovers' card. It may in time bring great happiness into your life, but for the short term, it means you're going to have to choose.

So what's it to be? Do you choose love over fidelity? Duty? Or perhaps even friendship?

Luckily for me, Valentine decided to go to the launch he was invited to at the Clarence Hotel after work, the one for toilet bleach or aromatherapy loo rolls or whatever it was. Off he went, lamb to the slaughter, while I slipped him our address and went on ahead to prepare the way.

Now, I have to tread carefully here. There is no surer way to guarantee that any set-up will fall dramatically flat on its face than if you let either party involved know that they are, in actual fact, being set up. This requires stealth, tact and diplomacy worthy of the United Nations Security Council.

OK. I have it. Brilliant. I'll go down the faux-casual route of, 'Oh yeah, Jo, by the way, there's a new guy from the office who's popping over later to watch the match, if that's cool with you.' Yep, that sounds good to me. Perfectly plausible. If questioned any further (Jo can be nosier than a sniffer dog if she senses there's any mischief afoot; honestly, she'd give Jane Tennison from

Prime Suspect a right run for her money), I'll just play the card of, 'Oh, but I felt so sorry for him, the poor guy, its his first night in the city and he doesn't really know anyone.'

Yes, bingo. Jo is known far and wide to be a great collector of waifs and strays; she's always taking people into the house that she meets through Amnesty and who have nowhere else to stay.

The main thing is for me to be very cool and calm about the whole thing, play it all down and hopefully she won't suspect a thing. Oh yes, and at all costs avoid eye contact with her, otherwise I'll start to blush and she'll cop on instantly, or worse, ask me straight out if this is a set-up, in which case I'll start stammering and coming out with all sorts of inconsequential shit and Jo will see through me quicker than an envelope with a transparent window. I am the worst liar alive.

Anyway, I get home, fish about in my bag for door keys and, as usual, walk right into a kitchen-sink drama. A Tennessee Williams play without the hot sun and lack of air conditioning and bottles of bourbon floating around a villa in the Deep South. Jo and Charlene are sitting at our kitchen table, having a mature, adult, balanced discussion about the whole Oliver situation.

Well, more correctly, Jo is attempting to have an adult discussion; Charlene is just flicking through the pages of this week's *Hello* magazine.

'Wouldn't my life be so much simpler if I'd been dating a footballer?' muses Charlene. 'You know, like the WAGs. All I'd have to do would be trade in Jack Hamilton for someone further up the premiership. Easy–peasy, really.'

'Hi, hon,' says Jo as I come into our toasty warm kitchen and stick the kettle on.

'Hi, girlies.'

Charlene blanks me for about three seconds, then caves. 'OK, OK, I'll just be the bigger person here,' she says, shoving the magazine away from her. 'I'm sorry if I embarrassed you in work today, but I'm not sorry that I asked Oliver out. There. I hope the air is all nice and cleared. So, anyway, what do *you* think about my new date, Jo?' she asks and I swear to God, I almost think she's trying to goad me. 'Do you approve? Don't worry, if your answer is no, I won't be upset.'

'OK then, my answer's no.'

'*WHAT* DID YOU SAY?!' she almost wails.

I just roll my eyes and try very, very hard to conceal my irritation.

'Sorry, but I'm with Cassie on this one. Of course I'm glad you took a few minutes to mourn Jack, but from what I've heard, your behaviour this morning was a disgrace. Or, to put it in crude terms, make a sentence out of the following words: Shit on own doorstep don't ever. You could easily go after someone else, Charlene. You're not *that* ugly. Are you honestly telling me that this famous Oliver is the only single, available guy for miles around—'

'I think I can die peacefully without ever hearing the end of that sentence, Josephine. Look, I'll only say this once, because frankly I'm getting tired of *constantly* having to defend my actions all the time in this house, but you are both aware of the pressure I'm under to find my life-partner.'

'I have a vague recollection of you mentioning that somewhere before,' I say firmly. And if that sounds a bit rude, I'm not really all that sorry. I'm still furious with her and I just can't help myself.

'So, I like good-looking men,' she goes on, and by now I swear to God I'm actually beginning to feel a vein pulsing in my forehead. 'I don't particularly care whether they were born good-looking or not, once they are now. Why are you both frowning at me? Those lines don't go away, you know.'

Right, that's it. I don't think I can take much more. I have to say something or else I'll end up screaming at her. 'Charlene, two things. First of all, I like my job and I'd really like it if the producer and production team, who, let's remember, are in fact all working professionals, didn't have to witness you parading one fella under another one's nose with no other end in sight than to stir up a bit of jealousy. It's childish, it's embarrassing, it's stupid and, trust me, as a tactic it's doomed to fail.'

'Oh please, who made you such a wise woman? What, have you bypassed being a mere psychic and now suddenly you're like this . . . shaman or something?'

I have to keep talking, I just have to, or I swear to God, I'll smack her. 'Number two, *Oliver*? Does it really have to be Oliver?'

She's gone back to her magazine now. 'Just so you're aware, Cassie, I'm tuning you out. So you can stand there and pretend you're talking to your imaginary boyfriend. Ooh, look, here's an article about Wayne Rooney and his family. Reminds me of all your ex-boyfriends. A who's who of uglyville. To these guys, every day is Halloween.'

'What is it about Oliver, anyway?' Jo asks, ignoring Charlene and looking at me keenly.

'Can't put my finger on it yet. But, don't worry, I will. There's something . . . I just have a horrible feeling. I didn't pick up anything from him initially, then on the day of the clearing he was just plain irritating, but now . . . now I'm feeling a huge negative energy practically *hopping* off him. I can't see what, at least not yet, but I think there's something really bad.'

'Are you even listening to this?' Jo challenges Charlene, but, nose in her magazine, of course she isn't. Honestly, the girl has the attention span of a malarial fruit-fly.

'No, sorry, I'm too busy reading about George Clooney. I don't know about you pair, but he's kind of beginning to bug me. I'm getting sick of all this "Oh, the political weight of the whole Northern hemisphere is on my shoulders while simultaneously every woman in the world wants to shag me."'

'All I can tell you, Jo,' I say, 'is that if Oliver came with sound effects, there'd be thunderclaps and sinister laughter following him around the place.'

'Well, I for one am listening to you,' says Jo, bless her. 'I'm all ears. Your instincts have never in all the years I've known you been wrong, not once. You've never been anything other than straight and direct about these things. About anything, in fact.'

Then the doorbell rings.

'Who's that?'

Shit, I nearly forgot. Well, I don't have to be straight and direct about absolutely *every* teeny little thing, now do I? 'You see, well, funny story actually, there's this guy from work and he's new and – by the way, he's called Valentine and the thing is I said he could come over. To watch a soccer match here, that's all. Honestly, that's it, no other reason at all. Of course, that's if no one minds. You don't mind, do you?'

Charlene just ignores me but I swear it's physically possible to see Jo putting two and two together.

'Valentine. Hmm. Unusual name. Not an easy name to forget. So, let me just apply my mind to this. Now, this is just a wild guess, but by any chance could this possibly be the same Valentine who rang you on the *Breakfast Club* because he can't get a girlfriend?'

'Ehh . . .'

'So he's a single guy then, if I'm not very much mistaken.'

'Emm . . . is he? Honestly can't say for sure. Righty-ho, I'd better go and let him in.' Told you I was a *crap* liar.

Anyway, in comes Valentine, looking very sharp and snazzy in a navy blue suit with a light blue shirt that he's changed into. I make the introductions and start to open a bottle of wine he's (very thoughtfully) brought. The girls are perfectly polite and they all shake hands and I'm madly trying to pick up any chemistry that might be going on, but no joy. Well, apart from Charlene giving him this quick once-over, up-and-down look that she does, immediately making snap assessments about him and his character based solely on his clothes, haircut, shoes, the fact that he walked here, the type of wine that he brought and his accent. Personality doesn't even begin to come into it with her, until a guy has passed all of these initial tests. I don't care, though. In fact, the way I'm feeling right now she doesn't *deserve* a sweetie like Valentine.

He's just going to sit down when Jo reminds him the match is about to begin so they both head into our living room.

'I'll call you when dinner's ready,' says Charlene,

slipping on a crisp white apron like Bree in *Desperate Housewives*. (God knows where she dug it up from, it certainly doesn't belong to anyone in this house.) 'I made vegetarian risotto tonight.' She smiles up at Valentine, who's being perfectly polite back to both of them but, oh shit, I can't for the life of me pick up anything else.

'Well, not so much made it,' Charlene warbles on, 'as took it out of the supermarket carton. And it's just all so idiot-proof, you know. As soon as the oven bell goes off, it's done.'

'Why don't you just trust to the smoke detector, like you normally do?' is Jo's parting shot as she and Valentine head off. 'Or else you could pour some warm sauce over a leather boot; it'll end up tasting exactly the same.'

I was going to leave them on their own, but then (a) Charlene and I are pretty much a cat fight waiting to happen and I really am in no condition to be in a confined space anywhere near her, especially with all the sharp knives lying around the kitchen, and then (b) Marc with a C arrives and, on hearing that I've invited a handsome man round, immediately starts pumping me for info before going into the living room to get a good look at him.

'So he's called Valentine, hmm?' he says to me in the hall as I hang up his jacket. 'Well, I for one am just so thrilled you've introduced a new male into our little circle of love and dysfunction. You have no idea the constant pressure it is for me being the only guy in the group. That and the fact that I'm by far the best-looking.'

Right. All thoughts of leaving the would-be set-up pair alone have effectively flown out the window, so I join them, bringing the bottle of wine with me, pouring a glass for everyone and a particularly large one for myself. Something tells me it's going to be a long, long night.

It's almost half-time, the score is one-all and Valentine is way too engrossed in the match to even cop on that Marc with a C is actually flirting with him.

'I ate a full-fat profiterole before I went to bed last night,' he says, about two seconds after they're introduced. 'Then I spent the entire night lying in bed, staring at the ceiling, just waiting for my impending heart attack. So you'll excuse me if I look as if I'm in need of a blood transfusion. I'm approximately twenty five per cent better-looking than this normally.'

I know, I know, you'd think he was completely and utterly wasting his time, but then Marc with a C is always telling us that in the parallel universe he lives in, the only difference between a gay man and a straight man is three pints and two shorts. You have to hand it to Marc with a C; if nothing else, he really is a tryer.

Anyway, at half-time (or the interval as Charlene, who

has now joined the boys, keeps calling it) I manage to collar Jo on her own in the kitchen to see if there is any white smoke.

'Cassie, are you trying to set me up?' she asks me straight out, direct as ever.

'Emm, well, would it be a problem if I were?' No point in lying, I'm just too bad at it.

'Look, Cassie, I appreciate what you're doing, I really do, but he's not for me.'

'Oh, come on, you haven't given him a proper chance. What's wrong with him?' Shit, so much for my skills as a matchmaker. I thought his all-round, unaffected, good-guy loveliness would win the day with her. I honestly did.

'Nothing, nothing. He's . . .'

'Come on, spit it out.'

'When I asked him who he would vote for in the next election, he claimed he wanted to vote for both guys because they both seem "nice".'

Right. Not a good idea to say this to Jo. At least, not unless you want your teeth metaphorically kicked in. 'Fine, so he may not be politically minded like you, but, you know, that's just a detail. Look on it as a possible hard edge which could be gradually sanded down over time.'

'If I were interested, which, sorry, babe, I'm just not. Nice try, though. Better luck next time. So, are you OK?'

'How do you mean?'

'You looked ready to put a knife through the Tipsy Queen earlier.'

I sigh so deeply it almost causes me pain and Jo pats my arm understandingly.

'That's the thing about her, I guess,' she says. 'Much and all as we love her, she is always, always driving *one* of us up the walls. And it's the perpetual role of the other one to say, "But she is our mate," which I'm dutifully saying to you now. Don't worry, it'll be your turn to say it right back to me soon enough. And I'll remind you of how you're feeling tonight and please God we'll all be able to laugh.'

'He's sweet, but, let's face it, kind of boring,' is Charlene's verdict on Valentine when she eventually joins us in the kitchen, probably afraid we're talking about her behind her back. Which we were. 'Now, he does have his own business, I found out, so that made me perk up a bit, because I thought, ooh, we could have a possible ATM on our hands here.'

'A possible *what*?' says Jo.

'Automatic telling machine, idiot. But then I made the mistake of asking him about it. What a yawn-fest. He went on about how his company makes tyres for the wheels of Boeing 747s. I just tuned out. M.E.G.O. Bigtime.'

This is Charlene-speak for 'my eyes glaze over', which

she uses whenever she finds a guy boring. I, however, am still simmering with anger at her. I can't answer the girl, I can't look at her, I can barely be in the same room as her. I help myself to another large glass of wine and knock it back in one go.

She continues to drive me nuts over dinner, giving Valentine her whole back history in the lead-up to the row with her father, by way of a Judy Garland biography. 'After my mum died, I felt so unloved at the age of fifteen that I almost turned to drink and drugs to help me cope. Have you ever felt that desolate and unwanted, Valentine?'

'That's terrible,' he says kindly. 'I'm really sorry.'

Now there's a depression hanging cloud-like over the table and, as ever when Charlene talks about her childhood, none of us really knows what to say. It's like the ultimate conversational trump card, nothing can top it, so instead we all just sit there in morose silence.

The clink-clink of knives and forks is driving me nuts. I am a bit squiffy by now and am perfectly happy to try and change the subject. 'Newsflash,' I say, suddenly remembering what happened in work earlier.

'Ooh, I love a good newsflash,' says Marc with a C. 'What's up?'

'I've been asked to go on *Late Night Talk*. For a Halloween special.'

They all give me a spontaneous round of applause. Well, all of them except for Charlene, that is.

'How fabulous for you,' is all she says. 'I can't wait to tell Oliver next time we talk.'

This shuts me up. I mean, does she really *have* to keep dropping his name into the conversation at every available opportunity? I need to get more alcohol into me or else there will be bloodshed.

There's another bottle of wine in the fridge, which I open and pour everyone, myself included, a very large glass.

Thankfully, after a while, things brighten up around the table a bit; Valentine is the perfect guest, laughing at everyone's jokes and banter, even though half the time he doesn't know who we're talking about.

'Lovely meal,' he says appreciatively to Charlene.

'Wasn't it?' says Marc with a C. 'You know, I'm sure our little domestic goddess here spent hours slaving over the take-out menu.'

'Now, now, thin ice,' she says, waving her finger at him.

'Just out of curiosity, what else did you achieve today, sweetie?'

'Well, the milk in our fridge is now good cheese.'

They all roar laughing. I'm the only one who doesn't. Jo cops it, just as we're clearing up. 'You OK, hon?'

'Our dearest Cassandra is in a snot with me, I think,'

Charlene smiles sweetly at Valentine. 'It's kind of a long story, but basically she doesn't approve of who I'm dating. And somehow, in this house, that makes me la crème de la scum.'

'I don't think Valentine is really interested in this,' I say in a firm don't-push-me-do-you-have-any-idea-how-close-I-am-to-exploding tone of voice.

'And the mortal sin I committed,' she goes on, blithely ignoring the daggers look I'm giving her, 'is that I went straight from seeing one guy to another. I know, I know, it beggars belief.'

'I often go straight from one date to another,' says Marc with a C, probably under the impression he is lightening the mood. 'I like to keep all my balls up in the air, if you're with me.'

'What can I say?' Charlene says, looking right at me now, knowing full well the effect she's having. 'I guess some of us find it easier than others to find boyfriends. Why are you looking at me like that, Cassie? Are you hearing voices in your head? 'Cos if you are, let me tell you something, none of them have dress sense.'

Right, that's it, gloves off. I honestly think I'll have to be held back and obviously so do the others because they're both in like Flynn to diffuse this.

'Back off right now, Charlene,' says Jo warningly, 'or you'll have me to answer to.'

'Ooh, and we'll have a saucer of milk for table five,'

says Marc with a C, eyes lit up, but then he loves a good ding-dong. Gives him a chance to exercise his legendary conflict-resolution skills.

It's Valentine to the rescue, though. 'Look, I'll tell you what. I have to go to some Comedy Cellar now, sure don't ask me why, but, the thing is, why don't you come with me, Cassie? I'm not going to know a sinner there. I'd love the moral support.'

Brilliant idea. Love it. Anything that gets me out of this house and away from the Tipsy Queen is fine by me. 'Gimme two secs to ring a taxi and lash on a bit of lipstick, in that order.'

There's a half-drunk glass of wine on the table in front of me. I knock it back in one.

Oh dear. I don't quite realize how much I've had to drink until the crisp, cold October night air hits me.

'You all right?' says Valentine as we bounce around the back of the taxi on our merry way into town.

'Fine, fine. I'm just sorry you had to witness that little scene, that's all.'

'Don't be worrying. Sure, I grew up with three sisters, which was kind of like being a permanent ringmaster on *The Jerry Springer Show*.'

He doesn't ask me any more, perfect gentleman that he is, which suits me just fine.

A great night out, a bit of a laugh and maybe even a

few more drinks is just what the doctor ordered right now. A bit of uncomplicated fun, that's all.

'The Comedy Cellar' is actually a misnomer, as it's basically just a room at the back of a pub in the city centre. It's packed and buzzy as we arrive (a bit late) and the comedy improv is in full swing. God, this is the perfect antidote to the tense evening I've had so far. There's a brilliant crowd, all heckling and boozing and shouting up suggestions at the comedy troupe onstage.

'Can we have a location for this sketch?' says a tall thin comedian from the stage, who kind of looks like a young Rowan Atkinson.

'A toilet cubicle!' some wag from the audience shouts back.

'OK,' says the Rowan Atkinson lookalike. 'So then I'm an Academy Award winner who doesn't speak English and all the others think I'm an illegal immigrant who's set up my own country with my own flag and claimed diplomatic immunity inside . . . a toilet cubicle.'

The crowd roar and cheer and, as Valentine and I find an empty booth at the back of the club, the sketch gets under way.

'Let me get you a drink,' says Valentine. 'Another glass of wine?'

'Mmm, love one,' I say and I'm just about to insist that I pay, because he invited me, when a tall, very pretty, dark-haired girl over by the bar catches my eye. I can see her looking over at us, or more particularly, in Valentine's direction. Out of nowhere I get a flash.

She's not Irish, she's ... Danish? Could that be right? A student, I think. Something to do with computers. Ohhh, she won't be going home alone tonight and that's for sure. I think of all the hordes of women wanting to date our Valentine, she's first up ...

'Cassie? Are you all right?'

'Sorry, sorry. It's just – do you see that girl over by the bar? Long, dark hair, leather jacket?'

'What about her?'

'Nothing, I just think this might be your lucky night, that's all. Go. Flirt. Have fun. Ask her to sit over here with us, if you like.'

'Jaypurs, that is something else, the way you can see things that haven't even happened yet. Unbelievable.'

'Why thank you very much, I'll be here all week,' I say, messing and dropping a theatrical bow. God, I must be drunk.

'And can you do it all the time? On demand, kind of thing?'

'Hmm, not on demand, no. Sometimes it can even be a bit tricky. I have to be relaxed and open and I really have to concentrate, which for me can be a bit of a problem. Oh, and one other absolute requirement. The most important one of all, probably.'

'What's that?'

'Shh. You won't tell anyone, will you? My secret would be out and I'd be ruined.' OK, now my head is starting to spin a bit from all the wine I've drunk. Will I tell him or will I not? Ah, what the hell.

'Not a word. Scout's honour.'

'There's this guy and, oh Valentine, I just fancy him so much. I'm seriously warm for his form, as Marc with a C would say. Anyway, the thing is, I've discovered through a highly embarrassing process of trial and error that whenever he's within a ten-foot radius of me, I'm about as much use as a chocolate teapot. Can't see a bloody thing. Nothing.'

'That's amazing. Lucky you found out. So do you just avoid him when you're doing your column?'

'The column, believe me, is the doddley part of my working day. The hard part is when I'm on TV.'

'Why's that?'

'Because that's where *he* works. Can you believe it?'

'So what do you do when you're out at Channel Seven? If this man is around, I mean?'

'What I always do. Wing it. Hope for the best.'

'Ah now, come on, Cassie, you can't leave me in the dark like this. I'm not letting you off the hook till you tell me who he is. A cameraman, maybe? Or somebody famous, someone I might know? A newsreader? That fella that does the National Lottery? The girls at home are all mad about him.'

'My lips are sealed.' I giggle, thinking: bit late for any kind of discretion now.

'Well, he'll be a lucky man, whoever he is. A gorgeous girl like you? Sure, all you have to do is pick and choose.'

Oh, isn't Valentine just *adorable*? Lucky, lucky Danish girl.

'I wish my life was that straightforward, I really do. But there're . . . Well, let's just say that there are complications about this guy. He kind of falls into the untouchable category.'

'Oh right. Sorry, I didn't mean to be nosey.' And I can immediately see what he's thinking. The fella I fancy is married. With a large family. And I'm the worst kind of wannabe home-wrecker.

'Valentine, I promise, whatever you're thinking, it's not the case. Honestly.'

'Right, grand. Sure, I was only thinking that if the Channel Seven guy isn't for you, there's a fella just come in the door who hasn't stopped staring over at you.'

'What? Where?' Someone who recognizes me from TV, maybe? Ooh, how cool is that? I've always fancied being recognized, maybe even asked for my autograph . . . Hmm . . .

'There, he's coming over.'

I don't believe it. Serves me right for being so bloody indiscreet. My karma really is instant. It's Jack, with Lisa, the stage manager, who's looking so young I'm almost wondering how they let her in without ID. She spots a guy at the bar, waves and goes straight over to him. Then I barely have time to gather my thoughts before Jack's standing in front of me, looking yummy, as usual, in jeans and a chunky cable-knit sweater in deep green, exactly the same colour as his eyes.

Stop your bloody drooling, Cassie. For once in you life, can't you just act cool?

'Hi, Cassie, great to see you!'

'Emm . . . hi there . . . emm . . . Jack.'

Brilliant, Cassie. My, what an incredibly gifted orator you are.

'So, what are you doing here?' he says, hugging me warmly. 'Didn't know you were a stand-up comedy fan.'

'Didn't know you were either.'

'That's a pal of mine up there,' he says, looking up at the stage and indicating the Rowan Atkinson lookalike. 'Jim Keane. We were in college together.'

'Oh, right. Well, I came here with Valentine' – Oh no! That makes it sound as if he's my date. Back pedal, fast, very fast – 'who's just started work at *Tattle* magazine. Only today, in fact. Ooh, he rang up the *Breakfast Club* on Monday, do you remember?'

401

'Ah, you're *that* Valentine!' says Jack, shaking him warmly by the hand. 'How could I ever forget that call? Hey, you'll have to call out to our production office at Channel Seven sometime. There must be at least two dozen messages waiting there for you. All from women, all wanting dates, no less.'

'You work at Channel Seven, do you?' says Valentine, all innocence. 'Maybe you know this mysterious fella Cassie's been telling me about? You know, the one who makes her lose her gift whenever he's around?'

'What was that?' says Jack, all ears.

Shit. Now, I may be a bit tipsy, but the bit of my brain that's relatively sober is screaming at me MASSIVE damage limitation required – now. 'Oh, don't mind him, he's only messing. Valentine, come on, your round.'

Brilliant, get him up to the bar. Just get him away and then I'll come up with something . . . anything . . .

Valentine, however, shows absolutely no inclination to budge. 'Do you see, I was only asking Cassie if there was anyone special in her life, and she was telling me there *is* someone, a guy that works on the TV show who she can't go near for some mysterious reason—'

'Valentine, I really can't tell you how much I'm just *gagging* for that glass of wine,' I almost snap at him in a shut-up-for-the-love-of-God tone of voice. He may be a lovely, warm-hearted man but bloody hell, tact is not one of his more obvious qualities. However, I continue to glare at him and it seems to work.

'Oh right so, on the way, and what'll you have, Jack?' he asks, *eventually* taking the hint.

'Guinness would be great, thanks.'

He heads for the bar, leaving Jack and me alone. We sit down in the booth and I immediately make a valiant effort to try to get off this highly embarrassing topic.

'So, emm . . . you're here with Lisa?' Oh shit, did that sound as if I'm suspicious that there's something going on? Because I'm fairly sure there isn't. No, scrap that, I *know* there isn't.

'Yes, she wanted to come with me. To meet her *boy-friend*.' He points up the word slightly as if to say, 'I am here on my own, actually.'

As am I. OK, change the subject.

'So, that guy onstage is a friend of yours, then? He's hysterical. So funny. Kind of reminds me of—'

Jack's having none of it, though. 'So you have a crush on someone out at Channel Seven?' He looks down at me in that twinkly-eyed way he has when he's teasing. 'Anyone I might know?'

My stomach starts to flip and . . . oh shit, I'm really in trouble here. He's sitting close to me, so close I can smell that yummy aftershave he always wears.

You're going to have to say something, Cassie. You can't just sit here, mute for the rest of the night . . .

'Oh, pay no attention to Valentine, he's just trying to embarrass me, that's all. You see, I tried to fix him up with my best friend Jo earlier. You remember Jo?'

'Yes, I remember Jo.'

'With zero per cent success, so then we got here and I had a flash about – do you see that girl over there at the bar?'

'Certainly do.'

'I had a flash that they'd end up together, for now at least, because you see the thing about Valentine is that there're going to be literally hundreds of dates ahead of him – for the foreseeable future, that is—'

'Emm, Cassie?' he interrupts gently.

'What?'

'I hate to cut you off mid-ramble—'

'I wasn't rambling.'

'Yes you were. Grade A rambling. Answer the question. Who's this guy who's taken your fancy at Channel Seven?' He's smiling down at me now, almost as if he's daring me to answer him.

'Oh look, they're asking for us to shout up more suggestions at the stage,' I almost stutter.

'You are so great at changing the subject.'

'Was not.'

'Was too. OK then. Have it your way. If you don't tell me, I'll just have to guess. Doubt that it's Oliver—'

'No bloody way!'

'Besides, based on what I saw this morning, I think he might be, shall we say, involved elsewhere.'

Then he did see Charlene throwing herself at him. Oh God, this is just so embarrassing. I glance back over to the bar to see if there's any sign of Valentine getting back with those drinks, but he's too busy chatting up Danish girl.

Jack doesn't let up though; it's almost as if he's having great crack with this.

'And for some reason, you can't go near this guy.'

'You know, you're being very rude to your friend up on stage. You should really concentrate on the gig.'

'He'll understand. How often do I get you all to myself?'

Oh my God, did he really just say that?

'I'm just idly wondering here ...'

'Where are our drinks? Isn't Valentine taking ages?'

'... if the reason this guy is so out of bounds *might* just be that ...'

I know what he's going to say before he even says it.

'... he briefly dated a friend of yours.'

We look at each other for what seems like a long, long time.

He breaks the silence. 'Cassie, for the record, my so-called involvement with your friend consisted of one night, where, yes, I admit I did kiss her, but she was falling-over drunk, couldn't get a taxi so she came back to my place, where I put her on the sofa and let her sleep it off. Then she kept calling and calling so I met her for a quick drink and then, shortly after that, I realized that, nice as Charlene is, I couldn't be involved with her any more.'

'Why?' I'm on the edge of my seat. No pressure or anything, but my entire future happiness could depend on the next sentence that comes out of his mouth.

'Because it's not right to be with someone when you fancy their best friend, now is it?'

Oh my God. I can't speak, I can hardly breathe.

'Cassie, I don't want you to think badly of me. I promise you, I didn't string Charlene along, whatever you might think. I tried to finish things with her on at least two occasions. Firstly, when she invited me to her house for a pizza after work, I thought: This is perfect, I'll talk to her, explain that I'd prefer it if we were just friends. But when I got there, I found she was having a formal sit-down dinner for what felt like about two hundred very scary-looking people.'

I shudder, just remembering that awful night too . . .

'Then a couple of days later she called out to Channel Seven and I thought: Right, *this* is the perfect time. I'm not someone who can just have these God-awful break-up conversations over the phone. So I took her for a drink, but it turned out she had a family crisis going on, so what could I do? I was stymied, there was nothing else for me to do but postpone the inevitable. You know, there's never a good time to say these things, but if something's not right, it's not right.'

His hand is so close to mine now, so close we're almost touching. It's driving me nuts. The physical attraction I'm feeling for him right now is so unbelievably over-whelming . . .

Think of Charlene, think of Charlene. There are rules about this sort of moral dilemma . . .

But it doesn't work. Maybe I'm too drunk, but when Charlene comes into my head, all I can think about is that awful row we had today and how furious I was – still am – with her.

'Cassie?' he asks gently, looking directly at me.

He's moved in even closer. And I'm not imagining it.

'Do you think it would be OK if you and I, some-time, in the future I mean, when – you know – when everyone's moved on a bit . . . And just so you're clear, by everyone, I mean Charlene. Anyway, my question is, would it be OK if I . . . ?'

He doesn't get to finish his sentence. I look up at him; he smiles down, and we kiss.

Chapter Sixteen

THE TAROT DECK
THE THREE OF SWORDS CARD

Oh, not good. A time of hugely intense emotion, pain and distress. Can often symbolize a separation of some kind from a loved one. A tough time, involving friction, dispute and a lot of malicious gossip. This period will be nothing short of torment while it lasts, deeply painful for all three people concerned.

That's the thing about this card, you see. It almost always involves a triangle . . .

In the end, it's like Chinese whispers. Awful, awful, beyond awful . . . I wake up and have to stare at the ceiling for ages before last night all comes flooding back to me. OK, it's not so bad. As they say on all those TV shows set in the White House, you know, like *The West Wing*, I have spin control. All I did was kiss Jack, that's it.

At least I think that's it. Shit, why did I have to drink so much? My hangover is already starting to kick in and I'm not kidding, it feels as if a troupe of Irish dancers are doing Riverdance inside my brain. That and the fact that my mouth is as dry as parchment.

No, no, hang on, this mightn't be too bad. I remember Jack putting me into the back of a taxi – good. Then I remember him hopping into the taxi beside me – OK, maybe not so good. Then I remember the taxi taking me home – good. Then I distinctly remember not inviting Jack in – better than good, excellent. I am a model of virtue and discipline. Practically nun-like, you might say. Yes, just keep telling myself that.

The situation may yet be salvageable. I mean, I'm not so much of an old trollop that I spent the night with him. And one drunken snog doesn't exactly make me Mata Hari, now does it?

The only thing that's making me feel, if possible, *worse* than the hangover I'm nursing is the one, unavoidable hurdle that lies ahead. Oh God, the very thought of it is making my tummy churn so much that I have to concentrate really, really hard on not getting sick when suddenly my mobile phone rings.

Shit. Can't find it.

I spill the contents of my handbag out on to the bedroom floor and eventually, yes, there it is, under a mound of lipstick, hairbrushes and yellow Post-it stickers with predictions for the magazine scribbled all over them.

Oh, thank God. It's Jo.

'Hey, hon, are you OK?'

'Yeeee . . . no.'

'Oohkaaaaay,' she says in that drawn-out way she has when she can sense there's something up. Told you she could sound you out quicker than a sniffer dog at Dublin Airport. Any day. 'Something to do with last night, maybe?'

'Maybe.' I can't tell her over the phone, just can't. Mainly because I already know precisely what she's going to say, in her role as the group's moral barometer. And I know what's ahead deep down myself, except I'm just trying to postpone the inevitable, that's all. Until my head stops thumping, at least.

I have to tell Charlene.

Everything, in glorious Technicolor. I know it's unavoidable, I know it's just a question of getting it over with and that's all there is to it. I just need to talk things over with Jo first, that's all. She'll help me to think straight, put all this into perspective and – who knows? – maybe even come up with a few good lines for the speech I'm going to have to deliver to Charlene at some point during the day.

'So, how soon can you meet me?'

'Oh, this sounds like an emergency.'

'If this isn't an emergency, I don't know what is. Advice needed. Rapidly.'

'OK, how about Browns in half an hour?'

'Bless and double bless you.'

'Are you sure you're OK? You sound brutal. Never even heard you coming home last night. It must have been all hours.'

'Trust me, it's better if I tell you face to face. You're less likely to judge me.'

'I could never judge *you*,' she says and I can almost hear the worry in her voice. God love her, now she's probably thinking either (a) I caused a hit-and-run accident or (b) in a sudden blood rush to the head, I held up a late-night cashpoint on my way home.

'See you in half an hour, hon,' I say, deliberately hanging up, knowing full well that if I don't, she'll only wheedle it out of me anyway.

The house is stone-dead quiet, which is fantastic; it means Charlene's out. I glance at the clock on my phone. It can't be half-eleven, can it? Bloody hell, how long was I asleep for?

411

I'm just about to jump into the shower, in the vain hope that it'll clear my head, when I notice there's an unread text message on my phone. From Jack, sent at three a.m. this morning.

HEY SLEEPING BEAUTY. HOPE U ENJOYED TO-NIGHT AS MUCH AS I DID. WILL CALL U AFTER WORK TOMORROW. DINNER MAYBE? JXXX

Oh God, my heart does a somersault. He wants to see me again. Socially, as a date, I mean, a proper date, outside of work. Thank God he doesn't regret last night, at least. I don't know what I'd do otherwise, but one thing is for certain: this *isn't* someone who I can write off and say I never fancied him anyway. No use invoking the catchphrase here; it just won't work. Not this time. For once in my life, I have absolutely no idea what lies ahead; all I know for certain is that, as far as Jack is concerned, my catchphrase is completely and utterly defunct.

You know, maybe, just maybe, everything will be OK. I know it's asking a lot, but who's to say Charlene won't be completely cool about this? Maybe she'll even be happy for me. Yes, I know I've transgressed an unwritten rule of friendship by snogging the face off her ex not two days after they broke up, but, you know, miracles do happen, don't they? And she did ask Oliver out only yesterday, didn't she? OK, so he's clearly a rebounder and this is the same Oliver who I haven't had a single good word to say about pretty much since I met him . . .

Oh, who am I kidding? I'll be doing well if she doesn't rip out one of my ovaries.

I have a lightning-quick shower, get dressed, lash on a bit of make-up and am out of the door fifteen minutes later, walking as fast as my throbbing head will allow to the coffee shop where I'm meeting Jo.

The important thing here, I remind myself, is to be completely straight and upfront with Charlene. I mean, if the boot were on the other foot, if she'd had a fling with my ex, yes, of course I'd be . . . a bit taken aback, naturally, but the two things I'd appreciate most of all on her part would be (a) honesty and (b) directness. A quick coffee/strategy meeting with Jo, then I'll call her and come and meet her wherever she is. Get it over and done with early – well, relatively early in the day. Not to mention while I'm still a bit anaesthetized with last night's alcohol.

I'm late and I'm running now when another text comes through on my mobile. I nearly drop my handbag in my rush to find my phone, I'm so convinced that it's Jack again. Serves me right for being cocky. It's Jo.

WAS JUST LEAVING AMNESTY WHEN CHARLENE CALLED IN. SHE KNOWS.

EVERYTHING. SHE'S COMING WITH ME TO
MEET U. FOREWARNED IS FOREARMED.

Oh shit.

It's only much, much later that I get a chance to figure
out the chain/trail of shame. Piecing it together roughly,
it appears to have proceeded something along these
lines.

Location: the Channel Seven make-up room
Time: 7.30 a.m. this morning approximately

LISA TO DAMIEN, THE MAKE-UP GUY: Hot gossip from last
night! Now I'm not one to blather out of turn, but I was
at the Comedy Cellar last night and I did happen to see
our executive producer kissing the face off our resident
psychic.

Time: 7.35 a.m. approx.

DAMIEN TO MARY (*as he's lashing on her foundation*): Ooh, do
you wanna know what I heard? Jack and Cassie are going
out with each other. For definite. They were seen together
and everything. Apparently, this has been going on for *ages*.
You heard it here first, baby.

Time: 8 a.m. approx.

MARY TO THE FLOOR MANAGER: Just while you're talking to
Jack there on your headphones, will you congratulate him

for me? I'm over the moon that he's moving in with that lovely young girl. I'm very fond of Cassie. You can tell him I totally approve.

Time: 8.05 a.m. approx.

FLOOR MANAGER TO OLIVER (*during a commercial break*): Nice piece of stuff Jack's been seeing all this time. Lovely legs. I always wondered how she landed such a prime slot for herself so fast and with no telly experience or anything. Now we know, I suppose.

Time: about 30 minutes ago, but then I'm only guessing

OLIVER (*traitorous git that he is*) TO CHARLENE: Well, your ex didn't exactly let the grass grow under his feet . . . madly in love with your flatmate . . . all over the station, etc. etc.

Unbelievable. Just unbelievable.

By the time I get to Browns, they're both in there at a quiet table at the back of the shop, which could turn out to be very handy in the event of bloodshed.

Charlene is looking very red-eyed. Bad sign.

I decide to speak first, on the principle that attack is the best form of defence. 'OK, Charlene, straight off, I want you to know that I am so, so sorry. You have no idea how sorry I am, but you have to let me explain—'

She doesn't let me get to the end of my sentence. 'You're sorry that I found out, you mean?'

415

'Will you let her finish?' Jo says to Charlene. I'm so grateful she's here. At times like this, having a referee is always handy.

'Well, (a) I was drunk and (b) it was only a snog. That's it. I was back home, alone and in bed by . . . well, I can't remember when exactly, you were both long gone to sleep, but that's all it was. I promise you.'

Charlene starts to sniffle. 'Jack could have been the love of my life, you know.'

'Oh come on,' says Jo, but she's actually being gentle. Trying to lighten things up a bit, bless her. 'You said that about each and every one of Westlife.'

'So you're taking Cassie's side in this? Oh well, there's a surprise.'

Now I swear I can practically see the hackles on the back of Jo's neck slowly, very slowly, beginning to rise. 'You know, maybe you need to grow up here a bit. Two single people got together last night. So what? Is it really such a big deal? As they say in the States, build a bridge and get over it.'

'Don't you dare speak to me like that, Josephine. How do you think I feel? I had to hear this about fifth-hand from Oliver. Everyone at Channel Seven seems to know all about it, but not me.'

'Look,' I say, trying to calm things down. 'I know it's terrible the way that you found out, but honestly, I only woke up half an hour ago. *Of course* I was going to tell you. It's hardly my fault if events took over, now is it?'

'Well, it's not my fault if you've broken an unwritten rule of friendship. Stay away from your girlfriend's exes.'

There's a silence. That's kind of the ultimate bring-down and she has me there.

'Now, in all fairness,' says Jo, a bit more calmly now, 'it's not as if you haven't moved on yourself. If I can just jog your sieve-like memory, what about Oliver?'

'Yes,' she sniffs, 'my rebound guy. You know what really upsets me more that anything else, Cassie? Only yesterday, you were picking a fight with me, demanding to know if he was the only guy in town I could have gone after. They were your exact words. So here we are, twenty-four hours later; same question back to you.'

OK, if I didn't feel bad enough before this, I really do now.

She plays her advantage to the fullest. 'There you were, up on the moral high ground, like some kind of ethical watchdog, telling me how I could and couldn't behave and then you go out last night and . . .'

She trails off, thank God, and she doesn't even know the half of it. How is she to know the way I've felt about Jack pretty much since the night they met? When I clearly saw that I would fall for this guy and *I didn't tell her*?

Guilt sucks, it really does. I will fry in hell for this,

and that's if I'm lucky and God's in a good mood on Judgement Day. Oh, and Charlene's started to cry now, just to make me feel worse.

'The image of you two together is, like, seared on my retina for ever,' she says, dabbing her eyes. 'How could you, Cassie? I thought you were my friend?'

'Come on,' says Jo after a long pause and a concerned look over in my direction. 'This is bad enough without the emotional guilt thrown in. You have a chance to be the bigger person here, Charlene. Can't you just accept that this has happened, put it behind you and move on? This conversation demeans everyone.'

'I don't think so,' she says, getting up abruptly. 'Just so you're aware, Cassandra, you have now officially become top of my list of enemies, bypassing George Bush Junior and that incredibly lucky cow who married Russell Crowe.'

'Charlene, sit down, please, let's be adults here,' I say, half aware that everyone in the restaurant is now looking over at this highly entertaining side-show.

'Forget it,' she says, pulling on her coat, and for a split second I think she's going to throw her half-drunk cappuccino over me in a Bette Davis–style diva gesture. 'I think you're aware of my personal motto. Forgive and remember.' And out she goes.

I slump back into the chair, shaking, actually shaking.

'Are you OK?' says Jo, squeezing my hand.

'Mmm.'

'Tantrums and tiaras, that's all that's wrong with her. She'll get over it.'

'Mmm.'

'Her behaviour is completely irrational, you do know that, don't you?'

'Mmm.'

'Cassie? Are you listening?'

'Sorry. I'm just thinking about . . .'

'What? Tell me.'

'It's just . . . I like him, Jo, I really do. And I don't know, but I think he might, just conceivably *might*, feel the same way about me. And that this could, for once in my life, you know, actually *be* something. This could have legs. He could be a keeper.'

'But that's wonderful news,' she says, smiling at me. 'I've never heard you say that about anyone before and I'm thrilled for you, I really am.'

'Except that I think we both know how Charlene is going to see it. Jack versus her. A twenty-year friendship versus a potential lover. No matter which way you look at it, one thing is for certain. She's going to make me choose.'

Chapter Seventeen

THE TAROT DECK
THE JUSTICE CARD

OK. Who among us hasn't heartily wished that they could turn the clock back, at some point in their lives? This card symbolizes that it's time to make amends. Speak your mind, clear your conscience and if you feel an apology is warranted, offer one immediately. If it's accepted, all will be well, harmony will be restored and the past can be put to rest.

If not, you're going to hell anyway. You might as well dance . . .

Needless to say, I'm beyond useless when I do eventually get into work. Can't see a thing. Nothing.

I spend the guts of a full hour with one letter in my hand, madly trying to pick up something with absolutely no joy. And it's a great letter too, one I'd normally be able to deal with in no time. One I'd really enjoy giving out advice to, as well.

Dear Cassandra,

I am stuck in such a rut and desperately need your help. The problem is that the last few relationships I've had have all involved men whom I always seem to meet when they're in the throes of a crisis. Example: the last guy was going through a very messy, painful divorce, two small kids, you know yourself. Awful, just awful. So what did I do? Picked him up, put him back together again and made him all better.

And then he left me. It's as if they see me as some kind of emotional fixer, but the minute they're good as new and ready to go out and face the world again, they don't want to know me because, let's face it, I knew them when they were broken. I'm a reminder of bad times. In some warped way, I symbolize the past and now, of course, they hate their past. Do you ever see the pattern breaking, Cassandra? I so don't want to be alone. Happily married to the right guy is what I want, if it's not asking too much.

Please, please help me.

Lost and lonely in Dublin. xxx

The Dragon Lady's not here, so the office is noisy and buzzy, but even tuning out all the normal high-jinks and gossip doesn't work. And there's no sign of Valentine, the one person I'd actually have loved to talk last night over with. Probably still with Danish girl. Oh well.

At about five-ish, I throw in the towel and decide to call it a day.

'All right, old thing?' Sir Bob asks me as I gather up my things. 'Not at all like you to be so quiet. And if you don't mind me saying, you're looking most dreadfully pale.'

'Late night last night, that's all,' I say, doing my best to laugh it off. 'I'll be back on form soon enough, don't you worry about me.'

He escorts me to the lift, thorough gentleman that he is, says nothing, asks nothing, just presses the ground-floor button for me and waves me off.

Probably thinks I have 'women's problems', as he'd most likely say.

It's already pitch dark and as I'm walking home, desperately trying to clear my head and decide what in the name of God I'm going to do, Marc with a C texts – one of his why-leave-a-brief-message-when-a-radio-play-will-do-instead-type texts.

AM WITH CHARLENE. JUST TO LET U KNOW THAT SHE'S MOVED OUT OF YR HOUSE AND BACK INTO HER OWN. DIDN'T WANT U TO GO HOME AND THINK YOU'D BEEN BURGLED. SHE'S V UP AND DOWN BUT AM TALKING TO HER, WORKING ON HER AND V. HOPEFUL SHE'LL COME ROUND EVENTUALLY. LIKE IN A YEAR OR SO. ANYWAY, I STILL LOVE U, MXXXX

Bloody hell.

There's a taxi with the light on just driving past me. I don't even hesitate, I barely even pause to weigh up whether this is a good idea or a bad idea. I hail it down and jump in. My phone beeps again as another text comes through.

This time it's Jack. Again.

LET ME KNOW UR OK. THAT DINNER INVITE IS STILL OPEN. J.X.
P.S. U AND ME R THE TALK OF CHANNEL SEVEN, SO IT SEEMS!

'Where to, love?' the driver asks me.

I don't even think about it, just give him Charlene's address. I can't contact Jack, at least not just yet, so I switch my phone off. I have to do this first. Get it over with. It won't be pleasant or easy, but it would be on my conscience if I didn't.

For the first time in my life, I'm actually nervous walking up the long driveway to Charlene's house/mansion. Marilyn's car is parked there, but there's no sign of Mr Ferguson's. Phew.

Marilyn lets me in and is so warm and welcoming, I'm left thinking: Does she even know what happened? That, in the space of twelve hours, I've been demoted from best friend to spawn of Satan?

Hard to know. On one hand, Charlene can't abide the sight of Marilyn, but on the other, whenever she's going through a crisis, everyone, and by that I really do mean everyone, right down to her eyebrow-waxing lady, *knows*.

'Hey, am I allowed to say congratulations?' I ask as Marilyn takes my coat.

'Of course,' she says, blushing very prettily. 'Thanks so much, Cassie. It was a bit of a shock, but I think – well, I hope that, in time, Charlene might, you know, come around to the idea. She's just upstairs in her room, with Marc with a C, if you want to go on up.'

'Thanks,' I gulp, dreading it.

'Cassie, do you mind if I say something?'

'Of course not.'

'The thing is, it really was a terrible row between Charlene and her dad, but you know, there's nothing

I'd love more than for us all to build bridges. Maybe she and I will never have the friendship you all do, but, well, I'd like her to know that I'll always be here for her. I know this is hard for her, I really do, but there's nothing that would give me more happiness than for her to be involved with this baby. Is that asking too much, do you think?'

'No, not at all. I'm really over the moon for you,' I say, hugging her warmly, really meaning it. Wow. Lucky little spirit to be born to such a fab mother, I'm thinking. And it looks as if Charlene might, in time, come round to the whole idea, given that she's physically moved back here, so . . . well, it's an ill wind and all that.

Of course, the *main* reason she's back home again is because she can't bear to share the same airspace as me, but that's what I'm here to deal with. I hope. Anyway, I'm on my way upstairs, just thinking about how lovely Marilyn is and how lucky Charlene is that her father isn't marrying some gold-digging horror story, as he could so easily have done. OK, so maybe she and her father will never see eye to eye, but at the very least Marilyn is a good soul and Charlene'll always have her in her corner.

'Hey,' says Marilyn, interrupting my happy thoughts about her. 'Any flashes on whether it's a boy or a girl? I'm only asking, because, for Charlene's sake, I think a boy might be that bit easier for her to come to terms with.'

I don't even have to think about it. I get an instant flash. Wow again.

It's Mr Ferguson and Marilyn, standing in a church, at the baby's christening. They're both beaming with pride, gazing down at this tiny bundle, swathed in oceans of Chantilly lace.

'Will the godparents step forward, please?' an elderly priest asks the congregation.

This is a minor miracle. The godfather, who I don't recognize, steps up to the font and beside him, looking strangely pleased and even proud to be godmother, is Charlene.

'By what name do you wish the child to be known?' asks the priest.

Marilyn looks adoringly down at her little bundle, then back up again. 'James Henry Charles.' She smiles and I'd swear I can almost see her winking at Charlene …

'You know, don't you?' says Marilyn, correctly gauging the look on my face.

'Yeah, but I'm not telling.'

'Ah, go on.'

'Nope. My lips are sealed. But you are going to be so *happy*.'

She goes back into the drawing room, delighted with life, and I head upstairs, feeling a little bit more confident

426

now. This mightn't be so bad. I mean, Charlene's had all day to get her head around what happened. OK, so she did move out, which could be interpreted as a bad sign, but then I am here, I have made an effort to at least try and find some middle ground. To show that I do actually value our years of friendship.

Above a fella. Yes, even a fella as divine as Jack.

Right, just hold that thought, Cassie.

I knock gingerly on her dressing-room door.

I have to wait for ages before Marc with a C eventually opens it. 'Hey, honey,' he whispers, kissing me. 'Thanks for coming.'

'Why the low voice?' You'd swear there was either (a) an invalid or (b) someone just out of an intensive-care unit in the room with him.

'Who is it?' I can hear Charlene asking from her bedroom, which is a kind of inner sanctum through a big French double door.

Deep breath. 'It's me.'

There's a pause and now I can hear her getting out of bed.

'You must prepare yourself for a shock,' whispers Marc with a C in that respectful tone of voice people use whenever there's been a bereavement. 'I'm not kidding, she has Macy Grey hair.'

Charlene appears at the doorway, wearing her comfy pink fleecy pyjamas which I happen to know she only ever wears when she's in the throes of a crisis. She looks at me in deep disgust, that same disdainful sneer she reserves for women who wear last season's lip colour.

'Oh, it's you,' she says. 'I thought it might have been Jo. You remember Jo? My friend who didn't run off with my ex a day after we broke up?'

'How are you?' I ask, ignoring the jibe and deliberately keeping my voice cool.

'Do you really want to know how I am? Because I'll tell you.'

'Charlene, look—' I say, but Marc with a C interrupts me.

'Can I just say one thing? If we were all French, there'd be no problem.'

Bless him, I think he's trying to lighten the mood, but some instinct tells me to just keep on talking while I still have the chance. 'Charlene, I hated the way we left things today, but I really have to tell you—'

'Is that why you're here?' she says. 'Don't Hallmark make sorry-I-ran-off-with-your-ex-boyfriend cards?'

'Come on, sweetie, let her finish,' says Marc with a C.

OK, this will be awful, but I'm going to try to get it all over with in one sentence. 'I think – I honestly feel that . . . Well, look, here it is. I think that I might have feelings for Jack, I really do, and I'm not certain but I think that he might have them for me as well and – the thing is, this has been on my mind all day – I really feel the right thing to do is to be completely straight with you. It wasn't a fling. At least I don't think that it was. He has asked me out and I think I'd like to take him up on it. But obviously not if it's going to upset you or mean the end of our friendship. And I want to know where you stand on this.'

Marc with a C gives me a round of applause. 'Brave, brave lady,' he says. 'So now over to you, Charlene. Come on, let's try to find some common ground here.' Now he's starting to sound like a relationship counsellor. 'Cassie has been honest with you, so – maybe – you could meet her halfway and admit that you have moved on as well, with whatshisname, that reporter guy, so can't we just all put this behind us and go back to being a happy family? For my sake?'

'Brilliant,' Charlene snaps back at him, a bit ungratefully considering that all he's trying to do is help. 'Tell you what, when you're finished here, why don't you go out to the Middle East and solve that little problem with a nice big group hug?'

There's a very long, very ugly pause.

Big mistake coming here, I'm thinking. She's not prepared to listen to reason, in fact, she's probably prepared to drag this out till Christmas. At least I tried. Conscience clear. Well, clear-ish.

I'm just about to say my goodbyes when she comes right in tight to me in a move I'd swear she copied straight from Joan Collins on old re-runs of *Dynasty*, which I happen to know she knows almost every line of by heart.

'I just have one thing to say to you, Cassandra, before you go. There is a thing called karma and what you've done *will* come back and bite you in the arse. And when it does, all I can say is, I hope it bloody well hurts.'

Chapter Eighteen

THE TAROT DECK
THE TEN OF SWORDS CARD

Awful, just awful. The card has a picture of a person lying face down in the snow, with ten swords stuck into their back and blood oozing everywhere.

A distressing and very upsetting time for all concerned. The only chink of hope is that if you look closely enough at the card, there are stars twinkling in the dark night sky giving some hope that time heals all wounds and that the dawn will, eventually, come. Mind you, you do have to look really, really closely . . .

Maria von Trapp has just come on stage in her nun's habit singing about the hills being alive with the sound of music and Jo's sitting beside me in the freezing parish hall, nudging me to stay awake. Thank God too, because I was about to drift off and the next scene is when Mum makes her grand entrance. According to the programme, she's playing Sister Mary Bernadette and her big chorus number is 'How Do You Solve A Problem Like Maria?'

OK, so maybe the scenery is a bit shaky and maybe the singing is not up to Broadway standard, but, still, we're all here to support her and cheer her on. Well, Jo and I are here, that is, with my proud dad sitting in the row in front of us, digital camera at the ready, all set for Mum's big scene.

Charlene didn't come and Marc with a C elected to stay at home with her. She never even phoned to say she wasn't coming. Nothing. It's like I've been completely dead-headed. It's been a horrible, horrible week, best summarized in the words of my friends, or at least my friends who are still speaking to me, as follows:

JO: We are *constantly* giving in to Charlene and her emotional blackmail and I for one have had enough. In much the same way as it's wrong to negotiate with terrorists, this time we need to stand firm, whatever the cost. Charlene is acting like a spoilt five-year-old and, trust me, the best thing all round is not to let her appalling behaviour win the day. In the long run, we're doing her a favour. A true friend would have seen that you and Jack genuinely seem to like each other and would have selflessly stepped aside. The good old Tipsy Queen, however, is acting as if she was married to him for about five years. You'd swear she owned him and, as you know, I am opposed to ownership on every level. Stay strong, Cassie, and whatever you do, don't budge an inch.

MARC WITH A C (*still doing his best Florence Nightingale impression*): OK, so I've been staying at the mansion and the lie of the land is thus. Yes, she's still doing the whole martyr/betrayal act but I do think, in time, she'll come round. As I always say, patience is a virtue as well as an opera. There have been an awful lot of phone calls toing and froing between her and that guy Oliver, but I think she's mainly ringing him to give out about you and Jack. No offence, sweetie. Don't take it too personally.

Oh shit, I better stop daydreaming.

The nuns have just come out now and there's a huge round of applause, dragging me out of my reverie. There's Mum and her friend Margaret, looking, well, actually a bit over made-up and glamorous for two nuns who live in a convent in Salzburg circa 1938. Dad's on his feet with the camera just as they burst forth into song. Anyway, before you know it, they're done (flawless performances, everyone remembered their words and

Mum only winked down at us twice, very professional), Maria's been dispatched off to the von Trapp residence to take care of the seven children and . . . whaddya know, I'm drifting off again.

I haven't been able to concentrate on a single thing these past few days. I'm way behind with work, I've yet another deadline looming and I haven't even begun to tackle the mound of letters that's waiting for me. I did, however, hear from Jack. He called me when I was supposed to be working but was actually more gainfully occupied gazing out of the window. One of those days.

He was sweet and funny and lovely, as usual. Asked how I was and I told him. About my awful, misguided visit to Charlene's house, the guilt that's been laid on with a bloody trowel, the whole works. Plenty of guys would have tried to talk me round, but he didn't and I really liked that he didn't. Honestly. We were both very adult and grown-up about the whole thing, really. I think he's feeling like a bit of a heel himself, in fact.

He said he felt awful that I was feeling so awful but understood what I was going through, or rather, being put through. Anyway, I can't remember if he suggested it or if I did, but we agreed not to see each other. For now, anyway.

'Let's let the dust settle a bit,' I think I may have said to him. I can't be sure, it was all a bit of a blur. Anyway, he was fine about it, absolutely cool, and agreed that was the best thing all round.

Yes, I know I'll have to do the *Breakfast Club* soon enough, but it's possible to avoid him until then, isn't it?

Course it is. A bit of breathing space is what we all need right now, just till things blow over.

Yes. This is unquestionably the *right* thing.

What I can't figure out then is: why does it feel so wrong?

I must have been daydreaming for ages because Jo actually has to nudge me awake for the interval. She's absolutely brilliant, as usual, chats away to Dad as if there's absolutely nothing amiss. He does ask what happened to Charlene and Marc with a C and she covers beautifully. 'Unavoidably detained,' she smiles and gets away with it. Luckily, Dad's too busy going around talking to neighbours and pals to give it too much thought and before you know where we are, Mrs Walsh from the refreshments committee is ushering us back into our seats for Act Two.

Pretty soon, I'm drifting off again, except this time to the strains of 'Edelweiss'.

Valentine did finally turn up at the office, looking like he hadn't slept in days, which, in fairness, he probably hadn't. I took one look at him and immediately dragged him down to Starbucks for a badly needed max-strength cappuccino.

I'm not joking, for the half-hour or so that we were sitting there chatting, his mobile must have beep-beeped about a dozen times, all women, all looking for dates, all wanting a piece of our Valentine. He looked kind of embarrassed every time it happened, but also delighted at the same time. Anyway, it seems Danish girl has now been replaced by his next-door neighbour in the apartment where he's staying while he's in Dublin. Blonde and very pretty, according to him, although at some breakfast launch do only that morning, he did meet yet another gorgeous girl who runs her own PR company. Phew. I have a hard job just keeping up.

Anyway, sweetheart that he is, he asks about Jack and I tell him. Everything. I omit no detail, however trivial. I'm glad I did too, because it's brilliant to get a man's perspective on the situation. Well, a straight man's perspective, that is. What's even more brilliant is that Valentine was there, in our house, on the night in question, your honour. So, as I pointed out to him, he saw first hand how much Charlene was driving me completely and utterly scatty.

Not that it's a defence to say she was driving me nuts, I'm only reminding him of my mental state at the time. Oh yes, and not to forget that I was pretty much off my trolley with cheap wine.

Wine and dementia. Lethal combination.

He listens to every word I'm saying and doesn't rush

to judge. 'Charlene is your friend and all you owed her was the truth and that's what you told her. Friends want their friends to be happy, don't they? She'll come round in time, you just wait and see. And for what it's worth, I think you're doing the right thing with Jack,' he said to me, gently squeezing my hand. 'Bit of time out is no harm. Sure, if you were to go out to dinner with him tonight, you'd be so riddled with guilt, you'd both end up miserable. Just remember this, Cassie: if he's a nice guy and if he genuinely likes you, he'll wait for you. You're a girl that's worth waiting for.'

I keep saying it over and over in my head, like a mantra. It's the advice of the millennium. *If he's a nice guy, he'll wait for me.*

Won't he?

Shit, as usual, there's never a psychic flash handy when I actually could do with one. Another sharp nudge from Jo and I realize that everyone's clapping and the show's actually over. The von Trapps are safely over the Alps and everyone's on their feet cheering.

God, at times like this I really don't know what I'd do without Jo. She's just so fab, coming back to the dressing room with me and Dad afterwards to congratulate Mum and the rest of the cast. Boy, do I owe her big time.

The dressing room is actually just a big storeroom off the side of the stage where nuns and Nazis are all cracking open the champagne, high as kites on the euphoria of finishing a show where nothing went wrong.

We eventually find Mum, wearing the Japanese kimono I gave her last Christmas, with, I'm not kidding, an actual turban on her head, as she takes off one layer of make-up and replaces it with another.

'Does this make you feel like Liza Minnelli?' Jo whispers to me. 'You know, and she's Judy Garland? Mother and daughter both in showbiz-type thing. Just think, you're playing Carrie Fisher to her Debbie Reynolds.'

'Oh, there're the girls!' says Mum, spotting us and giving each of us a huge hug. 'Thanks so much for coming! Did you enjoy the show? Did you see me waving at you? Oh, what did you think of the costumes? I don't want to blow my own trumpet, but Mrs Nugent our director thinks Margaret and I might very well get a nod for a nomination for the best costume design award this year! Could you imagine? Us, winning an award! Oh Margaret! Look, it's Cassie and Jo, come on over here and say hello!'

Then Margaret our next-door neighbour is over, still in her nun's costume, glugging back a glass of champagne. Dad's busy photographing everything and everyone and Jo and I politely shake hands with Margaret, congratulating her on a great performance. Oh, and the costumes too, of course.

Mum is still on a stage high and barely lets anyone get a word in. 'Can you believe the girls came all this way to see us, Margaret? Aren't they just great, now? Oh, and remember Cassie has a big night ahead of her on Halloween! Nothing for you to be worried about now, love,' she says, misinterpreting the worry lines across my face. 'Sure, you're well used to television at this stage, aren't you, love? Walk in the park. I just can't believe our little Cassie is going on the *Late Night Talk* show! We're so proud, darling. I'll make sure the whole musical society is watching and don't you worry, Daddy will have the VCR recording.'

Oh, bloody hell. As if I didn't have enough to worry about.

Chapter Nineteen

THE TAROT DECK
THE DEVIL CARD

Not good. Symbolizes a vicious, strong and forceful element in another, which is about to be unleashed with devastating consequences. Can indicate a power-hungry person, who will stop at nothing, absolutely nothing, to succeed, even if that success is at the price of another's downfall.

The devil is considered a trump card, meaning that it's pretty much unstoppable.

In other words, there's only one thing to say: good luck. You're going to need it . . .

Going into Channel Seven at night-time is a weird experience. And it's Halloween and there're bonfires everywhere and fireworks going off all over the place and kids with their little faces painted trooping around the streets trick-or-treating. Normally I'd be excited and looking forward to the night and, well, feeling anything other than the way I do right now. Which, to be honest, is numb. Completely numb.

I got a call earlier to ask me to turn up at the station about an hour before transmission, just to get made up and settled, I suppose. I'm not in the least bit nervous, which is unlike me. I think I'm still just too punch drunk with recent events even to be worried about this. So, I park my car and head to TV reception, and the only thing that's going through my mind is how quickly I can reasonably get out of here.

Jo, bless her, has agreed to sit in the studio audience, so I won't see her till after transmission. Marc with a C is coming along too, as diplomatic as ever, just to prove that he's absolutely *not* taking anyone's side in the Great Barrier Reef, as he's nicknamed this stupid bloody feud.

'I've given this a great deal of thought,' he said to me on the phone this morning, 'and the fairest thing really is if neither of you see Jack, ever again, as long as you live. OK, sweetie? That's my two cents' worth and see you *ce soir*!'

I asked after Charlene and he immediately changed the subject, which is only making me think that she's continuing to wish a pestilence on my house and that I put on two stone. Ho-hum.

Oh, and Valentine has promised to come along too, which I'm very grateful for, as are half the *Tattle* magazine office, mainly because I'm under strict instructions from all of them to suss out who he brings along with him as his date.

Anyway, I really am glad that I'll have some support out in the audience tonight. Apart from them, I won't know a single soul here. No, not strictly true, there's Richard Bryan from the National Ghost Convention, who's the person who put me forward for this in the first place. I've never met him but I'm presuming he'll be here. I never made it to their convention either (if you could call it that) at Kilmainham Jail today. I could have, I suppose, only, well, I had to work, didn't I?

Yes, of course, very busy working girl. I was in the office all day. Gazing out of the window for most of it, hardly getting any flashes and nearly jumping six feet in the air every time the phone rang, just in case it was Jack.

Which it wasn't.

Not even a text, nothing. And no calls to do a slot on the *Breakfast Club* either, which, under the circumstances I suppose, is a good thing.

A stunningly productive day, as you see.

Anyway, the first person I see when I get to reception is, surprisingly, Lisa. 'Hi,' I say, hugging her warmly, 'what are you doing here?'

'Hey, Cassie! Great to see you! I'm gonna be working with you tonight. *Late Night Talk*'s regular stage manager is out sick, so they rang me to see if I could fill in at the last minute. What can I say? I have no morals and I need the cash.'

I'm really delighted; it's just great to see a friendly face before I go on. She leads me through reception and into a tiny dressing room with a big basket of fruit sitting there waiting for me. There's a slightly awkward pause where I'm just hoping against hope she doesn't mention Jack. The last time I saw her was the infamous night in the Comedy Cellar and I know that she knows what happened and, well, it's just that there's a very good chance that if she does give me the third degree, it might well end in tears.

She doesn't though, which is fab.

'Wow, this is all very A list, isn't it?' I say, indicating the towering fruit arrangement, dying to keep the conversation away from – well, you know. Seriously though, it almost looks like something Carmen Miranda would perch on top of her head.

'Only what you deserve.' She smiles. 'Emm, Cassie, do you mind if I have a quick private word with you?' Then she closes the door, as if she doesn't want anyone to hear what's coming next.

Shit, she's going to ask me if I'm seeing Jack.

OK, Cassie, keep the head.

This is a perfectly normal, lovely girl who isn't out to cause me any upset or embarrassment, she's just looking for a nice juicy bit of gossip, that's all. As I probably would myself, if I were in her shoes. I mean, at the *Tattle* office, that's pretty much all any of us do, all day long. Presuming the Dragon Lady isn't in residence, that is. If she asks, I'll just laugh the whole thing off and brush it aside.

Great plan.

Oh yes, and claim that I was pissed drunk. Which is the truth, anyway.

'The thing is,' she says so slowly that I'm now really starting to worry, 'the producer was wondering, now – only if it's absolutely OK with you . . .'

Shit. The producer. Shit, shit, shit, I forgot to ask who the producer was. Can't be Jack. No, it can't be . . .

'The thing is, she has this idea . . .'

Phew. I'm safe. 'Yeah?'

'Well, it's just because it's Halloween and everything. She sort of thought . . .'

'Yeah?'

'That the guests tonight appear . . .'

'Yeah?' Now I'm thinking: What, naked?

'In fancy dress.'

'*What?*'

'It's only for a laugh, that's all. All the other guests have agreed to it. Oliver Hall has already nabbed a Captain Jack Sparrow costume for himself. You should see him. He's upstairs in make-up prancing around the place like he's Johnny Depp.'

My jaw drops to my collarbone and I look at her in total shock, which poor Lisa misinterprets. I'm honestly not a bit bothered about going on in costume, but *Oliver*? What the hell is he doing here?

'Oliver Hall? He's going on tonight as well?'

'Yeah. But look, Cassie, if the costume thing is a problem for you . . .'

'No, no, not at all. Emm, I don't want to appear nosey or anything, but can I ask you what Oliver's going on to talk about?'

'He's going on with you.'

'*WHAT?*' OK, now I think I might just need a brandy.

'Didn't anyone talk to you about this, Cassie?'

'Well, no,' I say, racking my brains to think. Did anyone call me or email me and did I just forget, like I normally do with anything really important?

No, no, I know I've had a lot on my mind, but I'm fairly sure that they didn't.

Lisa checks the show's running order on a clipboard

445

she's carrying. 'Yup. There's an environmentalist on first, then you and Oliver up next, then we go to a commercial break.'

Jesus, I need to sit down. 'But, Lisa, to talk about what? I thought I was just here to have a chat about Halloween and, I dunno, maybe it would be a bit like on the *Breakfast Club*, where people ring in and . . . you know . . .' I trail off lamely. The unspoken part of my sentence is 'and I'll just be able to wing it like I normally do.' Shit, here I am about to go on live television, completely and utterly unprepared. Serves me right for spending the last few days going around in a complete and utter daze.

You roaring bloody eejit, Cassie, you are about to get your comeuppance and boy, do you deserve it.

'OK, stay cool,' says Lisa, popping a chewing gum into her mouth. 'I'll find the producer and see if I can find out a bit more for you. Relax, you'll be grand. For God's sake, you're Cassandra. Everyone knows you're *brilliant*.'

Yeah, everyone except me, I'm thinking. Oh, sweet baby Jesus and the orphans.

An hour later I'm ready to go on, feeling as sick as a parrot and within an inch of sacrificing my name and reputation (if I still have one, that is) by committing the most unprofessional act of all and running away.

It's sorely tempting. By the time I get down to wardrobe, the only two remaining costumes are Marie Antoinette or Alice from *Alice in Wonderland*. I try both of them on but Marie Antoinette's corset is making me weak and light-headed and, given that there's a good chance I might pass out anyway, I opt for the far safer bet of Alice. Blue hairband, big white starched apron with a bow, the full Monty. I look ludicrous. Marc with a C and Jo will crack up when I appear in this, and who could blame them? But for the moment that's the least of my worries.

I'm pacing up and down in the dressing room, all made up with big red rosy cheeks that make me look (if possible) even dafter, when Lisa knocks on the door.

'You're on,' she says. 'Feeling OK?'

'It'll all be over in ten minutes,' I say, squeezing her hand. 'Tell me it'll be all over in ten minutes and just keep telling me that and I'll be grand.'

'Cassie, you of all people have nothing to worry about. You're an old hand at this by now. To be honest with you, I'm much more worried about Oliver.'

I look at her in disbelief as we walk down the corridor towards the studio door.

'Yeah, he's acting like he's Steven Spielberg or some-one,' she says. 'Well, you know the way he goes on. He's prepared a video clip to show and everything. God knows what's in it, though. Anyway, the producer says to tell you that there's absolutely nothing for you to worry about. There might just be a bit of a debate about whether or not psychics and fortune-tellers are for real or, you know, if they're all just chancers out to make a quick buck.'

For a second, I think I might just faint. Or throw up. One or the other.

'Oh, not that you are,' she adds hastily. 'I'm only telling you what the producer said. Hey, don't shoot the messenger. You just do what you do on the *Breakfast Club* and I'm sure you'll win everyone over.'

Suddenly, after dismal days of hardly getting any flashes at all, now I get the strongest gut instinct I've had in a long, long time not to go on the show.

RUN, my inner voice is saying. *Get out of there. Say whatever you have to say, make any excuse you like, just do not, repeat, DO NOT under any circumstances go through with this.*

'Lisa, do you think I might just—'

'Are you OK?' she asks again, opening the studio door and ushering me inside. 'Do you need me to get you some water?'

'No, it's just that . . .'

'Let me get your radio mike put on and I'll be right back to you. I reckon you're on in about four minutes.'

Shit, shit, shit. No way out, then.

OK, nothing for it but to put on a brave face and remember, whatever happens, it'll all be over fast.

Bloody hell, why couldn't they have put me in a costume with a mask, so at least no one would see my face and hopefully my on-air humiliation would be kept to a minimum? Lisa and I are standing just behind the *Late Night Talk* show set, and have to whisper now, as the last guest is just wrapping up. A sound man who I don't recognize bounds over to clip a tiny microphone on to the apron of my horrendous Alice costume, then suddenly a voice from behind me makes me jump out of my skin.

'Lost a white rabbit then, have you, Alice?'

I'd know that faux-American accent anywhere. I turn around to see Oliver, looking, if possible, even more ludicrous than I do, in a *Pirates of the Caribbean* outfit, sword in scabbard, Rastafarian wig, the works.

'Hi, Oliver,' I whisper, not even bothering to sound polite or, God help me, pleased to see him.

'All set then?'

'Mmm.'

'Well then,' the smarmy git says, before disappearing around to where we're supposed to make our entrance from, 'may the best man win.'

Did he just say 'may the best man win'? What is this, the world heavyweight championships? God Almighty, what have I let myself in for?

There's nothing for it, I have to wait beside him for our cue to go on. The doorway in the set is narrow and small so I practically have to stand on top of him, trying desperately to look as dignified as I can, considering

I have a big blue hairband on my head and a boob-flattening apron so wide it's practically hitting off the sides of the scenery.

I can't see what's going on out front, but I can hear perfectly. The presenter, a former stand-up comic called Ricky James, is busy wrapping up the previous item.

'So, best of luck with the sponsored sit-in for Greenpeace. Wow! A seventy-two-hour-long protest! And remember, anyone who wants to go along and lend their support, he'll be shivering his tush off in Temple Bar from eight a.m. tomorrow morning. Good luck from all of us here. Please put your hands together for . . .'

A thunderous round of applause drowns out his name and a split second later Greenpeace man walks right past me, on his way out. Very tall. Blond. The type that you'd swear just stepped off a Viking warship. Oh dear, now, of all times, I feel a flash coming on.

'And now, ladies and gentlemen,' I can hear Ricky saying, loud and clear, 'given the night that's in it, we have a *Late Night Talk* special coming up. Will you please give a warm welcome to Oliver Hall, a man who needs no introduction. Many of you will know Oliver for his stunning and insightful investigative exposures over the years . . .'

Ricky James is still introducing us and . . . Oh my God, I don't believe this.

'Cassandra, wake up, we're about to go on,' Oliver is hissing at me.

There's Greenpeace man staging his sit-in in town, and – there's no mistaking it – I can see Jo, standing right beside him, almost holding vigil with him. They're both clutching on to candles, smiling at each other. I have the strongest feeling this man could be for her. He could really be a contender – a keeper. Finally, my best friend has met her elusive D.S.M....

'Cassandra? Earth to Cassandra?'

'What? Oh, sorry. I was, emm, a bit distracted.'

'By the way, Charlene is here. Just thought you'd like to know.'

'What did you just say?'

'Yeah. I invited her and she came to support me.'

He did that on purpose. I know it. Bloody bastard waited until the nanosecond before we went on before he mentioned it, knowing right well it would throw me.

Don't let him, Cassie, whatever you do, do not let him ...

Ricky's still doing the introductions. 'And he's appearing tonight with someone new to television but already a familiar face to audiences thanks to her regular slot on the *Breakfast Club*. Please give a warm *Late Night Talk* welcome to Oliver Hall and Cassandra!'

Shit.

A bit disorientated, I follow Oliver out on to the front of the set. The lights are so glaring, they make me blink and I'm aware of thunderous applause and a lot of laughter, probably at our ridiculous costumes as much as anything else.

'Thank you so much for joining us, you're both very welcome,' Ricky James is saying, shaking my hand. He's wearing a Spiderman costume and looks just as daft as Oliver and I do. Which I suppose is something.

Next thing I know, I'm plonked on a very uncomfortable leather swivel chair beside git-face. I smile and I think I mutter something, but all the time I'm looking out into the audience to see if there's any sign of Jo. Or Marc with a C. Or Valentine – just a friendly face. But no joy. The lights shining in my face are too bright, far brighter than they ever are on the *Breakfast Club*, and I can't see a bloody thing.

Ricky's sitting behind a desk, still chatting away. I'd better pay attention. Plenty of time later to tell Jo what I saw.

'. . . two diametrically opposed sides of the coin here, ladies and gentlemen. Cassandra, who as I'm sure you'll all know is probably the most famous psychic in the country at this stage, and Oliver Hall, scourge of many a global corporation and, may I say, thorn in the side of many an unsuspecting personality. So, Cassandra, let's start with you.'

I've been drifting and almost jump when I hear my name.

'You have a sixth sense, you believe in the unseen and make your living out of giving messages of hope to I'm sure many thousands of readers and viewers at this stage.'

'Emm, yes, Ricky, that's right. At least, I hope it is.'

Now they're all looking at me as if I'm expected to elaborate, but I'm too busy thinking: Was there a question buried in there?

He keeps on going. 'And you get accurate results?'

'Well, it's very simple, I just tell people what I see and – that's it, really.' Bugger it, why am I so unprepared? 'It's not as if I keep a score sheet or anything,' I add lamely, trying to make a joke, but I'm sure I look beyond pathetic.

There's an awful silence and I'm horribly aware of a camera pointing right at me.

Then Ricky turns to the audience. 'So, how many people here tonight have ever visited a psychic or a fortune-teller? Can we have a show of hands?'

I do my best to peer out into the darkness, but it's a waste of time. The lights are just too bright.

'And, of all those people, how many felt that it helped them? Or did any of you feel you were being ripped off?'

I'm still squinting like Mr Magoo and still nothing. Then I hear a woman's voice from the audience.

'Ehh, hello, Ricky? Can I just say that I went to a guy in the George's Street arcade a few years ago and he told me I'd break up with my boyfriend – and guess what? I'm married to him now. Two kids and everything.'

'So lucky you didn't listen, then,' Ricky is saying.

Laughter, then another voice.

'Well, can I just say that I've actually written to Cassandra twice in the last few weeks and I never even got a reply.'

Oh, now that's unfair, I'm thinking. I do my level best to get around to everyone who writes to me, but if you only saw the sheer volume of letters I get . . .

'Anyone who reads their horoscope needs their head looked into,' I can hear a man's voice saying.

Another woman's voice. 'Well, Ricky, I went to a fortune-teller on my holidays and she said I'd move house, which I did. She also said there'd be a number seven on the door, which there wasn't, but I suppose you can't really have everything, can you?'

Then an older woman from somewhere says, 'I went to one who charged me fifty euro to tell me I'd cross water. I mean, how useless is that? Sure, I have to cross the river Liffey every day just to get into work.'

Then Ricky turns to me. 'So, Cassandra, anything you'd like to say at this point?'

Shit. What exactly does he want me to come out with? Am I expected to justify myself here?

Say something, say something and try to sound as if I've actually done some preparation for this medieval torture . . .

'Ricky, it's like this,' I begin, doing my best to sound intelligent, but then remembering that I'm dressed up as a Disney character. Nothing for it but to smile and try to look as if I'm here for the laugh. 'It's not like I have a job description or anything. All I'm here to do is help people. Ever since I was a small child, I've been getting these flashes. I see things and then I tell people what I see. Simple as that. Haven't had any complaints so far.'

There's a tiny wave of applause from the audience and I instinctively know that Jo started it.

'So do you see me winning a TV award for presenting this show?' Ricky asks cheekily.

''Fraid not. As I always say, being a psychic isn't something that's on tap, twenty-four hours a day. Oh, and it doesn't work for Lottery numbers either. Unfortunately.'

A polite ripple of laughter.

'So, given that you want to help people who come to you, the question is, how do you *know* that you are actually making a difference?'

What do I say to that? 'Well, Ricky, I don't, that's the thing. We're not dealing with an exact science here.'

Another awful pause and I'm still aware of the camera pointing right at me. Then something Jack once said to me comes back to me. Thank God. 'As someone once said to me, for those who believe, no explanation is necessary, for those who don't, no explanation is possible.'

Ricky looks at me with an is-that-it? expression on his face and all I can think is, I've just made a show of myself, live, on national television. Why couldn't I have talked about some of the success stories I've had over the years? Why couldn't I have told him that, to my know-ledge, I've never *once* been wrong? Serves me bloody right for just drifting in here in a daze, without doing my homework.

Grin and bear it, Cassie, it can't go on for much longer.

'Right then,' Ricky says slowly, 'so maybe if we could turn to you, Oliver. I understand you have some thoughts on this subject?' No sooner has he moved off me than I'm filled with smart-alec indignation at all the things I could have said, should have said. Anyway, too late now, for the moment, at least.

'Yes, thanks, Ricky,' Oliver says, checking to see which camera he's on and then beaming into it. Slick. Practised. Professional.

Smarmy git that he is.

'Ever since I returned to Ireland, I've been fascinated with the whole psychic phenomenon that seems to be sweeping the country. Never before have we, as a nation, been so anxious to turn to astrology, palmistry and clairvoyants, to look for answers about what the future holds for us. Perhaps it's because we're not attending church as diligently as our parents' generation once did. Perhaps we're subconsciously searching for something to fill the spiritual void in our lives, as it were. Man is a spiritual being and, historically, has always looked to the sky for guidance. The Romans had their soothsayers; in today's society, we turn to people like Cassandra.'

He gets a big round of applause and I'm left thinking: Why didn't I say that? He sounded so intelligent and *prepared*.

Bastard.

'And I understand you're putting together a documentary on this very subject, aren't you?' Ricky asks him.

'Yes, indeed. In fact, I've been following Cassandra for the past while, with her permission, naturally, just to see first hand what these so-called mystics do for a living. I think it'll make for very interesting viewing.' Then he turns to address the audience directly. 'Anyone like to see a clip from it?'

A couple of 'yeah, go ons' from the audience.

'I can't hear you,' says Oliver, whipping the crowd up and sounding like the ringmaster at a circus. 'Are you sure you all want to see a clip?'

'Yes! Show it! Go on, then!' comes from the audience.

'OK, let's roll it,' says Oliver, sitting smugly back into his chair. 'Let's let our wonderful audience judge for themselves if there's anything credible in the whole psychic phenomenon.'

Jesus, the man has the nerve of a matador. The studio lights dim a bit and everyone turns to the screen behind us.

OK, the sensible part of my brain thinks, this could just be my salvation. I mean, yes, Oliver was trailing around the past while, driving me nuts more than anything else, but everything was fine, wasn't it? I mean, I was getting my flashes, doing my thing, all successfully, wasn't I? So what's to be worried about?

And more importantly, why do I feel as if I want to pass out?

Oh shit. Now I feel a flash coming on. An awful one.

It's me, still in my stupid-looking Alice costume and – I don't believe this – I'm back in my dressing room, bawling crying, really howling to the four walls …

No time to dwell on it, though. I'm pulled out of it by the sound of my own voice.

I do not believe this. There I am on the screen above, in glorious Technicolor. I'm sitting on the *Breakfast Club* set, with a blank expression on my face.

'Emm . . . it's . . . well, you see . . .' I'm saying on the video clip, for all the world to see. 'This time with George could turn out to be very precious. Umm . . . for both of you. I think.'

I look petrified, I look like a complete dope and then I remember, as I'm going through the horribly surreal ordeal of having to look and listen to myself, that caller. She was the woman who moaned about her husband and I saw him dead within a few short months. What could I have said? I could hardly tell the caller that she was about to be widowed, now could I?

'Excuse me, Ricky? Could I just say something here?' I say in a tiny voice, but I'm drowned out by my own voice on the screen. Jesus. It's me again, same outfit, same *Breakfast Club* slot.

'Emm . . . well . . . the thing is . . . I can't see whether—' Then a shot of me looking like a goldfish, with my mouth gaping open. 'What I'm trying to say is, well,' I'm saying, in a deafening voice on screen, 'sometimes the worst thing that happens to you can often turn out to be the best thing.'

Then it comes back to me. Yes. The woman who wanted to marry her boyfriend and I saw him moving out and leaving her a note. There's another shot of me umming and ahhing, then I say, '. . . trust in the Universe.' And the studio audience laughs. They actually laugh.

And part of me doesn't even blame them, I look like

an idiot. The bastard has edited me to look like a half-wit.

There's worse to come: a shot of me at the Hendersons' house on the day I did the clearing for them. That beautiful little spirit boy who didn't know that he was dead. Dear God, I can hardly believe it.

It's Liz and her neighbour Louise, being filmed at the kitchen table where I left them that morning. Liz Henderson, the very woman who was so reluctant to be filmed, is now filling the screen for all to see, chatting away with her new friend.

'So now that Cassandra's left the building, as it were' – I can hear Oliver's voice off-camera – 'what do you think she actually did for you?'

Then a close-up of Liz, smiling. 'Well, you know, she didn't really do anything.'

And that's it. *No*, I'm silently boiling, how can you sit there and say that? If you only knew what I had done that day – but then I get a flash. That isn't what Liz said at all. Or at least, not everything that she said. Oliver edited her sentence in half, purposely to make me look even worse.

Now I see Liz, back at that kitchen table, saying, 'She didn't really do anything that got in the way, but the difference in the house is astonishing. I'd hardly know the place.'
Then Louise is saying, 'Oh, I completely agree, the girl did

absolutely nothing intrusive and I should know, I was here the whole time.'

Except that's not what Oliver, the bastard, is showing. He's cut it down so now Louise is up on screen saying, 'Oh, I completely agree, the girl did absolutely nothing.' And that's it. Now the studio audience are roaring laughing at me and I can feel hot, stingy tears beginning to well up in my eyes.

'No, no, that *isn't* what they said, or . . . at least, not what they meant,' I'm desperately trying to get out, but I'm wasting my breath. The camera is focused on the screen above me and I'm completely drowned out.

The torture's still not over. We're back to the *Breakfast Club* set and there I am with Mary sitting beside me. 'I hate to tell you, but I'm afraid I can't help,' I'm saying crisply, all matter-of-fact. 'I can't see anything. Sorry, but there it is.'

More laughter from the studio audience and now I want to scream. That was that awful, bossy woman who rang in and I couldn't see anything because I took a dis-like, a very rare dislike, to her. But Oliver has made it look as if this happens to me every day of the week.

Then comes a shot of me whispering to Mary, which happened during a commercial break, I remember, because I was explaining to her why I blanked, but of course now it looks like I said it live. 'I'm worse than useless,' I hear myself saying to Mary. 'As far as your future is concerned, I'm as blind as a bat.'

OK, now I actually want to scream at the *unfairness* of it all, but I can't because there's more humiliation to come. Oh Christ. Here I am again, leaning forward and stage whispering into the mike, 'Anyone who believes in ghosts is a big silly pants.'

'The caller was a little girl!' I say at the top of my voice but still no one can hear me. 'She was frightened and I was trying to calm her down!'

The studio audience are still guffawing as the clip finally comes to an end.

'Well,' says Oliver, turning to camera, 'as I always say, I just present the facts in an unbiased manner and let the viewer decide. I hope you'll all tune in to my documentary, it'll be on your screens, twentieth of November, nine p.m. Hey, don't miss it!'

'But that's not FAIR!' I almost scream at him, with tears starting to roll now. 'You edited me to make me look like I hadn't a clue—'

'And I'm afraid we've run out of time on this item. We'll have to leave it there and go to a commercial break,' says Ricky to the audience. 'Oliver Hall and Cassandra, thank you so much for your time.'

I don't believe it. They never even gave me a chance to defend myself.

The next few moments are a haze. I desperately want

to see Jo and Marc with a C or even Valentine, but next thing Lisa comes out and ushers me and Oliver off the set. I can barely see straight, the tears are stinging my eyes so much.

We get out to the corridor where the dressing rooms are and Oliver strides on ahead of me but I don't let him. He is *not* getting away with this.

'What exactly did you think you were doing in there?' I almost splutter at him, angry tears streaming down my Disney cartoon make-up. 'You made a fool out of me, and you know right well that . . . that . . . what you showed was a load of crap. It wasn't like that . . . It was . . . edited to make me look like—'

'Cassandra,' he says and I swear I want to punch him. I physically want to punch him. 'I just record what I see around me, that's all. May I remind you that you did give your permission for me to film what I saw. Now, if you're unhappy with what I shot, frankly, that's your problem. The viewers are paying their licence fees and they have a right to know what goes on behind the scenes.'

'You absolute BASTARD,' I try to scream at him, but I'm too upset and my voice sounds tiny.

'Hey, you're the one who charges money to umm and ahh and fill people's heads with crap like "trust in the Universe". High time charlatans like you were exposed, in my opinion.'

'How bloody *DARE* you . . .'

But Lisa's straight in, thank God. 'Cassie, come on, let's get you to your dressing room,' she says, firmly steering me out of Oliver's path. 'Let me get you settled and then I'll run to the bar and bring you the largest gin and tonic I can get my hands on.'

I can't answer her. All I can do is sniff and snuffle and allow myself to be led away.

It's over. My career is as good as finished. I'm a national laughing stock and I'll never survive this. My reputation is in tatters. No one will ever come to me for help ever again. Why would they? Why would anyone write into someone who's just been spectacularly exposed as a fake?

We go into the dressing room, she leaves me in peace and I collapse on the sofa in a fit of deep, uncontrollable sobs.

A few minutes later, there's a gentle tap-tapping on the door.

'Come in,' I say in a tiny voice, expecting it to be Lisa. Badly needing that drink.

But it's not. The door opens and in comes a very contrite, very humble-looking Charlene.

Chapter Twenty

THE TAROT DECK
THE SUN CARD

Ooh, lovely. High time a bit of good fortune came your way. Symbolizes special relationships all around. Which will bring great happiness to one and all.

OK, in the short term, there may have to be some, shall we say, heated discussions, but stick with it and, if you're very, very lucky, things just might work out.

This is a card of miracles, and if ever anyone was due a miracle of biblical proportions, it's you, baby . . .

Charlene hasn't come here to say, 'I told you so.' Which, considering the last time we spoke she told me that there was a thing called karma which would eventually come and bite me on the bum, is a major relief.

'I'm sorry,' she says simply.

'No, I'm sorry.'

'What have you to be sorry for?'

I just look at her, still in floods of tears, with my Alice in Wonderland make-up dribbling down my cheeks. I can't bring myself even to say Jack's name. 'For . . . you know,' I trail off.

'Well, I'm sorrier,' she says, sitting down beside me on the sofa and slipping her arm around my waist. 'You were right about Oliver and I didn't listen to you. I can't believe he did that to you. I nearly died. He made you look like . . . like . . . oh God, I don't even want to finish that sentence.'

This starts me off bawling again.

'Shh, shh,' Charlene says, fishing around in her handbag for a Kleenex, which I gratefully grab from her.

'It's my own bloody fault,' I say, wiping my eyes. 'I wished him for you, you know. Before I knew what he was like,' I hasten to add.

'No, if there's a blame game, I get first dibs,' she says, really looking sorry. 'My humble muscle has just kicked in and we all know that doesn't happen too often, so just let me finish. Here it is. I have a confession to make.

I was the one who told Oliver you were going on *Late Night Talk* in the first place. So, if it wasn't for me and my big mouth . . .'

I pause to blow my nose. Very attractive.

'He set you up, Cassie. Completely and utterly. But you have to believe me, I didn't know what he had planned. Honestly. On my future deathbed.'

'I do believe you.'

'Thank you, sweetie.'

She squeezes my hand and I squeeze it back.

'I missed you.'

'I missed *you*.'

OK. Nothing else for it. Seeing as how we're having confessionals, I may as well get it off my chest. 'Charlene, there's something else that I really want to say to you, that I *have* to tell to you—'

'No, no, there's no need,' she says, looking all noble. 'Jo and Marc with a C have been at pains to point out my appalling behaviour. You were so generous and kind to me; you took me in when no one else would and in return I was horrible to you. I don't want to fall out with you over a guy, Cassie. We've been friends for too long. If you want to see Jack, you have my blessing.'

OK, I know it sounds like something the Pope might come out with, but she really, really does mean it. When she's being insincere, she stares off into the middle distance, another pose courtesy of Joan Collins on *Dynasty*, but not now. She's looking straight at me, white as a ghost.

'I haven't been seeing him,' I tell her, gently. 'How could I when I knew that it was hurting you? Anyway, long story short, we agreed to leave it be.'

'Well, call him,' she says generously.

'Can't,' I say, shaking my head. And it's the truth. I've just been through too much in the last few excruciating minutes to even think straight.

There's a comfortable, easy silence while I compose my thoughts.

'Charlene, can I ask you something?'

'Of course, sweetie.'

'How bad was it out there? When Oliver showed that awful clip?'

She doesn't answer, which immediately makes me think the very worst.

'Tell you what,' she says, getting up. 'Why don't you and me go to the hospitality room and have a nice stiff drink? I think we could both use one.'

I'm in no fit state to argue with her, so I get out of the horrendous Alice gear and back into my comfy jeans and a warm sweater.

Lisa pops her head around the door, says a quick hi to Charlene and plonks a full-to-the-brim gin and tonic into my hand, bless her.

'Thanks, lifesaver.'

'You're so welcome. Jesus, if I get my hands on that bastard Oliver Hall, I'll murder him on your behalf. The guy is unbelievable.'

There's another silence. Neither Charlene nor I are about to argue with her on that particular point.

'Well, I gotta get the next guest on,' Lisa says apologetically, 'but I'll see you in hostility after the show, OK?'

'Hostility?' says Charlene innocently.

'Sorry, that's what we call the hospitality room here. Just taste the wine and you'll see why.' She winks at me and disappears as Charlene and I leave the dressing room.

When we do get to hostility, sorry hospitality, Jo, Marc with a C and Valentine are all there. In fact, we have the place to ourselves, as the show isn't even over yet. Which means they left, just to support me, to see if I was OK.

Oh God, here I go.

The very fact that they're here to bolster up their pathetic friend in her hour of need and . . . all their *encouragement* makes me start snivelling all over again. 'You guys,' I say, hugging them all. 'What would I do without you?'

'Well, just take a look at the miracle of Halloween,' says Marc with a C, trying to cheer me up.

'What's that?'

'You, baby, and our dearest Charlene back best

469

buddies again. Oh, there's nothing I love more than a good reconciliation in the final act. If I were wearing pearls right now, I'd be clutching them.'

'As I always say,' says Charlene, equanimity restored, 'guys may come and go, but friends and Manolo Blahniks are always here to stay.'

'You know, this could turn out to be a blessing in disguise,' says Jo, pulling a chair out for me and sitting me down.

'If it is, it's a very good disguise,' I say dully.

'No, what I mean is that now you know what that horse's bum Oliver has put into his documentary, maybe you could try to get it pulled, on the ground that he completely misled you. Couldn't you? I mean, he only got you to take part under false pretences and you agreed in good faith.'

I look at her blankly. I know she means well, but the thought of having to have any more dealings with that malevolent bastard . . .

'All I mean is that we may be able to do a bit of damage limitation,' she says softly. 'It's not the end of the world.'

Only a great pal like Jo would come out with something like that after my public humiliation live on the national airwaves. 'Thanks, hon,' I say, taking a big mouthful of gin and tonic. It burns as it goes down and almost makes me choke.

'Jaypurs, I know a few lads down home wouldn't be long putting manners on that Oliver Hall fella for you,' says Valentine kindly. 'Just say the word, Cassie, that's all you've got to do.'

'I love it,' Marc with a C says to him. 'Protectiveness and brotherliness, all wrapped up with just the merest hint of violence. Why are men like you never, ever gay?'

Valentine looks a bit embarrassed, but Charlene comes to his rescue.

'Hands off,' says Charlene. 'Valentine, would you mind getting me a teeny glass of champers from the bar? This wine tastes kind of like fermented battery acid.'

'Of course, you stay there,' he says, getting up. 'Anyone else want anything?'

Jo and Marc with a C put in their orders and then I get a flash.

Dear God. In a million years, I would never have seen this one coming.

It's Valentine, now a major celebrity in his own right and … bloody hell. He's with Charlene. Yes, it's definitely her, he has his arm protectively around her and she's snuggled up against him. There are press cameras and reporters clustered all around the pair of them and she's flashing – I do not believe this – an engagement ring for all to see. It's stunning, and, boy, will it put Anna Regan in her place.

*'Not quite love at first sight, but we got there in the end.'
Charlene is beaming as a load of flashes go off in her
face. 'Can you believe I landed him? He's the most eligible
bachelor in Ireland, and he isn't even bald!'*

'What's wrong, what's the matter?' says Jo, clocking
that I've drifted off. 'Are you seeing something?'

'You'd never believe me if I told you,' I say. 'I can
barely believe it myself.' And it's the first time all evening
I think I've cracked a smile.

Things slowly get better. The show must have wrapped
up by now, because some of the other guests start drifting in, led by Greenpeace man, whose name I couldn't
hear for applause. The guy I saw for Jo.

My God, this is just incredible. It's almost getting to
be like the ballroom of romance in here tonight. Now,
if I could just see a special someone in the pipeline for
Marc with a C . . .

I can't, but two out of the four of us happily matched
up isn't bad going, is it? Anyway, considering the misery
I've just been through, this certainly is a very welcome
distraction. Can't ask for miracles.

A few minutes later, the audience have all begun to
drift in and the bar is rapidly filling up. I'm beginning
to be aware of a few pitying looks being thrown in my
direction and if I could lip read, I'd swear people were
saying, 'There's the poor girl that made a show of herself

earlier. You know, the one that claims to have a gift but when it comes down to it, is beyond useless.'

Shit.

I take another gulp of lovely, nerve-calming gin and tonic and then whisper to Marc with a C, 'I think I might very subtly exit stage left. If you don't mind?'

Marc with a C looks around. Jo has gone off to congratulate Greenpeace guy (I'm seeing a J in his name for some reason, and he's . . . yes, got it. Pisces. Definitely a Piscean). And Charlene and Valentine are chatting away very amicably in the corner. 'Don't think the others would even notice,' says Marc with a C. 'As one who entirely understands your need to be where other people are not, let me walk you to your car. Least I can do.'

I smile at him, grab my bag and the two of us slip out, unnoticed.

I'm not being rude, you understand, it's just that I don't know if I'd be up for anyone coming over to commiserate with me. For being such an out-and-out failure, I mean. I'm so close to tears that really the best thing all round is for me to put as much distance between myself and Channel Seven as is physically possible.

Marc with a C links me as we head down the corridor, past TV reception and on out into the car park. It's pitch dark and freezing cold and there're fireworks going off everywhere.

'Wouldn't this be romantic, if only you and I were an item?' he says as we stroll companionably towards where I parked my car. 'My God, did you see the way that Valentine guy was throwing himself at Charlene? There are baboons out there with more subtle dating rituals.'

'Now, now, don't get narky just because it's Halloween and you and I are dateless,' I say, and then a flash comes. 'Joe! That's it!'

God, that really did come out of nowhere.

'What, what? Joe who? Is that the name of the next guy I'll date? Do you see it?'

'No.' I smile. 'It's the name of the guy that Jo—'

'Ahh, I get it, Joe and Jo. How original,' he says. 'Greenpeace man. Now don't think me gossipy, but did you get close enough to smell him? Dear God! I thought: Has this man ever met a clove of garlic he didn't like? Anyway, he and our Jo will be a match made in eco-warrior heaven. Well, cheer up, babes, at least you and I have each other to console on the long winter nights ahead. Sure you'll be OK?'

'Mmm, and thank you again, so much,' I say, reaching up to hug him. 'I'm going home, hot bath, straight to bed and tomorrow . . . tomorrow . . .'

'. . . is another day, Miss Scarlett,' he says in a truly awful Southern accent.

I'm just about to open the door when another car

pulls up right beside mine, beeping the horn at me. It's so dark, I can hardly see who it is, but the beeping keeps up and I keep squinting, and then . . .

The door opens and out steps Jack.

Marc with a C almost falls over. 'A *deus ex machina*!' he says theatrically. 'Love, love, love it! Well, I'll be tactful and leave you two in peace but, Cassie dear, I will expect a text with updates every hour on the hour.'

He practically skips back inside, leaving Jack and me alone.

There's a long pause as we just look at each other. I'm suddenly aware that I've been crying and am all red-eyed and tear-streaked. But, thank Christ, at least I'm not dressed as Alice in Wonderland any more.

He breaks the silence. 'I liked the Disney look on you, Cassie. You were adorable.'

I can't help laughing, but it's a laughter-through-tears type thing. 'You saw it then. You witnessed my public downfall. All Oliver was short of doing was putting me in medieval stocks and getting the studio audience to throw rotten tomatoes at me.' I'm doing my best to make light of it, to sound bright and breezy, but it's not working. The tears I've been holding back start to flow and before I know where I am or what's happening, he's folded me in his arms and is hugging me tight.

'Shh, shh, come on, Cassie, it wasn't your fault.'

I try to say 'Of course it bloody was, who else's fault

could it possibly be?' but I think it might have come out as 'Waaaaahhhhh! I'm such a miserable failure!'

'Hey, hey, hey,' he says, not letting me go. (And I'm not letting him go either.)

'I was the one who told you that Oliver Hall was a widely respected journalist. I may even have used the word trusted, but I'm kind of hoping you won't bring that up. At times like this, a good memory is unforgivable. If it's any consolation, one of the reasons I jumped in my car and came around here was to punch the bastard in the jaw for putting you through that. It was unforgivable, unethical and, I'm telling you right now, he'll pay.'

'One of the reasons?'

'And to see if my star was OK, of course.'

I smile, still feeling a bit wobbly. But so glad he's here.

'Listen to me, Cassie,' he says, taking me by the shoulders and looking me straight in the eye. 'Everything's going to be fine. Over my dead body will I allow that documentary to be broadcast. Small comfort, I know, but it's the least I can do.'

'Thanks,' is all I can say, in a tiny voice.

'You're not to worry, Cassie. The nightmare ends here.'

'I haven't lost my slot then? I'm not fired?'

'You daft lass, why would you be fired? You're one of our biggest assets and don't you forget it.'

He grins at me and I do my best to smile back and there's another awkward moment. He's just being professional. That's the only reason he came round here.

This is not the end of the world. Oliver, the unctuous git, can do me no more harm, I've still managed to hang on to my slot, so this is all good then, isn't it?

Yeah. A happy ending, I suppose.

It just doesn't really *feel* like one, that's all.

Come on, Cassie, you can't have everything. You've got your friend back and that's worth its weight in gold.

A loud firework goes off in the background and I nearly jump out of my skin and he laughs at me. It's one of those Catherine wheels, multicoloured, and it's just stunning. We both stare up at the sky, side by side, in silence.

This is getting awkward. Say something, Cassie, say anything. Just try not to sound like a gibbering eejit.

'Thanks, Jack,' I say eventually.

'For what?'

'Coming here. Making everything better. Being the human equivalent of six Valium. Calming me down.'

He slips his arm around my waist which makes me freeze inwardly, thinking, Aghhh! His arm is around my waist!

'Cassie, I'm suddenly very aware that we're in a car park. It's just that I can think of better places where you and I can talk, can't you?'

477

Half an hour later, we're tucked in the corner of a tiny, gorgeous Italian trattoria in Temple Bar, where Jack is obviously a regular, because we're treated like minor royalty when we arrive. The tables are cosy and intimate, covered in red-and-white gingham tablecloths, with candles stuck in bottles. You get the picture. It's snug and romantic and Dean Martin is singing 'That's Amore' in the background and it's exactly what I need right now.

Jack orders a bottle of red wine and a yummy, comforting plate of pasta for both of us and I don't put up any arguments. After everything that's happened, this is like the perfect end to the most miserable day.

We talk and talk for what seems like a very short time, but we must have been there for hours because in no time they're putting chairs on top of tables and locking up. We're the last two customers here.

I tell him all about Charlene and her about-turn and Valentine and the flash I had and maybe it's because I'm actually a bit squiffy now, but . . .

'So, any flashes about me?' he asks, leaning forward and playing with my hand.

And I tell him. Everything. All about how I can't see a bloody thing when he's around, and he roars laughing and says they'll have to have a barring order on him next time I'm doing the *Breakfast Club* and then, before I know how it even happened, he leans in and kisses me.

And I kiss him back and it's wonderful.

'So,' he says, gently playing with my hair, 'here we are.'

'Mmm,' I murmur, moving in as close to him as I can get, considering we're in a public place.

'Now, I may not be psychic like you,' he whispers in my ear. 'But go on, have a guess what I think your future holds.'

Oh dear. Never a flash when you need one.

'Haven't a clue,' I whisper back at him, kissing his cheek and snuggling into him. 'But I can't wait to find out.'

Dear Cassandra,

First of all, congratulations on finally getting your own TV show. I'm thrilled for you; it's about time. I saw a stunning picture of you at your show's launch party in *Tattle* magazine and you looked a million dollars. Is it true that you're dating the producer, Jack Hamilton? I saw a photo of you both and you look like such a cool couple. Come to think of it, I also saw you together at that dizzy socialite's engagement party in the Four Seasons a while back – Charlene something or other, isn't it? The one who's getting married to the columnist from Valentine's Day.

See? What can I say? I get my hair done a lot and am always abreast of what's happening in the world of *Tattle*.

Sorry, I digress . . .

Anyway, here's my question. Nothing but happy people beaming out at me from all the glossies – when, oh when, will it be my turn?

No pressure, Cassandra, but you are like this beacon of hope for single gals like me. I cannot do any more bad dates. I'm so tired of my friends saying to me, 'But how do you meet all of these headcases/losers/weirdos?'

The answer is simple. I answer their ads.

My dating history can pretty much be summarized as follows: the triumph of optimism over experience. But you did it and I'm happy for you and I know I can too. Come on, Cassandra, I know you won't let me down! You've found someone lovely and so too can all your readers!

All I need to know is . . . when, oh when, will it be my turn?

Yours, in everlasting hope . . .

THE END